SUDDENLY THE GROUND SEEMED TO ERUPT ALL AROUND TRENT'S *TIMBER WOLF*

as if he were suddenly cast into the middle of a raging thunderstorm. Sod splattered onto his pitching OmniMech, and flames licked upward at him from the exploding ground.

His targeting computer demanded his attention as he rocked. *Artillery—and Arrow Missiles.* His enemies were not facing him in a direct fight but, instead, wanted him dead without honor.

The second barrage did not rip at the soil but found its mark on his already battered *Timber Wolf.* One of the Arrow VI missiles went off on his foot, then another dug deeply into his shoulder, ripping his left weapons pod away from his 'Mech's torso with a thunderous blast that filled his ears and head. *My* Timber Wolf *is dying all around me. I must do something—and now!*

BATTLETECH®

Exodus Road

Twilight of the Clans I

Blaine Lee Pardoe

A ROC BOOK

ROC
Published by the Penguin Group
Penguin Books USA Inc., 375 Hudson Street,
New York, New York 10014, U.S.A.
Penguin Books Ltd, 27 Wrights Lane,
London W8 5TZ, England
Penguin Books Australia Ltd, Ringwood,
Victoria, Australia
Penguin Books Canada Ltd, 10 Alcorn Avenue,
Toronto, Ontario, Canada M4V 3B2
Penguin Books (N.Z.) Ltd, 182-190 Wairau Road,
Auckland 10, New Zealand

Penguin Books Ltd, Registered Offices:
Harmondsworth, Middlesex, England

First published by Roc, an imprint of Dutton Signet,
a division of Penguin Books USA Inc.

First Printing, August, 1997
10 9 8 7 6 5 4 3

Copyright © FASA Corporation, 1997
All rights reserved

Series Editor: Donna Ippolito
Cover art by Bruce Jensen
Mechanical Drawings: Duane Loose and the FASA art department

 REGISTERED TRADEMARK—MARCA REGISTRADA

"Gentlemen, you can't fight in here. This is the war room. . . ."

—from *Dr. Strangelove*

This book is dedicated to a number of people in my life who are important. First and foremost, my family—beautiful and loving wife Cindi, dynamo daughter Victoria, and adventurous son Alexander. If not for my family, I would not be who I am today, nor would I try to be more than I am.

To Dan Q. Plunkett and Cullen Q. Tilman of Enterprise Management, two remarkable men in this or any century. From them, I have learned to master the mistakes of the past—and in their own way they helped forge Trent into being, though I doubt that they knew it. Kari Pardoe, as well as Trisha and Sarah Miller deserve some mention as my bloodkin.

Exodus Road is also dedicated to Central Michigan University, where I earned my bachelor's and master's degrees. What I learned there was beyond classroom and the many fond memories of the basement of Grawn Hall and the Malt Shop are always with me.

My thanks to Bill Keith for helping me at Gen Con with the character of Trent and for having me bone up on my Benedict Arnold. Traitor heroes can be difficult at best. Donna, as always, for your patience. My thanks as well to Sobhna Garg for her assistance in the naming conventions used for some of the ships and for Huntress locations. I also fully acknowledge the political slings and arrows that the real-life Russou faces. Credit for this book must also go to all of my former and (possibly) present employers, thanks for the political insights that allowed me to make the Smoke Jaguars so corrupt and dark. Odd how office politics can surface in fiction, eh?

Also thanks to the other BattleTech authors who will continue to fan this spark into a flame. Writing in the BattleTech universe takes a great deal of coordination and cooperation with others. My sincere appreciation to my comrades in arms, Mike Stackpole and Robert Thurston, for our meeting at Gen Con where we laid this groundwork and to the others whose books will follow in the path of the Exodus Road. See you on Huntress, lads!

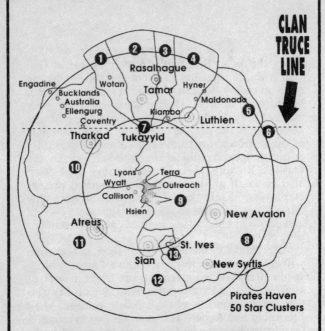

MAP OF THE
INNER SPHERE

1 • Jade Falcon/Steel Viper, 2 • Wolf Clan, 3 • Ghost Bear,
4 • Smoke Jaguars/Nova Cats, 5 • Draconis Combine,
6 • Outworlds Alliance, 7 • Free Rasalhague Republic,
8 • Federated Commonwealth, 9 • Chaos March,
10 • Lyran Alliance, 11 • Free Worlds League,
12 • Capellan Confederation, 13 • St. Ives Compact

Map Compiled by COMSTAR.
From information provided by the COMSTAR EXPLORER SERVICE
and the STAR LEAGUE ARCHIVES on Terra.

© 3058 COMSTAR CARTOGRAPHIC CORPS.

Prologue

Mist Lynx Training Facility
Gray Ridge Mountains
Londerholm, Kerensky Cluster
Clan Space
3 October 3037

Star Commander Porcini stood on a rock, towering over the dozen cadets in his charge. Dark gray and purple clouds hung over the Smoke Jaguar training camp high in the Gray Ridge Mountains. The terrain was rugged and stark, but the spot offered a stunning view of the treacherous jungles nearly seventy kilometers down the slopes. He was their Kit Master, as Jaguar training officers were known, and liked to bring his young charges here when weather permitted. Today he had made them jog up the steep slope as part of their morning regimen.

Porcini wore a light gray jumpsuit that looked as if it had seen many seasons and its share of action in places far from Londerholm. He stared down at the sibling company in his care, his face as hard-edged as the rock on which he stood. He showed no pride in them, only a kind of dark contempt. Perhaps he was not pleased with their performance that day or that week or that month. More likely, as Trent would think back in years to come, Porcini hated the cadets because they were on their way to becoming warriors—the pinnacle of Clan society—and he could no longer look forward to the glory of that life. Among the Clans, especially the Smoke Jaguars, a warrior of Porcini's age was already considered obsolete.

To the members of the Mist Lynx sibko, however, he *was* their life, their enlightenment, their window on the universe. The Kit Master was an example of what they might hope to be one day—a trueborn warrior. To them there was no outside world, no other planets, no Kerensky Cluster, no galaxy. There was no place to go, no place to visit. This was their home, one they had never left in all their lives and all the years of training. The camps, the study, the drilling, the practice, the constant testing, these were their entire universe. All they knew. At least until they either flushed out in failure or won the final Trial of Position that would qualify them as full-fledged Clan warriors.

And today was a day like so many others, but Trent would remember it all his life for what it taught him about himself and the way of his Clan. On this day he took a stand, little dreaming where it would lead him many years and many light years from this time and place. On that misty morning, one burned into his memory like a hot brand, Trent made his true place in Clan history, more than if he had earned a line in the *The Remembrance,* the long epic poem that every warrior revered and learned by heart.

"You have all been trained in our history, but today I want to teach you something beyond history, something about who we are as a people. You, Cadet Sobna, tell me, who are we?" Porcini's question was, like so many others he posed, obviously a trap.

"Aye, Star Commander," Sobna said, buying herself a few scant moments as she organized her thoughts. "We are Smoke Jaguars, true heirs of the legacy of the Star League! We are the hunters of our enemies, the wreakers of havoc, the stalkers in the night. We are fearless in combat, the true embodiment of the warrior code!" The dark-haired girl spoke firmly and with a conviction that had been hammered into her brain almost since the day she emerged from the iron womb—the genetic engineering vat that had spawned her.

"You utter words from books and lessons, petty words in the mouths of unworthy children. You do not know yet what it means to be a Smoke Jaguar," Porcini scoffed. "Your battles are with simulators and with your bed mates." His scowl of disgust was so fierce that Sobna bowed her head in shame. Sibko members were genetically bred from the same donors and at the same time, and were then reared and trained together from their earliest days of memory. Life in a sibko was one of constant martial training and intense competition.

Failure, even minor, was feared. Porcini's cold gaze drifted to the equally dark-haired Russou, who seemed eager to take on the question.

"Cadet Russou, who are we?" Porcini commanded.

Russou faced him squarely, without fear. "We are the ordained ones, the ones destined to one day re-forge the Star League. Of all of the Clans, the Smoke Jaguar alone hunts for the thrill of the hunt alone. We are stalkers, patient, swift, and brutal. When the fog of war has lifted, we alone will bear the banner of the one Clan, the ilClan, and the flag of the new Star League."

Young Russou's whole face lit up as he spoke the dream of all the Clans, that they would one day return to the Inner Sphere, that they would reestablish the glorious Star League under their rule. And like every other Clan, the Jaguars believed it was their Clan that would rise to power over all the rest.

Star Commander Porcini turned away slightly, then pivoted back suddenly, slapping his leather glove across Russou's face with such force that the young cadet spun away under the impact. As shamed as Sobna had been, Russou grabbed at the stinging red mark on his face. Resistance was futile and foolhardy.

"You too know the words, and the words you utter contain the truth, but they still do not say who we are. And coming from a cadet who has never fought a battle in the name of his Clan, they border on mockery of all true warriors."

Porcini shifted his gaze to Trent. In the years that would come, Trent would remember this moment in the twelfth year of his life as a cadet, would remember the utter contempt on the Kit Master's face—a look of near hatred.

Porcini locked eyes with Trent. "You, Trent—you believe that the blood of the Jaguar flows in your veins, *quiaff*? Then, tell me, who are we?"

Trent studied the training officer for a moment, heart pounding and hands trembling as he searched his mind for a response. "No words, Star Commander," he said finally. "Words alone do not make a warrior or show the true nature of the Smoke Jaguar. Only battle can do that. I challenge you to combat in a Circle of Equals to give you the answer you seek."

Star Commander Porcini smiled, a dark, almost lustful smile. He gave a single nod. "Answered well, Cadet, and you shall have your wish. But for me to face you would be idle folly. I am a warrior and you a mere kit. But I will grant you the opportunity to prove your point. Jez will stand as my proxy." He motioned to the girl standing nearest to him.

Jez. Up until that day Trent had managed to keep her at a distance despite their cramped living conditions. Sibkos were usually a tightly knit, close group, but Trent could never feel any kind of closeness to Jez. No matter that he had seen her every day of his life, that they shared the same precious genetic donors, no matter that sibmates ate, drank, studied, trained, slept, and succeeded or flushed out together. Trent could never feel he had anything in common with Jez. She was always the favored of the Star Commander, but not because of any intrinsic worth. It was more that she always seemed to push herself to the forefront by stepping on the backs of others. She came forward now as the others formed a circle around her and Trent.

Years and years later, after the passage of many battles and many journeys, after the death of many comrades, after betrayals and humiliation, after victory over his enemies and the loss of everything he had ever known, Trent would still remember that day he fought Jez in the Circle of Equals.

Her long black hair was braided down her back, and the tawniness of her skin was tanned even darker. She was as slim and strong as Trent, but he did not share the slight Oriental tilt of the eyes that Jez and some others of his sibmates showed. She licked her lips as if she savored fighting him—or, at least, so he remembered. Perhaps memory clouded the truth, but it would always seem to Trent in later years that she was not just getting ready to fight him, but to kill him if given the chance.

He dropped into a crouch, lowering his center of gravity as he reached out with his hands. He had seen Jez fight before, and knew what to expect. She always went on the offensive. It was her hallmark. She struck fast and furious, hoping to take out her foe in the first few seconds of combat. In later years he would remember this well and use it against her then as he did on this day.

She will attempt to leap on me, get to my rear. I've seen her do it before. Trent, like the others of his sibko, was trained in the martial arts, and his mind raced with the various possible countermoves. Star Commander Porcini raised his hands in the air as he spoke from the Circle of Equals surrounding the two cadets.

"As it was in the time of our founders, such tests are

settled by battle in view of the peers. Let none break the Circle, save the weaker and the inferior. To the victory goes justice and the right." He clapped his hands three times as the members of the sibko chanted in unison, "Seyla!"

Jez sprang even as the solemn word was uttered, her eyes seeming to blaze with hate. Trent was ready. He grabbed her even as he let his own body drop into a roll, lifting and flipping her over his head as she attempted a grapple. He completed the roll and landed squarely on top of Jez as she tried to turn over. She grabbed at his hair to pull him to the side, but Trent jabbed his palm into her windpipe.

The blow was true. Her eyes seemed to double in size as she gasped for breath that did not come. Trent did not wait for her to regain her wind. As she let go of his hair and grabbed at her throat, he rolled off her and pulled her to the edge of the Circle of Equals. The other cadets stepped aside to let him through. Once he got her outside the Circle, he had won.

Jez lay gasping for air as Trent rose to his feet and faced the Star Commander Porcini. "That is my answer, well delivered and done. That is what a Smoke Jaguar is."

"Well delivered and done," was all Porcini said as if nothing had just transpired. "You understand what it is to be a Jaguar cadet—this much you have proven. Now you must learn what it is to be a warrior." He swept his leg out and sent Trent sprawling. Trent was totally unprepared for the attack. It came like lightning and left him lying flat on his back on the stony ground.

Trent never understood why the Kit Master had behaved this way. He had defeated Jez in a fair contest, only to be humiliated. It seemed unfair that the vastly more skilled warrior would knock him down, especially after Trent had managed to beat him at his own lesson.

Many things began for Trent that day. His rivalry with Jez, his disdain for Clan politics and intrigue, everything seemed always to lead back to those moments high in the Gray Ridge Mountains of Londerholm. An insignificant day in the life of a warrior in training—a day like any other—yet like a pebble in a pond, its ripples were far-reaching. It was a starting point, but it was also the beginning of the end. Perhaps the end of the very people who had spawned him.

"One day," Porcini said, picking up his thread as if nothing had happened, "one day you or your bloodkin will take our people down the Exodus Road. My task is to make sure that you are prepared for such a journey. When the grand crusade to liberate the Inner Sphere begins, you will stand ready as true Jaguar warriors."

They all knew the story of how the Clan forefathers had long ago left the Inner Sphere to escape the pettiness and greed and vicious wars that had destroyed the glorious Star League, mankind's greatest achievement. In the centuries that followed the Clans were born, but they remained hidden deep in untracked space far from the Inner Sphere. There, they had evolved on their own, adopting genetic engineering to create and maintain their warrior caste. Every Smoke Jaguar knew that the Clan's single most important goal was to one day return and reclaim their heritage.

"This 'Exodus Road,' what is it, Star Commander?" Russou asked obediently.

"It is the path General Kerensky and the Exodus fleet took from the Inner Sphere to our homeworlds. The Star League, the glory of mankind, had fallen. Aleksandr Kerensky saved us as a people by taking his followers away from the chaos that was to come.

"For almost two years they traveled into the unknown depths of space, until they came finally to five worlds that would become their refuge from the chaos of the Inner Sphere. The way was long and hard. The great Kerensky rescued our people from the age of war and destruction that has consumed the Inner Sphere in the centuries since then. After his death, the general's son Nicholas completed his father's work by creating us as warrior Clans in fulfillment of his own great vision.

"The Exodus Road still awaits us. Just as it once brought our people here to the Kerensky Cluster, it will be the path back when the time comes for the Clans to return to the Inner Sphere. The Exodus Road is our secret, and our greatest defense. No one in the Inner Sphere suspects either its existence or ours, and thus we need never fear them coming here to taint us as they taint everything they touch."

Exodus Road. Every time Trent heard those words in the years to come, he would remember this day, his fight with Jez, and the unfair treatment by his Kit Master. Trent would travel the road three times in the service of the Jaguar, and two more in the service of his own soul.

But all that was to come. Much else would happen before his future would take shape from this moment. Just how much, the young Trent could neither have dreamed nor imagined.

BOOK ONE

Anvil and Forge

From Kerensky's Stars came the Eight Hundred
Beneath a banner of Truth and Righteous Light
To lift up those who had suffered and to smite down
With fearful vengeance those who had ruled
In the name of Vanity or Greed.

—The Remembrance, Passage 98, Verse 28

There will be a time when our descendants
Return to reclaim what is our right.
With honor swelling their hearts, they will crusade
Against the dark emotions that have dimmed
The Inner Sphere for so long.

—The Remembrance, Passage 3, Verse 41

True warriors do not follow paths, they make them. It
is not just their desire, it is their nature

—Nicholas Kerensky

Racice River Delta
Tukayyid
Free Rasalhague Republic
2 May 3052

Star Captain Trent barely noticed the dense trees that filled marshes of the Racice River Delta as he rushed up to the large open clearing, his *Timber Wolf* sinking into the muck as he came to a walking pace and searched for targets of opportunity. This was the only large clearing they had encountered for kilometers of swamp and bog. His Starmate, Schultz, moved to flank him in a *Mad Dog*. The *Dog* was so shattered and mauled that Trent was amazed it could even move, let alone fire. So many warriors had fallen in the fighting. He and Schultz were all that was left of the Binary that had been his command.

The sight of the *Mad Dog,* moving with its bird-like gait, stirred Trent even after all his years as a MechWarrior. For the past six hundred years 'Mechs had dominated the battles and wars of mankind. Roughly humanoid in shape and rising up to twelve meters tall, a single 'Mech carried enough firepower to level a city block. It could operate in almost any terrain, be it the vacuum of space or the depths of the sea. Even this swampy morass. And animating them were the warriors who sat high in their cockpits, using their own neural feedback to help pilot the massive machines of death.

To Trent it was fitting that the cream of Clan technology

was here to crush the Inner Sphere's last vestige of hope. The might of the Clans returning to conquer the Inner Sphere had made the invasion a stunning success. Planet after planet had fallen to them as their armies rolled relentlessly toward Terra.

Then ComStar, the techno-mystical cult that occupied and preserved Terra, had decided to take sides. Using secret intelligence they had gathered on Clan honor and traditions, they had challenged the Clans to a proxy battle on Tukayyid. If the Clans won, they could claim Terra at last. If they failed, the invading Clans would have to abide by a fifteen-year truce. Such a truce would leave a warrior like Trent too old to take part in the invasion when it resumed. That was why losing the fight here and now was not an option.

Each Clan was to conquer two cities in the fight, and the Jaguars had won the right to strike first. While Alpha Galaxy dropped into the nearby Dinju Mountains to approach their target, his own Beta Galaxy, the Mist Weavers, had dropped into the swamps of the Racice River to reach their target city of Port Racice. Victory and the kill was to be quick, but instead of an honorable battle on a field of honor, the Com Guards had used the bogs and deep pools to stage a series of ambushes. They had mired down the Mist Weavers with artillery barrages, turning what should have been a quick victory into a prolonged and costly fight . . . one that was not going in favor of the Smoke Jaguars.

"Silver Paw to Cluster Command," he barked, as a series of explosions rippled among the nearby trees. "We are in Sector Five-fourteen."

There was a hiss of static, some from Com Guard ECM, some from damage. The strained voice of an officer—not his own Star Colonel—replied. "Silver Paw, this is Dark Vigil. The command post has been overrun. We are pulling back. Elements of the enemy are in your area. Link up with Blood Streak Star and pull back as our rear guard. We will reorganize in the delta, *quiaff*?"

Blood Streak Star . . . Jez's command. A part of Trent hoped that Jez had met her fate against the meat grinder of the Com Guards. These were not the untested warriors that Khan Lincoln Osis had led them to expect. Their first engagements had been against green troops, no match for the Jaguars. Now it was different. Word had reached him that saKhan Weaver had died in the fighting. With her death, what was left of Beta Galaxy was pulling back, regrouping, still groping for some kind of victory.

Worse, the Com Guards had nearly destroyed his Binary, Bravo Striker of the 267th Battle Cluster. Schultz was all that was left, more by luck than skill. Temper had perished in an ambush by Com Guard infantry. Silvia had died in her cockpit while a Com Guard fighter strafed the battle zone. Winston had died embracing an enemy *Crockett,* letting his fusion reactor go critical as he held his foe in a death-hug.

It was *supposed* to have been a lightning-fast victory against inferior Inner Sphere warriors. He let his eyes rove briefly over the trees and the dark shadows among them, and in that brief instant understood the meaning of this moment. This was Tukayyid, the largest battle fought since General Aleksandr Kerensky had liberated Terra from Amaris the Usurper three centuries before. But that was not all.

Trent was a Smoke Jaguar, and he knew that such a mighty conflict must surely result in heavy losses. New warriors would now have the chance to fight for and claim the bloodnames of those who died on the battlefield. The thought of winning a bloodname stirred Trent to his core.

He had met with Star Colonel Benjamin Howell just before the Jaguars dropped onto Tukayyid, and Howell had agreed to sponsor Trent for any Howell bloodnames that came open when the fighting was done. Trent believed it was only a matter of time before he too would stand among the bloodnamed of the Smoke Jaguars and all the other Clans. Claiming a bloodname was the greatest achievement to which a warrior could aspire. It meant his genetic legacy would become part of the sacred gene pool, and he would live on beyond his days.

All that remained was to defeat the Com Guards. He knew that his commanders considered ComStar's effort to end the invasion pure folly. They also viewed the quick strikes of the Com Guards as a waste of resources.

Trent saw the truth, that the Com Guards had played a game of hit and run so hard and fast that the Jaguars of Beta Galaxy were being worn down. Now, the Jaguars were in retreat, no matter how much their commanders called it reorganization. He had tried to tell the Star Colonel what he saw unfolding, how the Com Guards were crippling the Jaguars. But he'd been cut off in mid-sentence. The Jaguar high command believed they had the situation under control. They had ignored him.

Just as he was about to signal for Jez, Trent saw her *Warhawk* sweep into the far end of the clearing a kilometer away. She was following the Com Guard infantry she was routing, mowing them down with a barrage from her large pulse lasers. Or, at least the one that was still operating. He throttled his *Timber Wolf* to a full trot as he raced after her.

He knew Jez well enough to realize she would not break off pursuit no matter what the orders. They must have already commanded her to do so. That must be why they were sending him after her. Her willfulness would be her death one day. Perhaps this day . . .

Trent signaled Schultz as he rushed forward, locking on to her signal. "Cover my left flank as we go. We have orders to link up with Jez and pull her back to cover the Galaxy's rear flank."

"Aff, Star Captain," Schultz said as he matched the trotting pace of Trent's *Timber Wolf.* Trent checked his sensors and saw that Jez was ahead of them, moving in and out of the trees surrounding the swampy clearing. Her slow movement on the sensor display told him that a battle was raging over there, and he braced for it as he ran toward the shadows of the dense trees.

Suddenly he was buffeted by a powerful blast that lifted his *Timber Wolf* off the ground. There were impacts, not from weapons, but from pieces of Schultz's OmniMech battering his own.

The short-range sensors told him what was happening. A short-range missile carrier had opened up on Schultz the moment it had spotted him. More than thirty missiles had blown through the remains of Schultz' *Mad Dog* in less than two seconds. There had been no time for him to eject, no time to fire, only time to die. And Jez was facing two other Com Guard 'Mechs in the middle of what must have been a Com Guard forward command post or repair base concealed at the edge of the clearing. Infantry blasted away with shoulder-mounted missile launchers and manpack PPCs, slowly but surely, destroying her *Warhawk.*

Trent was not about to accept Schultz's fate. He locked onto the withdrawing SRM carrier and let go with his long-range missiles. The warheads raced across the smoke-filled base and into the carrier. Digging through its side armor, the blasts ate into the vehicle's magazines, setting off its weapons in a massive explosion.

He was pivoting just as one of Jez's attackers, a stark white *Crab*, broke off and fired a wild shot in his direction, missing by at least five meters. Trent was hoping for just such a shot, one that would let him intrude on Jez's fight without depriving her of any honor. He locked on with his last salvo of long-range missiles and let them fly the milli-second he heard the lock tone on the stout *Crab*.

Most of the missiles found their mark on the enemy 'Mech's right side, ripping its arm off and sending a shower of smoke and sparks into the air. At least two of the missiles streaked past the *Crab*, pounding into Jez's 'Mech. *That warrior is good. He has tricked me into doing damage to my own people* . . . The Com Guard 'Mech twisted at the torso under the impact of the blast, but quickly returned fire from its deadly large laser. The shot dug into the left leg of Trent's *Timber Wolf*, popping off the ferro-fibrous armor in a series of rattling explosions. The heat rose slightly in his cockpit as he moved to the left of the *Crab*, making it harder for the enemy 'Mech to maintain its weapons lock. Keeping his distance, Trent knew he could optimize his long-range weapons against the injured 'Mech.

He held his fire until he had cleared the distance between them, then opened up with his large lasers. The brilliant red lances of laser light reached out for the *Crab*. One beam hit the ground just past the aptly named 'Mech, sending a streak of smoke across the once green field. The other found its mark, cutting laterally into the hip of the *Crab*. Its armor sizzled for a second, then exploded as the shot sliced deeply into its internal structure. Myomer fibers, the "muscle" that propelled BattleMechs in combat, severed and burned, and a sickening green wisp of smoke rose into the air. The hip joint seized, if only for a instant, finally popping loose at the last moment as the *Crab* pilot desperately attempted to get his damaged 'Mech into a better firing stance . . . or so he thought.

Jez's fight with a nearby Com Guard *Thug* was turning into a deadly slugfest as the *Crab* spun back on her, fully exposing its back to Trent. He saw the *Thug* drop, its left leg blown off at the knee in an explosion of black smoke and shrapnel. Almost at the same moment the *Crab* spun to face her at nearly point-blank range. Jez never saw where the shots came from, and the assault was devastation. The *Crab*'s small and medium lasers sent out a wall of pulsating light, gouging into the armpit of Jez's *Warhawk*, stabbing upward because of the *Crab*'s lower posture. A secondary explosion from within the guts of Jez's OmniMech sent her left weapons pod flying into an infantry position while the *Crab*'s remaining large laser boiled off what remained of her rear armor.

Jez pivoted to face her foe, swinging the stump of her mangled arm like a club. In a difficult piloting move, the *Crab* pilot evaded the swinging arm by putting his 'Mech into a crouch. Rather than return fire, it moved in close and kept to the side of the *Warhawk,* giving Jez a kick that caved in most of the *Warhawk*'s leg. Trent was impressed. To dodge, turn, and still attack at such range was the mark of a warrior worthy of a Jaguar in combat.

Trent could not let Jez die. They were both Smoke Jaguars, no matter what were his feelings for her. Her 'Mech had taken a lot of damage, and if he didn't leap to her defense, she would die. Then he saw what the *Crab* pilot had done and could not help but feel admiration. *A worthy foe indeed.* From the way the 'Mechs were positioned and their close proximity, Trent would hit Jez's dying *Warhawk* if he fired at the *Crab* and missed. The choice was his. Hold his fire and move to her flank, possibly allowing Jez to die, or open fire.

For Trent, a Smoke Jaguar as surely as if the Jaguar's heart beat in his own chest, there was no choice.

As his targeting cross hairs arced down on the *Crab* and his weapons hummed with preheat energy, he suddenly hoped that the *Crab* pilot would somehow survive his attack. He or she would make a fine addition to Clan Smoke Jaguar as a bondsman. Any warrior willing to place him or herself between two foes and take both on at the same time was a worthy prize of battle.

Trent held his stance and fired with everything he had, hitting the rear flank of the *Crab* with a horrific blast of laser fire. The bright red and green laser beams sliced into the armor deeply and brutally, and slabs of armor sprayed off into the air. None of his shots had missed . . . Jez lived for now.

The *Crab* warrior held his own, firing steadily at Jez as she finally turned her 'Mech so she could retaliate. The Com Guard MechWarrior stayed with his 'Mech long enough for Jez's *Warhawk* to shred two tons of his armor in a wracking series of laser blasts doled out at devastating range. The superior Clan technology held. The *Warhawk* stood its ground, readying for a kill.

Trent's shots ensured that Jez would not have the honor of dying on the field. He had locked onto the *Crab*'s damaged hip region, and his lasers had done their job well. A burp of black smoke and green coolant spilled from the area he'd struck. There was a flash of flame as the hip actuator superheated and exploded violently, knocking the *Crab* down and out of the battle. Its pilot knew that the 'Mech was all but finished. Trent saw the cockpit blast clear and the ejection seat rise up on a white wisp of smoke over the battlefield. *Punch out.*

Jez swept the retreating Com Guard infantry with her lasers, hitting only one trooper, but pressing the others deep into their foxholes and trenches with the fiery display. Trent opened a broad-band signal to the entire area. "Pilot of the Com Guard *Crab*, I claim you as isorla in the name of the Smoke Jaguars."

His communications channel came to life as Jez spoke to him. "You dared violate my honor by firing on that *Crab*, *quiaff*? I shall face and kill you for your actions."

"The *Crab* fired at me first, Jez. No honor was lost. We have orders to fall back and act as rear guard. You will accompany me," Trent replied curtly.

"Orders to fall back? That is not the way of the Jaguar warrior."

"It is the way of all warriors to follow orders of superiors, and yours come from Galaxy command. We must leave now."

Jez did not get a chance to respond. From the eastern edge of the clearing a swarm of Com Guard BattleMechs rose from the muck and mire and took firing stance, lighting up Trent's short-range sensors. He saw the count of enemy targets on the display and felt his mouth go dry. *Ten!* Trent instantly understood why he had been ordered to withdraw. Apparently the Com Guards were heading straight at him. *Clan honor places victory above wasteful death. Standing and fighting here means death.*

The closest of the ten 'Mechs, a racing *Hussar*, was locking onto Jez at the same moment Trent triggered his extended long-range lasers. He reopened a channel to Jez. "Pull back now, Jez!" He began to move his *Timber Wolf* toward the center of the clearing and was preparing to break into a full run.

"Damn you," she said, finally conceding and moving toward him. "When this is done, you will die at my hand in a Circle of Equals."

"Later, then. For now, do your duty and move out!"

His sensors showed a Star of Smoke Jaguars closing in, rushing to reinforce them, but they were still precious seconds away. Jez's 'Mech moved past him, and Trent cursed her silently. No matter what he did or said, she would bend it to her purposes, twist the truth to fit her vision of the events. He did not need this, not with his chance at a bloodname so close at hand. *Perhaps she will die first. No question of honor must taint me when I am presented for the Trials . . .*

Suddenly the mud and swampy waters seemed to erupt all around his *Timber Wolf.* Fiery clods of muck, peat, and bog splattered against the *Wolf* as if the very ground of Tukayyid was exploding under him. As the 'Mech pitched, he compensated. Flames licked upward at him from the ground.

Trent's targeting computer demanded his attention as the 'Mech rocked. *Artillery—and Arrow missiles.* The enemy 'Mechs were not confronting him in a direct fight, but wanted him dead without honor. He turned his 'Mech to try and get free. It was a move he would never complete.

The second barrage did not rip at the soil but found its mark on his already-battered *Timber Wolf.* Artillery rounds shattered his shoulder-mounted missile racks, turning them into debris in an instant. A blast of warmth seemed to wrap his body as he saw the image of a ComStar *Hussar* still racing straight at him, its laser blazing as Trent's 'Mech staggered like a drunkard. One of the Arrow VI missiles went off on his foot, then another dug deeply into his shoulder, ripping the weapons pod away from the *Timber Wolf's* left torso with a thunderous blast. His 'Mech was dying, but Trent knew he had to survive. Somehow.

There was no time to fire or move. The *Timber Wolf* began to tumble as countless artillery rounds rained down on him. The 'Mech quaked under each impact, and Trent's brain shrieked as the battle computer sent a stream of neural feedback into his neurohelmet. Trent wanted to scream and may have, but the deafening echoes of explosions drowned out every sound around him. His secondary display lit up as jump infantry suddenly appeared all round him. The display imploded and cracked, its plasma crackling like green and orange lightning. Other controls popped and smoked. His mind sped like a wild horse, trying to find a way out of the disaster around him.

He reached to hit the ejection control when suddenly the viewport in front of him blew inward. A wave of flames roared to life before him. *Infernos!* Inferno missiles were filled with gelled petrochemicals that could generate incredible heat in a 'Mech. Given his crippled status, the use of inferno weapons meant a fiery death for him. Trent felt his body tense against the restraining straps as the flames engulfed his arms. His neurohelmet visor popped off from the blast, and flames lapped inward at his eyes. The smell of cooking meat filled his nostrils, and he knew that the smell was his own flesh.

Pain, harder and deeper than anything he had ever felt before. Every cell of his skin seemed to sear with a pain that cut deep to the bone. A bright white light seemed to take him, and all sound melted away. *Death. It had to be death. If only the pain would go as well . . .* Blindly, he reached into the light, groping either for the visage of death or for the ejection control, whichever he could find first.

$\equiv$ 2 $\equiv$

***Smoke Jaguar DropShip* Hunter's Den**
Outbound for Nadir Jump Point
Tukayyid
Free Rasalhague Republic
28 May 3052

It was the time of his eternal nightmare, a blackness of night that seemed to have no end no matter where he moved in it. In the nightmare, he saw the fire demons all around him. They were shaped like humans, but were made of fire. Like people perpetually engulfed in fire.

He was afraid in the nightmare, trying to run from them. He had been afraid before as a youth, but not like this. This was an indescribable terror when the demons burst forth, their unintelligible screams somehow muffled in his ears. Trent tried to run, but the furious shapes merely reappeared in front of him, bursting into existence from nowhere.

He didn't always run. At times he tried to punch or kick the fire demons, using every shred of his warrior's training and prowess. But he was no match for the flames. Worse yet was the pain that came when he did manage to strike out at them. He screamed, his voice reverberating strangely in the distortion of the dream. He knew the screams were his. And that the odor of cooking flesh was his own. This was no ordinary nightmare. It was beyond that.

What frightened him most was that the dream never seemed to end. He tried to wake up, push himself to the edge of it, but he couldn't seem to get free. Even the pain and fear were not enough to wake him. Still, he kept on trying. He had to. If this wasn't a nightmare, then it had to be hell. Trent didn't believe in hell, but if he were dead, what else could this be?

Fear was no stranger to him, but as a warrior he had learned to overcome it. This, however, was a fear that could not be vanquished. The flaming demons, their roaring, their searing, defied him. Amid the sound of his own screams, he heard a distant laughter. It was the fire demons. They mocked him, they eluded him, they tormented him. The sound was worse than the flames, the rage of his frustration burning him even more.

Then he heard a voice. This was something new, something that had not happened before. The voice seemed to call his name, echoing in his brain and heart. He rushed past one of the flaming demons, which reached out for him with its fiery fingers, singeing his arm. Trent paid it no heed. It felt like his feet were encased in lead, but he pushed on, moving toward the sound of the voice. Suddenly the darkness came alive with both light and movement. He tried to focus on the images, but they were blurred. As he moved forward, the light seemed to fade entirely.

"Star Captain?" the voice said, this time not echoing but clear. Trent opened his left eye and saw a face hovering over him. It was female and someone he didn't know. A film slightly blurred her image, but when he tried to raise his hand to wipe it clear, he couldn't. *One of my eyes will not open . . .*

"Do not attempt to move. You are aboard the hospital ship *Hunter's Den* en route to Hyner. I am MedTech Karen. You have been badly injured and are currently restrained while your wounds are treated."

"Victory, *quiaff*?" His voice was barely audible through parched lips and a dry throat.

The MedTech lowered her head slightly. "You ask of Tukayyid. On the third of May we departed the field of battle. Only the Wolves won both their objectives. The Jade Falcons and the Ghost Bears each fought to a draw, but with grave losses. We live now under a truce with ComStar."

Truce . . . neg! Trent's mind felt sluggish, but he understood the implications of her words. The battle of Tukayyid was to have been the proxy for control of Terra. If the Clans had won, then Terra would be theirs, it being only a matter of time before the rest of the Inner Sphere fell to their might. A loss meant not only dishonor but that the Clans must halt their invasion for fifteen years. A warrior like Trent would surely be too old to participate in the front lines when the invasion began again. Worse yet, the grand crusade of the Clans to retake the Inner Sphere and form a new Star League was on hold, ground to a halt.

It was as if he had traded one nightmare for another. The warrior caste of the Clans was nothing like the militaries of the Inner Sphere, which allowed their warriors to fight on into old age, decrepit and past their prime. No, the Clans kept their warrior blood hot and young. New warriors, genetically bred and then honed in the sibkos, manned the front-line Jaguar units. Older warriors, those now past the age of thirty or so, were cast aside to solahma units that offered little hope of honorable death.

Trent had no idea how long he had been unconscious, how long he had been wrestling with the flaming demons of his nightmares, but now the horror of that dream seemed preferable to the nightmare of waking reality. All hope was lost. All hope but one. And to that he clung.

A bloodname.

Star Colonel Benjamin Howell had promised his sponsorship. Despite the Smoke Jaguar defeat on the battlefield, Trent could still aspire to winning a bloodname. It meant survival beyond his days, a hope that his genetic legacy might one day serve the Clan further.

"How long?" he croaked as the MedTech moistened his dry lips with a damp cloth. His upper lip felt swollen, as if he had been punched in the mouth.

"You have been unconscious for twenty-six days. We dock with our JumpShip tomorrow. Do you remember what happened to you?"

Trent closed his one eye and winced slightly. Yes, he did remember. He had saved Jez, done his duty. There had been a massive artillery barrage and the Com Guard assault. Then there had been flames and fire. The smell seemed to rise again to his nostrils, the odor of burning flesh.

"Aff," he replied as she adjusted his bed position, raising him slightly so that he could see more than just the ceiling. The dull green color of the bulkhead walls told him that he was in an intensive care unit, and the designation of the ship as a hospital DropShip told him even more. He knew the colors all too well. It was not the first time in his life as a Jaguar warrior that he had been in such a place.

Trent did not know what to think or say. He had been injured many times before, but never to the point of unconsciousness for such a long period. Had they induced unconsciousness as part of the healing? Memories of the fire and of the terrifying images of the nightmare played through his mind as he thought on what had happened.

A new voice just outside his field of vision shattered his reverie. "How long has he been awake?"

"A few minutes, sir," MedTech Karen's voice replied.

"What does he know?"

"Only the results of the battle and how long he has been unconscious. Nothing of the extent of his injuries." Her voice was pitched low, but her tone told him everything.

Trent tried to stir his body to life, as if he were doing a physical inventory of himself. He shifted his feet, though only slightly and with an aching in his joints. Still, the legs and feet seemed to be there. His left arm was also responsive, but his right seemed immobile. Numb and lifeless, unable to obey the signals from his brain. *My arm, have I lost my arm? And my eye, it is covered. Have I lost that too?*

"Star Captain Trent." It was the new voice, and now the face of an older man came into his field of vision. By his age and dress, the man was obviously a member of the scientist caste. Warriors never reached such advanced years, but the lower castes perpetuated the old traditions of keeping the aged active. "I am Doctor Shasta. Do you feel any pain?"

"Neg," Trent said, voice weak but sounding clearer to his own ears. It was as if he was finding new strength with every breath, as if his body were waking from a long sleep. He felt no pain, but the disturbing absence of sensation in one arm and one eye left him wondering just what was the extent of his injuries.

The one called Doctor Shasta, his hair stark white and deeply receded, stared down at Trent thoughtfully. "You were badly burned. If not for the actions of our relief forces and your bondsman, you would have died."

Bondsman? He remembered the warrior he had claimed as isorla, the one who had piloted the *Crab* so daringly. "How bad?" he stammered.

"Your right arm and hand were badly burned. We have

used myomer implant surgery to restore their mobility and control. I had to reinforce your bones with carbon filaments as well. It will be several more days before we can calibrate the arm for use. Your face was also burned severely, and I could not repair your right eye. We have budded you another from your gensamp, and it will be complete in several days. That is why your head is restrained. The growth matrix is mounted on your face."

My eye is gone. They were growing him another, but how did a man fight in battle without his *own* two eyes? "Fight again, *quiaff*?" Trent asked in a rasping breath. His greatest fear was to hear that all this effort was being made to prolong his life with no hope that he would ever again lead men and women into battle.

The wrinkled old doctor shook his head almost hesitantly, as if he was not saying all. "You will pilot a BattleMech again, Star Captain. There is more to your injuries, but we will save that for later, when the time is right. For now, you need nourishment and rest. MedTech Karen will help you eat, then we will induce sleep."

Trent closed his left eye and felt a warm wet trickle down the side of his face. He clung to the words of Doctor Shasta. He would once again be able to serve the Clan, to stand and earn a bloodname in the Howell line. He would once again command warriors in battle. War must surely come again, and Trent swore to himself that he would be a part of it. This time, there would be no nightmares. He had faced the fire, he had survived it. He had met death, lain unconscious for many days. But he had come back. What could stand in his way now? Nothing would ever stop him again.

Trent awoke with the feeling of his entire universe seeming to pitch inward on him. He knew the sensation all too well, the nausea and disorientation of a hyperspace jump. The JumpShip and its DropShip riders had leaped from one star system to another, tearing a hole in the fabric of reality, if only for a millisecond. The disturbing sense of spatial vertigo common to a hyperspace jump had stirred him to consciousness.

He opened his eye and saw the room. It was the sixth time he had been awake since his long period of unconsciousness, each one longer than the last. More important, he felt stronger each time, as if his body were doubling in strength

with each awakening. He was always attended by MedTech
Karen, whose face and hands had become familiar as she
tended him. Even the synthetic rations tasted good to Trent,
and that alone told him just how seriously he must have been
injured.

He was permitted the use of his left arm and that gave him
control of the bed-angle controls. They had removed the
bulky genetic accelerator from the right side of his face,
which allowed him to lift the bed to a sitting position. He
had used his left hand to feel the synthskin wraps in place on
his other arm. He had also felt his face and the bandages that
seemed to mummify half his head.

This time Karen was not alone. Doctor Shasta stood at her
side. Trent suddenly realized that the man's presence had
significance, a sign perhaps of something more serious. "Is
everything in order, *quiaff*?" he asked.

Doctor Shasta cradled one arm at the elbow, chin resting
in his hand as he studied Trent. His expression was one of
concern, but he did not answer immediately. "We are going
to have to change your dressings, Star Captain. The time has
come to show you the extent of your injuries."

"You told me I would pilot a 'Mech again," Trent said
calmly. "For a warrior, there is no more."

Doctor Shasta smiled as he spoke, but to Trent it looked
like pity. "I have treated warriors for my entire career, Star
Captain. Each caste carries its burdens as well as its privi-
leges. You may yet learn that there is a higher price for the
right to command in combat again."

What was this? Insolence? By a member of a lower caste?
Doctor Shasta reached out with a pair of scissors and began
to remove the outer wrappings around Trent's head. Trent
remained still, but his breath, much to his surprise, was
racing. What *am I afraid of, the words of a mere scientist? I
will fight again. That is the only thing that matters.*

The entire process took ten long and tedious minutes.
MedTech Karen handed Doctor Shasta a small mirror, which
he in turn handed to Trent. Without hesitation, Trent held the
mirror in front of his face and looked out with his one good
eye at the image there.

Only a single bandage remained, and it held a patch over
his right eye. The flesh of his face was badly malformed. The
skin was gone, covered only with a wet, almost glossy synthskin that eerily revealed the veins underneath. Half the hair

on his head was gone, what was left apparently rescued only by the lining of his neurohelmet. All that remained of his right ear was a deformed bump of flesh. His nose did not bear any resemblance to its former state. It was almost as if his face had melted, leaving his nasal passages wide open and oozing with antiseptic cream.

The skin that had been his upper lip was half gone on the far right, exposing his gums and teeth. Trent understood now why he had dribbled some of his liquids on his chin—or what was left of his chin. The once firm jaw, the genetic hallmark of the Howell bloodline, was now all but gone. The skin and muscle tissue had been so badly eaten away that only some synthetic skin covered the thin remaining tissue and bone there. The horrible scarring continued down his neck and ended there.

Doctor Shasta had pulled off the dressings from his right arm, and Trent saw the price he had paid for ejecting and surviving. The hand seemed reddened but intact, but the forearm and upper arm were burned as horribly as if they had been exposed to the brimstone fires of hell itself. Replacing the lost muscle were myomer bundles, covered again with synthetic skin. The arm hung lifeless at his side, but somehow, Trent knew that it was functional. If anything, the myomer muscles would make the arm even stronger than before.

"My face . . ." was all he could say as he stared into the mirror.

The doctor nodded. "The synthetic skin will protect you from infection and is more durable than your natural skin." Trent looked over at MedTech Karen and saw the look of pity in her eyes, and it stung him.

"I bear the mark of a warrior," he said proudly, lowering the mirror. *Such scars and marks show that I have no fear in combat, that I fight fiercely and without remorse. It will be a sign to all who see me that I possess the true heart of the Jaguar.* But he also knew it would take time to get used to the face in the mirror. It was new, alien to him.

Doctor Shasta nodded slowly. "For all the days of your life, Star Captain. Our medical science could easily repair the damage, but our warrior caste does not permit us to squander medical resources for the sake of vanity."

Trent had no quarrel with that. The Clans, especially the Smoke Jaguars, abhorred waste. Such had been the way of the Clans since the time of Nicholas Kerensky. The Clans would never have survived without this policy. "I am not asking you to repair this damage. I will bear these marks with pride. They show me a true warrior to anyone with eyes to see."

Doctor Shasta shook his head slightly. "As you desire, Warrior. I have done what members of my caste are required to do. I have healed your injuries to return you to active duty as a warrior. I have rebuilt you to the extent allowed that you might rejoin the ranks of those who fight in the name of the Smoke Jaguar."

Trent smiled slightly. "Let those who see my face know that I did not run, but met the enemy head on."

Adept Judith Faber's last scream didn't go anywhere. The dark soundproofed room deep in the belly of the Smoke Jaguar DropShip *Hartel* absorbed her wailing as her interrogators talked above her limp body as if she wasn't there. She knew they must be outbound from Tukayyid, but she was only vaguely aware that she was on a ship. It was more like being in the bowels of hell. Judith could not see the faces of her tormentors, but she had endured their questions for several days.

The memories since her capture were a blur, twisted by drugs and the pain of torture. She had been only half-conscious when taken prisoner by the Jaguars. They had wrapped a cord around her wrist several times, then herded her aboard a Drop-Ship. In passing, one of her guards had told her of the Com Guard victory on Tukayyid, but her joy had been short-lived. With deadly efficiency, they had begun to interrogate her. First just interview style, then with drugs, electrodes, and neurofeedback sensors. She was not surprised by their extreme measures. She had, in fact, learned of these techniques as part of her mission briefing. Knowing about them was one thing. Living through them was another. All Judith had was her own strong will, a thin veil between agony and insanity.

"She passes, marginally," the deep voice said from outside her field of vision. It didn't matter to her any longer. The torment was almost too much to bear. She was ready to break, almost ready to tell her inquisitors the truth. Even death would have been a welcome release from the pain.

"Narco-interrogation is very effective, but ComStar has shown itself to be resourceful in our past encounters," the lighter voice, almost female, said. "She could have been treated with blocking agents to evade our interrogation."

"Is she at risk?"

"Perhaps," the suspicious voice responded. "But doubtful. Only a handful of our people claimed bondsmen in the fighting on Tukayyid. I find it odd that she did not want to be repatriated with the other Com Guards we captured."

"Her interrogation shows that she lost friends and subordinates in the fighting and that she felt much guilt for their deaths, even though she herself fought admirably. As we discussed yesterday, her guilt is deep, and it has proved to be a powerful weapon in breaking her thus far."

Judith hung on the pause by the suspicious voice, the one that had tormented and tortured her to surface the memories. "She has remarkable technical skill for one who was a warrior."

"It may be what keeps her alive and of use to us. Star Captain Trent claimed her as isorla," the deep voice said. "But we do not walk the path that the Wolves have chosen. She will never pose the risk of a Phelan Kell within our ranks— not if we certify her as a technician. And, that is my recommendation regarding her."

"She saved Star Captain Trent's life, *quiaff*?"

The deep voice did not answer immediately. "Aff. His support unit was overrun, and the technicians never recovered. She can serve as his tech, if Trent so chooses."

Judith heard the sounds of fingers tapping on a keyboard, methodical and quick. A few moments after they stopped, she felt a hand on her forehead. "I know you can hear my words, Judith. Your strength may return, but for now, you must be content only to listen, *quiaff*? You fought as a warrior, but that time has passed for you. You belong to the Smoke Jaguar now, and have a new role to fill. May the Kerenskys have mercy on you . . ."

Just before she passed out, Judith smiled to herself, knowing they would never know why. *It has begun . . . .*

Base Hospital
Smoke Jaguar Planetary Command
Warrenton, Hyner
Smoke Jaguar Occupation Zone
3 July 3052

Trent sat up in the bed and slid the fingers of his right hand into the glove-like device, adjusting the straps with his left hand. He activated it, and a series of controls and digital readout pads on the fingers and wrist came to life, showing an everchanging set of numbers. He made sure that it was hooked up to the computer interface in the arm of the bed, then he began flexing his fist. Each flex of the wrists sent myriad signals into the computer, which measured the control of his hand and wrist.

It was part of the ongoing therapy he had been forced to endure since his arrival on Hyner a week before. The damage to his arm was much more extensive than Trent had realized at first. Most of his natural muscles had been destroyed and replaced with thinner myomer bundle strands. While the arm looked atrophied and frail, it was covered in a sheath of synthetic skin that actually made it much stronger than before.

The problem was in getting used to it. Constant therapy of this kind allowed the Medtechs to calibrate the tensions of his new muscle fibers, which would eventually give him the control he would need in the cockpit. His fingers, though burned, were healed enough for him to regain some feeling.

That was what he missed in his arm, the feeling. The arm was numb, with sensation only in his hand. It took getting used to, but he was getting better at it.

His eye was a different matter. The genetically grown replacement worked fine, but the loss of the muscles in his eye socket had required some artificial enhancements. The doctors had mounted a set of small, low-strength myomer muscles and a micro-computerized control mechanism that let the implanted artificial muscles position and focus the re-grown eye. The result, a functional dark brown eye ringed with circuitry controls that framed the eye like a silvery monocle. Over the past few days the headaches associated with the implant and replacement had become almost tolerable.

Trent's physical strength was still depleted, though he was working with weights to remedy that. The drugs pumped into him from several medipatches kept him functional, but his overall strength was low. Each day he was awake more, and slept less. Still, the most exercise he got was traveling between the bathroom and his bed. According to the doctors, it would still be weeks before he would be fit enough to return to active duty.

When not working on the various routines that would return him to the ranks of the warrior caste, Trent studied the files in the computer terminal attached to his bed. He was looking for information on the fallen bloodnamed of the Clan to see what bloodnames might now be open. It was frustrating that the files contained too little data on the aftermath of Tukayyid for him to be sure.

He had his orders, though. He was being reassigned to Delta Galaxy, Third Jaguar Cavaliers, known as "The Stormriders." It was hard to know much about the unit, however, since it was being reformed in the wake of the reorganization of the Smoke Jaguars after the heavy losses on Tukayyid.

As the light of Hyner's later winter sunrise lit the walls, Trent saw a man in a crisp gray uniform without a single wrinkle come into his room. He recognized the man instantly as Star Colonel Benjamin Howell. Howell came over to the side of the bed and looked down at Trent, his face more tired and worn than Trent remembered.

"Star Colonel," he said, swinging his legs off the bed as if to rise to attention. A wave of the hand from Howell cut off his effort.

"There is no need for such formality between us, Trent,"

Howell said, taking a seat next to the bed. "I saw that you had been posted here too and thought a visit was in order."

"I am honored by your visit, Star Colonel," Trent said. "But I am afraid my personal effects, including my chess set, have not caught up with me yet." Trent had known Benjamin Howell for the past three years, and the two had become comrades. Their chess games were the stuff of legends among the rank and file of the Cluster's warriors. More important, Benjamin Howell had agreed to sponsor Trent for any bloodname slots that opened up.

The mention of chess brought a smile, if only for an instant, to the face of the Star Colonel. Then he was serious again. "I do not have time for such diversions these days, Trent. There is much happening within the ranks of the Smoke Jaguars. How do you fare?"

Trent reached up almost unconsciously and touched his scarred face and the nub of flesh that had once been his ear. "I have been better. But I will be ready for combat soon. My arm is stronger than ever before, and my scars look much worse than they feel. They have offered me a mask, but I have turned it down."

Howell shook his head, then spoke in a much softer tone. "Truth be told, I do not know what would be worse. To have gone to Tukayyid and died, or to now have to honor the truce."

"Will we honor it?"

"Affirmative. But like any agreement, it has loopholes. Places where we can stretch the terms and conditions. Our leadership will do that. That has always been our way—the way of the Jaguar."

"Perhaps you and I will fight side by side yet for the Clan," Trent said. "We will yet stand on the soil of Terra, *quiaff*?"

Benjamin Howell did not seem heartened by the words. If anything, his shoulders slumped slightly at the words. "Neg. There are two types of war that the Clans engage in. One is the direct fight—the battle on the field. The other is the war of words, of politics. In both we are a ruthless people. While I long for the fight in combat, I find myself a victim in the battles of politics within our Clan."

Trent was puzzled by these words. Not that he did not know about the politics of the warrior caste. He had not reached the rank of Star Captain without exposure to the undertow of intrigue that ebbed beneath the austere image the warriors presented. What puzzled him was that Howell seemed to be saying he had somehow failed to master these skills.

The Star Colonel ran his fingers through his hair, a gesture of frustration that Trent had seen before. "You do not know because you have been too ill to learn of all that happened to us on Tukayyid. We were crushed because the Com Guards saw our only weakness and exploited it. Both of our Khans were also reported dead."

His voice dropped almost to a whisper, as if he feared his words would reach ears not intended to hear. "A Council of the bloodnamed was held immediately to name a new Khan and I backed the nomination of Star Colonel Brandon Howell. I spoke freely, saying that we might have succeeded on Tukayyid if Khan Osis had not bid too low. I pointed out that it was only because of Brandon Howell's exemplary performance that we retained any honor at all. As it turned out, Brandon Howell was approved as new Khan of the Smoke Jaguars."

Trent had only seen summary reports of Brandon Howell and his performance on Tukayyid. He had proven himself to be a wary commander whose caution saved the Jaguar Grenadiers from annihilation. He had also heard the broadcast that Khan Lincoln Osis had died during the battle. Osis' survival and virtual return from the dead seemed to have shaken the leadership of the Jaguars. "And then Lincoln Osis was found to be alive, *quiaff*?"

"Affirmative. Brandon Howell assumed the role of saKhan, and Lincoln Osis took over leadership again. He had learned of my speech and my strong support for Brandon Howell. As a result, he viewed me as someone less than loyal to him. It was a taint I could not refute, and I saw the accusation in his eyes whenever he looked at me."

Trent nodded in understanding. Lincoln Osis had a reputation for utter ruthlessness. Nor was he known to be forgiving. "There is a saying I have heard. 'Khans come and go, but the warrior spirit burns eternal.' "

"That is well when the Khans are truly dead. But that is not what happened in this case. But, Trent, please believe how much I regret that you have had to suffer because of my mistakes. You have been a true warrior, a credit to our blood house. You do not deserve to be pulled down by my short-sightedness."

"But I am not—"

Benjamin Howell cut him off. "Neg. You do not know all. Many bloodnamed warriors gave their lives on the cursed soil of Tukayyid. The Trials of Bloodright for those names will begin soon. The Khan has asked me to sponsor one of his candidates for the Howell bloodname."

Trent felt his heart race at the words. *It is not possible . . . Benjamin Howell was to sponsor me.* To a Clan warrior, a bloodname was the highest of possible honors. Only a small few eventually won the right to carry a surname—surnames that had been handed down from those who had been among the original 800 from whom Nicholas Kerensky had forged the Clans centuries before. Winning a bloodname was the goal of every Clan warrior and the only way to ensure that one's genetic material would become part of the sacred gene pool.

Trent was shocked to hear that Howell did not intend to keep his word, and his anger seemed to roar in his ears like a stormy sea. "What did you say to him?"

Benjamin's frame shifted in his seat, unable to totally hide his discomfort. But he did not evade Trent's eyes. "I did what any warrior in my position would have done—I obeyed what my Khan asked of me."

Trent balled his fists in anger. He felt his natural skin flush, but a warmer glow came from the synthskin that covered part of his scarred visage. "Your word. Your honor. You betrayed your promise to me?"

"Aff. I had little choice."

"You could have refused him."

Benjamin shook his head. "You have always misjudged the importance of such maneuverings in our Clan, Trent. Khan Osis knows of my rally-cry against him. If I do not accept his request, he will make it his business to see me excluded from any military actions that arise in relation to this Truce.

"I am older than you. Though I do claim a bloodname, we share the difficulty of coming to an age where a warrior must wonder whether he will end his career in glory or in disgrace. The Khan determines who is in command of what unit. If I cross him, Lincoln Osis can have me posted to some forgotten asteroid along the Exodus Road. Or worse, send me back to the homeworlds as a sibko trainer. I have worked too hard and long for such to be my fate."

"There is something I can do," Trent said, pivoting his body and planting his feet over the edge of the bed. "I can challenge you to a Trial of Refusal. If you feel the urge to bend to the will of the Khan, I will bend you back." Trent did not conceal his anger.

Howell shook his head and got to his feet. "Be realistic, Trent. You are still too weak. Undertake such a Trial and I would defeat you easily. And if you did somehow win, Khan Osis would simply challenge me himself. In the end, I assure you he would be the victor. No, Trent. This is the best way—the only way."

Trent drew a long breath. He felt the cool air on his legs. Looking down at his body still swathed in the drab hospital gown, he had to admit to himself that he was not ready for combat. Even if he did somehow manage to defeat Benjamin in a Trial of Refusal, he would be wasting strength he needed to compete for a bloodname. And Benjamin Howell's words rang true. Lincoln Osis would make both their lives difficult if Trent attempted to defy his will. He bit his lower lip in frustration. *This cannot happen. Do political games now rule the Clan? That nomination was to be mine!*

"I will not be denied a bloodname," he said in a low tone.

"I cannot help you," Benjamin said. "Not this time. Perhaps if another bloodname becomes available . . ."

Trent shook his head. The anger lay coiled in him and he must contain its power until the proper moment to strike. "I do not wish your help, Star Colonel. I am a warrior. There is always another way."

Benjamin nodded. "The Grand Melee."

"Aye," Trent said. "It is my only hope now." Most candidates could only compete in the Trial of Bloodright because they had been sponsored by one of the holders of a bloodname. But one candidate was chosen not by nomination but by a free-for-all slugfest known as the Grand Melee. Any eligible warrior who lacked a sponsor could participate in the fight. It was a wide-open contest, with dozens of 'Mechs engaged in battle. Only one warrior would emerge as winner, and that person would be eligible to enter the Trials of Bloodright. Sheer survival was the key to success in a free for all like the Grand Melee.

"You may die there. You are still weak from Tukayyid."

Trent's eyes were hard, his voice just as stony. "I will fight there and find my destiny."

"So, you are the bondsman who has been posted to my bay?" the large man said as he paced around Judith in the bowels of the DropShip's 'Mech repair bay. The smell of petroleum lubricants filled the air, joined by the pervasive smell of sweat. Judith had been in such repair bays before, and the familiar noise of rigging gantries clanging around her provided an odd sense of comfort. "Your presence here is a mark against me, freebirth."

"I am sorry that you feel that way," she said.

"You should be," he said coldly. "I am Master Technician Phillip. You may be the property of a warrior"—he flipped a finger under the bondcord around Judith's wrist—"but here, in this repair bay, I am your master."

"I am Judith Faber—" Phillip cut her off with a slap across the mouth.

"Neg," he bellowed angrily. "You are Judith. You have no other name. You have nothing that I do not allow or grant you. Any other name you had died with you on Tukayyid."

"I understand," she said. Judith had been trained intensively in the society of the Clans and their ways. Now she was finally living in their midst. The rules had changed, and she was going to have to work with that. *Fine, Phillip. You want to be in charge. You can. The day will come when you learn respect for me. For now, you may play the role of the dominant male.*

"You know very little. Even if you are the brightest tech in the Inner Sphere, you know nothing compared to me. They sent you here because you showed some hope of learning how we do our tasks. Even though I have more important things to do, I will shape you into a real tech . . . or see you dead."

Judith didn't answer this time. This fellow obviously thought he was superior, and for now it was best to let him assume he had that power. Resisting him would only cause problems she couldn't handle at the moment.

"Now you have nothing to say, eh?" Again he slapped her across the face with the back of his hand. She recoiled in pain, but Judith was sure it would have been worse if she had dodged the blow when she saw it coming.

* * *

Trent stirred slightly in his sleep, sensing the presence of someone standing alongside his bed. Opening his eyes he saw her there in her gray leathers, only barely visible in the night light of the room. Her pistol hung from a holster on her shapely hip, and she stared at him with arms crossed. Trent was certain he knew who it was, but reached over and turned up the light to be sure.

She startled at first sight of his face, then a sneer spread over hers. "So, the rumors are accurate. You do live."

"Yes, Jez, I am alive." The fact that he had survived Tukayyid must be eating away at her. Especially since he had saved her life. *The last time I saw her, she swore to face me in a Circle of Equals. Now her bravado is faded.*

"And I see you are looking more attractive than ever, Trent." She laughed softly.

He might have answered that she was as sharp-tongued as ever, but decided not to give her the satisfaction. Nor did he drop his eyes or change expression in any way.

"My scars show me as the true warrior I am. You are alive too, Jez. Perhaps that is why you are here. You have come to thank me for saving your skin, *quiaff*?"

She threw back her head and laughed again. "Apparently the battle damaged your memory as well as your body, Trent. If you ever get access to my reports of the incident, you will see that it was *I* who saved *you*."

Trent shook his head and laughed in return, though not with the strength he would have liked. "It sounds like you have falsified what really happened there on Tukayyid. And with my 'Mech gone, I cannot produce any battle ROMs to prove you the liar you are."

"Truth is written by the victor, Trent. My OmniMech was also lost later in the fighting, leaving only my word against yours. Though the Smoke Jaguars did not win in the Racice Delta, my actions there have won me a nomination for the Howell bloodname."

Trent heard her words and felt the anger roar in him like a fire stoked to white heat. Benjamin Howell had told him that the Khan had ordered him to back another for the open Howell bloodname. Now Jez was telling him that she had falsified her version of the battle and won the right to compete.

Trent regained his mental composure, then locked his eyes onto hers, so that she understood not just his words, but the menace he intended.

"Unlike you, I follow the path of honor that the Great Kerenskys laid out for our people. There is no honor in the path you follow, and you would be wise to consider what you might be bringing upon yourself and the Smoke Jaguars. And though I cannot prove or disprove your account of what happened on Tukayyid, you will not best me without a fight, Jez," Trent replied.

He lifted his right arm and flexed his half-natural, half-artificial fist in defiance. "Remember this, and remember well. I have known you since our days in the sibko. I know the truth of what happened between us on Tukayyid. Knowledge is the ultimate weapon a warrior can carry into battle." The last line was one he knew would sting her. They were words their sibko trainer had drilled into them. How could she have forgotten?

Jez stared back at him, her eyes narrowed in cunning. "There is another old saying," she said. "To the victor go the spoils."

= 4 =

Trent stood at parade rest at the far end of the massive repair bay, arms behind his back, posture ever-straight. The rounded collar of his gray fatigues bore the markings of his rank and of his new unit designation, a roaring storm cloud with the eyes of a jaguar cutting through them in red. In the dim light of the huge bay, Trent cut an impressive figure, and only a closer look showed his scarring. No matter how long he spent healing, his body would always be marked by Tukayyid. The synthskin that covered his face was a lighter shade than the rest of him. His eye, ringed in a circle of circuitry metal, gave him an air of menace.

Trent was actually pleased with the way he looked, however, and was beginning to call the face in the mirror his own.

He had come to the repair bay to meet his bondsman for the first time. Phillip, the burly Master Technician, was leading her over to him now. The woman wore an old jumpsuit that was two sizes too large and worn through in some spots. Her long black hair was tied back carelessly. Her green eyes revealed a hint of her Oriental genes, but were puffed and weary. Trent realized that Master Technician Phillip must be making life difficult for her. He saw her half-glance at the Master Tech, and glimpsed the rage she was not totally able to conceal.

Trent waited calmly for the pair to come within speaking distance, and he noticed the bondsman's eyes curiously examining his face. His scars, his mark of pride from battle.

"You are Judith, *quiaff*?"

"Yes, I mean aff, Star Captain," she said, catching her mistake before he or anyone else could levy punishment.

Good, Trent thought, *she is learning her place.*

He drew in a breath and straightened his stance slightly. "I am Trent, the warrior who bested you in the Racice Delta and who claimed you in the name of our Clan. You are my property, my bondsman. You are not a person now. You have no life other than that which I allow you. Do you understand, *quiaff*?"

The words were required. The owner of a bondsman had to make sure that the bondsman knew his or her place. To Trent, it was simply the way of things—how things had to be, the Jaguar way. He had seen Judith fight on Tukayyid and knew that she was every bit the daring warrior that he was. She had shown herself cunning and fearless, which was why he had claimed her as isorla for the Clan. Now he had to tame her, break her spirit. But not too much. Just enough that she would remember who and what she was now.

Judith looked down at her wrist where the bondcord was wrapped three times around. She rubbed the cord as if it bothered her, then turned back to Trent. "Affirmative, Star Captain. I remember the fight all too well. Master Phillip has made sure that I know my place in the Smoke Jaguars." She rubbed higher on her arm where a dark bruise was evident, proof that Phillip had used more than verbal abuse with his new charge. Trent did not balk. Such was the way of the lower castes.

"Good. Then know this, your place in our Clan is among the technician caste. My own tech was killed during the recent fighting, and you will now serve in his place."

"Understood, Star Captain. The Master Technician informed me of my posting two days ago. You will not be disappointed with my work. I have learned much already about how to service and support our 'Mechs."

Trent saw a glimmer in her eyes, as if she had hopes in her new position. *She does not understand how Smoke Jaguars deal with Inner Sphere bondsmen.* "Judith, you will serve in this capacity for the rest of your years."

"I seek to prove myself to you, Star Captain. One day, I hope to pilot a BattleMech in combat again as a warrior."

Trent shook his head. "Negative, Judith. You do not

comprehend the truth of your new life. We Smoke Jaguars do not subscribe to the folly of the Wolves or the Ghost Bears. We do not take bondsmen from the Inner Sphere and allow them to enter our warrior caste. That would dilute our breeding. You have tested as a technician, and you shall remain a member of that caste and serve always that role."

Her expression did not change, yet Trent could not help but wonder how she was adapting to this new life. Among the Clans, being taken bondsman was not an unusual experience, but for someone like her the adjustment to her new status must be difficult. She had, after all, been a warrior—Inner Sphere or not, freebirth or not. And one of such skill that Trent considered her capture a prize. "What is the status of my OmniMech, Tech?" he barked.

Judith pulled herself into a stricter stance, almost coming to attention, perhaps more out of habit from her former life than out of respect for her new master. "You were assigned another *Mad—Timber Wolf*." She shook her head as she corrected herself, about to use the Inner Sphere name for Trent's Clan 'Mech. "I've been working—"

Trent stepped forward, getting right in her face. "You will cease using contractions, Technician. This is not the gutter of the Inner Sphere." He snapped at her like a training master at a raw cadet.

"Aye, Star Captain," she returned as Trent stepped back. "The engine shielding had just been replaced and is operational. I am in the process of replacing the leg and refitting the cockpit components that have been damaged. Your T&T will be functional in two days' time. I hope to have all armor replaced in a week. Weapons pod configuration can take place after that."

Trent shook his head to show that was not good enough. "My 'Mech must be fully outfitted, repaired, and readied for combat by the end of the week, I expect it to be configured in a primary configuration."

Judith's face wrinkled in a mix of anger and frustration. "With all respect, Star Captain, that is not possible. There is a shortage of technicians, and I am all that is available. The schedule I gave you was ambitious as it was."

The left side of Trent's face also wrinkled in displeasure, but the synthskin of the right side did not move, did not reveal any expression. "Did you not hear me the first time, bondsman? I am telling you that you will have to do better."

"I do not know how—"

Trent cut her off. "You are Clan now, Judith. You must learn to improvise. I do not care if it takes every hour of every day between now and Friday, you will have my *Timber Wolf* ready for combat."

"By Friday," she said, lowering her eyes in a gesture of submission.

"Good. On that day, I will take part in a Grand Melee. Let Master Tech Phillip tell you what that is and the importance of it. My BattleMech must be ready by then."

She nodded. "I will do as you ask, Star Captain."

"And then some," he added, pivoting hard and walking away from her.

The simulator cockpit bucked and swayed as Trent swung his *Timber Wolf* through another slugfest, this time with a *Warhawk*. While the primary monitor displayed an eerily likelife model of the OmniMech moving past him, he could not help but remember the last time he'd seen such a 'Mech, in the Racice Delta.

He brought his already damaged *Timber Wolf* into a run and zigzagged across the possible field of fire. The *Warhawk* anticipated his attempt to evade fire. It laid down a pattern of suppression fire with its PPCs, trying to box him in and limit his movements. Trent admired the programmers of the simulator. It was so lifelike that it almost had an intelligence of its own.

Rather than dodge, which would have permitted the *Warhawk* pilot to make a searing shot to his left flank, he rushed into a blue beam of charged particle energy. The simulator shook violently, and a wicked arc of azure charged particles danced like lightning across his cockpit. The temperature spiked in the close confines of the cockpit, induced by heaters tied into the program, and Trent's skin began to crawl with the heat. Especially his synthetic skin, which didn't sweat like its natural counterpart. Nothing was as it had been. Things had changed. He had changed . . .

He pivoted and fired a swarm of long-range missiles at the *Warhawk*, not waiting to see how many of them found their mark as the other 'Mech moved to a lower firing stance. The simulator bucked and heaved as he swung hard right. Three of the *Warhawk*'s PPCs lanced out at his *Timber Wolf*. Their simulated beams slammed into his torso, ripping at the Omni-Mech's internal organs. Trent watched in frustration as the last of his armor disappeared and the beams tore at his internal systems. Failure lights came to life on his command console, their red beams of death the only illumination in the cockpit. *Gyro failure. Engine shielding breach. Reactor hit.* Each light told the story, one he did not want to admit was possible.

Suddenly, all of the lights went dark. It was over. He hit the release that opened the cockpit pod of the stimulator with a hiss, and looked over at the tech in charge of loading and executing the program.

"Numbers," he demanded sternly, lifting off his neuro-helmet and wiping the sweat from the left side of his brow.

"You managed to take out the two lighter 'Mechs and inflict a total of thirty-four point five percent damage to the *Warhawk* before system failure."

System failure. The words echoed in Trent's mind. Technician talk for his death. He would have to do better, drill harder and longer. The Grand Melee was only seven days away. He had to be ready.

Trent licked his lips and nodded. "Load the simulator again. Run it with random encounters, all weight classes."

"Aye, Star Captain," the tech responded. Trent pulled himself back into the simulator pod and prepared for another run.

"You are working late again," Phillip said, startling Judith as she contorted her body to fit into the small access hatch just under the cockpit of the *Timber Wolf.* The usually noisy 'Mech repair bay was oddly quiet at this hour, making her every grunting noise echo eerily through the bay. Only her head and one arm fit inside the space as she adjusted the circuity with a portable unit.

At the sound of his voice, she emerged from the hole, her hair and arms slick and clotted with light green coolant and lubricants.

"Is there a reason, Tech?" he said.

"Aye, Master Phillip," Judith said. "MechWarrior Trent has ordered me to have his 'Mech ready by the end of the week—ready for a Grand Melee."

Phillip softened his tone. "He did at that. Well, then, I shall assist you, for time is running short."

"Thank you, Master Phillip," Judith said, bowing her head slightly. She had heard of the Grand Melee during her training. She knew she should have asked him about it, but another instinct told her not to. *He's hiding something, and the less information I provide him, the more chances he will have to slip up.* It was a hunch, but one she was more than willing to play.

"Perhaps I will work with you on this—to set you an example of our techniques and procedures," Phillip said, adjusting his coveralls over the considerable bulk of his belly.

Judith studied him for a moment and nodded. "I would appreciate that." She stood watching him as he moved around to the other side of the 'Mech and out of her sight. *And I know enough to check over everything you do . . .*

Trent emerged from the simulator, drenched in sweat, his legs quivering slightly as the muscles relaxed from his last run. The pod-like simulator hissed as its sliding canopy's retracting pistons released some of their pressure. He stood for a moment, then leaned on the simulator, not even looking at the tech who had run the simulation. The last run had been much better. Three destroyed 'Mechs of the same and lighter class. One other, a massive *Gargoyle,* had sent him into oblivion. But in the end, he had beaten the programming, the equivalent of facing live warriors.

He drew a long breath and felt his chest muscles strain from the exercise. Trent knew he had pushed too far in the past few days. His body was still recovering slowly and painfully from his injuries, and now that the simulations were over, a wave of weariness washed over him.

The all-out fighting of a Grand Melee would surely go faster than anything he'd yet achieved in the simulations and would require higher levels of endurance. He had yet to press himself that far because he knew his body was not yet ready. He had a week to prepare, a week to bring himself up to a level not merely to compete in the Melee, but to win.

Trent felt a pressure that only a trueborn could experience. He was a Clan warrior, but he was thirty years old. By Clan standards, he had reached his prime. There would be fewer chances at a bloodname in his life, fewer opportunities for new commands. Unless he won a bloodname, he would soon fade into obscurity within the Smoke Jaguars. The thought of becoming obsolete gnawed at him, drove him on. It was that thought, that hidden fear, that pushed him to the Grand Melee. Ready or not.

And if he failed, it would be a total defeat. At his age and without a bloodname he could easily end up assigned to a cursed solahma unit—aged and worthless warriors slated for suicide missions where luck might give them one last chance for the honor of a warrior's death. The Grand Melee was Trent's last and only hope.

The hulking man leaned over the desk to better read the information on his desktop display. He paused over one page of text on the screen, running one massive hand through his crew-cut blonde hair as he pondered the words.

His office would not have been considered small by most commanders, but it was totally out of proportion for a man of his incredible size. Were he a MechWarrior like many of those in his command, the office would have been wasteful, too big. But as an Elemental warrior genetically engineered to wear and fight in the massive Clan combat armor, Star Colonel Paul Moon was huge by normal human standards. He seemed to be sitting behind a child's desk rather than one suited to a military commander.

He turned his gaze to the blast-proof glass windows behind him and stared off into the city. Already a fog was beginning to rise with the break of day, the hot sun instantly turning the frost and light snow into steam. The Smoke Jaguar planetary command post did not offer much protection against the cold of Hyner. He thought he knew winter from his days in the sibko, back on the Smoke Jaguar homeworld of Huntress, but this freezing cold was something else.

The Star Colonel returned his eyes to the screen and saw the image of his junior officer newly assigned to his Cluster. *Star Captain Trent.* The man was a Smoke Jaguar MechWarrior, but despite the length of his service and participation in the invasion of the Inner Sphere, had not earned a high degree of distinction. Yes, his actions during the initial phase of the invasion had been admirable enough. Reports showed that he was highly competent, a skilled tactical officer.

But then came the record of his performance on Tukayyid. Moon had not been part of that fateful conflict, but some of his closest comrades had fought there—and died there. Instead of winning in short order as they had expected, the Smoke Jaguars had been virtually driven from Tukayyid. Worse, nearly two whole Galaxies had been destroyed. It was not the fault of their leaders. Lincoln Osis was a great Khan, having risen like a phoenix from the dead on Tukayyid. No, Paul Moon saw that it was not the leaders, but the warriors themselves who had failed against the Com Guards. Untried freebirth warriors—Inner Sphere barbarians—had beaten the alleged best of the Clans on that accursed planet.

Warriors like Trent. He was among those to blame for the humiliation of the Jaguars on Tukayyid.

Studying the man's service record, Paul Moon felt his contempt growing. Trent had risen to the rank of Star Captain, but had failed in an earlier attempt at a bloodname. Now he had filed a request to participate in a Grand Melee. *He will fail in this as well. The odds are against him.* The chances of winning a Grand Melee and going on to achieve a bloodname were so low as to be almost nonexistent.

As an Elemental, genetically bred to fight in the powered suits of battle armor Clan infantry wore to rend apart enemy 'Mechs, Moon viewed the warriors who piloted BattleMechs with a certain degree of disdain. Clan society held warriors in a slightly higher position then Elementals, yet he thought that was not entirely justified. He looked down at his massive arms, his forearms callused where the internal webbing of his Elemental suit had rubbed him over the years, and smiled. *Like all warriors who pilot 'Mechs, this Trent probably considers himself superior. I am bred to be larger, stronger, more deadly than any mere MechWarrior.* And Paul Moon was now in a position to teach a man like Trent the reality as he saw it.

The reports showed that this Trent had lost his OmniMech on Tukayyid, and that one of his other officers, Star Captain Jez, had stepped in and saved his life as he led a retreat. A retreat! That only added to Moon's disgust. A true warrior would have died in the trying instead of whimpering home like this Trent. To top it off, the man was in his thirties—passing his prime and headed nowhere. A mediocre warrior, not excelling, just surviving. Now he belonged to Star Colonel Paul Moon.

No, he did not like this man already. The sooner Star Captain Trent was gone from his command, the better. He and the taint of Tukayyid he carried with him were intolerable. Like a stink that could not be washed away. Trent would lower the morale of his fellow commanders. He and Jez were from the same sibko, yet it was she who had proven herself. Ironically, she had done it saving his paltry life in battle.

His fate is in my hands. I could perhaps rescue him, turn him into a warrior worthy of the name Smoke Jaguar. Perhaps, with time, he might yet be able to redeem himself. Star Colonel Paul Moon shook his head. No. Failings and weakness within the Clan had led to the shameful defeat on Tukayyid. Warriors like Trent had now crippled the invasion. They were not to be rewarded in the eyes of other trueborns but expunged.

5

Niederwald Crater
Hyner
Smoke Jaguar Occupation Zone
14 July 3052

The week was like a blur in Trent's mind. The work of rebuilding his physical endurance was not going as rapidly as he had hoped. On several occasions, he had passed out from over-exertion, but he ignored the MedTechs when they tried to slow him down. Trent knew this was not the moment to reduce his effort, but the time to go further and farther than ever before.

His bondsman had done a good job of readying his new *Timber Wolf*, though it would be hard to tell by its outer appearance alone. The *Wolf* was newly armored, but there had been no time for his bondsman to give it a special paint scheme. All it could boast was a dull, gray-green coat of primer, which in its own way gave the Omni a unique look.

Trent was pleased with how well it handled, especially since Judith had virtually no experience with Clan technology. She'd worked hard, approaching the task from a warrior's perspective. More than once he'd visited her for status reports and found her sitting in the cockpit not just running diagnostics on new systems, but trying them out in ways that no mere technician could do. It was a bonus he had not counted on, and he respected her for it.

As he stood next to the portable gantry overlooking the

Niederwald Crater, he saw that the task before him was far from easy. A meteor had hit Hyner ages before mankind ever thought of exploring space. The crater itself was five kilometers in diameter and its sides and bottom were strewn with rugged boulders, loose rocks, and dry scrub brush. The contest for the Howell bloodname was being held on Hyner because the rim of the crater offered spectators good protection, and the terrain of the basin was perfect for the close infighting typical of a Grand Melee.

Brandon Howell, the current head of the Howell Blood House, had selected the location. As the leader of the Howell line, the choice of the venue was his alone to make. Fortunately for Trent, the journey to the crater was a short one, a transit of only ten hours to the equatorial region where it was located.

The circle of spectators would form the Circle of Equals. Crossing that line after the start of the match would end one's chances in the Trial. Unlike the Falcons and Wolf Clans, the Smoke Jaguars preferred their Melees to be held in places where combat, not exit from the field, would determine victors and losers.

The other participants were poised all around the rim, and there was a large gathering of spectators. Most were other warriors, a small handful of them there because they had already been sponsored for the upcoming Trials for the Howell bloodname. Trent saw the slender, cat-like Jez among them, standing alone. These observers were here to see and take the measure of a potential opponent.

Trent grabbed the handhold on the leg of the *Timber Wolf* with his semi-artificial hand as Judith inspected the ankle joints and feet of the 'Mech one more time. He had admired her on the field, and now was pleased to see her adapting well to the Jaguars thus far. The Master Technician had brought him none of the reports of insolence that might have been expected from an Inner Sphere bondsman. In fact, according to Phillip, he was worried that she was adapting too well.

Trent had merely grunted when Phillip made that comment. His only thought was that freebirths must have addled brains to spend their time speculating in such an illogical manner.

She walked over to him, slipping a noteputer into her

pocket as she approached. "I have completed my work, Star Captain. There is no more to be done now."

Trent nodded, noting that her Clan dialect and speech was improving. He turned his attention to the crater and the inspectors who were making their way out of it, a sign that the fight would soon begin. "You have done well, Judith," he said carefully. He might have said more, but knew it best to withhold the praise.

"I did what was required of me." There was no pride in her voice, only an expression of duty.

"As a bondsman, that is what is expected of you."

"You are going to go down there and take them all on at once," she said, gesturing to the open maw of the crater. "I've watched you all week as well. The technicians who run the simulator say your scores were impressive despite still being on the mend from Tukayyid. Are you ready for this?"

"You will address me as Star Captain, bondsman, but given your work this week, I shall overlook this mistake. And to answer your question, aye, I am ready to secure my place in the Howell bloodline. The winner of this Grand Melee, the sole survivor, obtains the open slot for the formal bloodname competition. Then, through successive rounds of combat trials, a winner will emerge, one destined to carry the bloodname of Howell."

Judith looked out over the crater, following his gaze. "It is similar to the open arena matches on Solaris VII. I should think the key to winning would be survival more than inflicting damage, at least early on in the battle."

The mention of Solaris made Trent wince in disgust, but only the left side of his face registered any expression. The synthskin on the right attempted to wince with the left, but was more rigid, as if it were a cast mask. "Your Game World, this Solaris VII, will not exist when the Clans complete their liberation of the Inner Sphere. To compare it with the glory and honor of the Grand Melee is to belittle our traditions. You will learn this over time, bondsman.

"But you are correct in your statement that survival is the key in the Melee. I have run many simulations in the past week, trying to find the best way to survive the fighting. It would be early death for me to give in to the temptation to fight like the Jaguar."

"What do you mean?" Judith asked. "What is it to fight like a Jaguar?"

Trent looked at her, up at his 'Mech, and then out over the vast expanse of the crater once more. "Since my first day in the sibko I have been raised to fight with the heart of the Smoke Jaguar. Strike quick, fight strong, kill fast. It is the way of the Jaguar warrior and the style of fighting we engage in during trials and combat. *The Remembrance* tells us we have three strengths: *'The jaguar's spring that brings the enemy down, The jaguar's claws that rend the enemy's heart, The jaguar's taste for the enemy's hot blood.'*

"On Tukayyid, however, I learned a truth I will not soon forget. The way of the Jaguar warrior must include the cunning of the beast that gives us our name. The Jaguar is a hunter as well as a fierce fighter. He does not always rush in fast and furious, but measures his foe and plans what tactics might defeat him. This will be the key to my victory here."

Judith nodded, and gave him a long look, as though observing something she had not seen before. Trent picked up his neurohelmet and began the climb up to the *Timber Wolf*'s cockpit. As he rose, he never heard Judith wish him luck.

Trent began the competition some one hundred meters down from the edge where the spectators stood. He had heard the formal proclamation of the opening of the ceremony over his headset, but he had been busy checking and rechecking every system on his refurbished *Timber Wolf*. Its fusion reactor purred behind and under him as he scanned his nearby opponents, waiting for the flash on his secondary display to indicate the start of the competition. A *Hankyu* sat squatly nearby, its weapons and targeting and tracking systems concentrating on the gathering of 'Mechs near the bottom of the crater.

Poised to his left was a *Cauldron-Born*. This heavier OmniMech was of more concern. His sensors told him it was a Class A configuration, mounting a deadly Ultra Autocannon and two large lasers outfitted for extended range. And, unlike the *Hankyu*, the *Cauldron-Born* seemed to be scanning him.

The signal flashed on his display in bright red—the signal to begin the Melee. Trent's heart seemed to skip a beat when he saw it. Every muscle tensed as he swung his targeting reticle onto the *Cauldron-Born*, which had already begun to rush toward him. The other thirty-one 'Mechs taking part in the competition rushed forward and down into the crater, making the ground vibrate with a steady groaning tremor.

Trent's mind flashed for a moment to his last battle and the rumble of missiles exploding around him on Tukayyid. A chilled sweat rose over his body as he pushed the memory away. *No, this time would be different.* With his mostly artificial arm and hand holding the joystick, Trent nodded to himself, resolve stronger than ever. *It had to be different. . . .*

His long-range missiles let go the instant he obtained a target-lock. They raced out across the open crater field of broken rocks and dry tumbleweeds, lancing into the front of the stout *Cauldron-Born* just as its warrior was slowing to a firing stance. The warheads made a distant popping sound, but Trent paid no heed. Instead he moved backward on the hillside, making his *Timber Wolf* a more difficult target. Even the bright flashes of discharging PPC fire and missile blasts from the cloud rising down in the heart of the crater did not shatter his concentration.

The *Cauldron-Born* pilot let go with his pair of ER large lasers combined with a medium laser. The brilliant red beams stabbed through the wisps of white smoke that rose from his missile hits, scarring the hillside around him. The two large lasers missed their mark, but the medium laser was dead on, striking just to the left of Trent's cockpit like a sword cut. Trent heard the sick sound of armor plating sizzling and blowing off. The slight spike in temperature told him the shot was very close to his cockpit. The synthskin on his arm and face seemed to tingle with the rise in heat, and felt like a thousand spiders crawling across his arm and face.

Trent watched his secondary display, switching it to tactical mode to show the placement of the other 'Mechs. Most of the fighting was below him in the bowels of the crater. The *Hankyu* was moving down to join the fray, at least for now. Trent continued to move backward, keeping the distance between him and the *Cauldron-Born*. If Trent let the other 'Mech get too close, he'd be at the mercy of its Ultra Autocannon. And he did not plan on doing that.

He let go a volley of missiles again, this time combined with his own lasers. Trent had aimed low, hoping to inflict the most damage into the legs of the 'Mech closing in on him. One laser missed, the other hit above the *Cauldron*'s right leg knee, the leg that was higher on the crater wall. The *Cauldron-Born* fired its autocannon as the missiles slammed into their mark. Behind it was a flash of light from the other melee contestants, the signal that a fusion reactor had gone critical.

The first two autocannon rounds whizzed past Trent's right side just past the cockpit. He began to twist the *Timber Wolf's* torso as the rest of the rounds began to slam into his right and center torso. The Ultra Autocannon was a deadly weapon system, and the *Cauldron-Born* pilot was obviously a skilled marksman. The shots shook and rattled the *Timber Wolf* as if it were caught in a hurricane. The whole 'Mech swayed under the shuddering impact of the rounds, and Trent listed forward, leaning into the incoming fire to keep the giant war machine from falling.

The stream of shells moved suddenly upward, one hitting the massive shoulder missile rack, the others then passing into the crater wall and some even higher. Trent turned and was readying another salvo when he saw why the weapons fire had stopped. The *Cauldron-Born* had stumbled onto one leg, the left, on the edge of the crater, then it had teetered and fallen down, sending its shot wide. Trent's concentration of missile fire against the *Cauldron's* legs had been enough to make the pilot lose his or her balance, which sent the 'Mech roaring down into the crater amid a spray of rocks, dust, and shattered armor plating as the 'Mech tumbled.

A glance at his tactical readout showed Trent another 'Mech approaching from below—most likely jumping upward toward him. The *Timber Wolf's* armor had been badly damaged in the previous attack, but he was still holding the high ground. Locking onto the incoming 'Mech he saw that it was the *Hankyu* emerging from the battle below, and about to land on him at almost point-blank range.

At 30 tons, the *Hankyu* was not an ominous threat, but its range would all but eliminate Trent's use of missiles. Trent moved backward up the crater wall, struggling to keep the *Timber Wolf* upright on the incline. A flicker on his internal sensors showed a problem with his left hip actuator. The light flickered on, then off again, and the leg seemed slightly sluggish. How could it be damaged already? The Mech had not taken any hits to the area.

The *Hankyu* landed just seventy meters below him, its array of short-range missiles and small laser shooting up the hillside at Trent. Half the missiles dug into the rocks some ten meters in front of him, while the others plowed into his legs, going off like fireworks and shaking the *Timber Wolf* like a ground quake. The laser and flamer lapped up at him, hitting his left and center torsos. The cockpit temperature spiked with the hit, and Trent broke out into a beady, wet sweat.

He swung his machine guns on line with the target interlock circuits on his firing joystick and dropped the targeting reticule squarely on the head of the *Hankyu*, perfectly outlined between the shoulder missile racks. Trent fired both weapons in a steady barrage, the armor-piercing bullets and flaming orange tracers slamming into the cockpit dead on. Under normal conditions the machine guns were virtually useless, but at this range, they were perfect for in-fighting.

Trent stopped his backward crawl up the crater and brought his recharged laser on-line, sweeping it into the same targeting position as the *Hankyu* reeled from the direct hits to its cockpit. Trent fired again as the *Hankyu* let go with another wild salvo of short-range missiles. His single medium pulse laser burrowed in exactly where the machine guns had done their damage, penetrating the cockpit viewport with a stream of ruby-red light. The cockpit held, if only for a second, then seemed to implode. He saw the explosion and fire at the same instant that the wall of SRMs splattered his *Timber Wolf.*

The damage display showed that none of the missiles had done serious damage, but had spread out all over the 'Mech, hitting its arms, torso, and legs. Trent saw the flicker on the hip actuator turn into a steady red glow on the outline of his 'Mech, and he bit at his lower lip in consternation. The loss of the hip actuator meant that walking, already tricky enough against the steep angle of the crater, would be more tricky. He glanced at the *Hankyu* just in time to see it tip backward—its head cockpit in flames and belching black and green smoke as it fell. There was no sign of ejection, and Trent knew that his shot had been true.

Checking his secondary monitor, he saw that he was still operational but had been peppered badly by the battle thus far. Four damaged tubes had shut down in one of his shoulder missile racks, but his armor, which had been mangled almost everywhere, had thus far not been breached. Except for the damaged actuator, he was still a formidable foe.

The short-range sensors told him that the battle was continuing to rage in the pit of the crater below him, with over half of the participants already shut down or dead. That was fine. His position on the outskirts of the fighting was a good one. Rushing into the middle of that chaos of fire and death was not how the Grand Melee was to be won.

On his flank a *Nova* rose on its jump jets and landed at his same relative depth on the crater's slope. The *Nova* pilot must also have figured out that holding the high ground was the key. Trent toggled through the battle computer readout until he saw that the other 'Mech was configured in its primary mode—mounting a dozen ER medium lasers and the heat sinks to help support them. Getting in too close was going to be suicide for him.

Trent aimed higher up at the boulders and broken rocks above the advancing *Nova*. The ledge-like formation was impassable but could be used as a weapon. Just as he was about to fire, the *Nova* closed to its extreme range and opened up with everything it had.

The air came alive with pulses of red laser light streaking at Trent from his foe. The *Timber Wolf*'s legs and weapons pods vibrated as their armor shredded under the impact, and Trent fought the controls as the 'Mech teetered under the assault. One laser slammed into the side of his cockpit and a throbbing ripple of neural energy pulsed between his eyes, fed back through the neurohelmet. Trent closed his eyes in agony, fighting the sensation of vertigo and nausea that was common with such a cockpit hit. He watched as his communications system shorted out, leaving a faint odor of ozone in the air.

His missile barrage of thirty-six long-range warheads raced outward not seeking the *Nova*, but the rock face above it. Hitting immobile rocks was much easier than aiming at a moving and firing enemy. The entire section and its boulders erupted in a cloud of smoke and dust before the advancing pilot could react. The landslide raced downward at the *Nova*, catching it squarely and pushing its legs down the hill while the upper body seemed to remain in the same place. The pilot fought hard to maintain his or her balance, but it was a hopeless cause. The *Nova* dropped hard, but only slid a few meters before coming to a stop, leaving a trail of broken and shattered armor plating on the rocks and dirt. Almost immediately, the *Nova* warrior began the process of trying to right the 'Mech.

Trent decided to move further back, to get out of the range of the *Nova*'s weapons should it get upright. As he tried to take a step, the hip actuator locked up, refusing to move. The *Timber Wolf* rocked as a new ripple of heat rose in the cockpit. *Stravag!* He tried again, throttling more power to the legs of the BattleMech's myomer muscles, but the hip refused to move, and the incredible shaking almost made him lose his balance.

He was unable to move the 'Mech. If he was going to win, he would have to do it from here.

He locked back onto the *Nova* at the same time that the other 'Mech regained its feet. This time he let go with a wall of laserfire and his own deadly array of missiles. The lasers hit first, gouging the left leg of the *Nova* just shy of the hip, the leg that had borne the brunt of its fall. Green coolant splattered and sizzled onto the bright brown rocks like blood as his weapons dug deeply. The missiles spread out all over the *Nova*, sending up billows of white smoke as armor plating shattered.

The *Nova* did not fall, but stood motionless after regaining its feet, telling Trent that he had either done considerable damage or the 'Mech was unable to move due to massive heat build up from firing all its weapons—possibly both. He tried once more to move the *Timber Wolf*, but the hip refused to give way, frozen in place. The *Nova* held its fire a moment, cooling down, then it took careful aim with its right arm and unleashed another barrage of six lasers. Trent averted his eyes as half a dozen red spears of laser energy reached out for him, blasting into his OmniMech.

He felt the two heat sinks give way before he ever saw the damage indicator on his display. The *Timber Wolf* let loose a metallic moan as the weapons pod dropped and shattered free at the right elbow joint. The sudden loss of weight made him have to fight for the *Wolf*'s balance as it listed on the hillside. Two laser hits to the feet of his 'Mech only made the fight worse, but his skill prevailed.

The *Nova* was running horribly hot and was recharging its lasers as Trent opened up with his remaining lasers. The bright beams cut like knives as he concentrated on the already damaged left side. Strands of myomer muscle broke free, depriving the *Nova*'s leg of support, and the 'Mech went down for a final time.

Before Trent could even check his tactical display, the *Timber Wolf* suddenly rocked from an attack from behind. The entire 'Mech tipped forward, and the ground seemed all too close to Trent as he fought to maintain his balance. The damage was far from light. The armor on the rear of a 'Mech was already weak, but the impact had penetrated deeply, hitting his fusion reactor housing and shooting the temperature in the cockpit up five searing degrees. Twisting his torso around, Trent saw the source of the assault. A *Mad Dog* mounting menacing Gauss rifles. *It is one of the last, if not the last survivor of the battle below. That makes this warrior all the more dangerous.*

The *Mad Dog* boasted two of the deadly rifles, but had only used one so far. Trent didn't wait for a weapons lock, but instead sighted by instinct and fired with everything he had. Half of the missiles and lasers missed, but the rest were enough to mangle the already damaged *Mad Dog* and let the pilot know he was serious. Trent checked his sensors and grinned in triumph—he and the *Mad Dog* were all that was left. The lone *Mad Dog* had emerged victorious from the firefight that until now had raged at the bottom of the crater. Trent knew that he had but to take down his foe, and the path to a bloodname was his. His mind raced over the possible moves he could muster from his crippled 'Mech.

He throttled the fusion reactor for all the power it could muster and pushed with his good leg in a valiant effort to budge the *Timber Wolf* from its frozen spot. There was an audible groan from under him as the internal structure of the OmniMech strained at the effort. Suddenly, the *Mad Dog* let go another Gauss slug, which flashed on Trent's targeting and tracking system for a millisecond before it collided with him. This round hit the *Timber Wolf*'s torso like a supersonic musket ball, digging deeply into the heart of the 'Mech to hit the fusion reactor and its shielding. The automatic safety controls kicked in and shut down the engine before Trent could react. The lights on his displays went dim, with only emergency lights flickering on. He felt the 'Mech totter slightly, then fall, slamming into the hillside.

It was all over now. Trent had no doubt about that. There would be no further bloodname Trials for him. The battle had been fought and lost. He howled in anger and frustration and pounded his fists against the controls in front of him. Shout and beat his fists as he might, it could not help him. Nothing could help him now, but Trent did not care. It was all he had left.

*   *   *

Judith reached the fallen *Timber Wolf* and saw from the look on Trent's face that he was past the point of anger—he was raw with rage. He had climbed out of the cockpit and was standing next to the battered war machine that she had put together from parts. She carried a portable repair kit and a medkit, but from the look in his eyes when he turned to her, he was interested in neither.

Before she could say a word he angrily opened fire. "You freebirth rat! My left hip actuator failed me in the fight. But for that, I would have won. You have cost me dearly, and you will pay for your mistake!"

Judith started at his words, but she took in a deep breath and carefully gauged her response. "I assure you, Star Captain, that I did not fail to check that system. Perhaps it was damaged?"

"Neg! I took no hits there," he spat. Had she been standing any closer, Judith sensed that he would have struck her merely to vent some of the rage boiling in his veins. His ruined face seemed almost demonic as he rode the tide of anger.

She stepped carefully over to the fallen OmniMech and climbed up the leg to gain access to the hip actuator. Trent's analysis was correct. She saw no damage anywhere near the joint. Using the access driver, she opened the outer armor plating to get to the actuator itself. Still fuming on the ground below her, Trent watched, but said nothing.

The access space was narrow and dark, but a portable light from her kit let her see the innards of the 'Mech. Lifting the insulation back she saw that the actuator itself was fused. Instead of the two single moving parts at the hip, they had overheated, becoming one. It was so hot that she could feel the heat even without touching the metal itself.

It was working fine before and after my repairs. She looked further back inside the access panel and immediately saw the problem. The coolant feed that passed nearby, designed to keep the hip cool, had fused shut. There was no breach from the outside, which meant some sort of internal failure. It was such a foolproof system that its maintenance was practically nil. Reaching up to the piping she found it severed and closed off.

Impossible. She moved her face in closer and saw that the piping showed signs of burning. A sticky substance covered its length on both sides that had been severed. She rubbed and smelled it, identifying it immediately. *Petroleum jelly?*

She understood instantly what had happened. After Master Tech Phillip had worked on the *Timber Wolf,* Judith had put in extra time following his moves carefully, inspecting and re-diagnosing every system she'd seen him touch. She didn't trust him, plain and simple. He had gone from an over-bearing and abusive toad to someone who was willing to bend over backward to help her. Now, despite all her best efforts, Phillip had somehow managed his sabotage.

"Star Captain, come up here if you would, sir."

"Why?" Trent fumed.

"You must see this, sir, then I will explain." It took Trent five minutes to reach her and see the spot.

"What is the meaning of this, Judith? You sabotaged my 'Mech?"

"Negative, sir." Judith felt her face flush at the suggestion. "But in a way, it is my fault. Master Technician Phillip was the only other person with access to this area. He must have done this."

"Done what?"

"This jelly pack was probably surrounding some sort of acid. During normal stress tests the *Timber Wolf* never got fully heated like it did during the Grand Melee. That's why it passed my check. I knew he was up to something, but I overlooked this entirely."

Trent paused, taking in her meaning. The implication was shocking. "What you are saying is that our Master Technician deliberately sabotaged my 'Mech for this competition, *quiaff?*"

"Yes, er—affirmative, sir," Judith replied. "He was the only person with the access necessary to plant such a device. He is also one of the few people with enough knowledge."

Trent crossed his artificial arm with his flesh one, and looked away for a moment in thought. "The truth of your words would be impossible to verify. Such sabotage is only investigated by the Master Technician—in this case the very person you accuse of the act."

Judith shook her head stubbornly. "I tell you this damage was not the result of combat, Star Captain, no matter what the Master Technician says or reports." She pulled on the coolant cable so that he could see it.

Trent weighed her words and whether or not he trusted her. Judith was new to the Smoke Jaguars—and an Inner Sphere bondsman to boot. Was *it possible that she was lying, quiaff*? He studied her face, thinking back on the handful of times he had met with her. What she was suggesting seemed unthinkable, yet he understood that for her to sabotage his 'Mech would be an act of suicide. From what he had seen of her on the battlefield, Trent knew that if she sought death, she could easily have found it there.

"The Master Technician—whose 'Mechs is he personally responsible for, Judith?" he asked.

Judith thought hard before responding. "He is in charge of the Star Colonel's armor. The 'Mech he tends belongs to someone named Jez."

Of course. That was all Trent needed to hear. Treachery might be impossible to prove, but he was sure that Jez had somehow engineered this. Furious, he pounded his semi-artificial fist into the side of the ferro-fibrous armor plating of the fallen *Timber Wolf*. The sound stretched out over the empty crater where it echoed like a death knell, then gradually dwindled to nothing in the twilight.

=== 6 ===

Smoke Jaguar Planetary Command Post
Warrenton, Hyner
Smoke Jaguar Occupation Zone
20 July 3052

Star Colonel Paul Moon heard a knock at the door and dimmed the display built into his desk. "Enter," he said.

A man stepped into the office, and Paul Moon's eyes widened slightly as he stared at a face that was scarred and deformed from what had obviously been serious burns. Despite a layer of synthskin, the face had an almost melted-rubber quality about it. Moon found the man's gaze slightly disturbing. He had one real eye and one ringed by a circle of circuitry and technology. Looking at this strange, almost alien face, Paul Moon wondered just how much of a real man was left in the physical form that stood before him.

"Star Captain Trent reporting for duty, sir," snapped Trent smartly, coming to attention before his new CO. He wore his field gray dress uniform, complete with its black and scarlet piping, in honor of the occasion.

For a moment Paul Moon said nothing. Then he stood, rising to his height of two and three-quarter meters. He glared at the scarred and mangled warrior in front of him. *Such disfigurement might be the sign of great pride with many warriors. But with this one, it is only a reminder of his disappointing failures.*

"So this is Star Captain Trent. I have read your file, Star

Captain, and I want you to know that I did not ask to have you posted to the Stormriders Cluster. With all of the reshuffling and reorganization since the battle of Tukayyid, I am forced to accept you into my command."

"I do not understand, Star Colonel. Is there some reason you would not want me to serve under you?"

"Aye," Paul Moon said in his deep voice. "Consider this, Star Captain. I get you, a warrior almost past his prime, a warrior without a bloodname, posted to my command. A warrior who has lost his BattleMech in each of his last two fights. A warrior, who, in the face of an enemy with no combat experience, failed to uphold the honor of the Smoke Jaguars in the most important battle our Clan has ever fought. Imagine, if you will, my lack of enthusiasm at having such a warrior in my ranks."

Trent's natural skin reddened slightly. "Permission to speak freely, Star Colonel."

Paul Moon nodded slowly. "Proceed, Star Captain."

"You have misinterpreted my codex, sir. There are facts you are unaware of and that the records do not reflect."

"Such as?"

"On Tukayyid I fought with honor. I was felled in combat when faced with overwhelming odds. If not for my actions, Star Captain Jez would be dead now."

Moon struggled to contain his anger. "Lies are unbefitting officers in my command, Trent. I have read the record of your exploits. The truth is that Jez saved you. Any further accusations against such an officer, and you will have me to face in a Circle of Equals. Something I assure you that you do not want."

"I do not lie to you, Star Colonel."

"You have no evidence to offer, *quineg*?"

There was a long uncomfortable pause. "Neg."

"Only your word." Moon did not disguise his sarcasm.

"My word as a warrior should be enough, Star Colonel. What true Jaguar warrior would invent such untruths?" Anger stung his voice. "And in the matter of the Grand Melee there is more. My bondsman and I inspected my 'Mech after the Trial for the Howell bloodname a few days ago. There were signs of tampering, sir—sabotage." His words hung in the air for a full five seconds as Paul Moon stared at him.

"Sabotage? Neg. Who would have performed such sabotage? Perhaps it was your own freebirth bondsman, *quiaff*? Had you not been so quick to take freebirth scum like her into our Clan, perhaps you would not have to stoop to such cries of 'foul.' "

"We found evidence, sir. It could only have been one of the other technicians, Master Technician Phillip, who had access to my actuator."

Moon shook his head on his tree-trunk like neck. "Negative, Star Captain. You speak of my personal tech. Why would he perform such an act? To what end? He has no way to profit from such sabotage."

"This I do not know," Trent said. "What I do know, sir, is that there is evidence of sabotage and that the only individuals with the skill to carry out the procedure were Master Tech Phillip and my bondsman. At the very least, such an act would invalidate the Grand Melee."

Moon crossed his arms and looked down at the officer across his desk. "You are grasping at straws, all in the effort to somehow win another attempt at a bloodname. I will have no part in this."

"But, sir—"

"This discussion is over, Star Captain. And I find you contemptible for hiding behind excuses for your failings as a warrior. If a mechanical failure cost you the melee and your chance at a bloodname, then that is the luck of the draw and the other warrior still won fairly."

"Star Colonel Moon—"

Moon cut him off with a voice that seemed to shake the room and everything in it. "End of discussion, Trent. Press me no further."

"I demand a Trial of Refusal over your decision, Star Colonel," Trent retorted.

Moon was pleased with the notion, if only for a second. But not for any reason that Trent would appreciate. Moon rather savored the thought of crushing Trent with his bare hands. But there was a higher calling in place, a higher command that he must heed. Such was the way of the Smoke Jaguar.

"Denied, Trent. First off, should I face you in a Circle of Equals, I would crush you alive. You represent the very reason our Clan is not standing on Terra as the victor in our invasion. And to my knowledge, no Grand Melee decision has ever been reversed in the history of our Clan. Defeating me would only take you to the Grand Council, and they would never overrule a decision won on a battlefield. And surely not based on the word of a freebirth bondsman and a washed-up warrior."

"You are denying me my future, Star Colonel." It seemed to Moon that the defiance had suddenly bled out of Trent.

"Neg," said Paul Moon, crossing his massive arms. "I am preventing you from further tainting the traditions and rites of our Clan."

Trent stared at him with his unsettling pair of eyes as Moon continued his blast. "You do not understand how you have insulted me already, *quineg*? It is not just Tukayyid. You actually claimed one of *them* as isorla—brought her into our camp. You took one of the warriors who bested you and brought her here as a bondsman."

"No insult was intended, Star Colonel. Judith's performance in combat was outstanding. I honor our Clan by claiming her."

"Neg. She only makes you look more hideous than you already do. She hangs around your neck like an albatross. As we all know, this Judith will never again fight as a warrior. And you, as one of my officers, should know that her very presence here taints you in the eyes of your fellow Smoke Jaguars. Were I you, I would kill her rather than have her around as a reminder of my own failings."

Trent said nothing, and Moon shook his head in disgust at his mute stare.

He reached down to turn up the display built into the desk and studied the screen for a moment. "I am giving you a command of a Star, Trent. By now you know I do this only because you bear a rank that demands such an action on my part. You will command Beta Striker Star under Star Captain Jez in Beta Binary. I plan to upgrade the unit to a Trinary if resources become available."

"Sir," Trent said, "I am a Star Captain. It is customary for one of my rank to command a Binary or Trinary." Within the ranks of the Smoke Jaguars as in the rest of the Clans, a Star Commander usually commanded an individual Star of five BattleMechs, while a Star Captain commanded two or three Stars—a Binary or Trinary.

Moon did nothing to conceal his enjoyment of Trent's humiliation. "While you were recuperating from your wounds, Star Captain Jez competed for the position and won it in a Trial. From the reports I have read, she is entering the final rounds of her bloodname trial as well—a fine addition to our Cluster." Again, Moon savored Trent's reaction, this time one of shock. "Is there a problem, Star Captain?"

"I was not included in this Trial," Trent said through clenched teeth.

"You have the right to challenge the decision of that Trial, but you will end up facing both her and the other officer for the position. And even should you defeat them both, then I would challenge you. And as you know, you cannot challenge Star Captain Jez until she returns. And if she has won a bloodname at that point, you will need the approval of a Khan to challenge her or persuade her to accept such a feeble plea. Should you somehow succeed against such odds, you would still be under my command. Rest assured that I would make your life unbearable for as long as I am in command of the Cluster. But then again, the choice is yours. Star Captain." Moon was anxious to bring this unpleasant interview to a close. "Now then, do you have a problem with Star Captain Jez as your commanding officer?"

"Negative, Star Colonel."

"Good." Paul Moon looked back down at his display. "Details of your unit configuration will be posted to your command files. I expect you to review them and prepare your unit for full combat readiness in one week. Are you capable of performing that duty, Star Captain?"

"I will not fail you, Star Colonel," Trent replied, firing off a salute.

"You have already failed me, Trent—me and every other warrior in our Clan," Moon said, not even lifting his eyes from the display. "You are dismissed."

Judith's quarters were in an old bunk house that had apparently served as military lodging somewhere in Hyner's past, most likely for planetary militia. The rest of the Smoke Jaguar command complex was newly built, while this older structure near the outer wall was a throwback to a time before the Clans.

Most of the building was used for storage, the old bunk beds dismantled and stacked against the wall except for her own, which was tucked into one corner. Storage crates otherwise filled the room. The Smoke Jaguar warriors and other technicians of the Cluster slept in their new quarters. This, however, was the place to which Phillip has assigned her, an old, cold warehouse. She had spent any free time she enjoyed when not tasked in the repair bay just getting the centuries-old latrine to operate.

Judith understood that the accommodations were fitting, given her place among the Smoke Jaguars. She was a bondsman. Thus far she had not met any other bondsmen, which also told her something of her status. They had placed her here, alone, isolated, not part of the others yet attached to them. It was symbolic and somehow just. She never thought about complaining, which would have been too "unClanlike." Instead, Judith simply adapted.

The chill of the wintry night had begun to settle in, and she pulled her blankets out of the small footlocker she had found in another part of the old bunkhouse. It was going to be another cold night, but she was thankful that at least a few of the heating units still worked. She was just spreading the blankets out on the bed when she heard the steady tapping of footsteps on the wooden floor outside her door.

No one had ever come here since she'd been assigned. Few except for Trent and Master Tech Phillip had even talked to her. Turning slowly to look toward the open doorway, she saw a shadowy figure approaching. She felt a brief stab of fear, but her training instantly kicked in as she looked about quickly for anything that might serve as a weapon.

Then she saw who it was standing in the doorway. Star Captain Trent. The mangled face was the same, yet this was not the same warrior of a few days before, after his Grand Melee. There was something brooding and defeated about this man who owned her, something she had not see before. Judith rose to attention. "Star Captain, I am surprised to see you here."

Trent tossed a bag on the floor between them. His scarred face wore a scowl, yet she sensed his weariness. "These are my dress boots. Clean and polish them by the morning. I am going to address my new command and wish them to see me at my best."

Judith bent over and picked up the bag. "Aye, Star Captain." She had learned that menial tasks were part of being a bondsman, yet Trent was neither abusive like Phillip nor as contemptuous as many of the other warriors. She had despised him at first, but now she saw something more in him, a complexity, perhaps a mystery. Among her many skills and talents, Judith liked complex things—be they puzzles or people.

Trent made no move to leave but stood there looking around Judith's less than Spartan accommodations. "Your quarters are quite private." He gave a short laugh. "One of the benefits of being a Jaguar bondsman."

"Aff," she replied, careful of her Clan talk. "I have not yet met any other bondsmen, and these quarters suit me well."

Trent shook his head. "You will not likely meet many other bondsmen in your life, at least none from the Inner Sphere such as yourself. Clan Smoke Jaguar rarely takes bondsmen. Many among us believe it would dilute our genetic lines, and others do not approve bringing freeborn warriors of the Inner Sphere into our midst. Our new commanding officer pointed that out to me when we met earlier."

"Yet you took me as a bondsman."

"I am 'different,' Judith. Which our new commanding officer is also pleased to point out. I saw your fighting against Jez, and saw that you had the heart of the Jaguar beating in your chest. You fought as I do, bold and daring. I was impressed. My claiming you as a bondman was a spontaneous act of admiration. I would do it again given the opportunity."

Judith gave him a look of surprise. "I don't understand. You are only a few years older than I am. You have plenty of years in the cockpit still."

Trent shook his head. "You are Clan now, Judith. I have heard stories of warriors in the Inner Sphere fighting into their fifth century, but that is not the way of the Clans. Combat is for the new generation of warriors. By the age of thirty, a warrior is at his or her peak. He must soon step down for a more advanced replacement, a newer, fresher warrior from superior genes. It is the way of the Jaguar, a way that you will learn." Trent spoke the words dully as if he were reciting them, no longer fully believing them.

She watched him carefully, and noted that he looked even more tired now as he spoke, as if the burdens of the day were overwhelming him. He uttered the words she might have expected, but the force behind them seemed weakened, as if he doubted their rightness. She wanted to ask him what happened to the older warriors, but given his mood, she thought it might make matters worse. "You mentioned our new commanding officer. I assume that you presented the evidence of tampering, *quiaff*?"

"Affirmative," Trent said with a bitter tone. "Star Colonel Moon has little care for me or for any evidence that *you* may have been able to find. He has refused to acknowledge my protest and has assured me that he and the Council would never reverse the findings of a test of battle. And"—Trent paused for a second—"he is correct. I was foolish to think otherwise."

"Then the matter is simply dropped?"

"Aye, Judith. I have a command again, however. A Star of warriors to lead and prepare." He seemed to perk up at that. "We are members of Beta Striker now, Judith. You will help me get their 'Mechs ready for battle."

Trent's eyes seemed to wander, as if he were looking past her, into the future, or perhaps into his own past. Either way, his face, despite its emotionless synthskin, seemed to become radiant as he spoke of command again. Judith took mental note of that. Perhaps it was something she might be able to use someday. If nothing else, it told her more about Trent.

She nodded. "And perhaps we can teach our new Star Colonel a thing or two about us, *quiaff*?"

Trent smiled slightly. "I would like very much to do just that, Judith." Silently he pulled out his combat knife from a small sheath on his belt. She blinked at the sight of it, wondering what he was planning to do.

"Hold out your wrist," he commanded. She did so as if hypnotized by his words.

Trent reached down and cut one of the three cords wrapped around her wrist. "We did not discuss this earlier, but each of the three bondcords you wear ties you to me as your superior. The first is the bond of integrity. I have severed this because you have shown me that you are honorable.

"The middle cord is the cord of fidelity. You have shown me faithfulness, but it has not been tested. When it is, I shall sever that cord as well.

"The last bond is prowess. Because you are a freebirth of the Inner Sphere I will never be granted the right of severing it. My peers in the Jaguars would never permit you to serve as a warrior. Should you ever prove your fighting skill to me, however, and this I swear, I will cut that cord—even if the whole of the Smoke Jaguars should stand against me."

Judith looked at her wrist and at Trent, nodding silently at the ritual she had just experienced. *He has the potential I was supposed to seek. Only time will tell whether I corrupt him, or he and the Jaguars corrupt me. . . .*

BOOK TWO

Tempered Steel

Politics is supposed to be the second oldest profession. I have come to realize that it bears a very close semblance to the first.

—Attributed to General Alekandr Kerensky

Politics is of great use to men such as myself. It helps determine who should be on the dangerous end of a PPC.

—General Aaron DeChevilier, second-in-command to
Alekandr Kerensky

As the insect feeds the bird,
As the bird feeds the wolf,
As the wolf feeds the smoke jaguar,
So all give life to the warrior
Who sheds his blood for their glory.

—*The Remembrance* (Clan Smoke Jaguar), Passage 121,
Verse 43

≡ 7 ≡

Beaver Falls
Hyner
Smoke Jaguar Occupation Zone
10 November 3054

Beaver Falls was a sleepy little hamlet about 50 kilometers to the southwest of Warrenton. Though tiny and isolated, it was a crossroads of sorts, sitting astride the intersection of Leesburg Pike and a lonely road known as Harper Creek that ran north and south and led to nothing but other small towns. A grand total of perhaps three dozen buildings, shops, and houses comprised the tiny village, and the falls were little more than a stream that broke over a three-meter rocky area of rapids in a place the villagers called Ketchum Park.

The structures themselves seemed to date back centuries, the long-faded bricks giving away their age. Some buildings showed signs of renovation, while others retained the facades they must have worn for decades. The population consisted mainly of the families of local shopkeepers and farmers, and peace and quiet was their way of life.

The hot humid winds of Hyner's early summer made Trent curse his allergy to the local flora as he sat waiting in the restaurant. His unit, Beta Striker Star, had been stationed nearby for close to five months for field maneuvers and training, and in all that time he had visited Beaver Falls only twice before. Both times he had been with Russou, whose unit was also stationed in the nearby countryside. As was their custom, the two Star Commanders met regularly to talk of things both military and otherwise. It was a good diversion, one of the few things Trent had to look forward to during nearly two years on Hyner.

Jez had stationed his Star out here, in the middle of nowhere, apparently more from spite than for any good reason. Jez, who had won the Howell bloodname in a furious fight a year and a half earlier, seemed more driven and ambitious than ever. Trent thought some of that might have to do with the neutral circuitry she'd had surgically implanted six months earlier. Only the most fanatic warriors risked the surgery involved with the implants, and hers showed through the skin of her face like a gray tattoo of the legendary Smoke Jaguar.

The neural implants gave a warrior an unsurpassed, direct neural connection with his or her OmniMech. This wireless link made control faster and more immediate and eliminated the need to wear a neurohelmet. But they were a mixed blessing. There were rumors that some warriors who opted for the implant eventually went insane. There were drugs to counter the problem, but Trent wondered if Jez might now be suffering mental disturbances because of the device linked to her brain.

He had brought Judith along today, though it was certainly not her place as bondsman to join the two Clan officers in their meal. She would be needed for some inspections he needed to make after this meeting with Russou, and she would wait for him in a park across the street from the little restaurant.

The House of the Lazy Duck boasted six or eight tables, which were mostly empty today. He looked around and decided to sit down toward the rear of the small dining room. His sense of smell was much impaired because of the artificial skin around his nose, but the strong aromas wafting from the kitchen were enough to penetrate even his clogged sinuses and long scarred nostrils.

As he took his seat to wait for Russou, Trent reflected on how well the past year and a half had gone for his bondsman. She was leaner now, more muscular, and she carried herself with an air of confidence despite her fall in status. She'd also cropped her black hair to shoulder length. She had insisted it was merely to keep it out of her face while working, but Trent suspected it was also a bow to a style favored by many members of the technician caste. She refused to admit that she was giving in to Clan ways, but that stubbornness was one of the things he appreciated about her.

Star Commander Russou dropped heavily into his seat across from Trent, startling him out of his reverie. "Greetings, you remains of a scarred surat," Russou said jokingly.

Trent grinned back, known that his synthetic skin and mangled features must make him look like a demon from the gates of hell itself in the dim lights of the restaurant. He remained proud of his scarring, and never minded the good-natured joking by Russou, who had been his friend since their days in the sibko.

"I may have lost my good looks," Trent returned, running one hand over the left side of his head, where he still had some hair, "but at least my genes have not failed me and left me bald like you, old friend."

Russou shrugged, for his retreating hairline was a simple fact. "This hole in the ground is almost as bad as the place where Jez buried my Star, but at least you have a good restaurant in your field of operations." Russou had also been posted to Jez's command when her Binary had been upgraded to a Trinary three months before.

"She never liked me and now it appears you are guilty by association," Trent said. "Now that she has a bloodname and the rank to back it up, we have no choice but to put up with whatever she decides to hand us," Trent reminded his friend.

"Aye," Russou said. "I did not expect us to end up like this, though."

"Nor did I."

"And how goes it with your command? Are you still making them toe the hard line, *quiaff*?"

Trent beamed as much as his visage allowed. "Aff. They are strong and good warriors all, most of them young and fresh. They came as replacements for our losses and are untested in combat. We veterans have experience, while they have enthusiasm."

Russou nodded. "The same is true of my Star. They have little wisdom of what the invasion was like. And even less respect for those of us who have fought in it thus far."

"That comes from our commanding officer," Trent said.

Russou nodded. "Our Star Colonel has his own interpretation of what happened even though he himself was not always involved in the fighting. I am tainted in his eyes because of my actions on Luthien." The Jaguars' humiliating defeat on Luthien preceded the further destruction suffered the Jaguars on Tukayyid. The end result of both campaigns was an almost total reorganization of the Smoke Jaguars in order to make up losses and to regroup. "And you, Trent . . . he does not speak well of you at all."

Trent shrugged. "I serve the Smoke Jaguar. He is but a man. Let him think what he will of me. All that matters is the truth, and I know what that is." Trent's conversations with Star Colonel Paul Moon had been limited over the past year and a half, but his CO had never treated him with less than utter contempt.

It was a mutual feeling matched by his sentiments for Jez.

The owner, an older female, came to the table and silently handed them menus. She seemed nervous, her actions quick and jerky. Her eyes also seemed to dart about the restaurant, as if looking for something or someone. Trent noticed her hands were shaking too, but she was not yet of an age to show such infirmity. He was unsure how much to read into it, if anything at all. "I have heard rumors of some sort of guerrilla activity here on Hyner."

"Aye," Russou said. "Our Trinary commander was kind enough to let me glance at a report she received. Apparently we did not wipe out all of the garrison force when we took this world. A few managed to survive and have been carrying out strikes against our forces. Minor raids, usually against convoys and troops transports."

"I did not know the extent of these activities," Trent said, wondering why he had not been briefed. He too commanded troops in the field. Such threats were a danger to them all.

Russou shrugged in reply. "Such guerrillas are nothing but filthy bandits. They do not merit our attention." He glanced around then. "I wonder what has become of our waitress?"

Sitting on a bench in the park across the street from the House of the Lazy Duck, Judith sighed and shifted in frustration. After all this time as Trent's bondsman, there were still times when he pulled her off her duties without explaining why or what for. Although she had forced herself to adapt to Clan ways and her subservient role as a bondsman, she would never totally understand her place in this strange society.

Stretching her arms for the hundredth time, Judith suddenly noticed two people she recognized as the owners emerge from the rear of the restaurant, then move rapidly away from the building in her general direction. She thought nothing of it until she saw the looks on their faces, as if they were fearful for their lives. She stood up quickly, sensing that something was wrong here, very wrong.

Laura Quong, the older woman who co-owned the establishment, ran up to her. "You must leave this area. You can come with us." Her breath was racing and her tone fearful and desperate.

"I do not understand," Judith said, eyes darting back to the restaurant where her bondmaster was.

"You're one of us, not one of them," said Mr. Quong, the husband. "We know you're a prisoner of these filthy Clan animals. You'll understand soon enough, girl. Come with us and you can be free."

Now Judith understood. She had heard reports of guerrilla activity in the region, mostly among the lower castes. According to rumors, members of the Second Arkab Legion, the Draconis Combine unit that had defended Hyner against capture by the Smoke Jaguars, had somehow survived and organized a resistance effort. She had spoken with the older couple many times before when she came alone to the Lazy Duck. They knew that she had been with ComStar, that she had fought on Tukayyid. Now they thought they were doing her a favor.

"You are mistaken," she replied. "I am part of Clan Smoke Jaguar. As are you."

"They can change the flag we have to fly, but they can never change what is in our hearts. They killed our son on Schuyler and have cut us off from the rest of our kin on Pesht. If you want to live, come with is. Otherwise, you are nothing more than a traitor in our eyes and in the eyes of those who represent the true government," Mr. Quong said coldly. He and his wife then both bolted away to where they had a vehicle waiting.

Judith stood there for a moment, watching and listening intently. The rumbling noise she heard in the distance was all too familiar and was getting closer. The sound was unmistakable. A BattleMech. The distinct thunder of at least one 'Mech closing on Beaver Falls, perhaps more.

Trent . . . I've got to warn him. She raced across the street to the House of the Lazy Duck.

Both Trent and Russou pushed back out of their chairs at the same moment Judith rushed through the door. Her arrival, coupled with the sudden realization that the owners had disappeared, accompanied by the deep rumble that shook the ground, had both warriors on their feet.

"Trouble, Star Captain," Judith heaved as she tried to get her breath. "Incoming BattleMechs."

"Guerrillas?" Russou asked.

She nodded, gasping a bit from her sprint. "Out the back. Now."

Russou looked out the window but saw no sign of the approaching 'Mechs. "We do not take orders from lower caste bondsmen. We are warriors."

The ground shook even more, and the rumbling footfalls growing louder told them that the enemy 'Mech was close. "Then take it as advice from a friend," Trent said, starting for the back door. Judith hot on his heels. "I suggest we leave now."

Trent opened the restaurant's back door at the same moment a *Warhammer* opened fire on the place. There was a cracking sound, like lightning hitting a tree. The hairs on Trent's entire body stood up as the 'Mech's PPCs blasted the building.

He and Judith both half-fell, half-rolled next to the big dumpster opposite the back door. Russou was not as lucky. He was still standing at the door at the moment the building exploded. Like a massive phalanx shield, both the door and Russou flew back into the fence next to the dumpster.

The House of the Lazy Duck came apart as a second volley of PPC fire tore into it. The building exploded upward, probably from the burst of a gas main. Debris crashed into the dumpster where Trent and Judith had taken cover, rattling the container like thunder. Trent tried to protect himself by curling up into a ball, and his ears rang from the deafening roar of the blast. Judith was next to him, also rolled into a ball. Dust and smoke filled the air, and only the cough of Russou a few meters away told them he was still alive.

Trent now saw the *Warhammer* for the first time. The machine stepped through the rubble of the restaurant, its giant feet grinding any remaining shred of it into mere dust and debris. The 70-ton 'Mech was a monster at a range of less than ten meters. Its firepower included a pair of PPCs for arms and a shoulder-mounted missile rack.

Having spent his whole existence training for the life of a warrior, Trent knew there were many ways to take out a BattleMech. Bare-handed was not one them. Watching the 'Mech, he noted the markings of the Second Arkab Legion still showing through a recent paint job of dark green. On the 'Mech's right chest, just over the deadly laser and machine gun, he could just make out some words and an insignia through the smoke and dust. It was a crudely painted symbol of the Smoke Jaguar, cut across with a red slash. The words "Kat Killer Five" were painted above it.

Apparently satisfied at accomplishing its mission, the *Warhammer* turned and began to lumber away. Trent suddenly realized that the 'Mech must have come specifically to kill him and Russou. *Cat killers, are they?* he thought. *They come like bandits, when our backs are turned. Too cowardly to face us like warriors . . .*

Trent rose, his whole body rippling with an excitement he had not known for some time. As Judith also stood, he went over and helped a badly battered Russou stagger to a half-standing pose. "What happened?" Russou asked, half-dazed.

"An enemy has come to break up the monotony of our routine," Trent said, giving both his companions his twisted grin. "And perhaps bringing us the chance to regain some honor."

The Hyner Planetary Command in Warrenton showed signs of life that Trent had not seen when he'd been here last time, a month earlier. As he and Russou stood on the parade grounds where Star Captain Jez had ordered them to meet her, he knew he was finally going to get orders that would lead to action. Not a mere garrison posting, unworthy of a true warrior. No, this time he would be assigned to go hunting bandits. Though still less than honorable work, it was at least a chance to take his unit into the field in battle. If nothing else, it would sharpen their skills and test them in combat.

Star Captain Jez Howell stood waiting for the two officers with hands clasped behind her back. Her dark hair was pulled back in a tight knot, and her lean, muscular frame had an arrogance about it. Trent and Russou came to attention before her. Trent looked straight ahead and made no eye contact, but this was not out of military custom but because of the contempt he felt for her.

"So, these are the brave warriors under my command who ran from a bandit enemy, *quiaff?*" she demanded.

Already she twists the truth, Trent thought, but he and Russou remained silent.

"The Star Colonel called in all unit commanders for the chance to bid for the right to track down these so-called Kat Killers. Such a mission is not worthy of a trueborn warrior, and at first I was insulted by the offer.

"But when Star Colonel Paul Moon pointed out that you two were present during a recent bandit raid and inflicted no damage to the enemy, he recommended that you be bid as part of the mission to apprehend and destroy this guerilla scum."

Jez Howell smiled, then licked her lips before resuming. "Thus I bid your two Stars to this mission. Your orders are to seek out these so-called Kat Killers and destroy them. You should know that not one other Star Captain wished to sully the honor of his unit by bidding for this mission. You will be briefed on all previous attacks and any other information known about these bandits in the next day."

Trent's mind and heart raced as he listened. Jez could say what she liked about the worthiness of the mission, and Russou too would probably find it disagreeable duty. But he could not wait. Bandits or no, here was a chance for him to return once again to the field, leading warriors into battle.

Judith looked at the door of the old bunkhouse that had been her home until she and the rest of the Trinary had been moved to the field location. She'd taken a walk to gather her thoughts and ended up here—mostly out of habit. It was the only place where she'd been able to be truly alone with herself and her thoughts. The Smoke Jaguars were an aggressive bunch, even for Clanners, and the warriors were dangerous in or out of battle. She who had once been a warrior was treated with scorn by those who were now her masters, but here in this bunkhouse she had learned to cope with her new place in life, her status as a member of a lower caste. The only thing that made it bearable was knowing that she had a reason to be here. A mission. If all went well, she would return to the Inner Sphere and one day be a MechWarrior again. She was about to reach for the door of the bunkhouse when someone touched her shoulder from behind. She turned and saw the mutilated face and body of her master, Star Captain Trent.

There had been a time when the sight of him had been revolting, but Judith now saw beyond the scars. He was a skilled warrior. She had seen that in the Grand Melee. And he was a warrior who had played by the strict rules of the Clans. And yet, somehow, this great warrior did not rise. The laws and traditions of the Clans turned against him at every opportunity. *There are other ways to reward such men, and when the time is right, I will make sure that Trent is honored properly.*

"Did you receive our new orders, Star Captain?"

Trent's gnarled lips pulled back in a grin, his gums exposed on one side. "We are tasked with tracking these guerrillas and destroying them."

"That is good news, Star Colonel, *quiaff?*"

"Not exactly, Judith. Fighting bandits is generally considered work beneath the dignity of a warrior. It is usually reserved for freebirth or solahma units. For me that matters not. I welcome the chance to once again fight battles rather than simulators."

"Guerrillas are not so easy to combat. History has shown that killing them often only breeds more rebellion," Judith said.

Trent nodded. "You can help, Judith. Some of the locals warned you the day of the attack on the House of the Lazy Duck, did they not? Such information can be of value, though once I might have scorned using it as not the way of a true warrior. Perhaps you can learn something that will help us bring this battle to a climax quickly."

Judith showed no sign of the surprise she felt. *He is asking me for assistance in finding the enemy. For him to do that is a sign of trust and of his willingness to work with me as a peer—whether he admits it or not.* "As you command, Star Captain."

Trent reached out and took her wrist. With one finger he lifted one of the two remaining bondcords. With a quick snap of his combat knife, he cut the cord. "Your cord of fidelity has been honored. Devotion to a bondsmaster, to a Clan, is necessary. Your actions in Beaver Falls proved that you are indeed loyal. With the cutting of this cord, you move closer to your own place in the heart of the Jaguar."

Judith looked at the cut cord in his hand, then up into his face. She gazed unblinking into his eyes, the one good one, the other a replacement surrounded by mechanical controls.

"I shall not fail you, Star Captain. . . ."

8

Jez stood next to the desk of Star Colonel Paul Moon at rigid parade rest as the other man entered the small office. Even seated at his desk, the massive Elemental commander of the Stormriders was nearly her height. She glanced quickly at Paul Moon, and saw that his expression was not just cold, but menacing, as if he threatened the man with death merely for saying the wrong word.

The man had short black hair and Oriental features. He wore the clothes of a common laborer, a loose-fitting brown shirt and green work pants typical of those who worked in the manufacturing plants in Warrenton. The air carried a strong scent, not the perspiration typical of a warrior, but the smell of dirt, sweat, and the stuff of back alleys. The man eyed the single chair in the room, probably wondering if it was appropriate to sit or stand before the Star Colonel. He opted to stand.

"You are the laborer Joseph, *quiaff*?" Star Captain Jez asked.

The man nervously nodded. "Yes, er, aff, sir."

"The duty officer indicated that you had information that would be useful to us regarding the terrorist group known as the Kat Killer Five," came the deep, almost thundering voice of Paul Moon from his seat next to Jez.

"I know where they are operating, at least lately," the man said.

"And how do you know this?" Jez put in. "Perhaps you are in league with them, *quiaff*?"

"No, no, that's not true," the man said, waving his hands as if to ward off her suspicions. "No. I know one of them. We met when the Second Arkab was posted here. Nasty man. He killed a friend of mine in a bar fight just before your arrival. I saw him and did some checking. He's one of them and somehow he managed to evade you when the rest of his unit left the system. I asked the right people, and they told me the location of the place he and his outfit are using as a base."

"And where might that be?" Jez demanded.

"North of the Glen where you beat them before. There's a box canyon in the hill country about seventy-five kilometers north. He and his friends are there. They're using an abandoned mining operation to hide their 'Mechs. They keep them in the mine tunnels where you can't spot them."

"Numbers?" Paul Moon asked.

"Two lances, er, eight 'Mechs, sir," the man replied, still visibly nervous. "They'll be hard to get to, from what I've been told. Those mines go back some distance."

"You can pinpoint this on a map, *quiaff*?" Jez asked.

"Yes sir—er, ma'am."

Paul Moon looked up at Jez, who gave him a small smile of satisfaction. Moon rose from his seat to his full height, dominating the small office. He blocked the sunlight from the window and cast a shadow over the laborer Joseph. "Why do you volunteer this information to us?"

"I don't like this guy who's one of them. Like I said, he killed a friend of mine."

Paul Moon lowered his gaze, tipping his head forward. "So, you do this for revenge, *quiaff*?"

"Yes, er, affirmative. That, and I thought there might be some sort of reward for the information."

"Reward?" Jez asked. "You still do not understand us despite the fact that we have held your world for some time now. We do not provide rewards to those who have an obligation to the Clan."

"But I—" Joseph tried to speak, but Paul Moon cut him off.

"Star Captain Jez will investigate your story. In the meantime, you will remain here."

"I don't—er, do not understand, Star Colonel. Why must I stay here?"'

Moon cocked his head and looked down at the other man from his towering height. "If it is a trap, Joseph, you will find the Smoke Jaguar extracts a high price for treason."

Trent stood by the mobile repair gantry where he and his Star were temporarily based. The small field camp was alive with activity, mostly warriors preparing security measures, motion and seismic sensors, and working on adjusting their portable dome-tents for the night. Judith looked at her bondsmaster and saw that in the dim twilight, his mechanically enhanced eye gave off a dim red glow from the circuitry controls deep in the back of his eye socket. In all of the time that she had known Trent, she had only noticed the glow once before. Now it was eerie, almost menacing.

"I have just returned from Planetary Command," he said. "A member of our laborer caste has volunteered the location of the rebel base. They are a ways from here, hiding in old mines in a box canyon. Star Captain Jez Howell has ordered Russou and I to secure the area and destroy the enemy forces."

"That was fast," Judith commented as she wiped the lubricant from her hands. "Maybe even too fast, *quiaff*?"

Trent nodded slowly. "I was thinking the same thing. Guerrilla warfare is unClanlike, but I believe I have come to understand how differently it is viewed by the people of the Inner Sphere. This planet has only been occupied by Clan Smoke Jaguar for a short time. It seems odd that any native of Hyner would volunteer such information to the commanders of the occupying force."

Judith smiled but did not answer. Trent tipped his head as if he was trying to read her expression. "You are smiling at me, Judith. Why?"

"I do not wish to overstep my place, Star Captain, but I must speak up. I would not trust that information either if I were you. A box canyon, mines . . . it all smells of a trap."

Trent nodded. "Aye, it does," he said. "The attack on Russou and myself was both planned and coordinated."

"Such an action would not be undertaken lightly," Judith added. "Anyone who would carefully stage a trap to kill two officers would not likely have so weak a link in their group—not one that volunteers information."

Trent felt as if she had spoken his own thoughts. That was the problem with Jez and even Star Colonel Moon. They did not know how to think like their foes. They approached everything only from a Clan perspective. He had been that way too, but Tukayyid had changed that. *Since Tukayyid, I have been treated like an outcast, and no one cares about what happened really happened between Jez and me there. Perhaps now I can prove what my true worth to the Clan is—again.*

"Do not think that because we are Clan that we are too rigid. I see the signs of a trap even if my superiors do not. I have fought the Inner Sphere militaries enough to see how they wage war. Given limited resources, this is the kind of battle I would fight if I were one of these so-called guerrillas. One on my own terms, on terrain of my choosing."

"I will have your OmniMech ready for action, sir."

Trent sat in his tent in the dim glow of the lantern as he hooked up the portable vidphone to a portable generator. The vidphone was small, compact, but allowed him to send a personal message to his current commanding officer.

He adjusted the disk controls, then activated the switch on the side of the projector, which would transmit his signal to the previously entered address, Star Captain Jez's office at Planetary Command. The screen flickered to life, and he saw the shape of Jez sitting behind her desk.

"Star Captain Trent," she said almost coyly. "To what do I owe this communication?"

"I have readied my Star to link up with Charlie Assault Star tomorrow," Trent said, knowing that Jez would not like the subject of a potential ambush, given their past.

"Good. I will join you at the canyon myself to oversee operations."

Trent paused and drew a long breath. "I have reviewed the maps of the area and the information provided you by your contact in Warrenton, Star Captain Howell. I have also spoken with my bondsman, an individual with experience in Inner Sphere tactics. As a result, I believe we may be leading our forces into an ambush."

Jez crossed her arms and glared back at him for a full five seconds of silence.

"That is all?" she finally asked.

Trent nodded. "Affirmative, Jez. Consider the nature of the terrain and how you obtained the information. It sounds like a trap, and we are marching straight into it."

"And you take the opinion of a technician over mine, a trueborn and a blooded warrior?" Her mention of the bloodname was a direct jab.

Trent felt his face flush, an irritating sensation where the synthetic skin covered his face. "I have come to trust Judith, bondsman or not. Look at the maps and think about how you obtained this information. This is a trap."

Jez gave him a thin smile. "Then you will need to be careful, Star Captain."

"You will not abort the mission, *quineg*?"

"Neg. I will not. You are a Smoke Jaguar warrior. These are bandits. Your orders are to crush them or die in the attempt."

Either way, Jez wins. "I could challenge you on this, Jez," Trent said coolly. "I have beaten you before in a Circle of Equals." They had faced off several times in their lives, both in and out of the sibko, and Trent had always defeated her.

"Aff, you could challenge me, but this order comes down from Star Colonel Moon. Meet him in hand-to-hand combat, and he will crush you to death simply to remove you as a blight on his duty roster."

Trent nodded slowly. He had been bred and born into the Clan way, yet everything that had shaped him and driven him now seemed to be working against him. How could a way of life that he had accepted without question so fail him when he needed it most? He fought down a feeling of betrayal.

"Very well, Star Captain Howell. I will meet you shortly. Together we shall see if you are ordering fine warriors to their deaths."

He reached down and toggled off the vidphone control. As the image of Jez disappeared, Trent remained sitting in near-darkness, lost in his own thoughts. He stared at the codex bracelet on his left wrist, the one that was still his own flesh and blood.

The codex was a warrior's life. The EPROM on it contained a record of the genetic DNA signature of the warrior who wore it as well as his or her entire service record. In all of his years, Trent had only taken the bracelet off to have it updated. Looking at it now, he thought back on his life.

He was a skilled warrior, and his record should show it. Even on Tukayyid, when, by all rights, he should have been killed, Trent had managed to hang on. Because he had survived a failed campaign, he now bore a taint. A taint not reflected by his codex, but by the whispers and sidelong looks of his fellow warriors.

Nicholas Kerensky, the founder of the Clans, had envisioned a society where only warriors engaged in combat and the rules of warfare were honored by all. Where truth and justice were tested on the field of battle. Right and wrong were clear-cut, determined by prowess shown in trials of combat. How could he reconcile this vision with the way his Star Colonel and his commanding officer treated him? No matter how he proved himself, they viewed him as worthless. They seemed to be operating under another code of conduct, one unknown to Trent. He could not even imagine what that code was, but found himself hating them for this aberration, this deviation from what the Clans were meant to be.

Have we strayed from the vision that guided Nicholas Kerensky in forging our superior way of life? With that thought, he reached over to turn off the tent light. He would think no further on this tonight. Some questions were best left unanswered. . . .

9

Baker Canyon, Stark Ridge Mountains
Hyner
Smoke Jaguar Occupation Zone
14 November 3054

Knowing that one is facing a trap does not always mean the trap can be overcome. It simply means you know something your foe does not know you know. Trent pondered this truth as he moved his *Timber Wolf* to a slow walking pace at the head of his Beta Striker Star. Some two hundred meters behind were Russou and the forces of Charlie Sweep Star. Between them was Star Captain Jez, anxious to rush the two Stars under his and Russou's command into battle.

The terrain was not going to be easy. Trent knew that from his studies of the maps of Baker Canyon, which the report named as the site of the Kat Killer Five base. Located in the foothills of the Stark Ridge Mountains, the area consisted of clusters of stout, cedar-like trees, steep slopes, numerous dead-end passes, and deep canyons.

The rock formations that poked up toward the white-blue Hyner sky would work to the advantage of anyone already holding the terrain. There were more than enough places to conceal BattleMechs and conventional forces.

The canyon itself was almost a kilometer and a half across, with a narrow opening a scant three hundred meters wide. The old mines from which the guerrillas were supposedly operating were at the far end of the canyon. The rest of the canyon floor was wide open, interrupted only by piles of millings from the now lifeless mine. The upper walls of Baker Canyon posed a threat as well. It would be possible to position troops and even BattleMechs like knights on a castle parapet on either side and along the far northern edge of the canyon. From that height, an enemy could rain down a shower of death and destruction while maintaining substantial cover among the rock formations and boulders that dotted the ridge. With so much terrain and so many hiding places, it was going to be difficult to cover both the floor and the rim of the canyon at the same time. But after studying the survey scans and topographical maps, Trent thought he knew what the enemy might do.

He had tried twice to convince Jez not to send his and Russou's forces driving into the canyon. He had urged using Russou's forces to secure the high ground and perimeter before moving in on the mines. But she would not be budged. Jez said that the mines were the key, and even if the whole thing were a trap, the enemy would strike from there.

There was no convincing her otherwise, and Trent knew it was because she refused to see these Kat Killers as anything other than bandits. That was her first mistake. It was important to remember that they were also MechWarriors. Inner Sphere freebirths or not, they had survived the Jaguar occupation of Hyner thus far, which made them foes worth taking seriously. The good thing was that Russou had agreed with Trent's view that the operation must be handled with great care and caution. Together, they had come up with a plan of their own, one that would allow them to respond to potential problems if this were indeed a trap.

The speaker inside Trent's neurohelmet stirred to life, shattering his concentration. "Jez to Strike Command. The objective is just ahead. Beta Striker, take the point. Charlie Sweep to follow." The orders were clear. If this was a trap, it was Trent's Star that would lead the way straight into its mouth.

I am Clan. My duty is to obey, no matter what I think of the orders. "Affirmative, Star Captain Jez. Beta Striker, follow on my mark in attack order Tango." Trent had worked out the deployment order earlier, without consulting Jez. Considering the models and the configurations of the 'Mechs they fielded, his plan offered them the best chance should the mine tunnel be filled with Kat Killers or if the bandits appeared on the surrounding high ground.

Trent would lead with his *Timber Wolf,* its deadly missile racks giving him the ability to reach the high canyon crests if the enemy appeared up there. MechWarriors Styx and Laurel in their *Summoner* and *Hellbringer,* respectively, would follow. If he had to take a position to ward off an attack from above, the *Summoner* would be critical, its jump jets permitting it a short flight to the canyon walls. Finally MechWarrior Ansel in his *Mad Dog* and Lior in her *Cauldron-Born* would sweep in. Both of those OmniMechs were good infighters if the trap were sprung from within the mines, especially the low-slung *Cauldron-Born.*

A cloud of dust rose as Trent walked the *Timber Wolf* through the entrance to Baker Canyon. He moved slowly, his short-range sensors sweeping the boulders and rocks that littered the floor of the canyon. The milling piles were not so easily handled. Filled with radioactive and metallic wastes, they blurred the sensors. Which was not something Trent had planned for.

"Laurel, go slow and form up on my left. Styx, come up on my right. The rest of you come in slowly and watch the ridgeline." Trent still considered the high ground surrounding the canyon to be the greatest threat, despite the masking that the milling mounds provided.

He was about to contact Russou when Jez's stern voice came over his neurohelmet headset. "Trent, you've slowed. I gave no such order. Advance now and let us get this over with."

Trent bit his lower lip to keep himself from saying something he might regret. "Aye, Star Captain," he said. His tactical display showed that she had moved ahead of Russou's forces and was rapidly closing on his unit's position.

He throttled up the *Timber Wolf* and concentrated his sensors forward. Laurel and Styx also advanced, moving along the outer edges of the canyon floor while Trent moved up the middle. As his Star advanced cautiously, Russou, obviously prodded by Jez, moved to the mouth of the canyon.

Always moving slowly and carefully, Trent piloted the *Timber Wolf* around the massive mound of discarded rocks and saw the opening of the mine. It was huge, obviously designed to permit MinerMechs to descend into the mountain. The gaping hole seemed to swallow up the daylight.

They could be down there with any number of BattleMechs. It was a perfect hiding place, or . . .

Suddenly there was an explosion somewhere in the distance. Trent scanned the area, but all he saw was a cloud of smoke up on the ridge line to the east near where Styx and Jez stood in their 'Mechs. Dust flew into the air, and a blur of something moved down toward the pair of OmniMechs.

There was a crash as a massive boulder slammed into Jez's *Warhawk,* followed by the almost sickening groan of ferro-fibrous armor and ferro-titanium steel. The *Warhawk*'s legs contorted under the impact and were crushed, flip-slamming the torso into the ground with incredible power.

"Beta Striker, concentrate on the canyon ridge," Trent barked as two more blasts rocked his *Timber Wolf.* An avalanche of rocks and debris raced downward to his left, where Laurel waited in her *Hellbringer.* She took a step back, but not before several tons of debris mauled her leg armor and nearly toppled her 'Mech.

Russou's voice came over the commline. "I am picking up multiple BattleMechs coming at us from the south."

Trent concentrated his sensor scans on the canyon floor. The distinctive red images on his secondary display indicated magnetic resonance readings, the kind made by the fusion reactors that powered the mighty BattleMechs. "I show two confirmed up above us on the ridge overlooking the canyon floor. Probably more we haven't seen yet."

As he spoke, Trent torso-twisted his *Timber Wolf* in the direction of one of the unidentified enemies, and his battle-computer came up with an image—a *Catapult.* He reacted immediately. He tagged the enemy as his, then signal-relayed to the other Jaguars as he opened up with both racks of his long-range missiles.

The missiles screamed up the canyon wall and plowed into the partially concealed *Catapult* as it moved to a firing stance. Three missed, scattering clouds of debris and creating mini-avalanches toward the far end of Baker Canyon, but the rest found their mark. Smoke, some gray, some black, billowed from the holes in the *Catapult*'s armor.

As Styx targeted the other 'Mech, Trent moved behind one of the milling piles to avoid a shot from the ambusher he had just hit. Jez's voice crackled to life over the speakers. "This is Star Captain Jez to all personnel. Fall back to the mine. We can take cover there."

Trent looked at the map and the placement of the enemy 'Mechs. They were moving to cut off the Jaguar exit and could hit them in the open. Jez's order looked correct, but only on the surface. Trent knew that the one who is being ambushed must not give his enemy an out. The open mine shaft was just such an out. *If I were the enemy, I would have rigged the mine with explosives.*

"Belay that order," Trent snapped. As he spoke, another explosion rocked the hillside near the opening where Russou's forces had lined up. This time four massive boulders dislodged from their timeless perch and plunged down onto a *Nova* in Russou's command. The squat OmniMech never stood a chance as the rocks crashed down on it, crushing it flat. Fire from the approaching lance of Kat Killer 'Mechs poured through the canyon entrance, peppering two more of Russou's 'Mechs. The Clan 'Mechs rocked backward under the impact, then laid down their own barrage of death and destruction. Depleted-uranium autocannon rounds, lasers, and missiles stretched outward to the south, where the enemy was. The Kat Killer 'Mechs were closing in from behind, attempting to push the Jaguars into the canyon.

"You dare," Jez commanded.

"Star Commander Russou, we are already in one trap, and I believe the mine is booby-trapped as well," Trent barked over her voice. "As the officer in command, I order you to attack out of this canyon. Elements of Beta Striker Star, pull back and provide cover fire support as needed."

"I am the commanding officer here, Trent," Jez cut in, her voice raged with anger.

"Star Commander Russou, Star Captain Jez has been injured and incapacitated. You will obey my orders."

There was a pause as Russou gathered his thoughts. "Aye, Star Captain Trent," he said finally. Russou's forces began to fire back as Trent's 'Mechs moved in toward them. Trent's *Timber Wolf* moved from behind its cover even as a spray of missiles erupted all around him. Two of the warheads hit his left weapons pod, blasting off armor that splattered against his cockpit viewport like the pelting rain of a summer storm. The *Catapult* still meant business and was going to have to be dealt with.

He locked onto it again with his missiles, the tone of the lock filling his ears with stark clarity. Just as he was about to fire, the Kat Killer 'Mech moved behind a rock, breaking

Trent's targeting lock. *We can sit here all day and trade shots back and forth.* Trent looked up toward the top of the canyon ridge where the *Catapult* was hiding. The sophisticated sensors of his OmniMech were designed to take out enemy forces, not study small bits of terrain. Trent had to trust his instincts and tactical acumen.

As his command moved into the canyon opening alongside Russou's forces, another salvo of fire poured through the entrance, raking a number of the Jaguar 'Mechs. Russou's Star began to advance to the south, followed by what was left of Trent's Star. He alone remained in the canyon, at least in his mind. He did not count Jez, her 'Mech downed and crippled on the canyon floor nearby.

Trent studied the tactical display to see if the *Catapult* had moved. The magnetic readings of its fusion reactor still showed the 'Mech safely hidden behind the boulder. *Very well.*

Trent side-stepped the *Timber Wolf* out into the open and locked onto the base of the boulder. With cold precision he switched the pair of long-range missile racks that topped the *Timber Wolf*'s shoulders to the same target interlock circuit. The TIC would let him fire both weapons with the same trigger. There was a metallic clicking sound in his 'Mech as the next reload of missiles slid and locked into the box-like firing tubes. He knew the sounds and the sensations without needing to check his weapons status. His thumb triggered all forty missiles at once.

Against a moving 'Mech, Trent knew that missiles sometimes miss. But it was impossible to miss hitting mere immobile rock. The warheads went off, raising a huge cloud of dust into the air, but Trent did not watch the physical image. He concentrated on his targeting and tracking system. As the boulder dislodged and rolled down the canyon wall toward the floor, he saw his targeting system switch to the now-exposed *Catapult*. Without hesitation and before the stunned Kat Killer could respond, Trent opened fire with his medium and large lasers, firing through the fog of dust and airborne debris.

The stabbing scarlet beams slammed into the right side of the *Catapult* just shy of where the cockpit joined the torso. Trent's battle computer displayed the precision of his shot even as a ripple of heat rose in his cockpit. Armor exploded away as the guerrilla BattleMech twisted under the impact and external explosions. As his missiles recycled for another shot, Trent thought the guerrilla 'Mech might tumble into the canyon because of the damage taken, but instead it suddenly burst into a ball of flame as its internal ammunition stores went off. The entire right side of the *Catapult* went off like a volcanic eruption. Black smoke and flames filled the dust cloud from his previous hit.

Trent lifted his head in time to see the actual 'Mech finish its spin and plunge head-first down the hillside. Almost mechanically he switched to his sensors and saw that the other 'Mech on the canyon ridge had already disappeared from the area. *All that is left now are Jez and the consequences of my actions.*

Her face red with anger, Star Captain Jez Howell stood amid the dust of the canyon floor swirling around her. Her 'Mech was only a scant few meters away, and behind Trent, Russou and his force secured the area. Three of the Kat Killers had been utterly destroyed. The remaining pair had fled and were already out of sensor range. *The battle is won, but not complete.*

Trent stood in front of his *Timber Wolf*, arms crossed, ready for the verbal dressing-down he knew was coming. She did not disappoint him. "You defied my direct and explicit orders," she spat, taking out the portable communicator and activating it.

"Affirmative, Star Captain. Your BattleMech was damaged and you were incapacitated. I fulfilled my duty as an officer in service of the Jaguar."

"I was still able to command," she snapped.

"I feared you injured, perhaps unconscious," Trent replied, putting up a deliberate facade of calmness.

"You lie," she said.

"Neg," Trent replied.

"Star Captain Trent," came a deep voice over the hand-held communicator Jez held. He knew the voice and the anger behind it.

"Yes, Star Colonel."

"Your actions showed a lack of courage. Your decisions allowed the bandit enemy to escape. Your failures will be noted on your codex for now and for all time."

Trent spoke almost without thinking first. "My actions saved the entire command," he retorted. "Had we proceeded with Star Captain Jez Howell's plan we would have been boxed in and killed. One of my warriors has already inspected the mine she had ordered us to enter. It was booby-trapped with several drums of petrocycline. Had we fled there, we would have been wiped out to the last warrior."

"Your findings are irrelevant, Star Captain," the disembodied voice of Star Colonel Paul Moon replied. "The issue at hand is your presumptive assumption of command and blatant disregard for the orders of a superior officer. Your codex will reflect your act of insubordination."

"Neg, Star Colonel," Trent replied. *Not this time . . .* "I invoke the right of refusal against Star Captain Jez's version of events. If I win, my codex remains untainted." He stared fiercely at Jez, who grinned broadly in return.

"I accept this challenge," she replied. "We fight unaugmented and we fight now."

"Star Captain Jez," Moon's voice said. "This 'warrior' is unblooded. You do not have to face him."

"Neg. He is mine and his blood will flow today."

She means this to be my death. Trent took off his gun belt. *I mean this as redemption.* Jez likewise took off her weapons belt and tossed it aside, along with the communicator. Russou and the other warriors gathered around them, forming a Circle of Equals.

The rules of such trials were simple. The one killed, disabled, or removed from the perimeter of the Circle lost. Star Commander Russou glanced at Trent and nodded once, slowly, and Trent understood the unspoken message. *I will take her down for the both of us, my friend.*

Jez dropped to a combat stance, low and ready to strike. Trent had seen her do this before, and for a moment he was standing on Londerholm with the members of his sibko so many years before. He had beaten her that day, but nothing else was the same. They were no longer equals. She might outrank him, but Trent did not feel inferior to Jez; he felt *beyond* her. He flexed his right fist, and the artificial muscles in the arm tightened around his reinforced arm.

Jez sprang, just as he knew she would. He sidestepped to the left as she reached out for him. She clawed madly at his right arm, hoping to tear flesh, but ripping only his synthskin instead. Trent pivoted as she passed, thrusting up and around with his arm, then dropping quickly as she hit the ground and started to roll away.

His knees came down hard on her kidneys, knocking the wind out of her and pinning her face-down now under his bulk. Raising his right arm high, he brought it down just below her right ear with incredible force. The artificial myomer muscles of his replacement arm moved it at terrific speeds and with so much force that he was sure she must have suffered some internal ear damage. Jez's body went limp under his as she went unconscious.

Trent rolled her over, and without hesitation punched her in the face, half-wondering if she was faking. Her nose bent and a spray of blood streaked where his fist pummeled her. He struck her two more times with the full force of his fury. His hits to her neural implants caused minor sparks as his fists thrashed at her face. These blows were intended to leave a mark on her, to disfigure her.

He looked at her body under his. Trent knew that she would have killed him if given the chance. He could do the same to her if he so desired. She was helpless in his hands. The temptation was strong, but Trent held back. *Losing to me, and before the eyes of the others, will be worse than death for her.*

Trent pushed himself off her, then rose and looked around him. The warriors of his and Russou's commands watched him in silence. His heart raced in his ears and his breath was ragged, the result of his adrenaline rush. Trent walked over and picked up the communicator Jez had thrown down.

"Star Colonel Moon, this is Star Commander Trent. My codex remains as it was, pristine." He tossed the communicator down on top of Jez's body and walked back toward his 'Mech.

≡ 10 ≡

Smoke Jaguar Planetary Command
Warrenton, Hyner
Smoke Jaguar Occupation Zone
1 December 3054

Joseph's entire body convulsed upward from the lab table
as the interrogator increased the neuro-feedback from the
wall unit. His screams went nowhere, absorbed by the specially designed walls. The dim lights, also part of the interrogation process, were controlled by the neuro-stimulation unit
that lined one entire wall. Another wall of the room was covered all along its five-meter length by a dull mirror. The
member of the scientist caste looked on dispassionately as
she watched both her subject and the multiple computer displays. The displays told her exactly what kind of agony she
was inflicting and whether his anguished answers were
indeed truthful and all that he knew.

From behind the mirror Star Colonel Paul Moon stood with
Jez Howell and Trent, watching Joseph writhe in agony with
each new wave of treatment. Trent had never observed neuro-
chemical interrogation before, but he knew it was effective.
Jez's face, still showing the dull purple-blue bruises he had
given her, seemed to light up with the torture of the infor-
mant. Paul Moon also seemed to relish the agony of the man.

Trent turned his eyes away from the sight. "What have
you learned from this man, Star Colonel?"

Paul Moon continued to gaze at Joseph, whose body

attempted once more to twist free from the bonding straps of
the white medical table. "This Joseph was working for the
guerrillas all along. The information he gave us was intended
to be bait for the Kat Killer trap."

That much I already knew. "Were you able to learn any
more from him?"

The Star Colonel watched as the technician administered
another wave of pain. Joseph's muted screams, while totally
silent to their side of the two-way mirror, seemed to reach
Trent. "This freebirth was only able to identify those in his
cell. They are being sought, but thus far have evaded our
attempts to locate them."

Jez added more. "We were able to capture one of the pilots
after their pitiful excuse for an ambush. He was near death
when Russou found him. This bandit who had the audacity
to turn a BattleMech against the Smoke Jaguars was more
revealing. Before his termination he provided us with
some useful information—the name of the one of the towns
these so-called Kat Killer Fives use as their base. The
tracking we did on the two surviving Kat Killers confirms
the information."

Paul Moon moved closer to the two-way mirror and activated his wrist communicator. The device tied him to the
internal base communications system, giving him the ability
to issue orders to almost anyone under his command. "Technician Rubin, is there any sign that this Joseph is still with-
holding information?"

The tech moved to the wall of displays in the next room,
then her fingers danced across the three keyboards as the
monitors displayed data and graphics amid a barrage of
flickering lights and colors. After adjusting her thick glasses
twice to read the information displayed, she turned and faced
the mirrored wall, activating her own communicator. "Negative, Star Colonel Moon. There is no indication that he has
any will left. We have a ninety-eight percent probability that
we have obtained all that is possible from him."

Moon smiled and gave Trent only a quick glance. "Very
well. Terminate him, Tech Rubin," he said in a low tone.
"And Rubin . . ."

"Yes, Star Colonel?"

"Do it slowly."

The tech stood mute for a moment, looking at the mirror on
her side of the wall, then turned away. With a flick of two con-

trol knobs, Joseph's body began to twitch as he once again fought back the waves of neuro-energy being fed back into his brain. His body jumped as he tried to physically fight it. His mouth was open to scream, but no sound reached Trent. A wet spot formed in the man's groin as he lost bladder control and his body seemed to quake more rapidly. Trent saw his face as it turned toward the two-way mirror. Every facial muscle strained and seemed to leap off his skull. Joseph, the would-be freedom fighter, vomited as he tried vainly to escape one last time. There was a splatter of spit in the air as his head turned. Then it was over. Between the neuro-overload and the choking on his own vomit, Joseph was dead.

Paul Moon turned away from the glass wall and faced Trent. "The Kat Killer Five, that accursed blight on this planet, is apparently hiding near your field camp, Star Captain Trent. According to the information received, they are using Beaver Falls as their base and hiding their 'Mechs in the ruins of the city of Quantico."

Trent was familiar with the ruins. He'd explored them in the course of setting up his field command. During the Star League era, Quantico had been a thriving metropolis, the second-largest city on Hyner. He had learned from briefings that it had been destroyed in the First Succession War, victim of a Lyran Commonwealth attack. Now all that remained were ruins and mounds that had once been skyscrapers and other buildings. It was conceivably a place where BattleMechs could be concealed.

"So, we mount a strike into these ruins," Trent said confidently. "I am familiar with the terrain. Give me a few hours, and I should be able to prepare a battle plan worthy of the Jaguar."

"Neg," Paul Moon said, crossing his thick muscular arms. "It is obvious that these guerrillas could not have operated this long without the support of the local population. It appalls me. We come here to liberate these barbarians, and instead they raise their fists against us in anger. The Jaguar offers peace and protection to the local populations.

"There will be no strike against Quantico, not yet. Instead we will crush the rebels' support. Without the support of the indigenous people of this planet, their activity will be slowly strangled. Accordingly, Star Captain Howell, you will take your Trinary to Beaver Falls and you will raze the entire village. I want you to leave no building intact. Crush it under the feet of your 'Mechs. Kill anyone and everyone there."

Trent felt his heart skip. The Smoke Jaguars were known for their swift suppression of local uprisings, but there had been nothing so severe since the attack on the city of Edo on Turtle Bay. Hohiro Kurita escaped from the prison there, and the local population had mounted a minor rebellion. The Smoke Jaguars dealt with the problem with the strictest adherence to the Crusader mentality. Quoting from *The Remembrance,* they ordered their flagship, the *Sabre Cat,* to destroy the city. The planetary bombardment killed more than a million people, and literally boiled the waters of the Sawagashii River. Those who somehow managed to survive were lasered or bombed by ground forces.

The massacre brought about two things. One, all rebellion on Edo ceased. The other result, however, was that some of the other Clans sanctioned the Jaguars in the Clan Grand Council. The practice of razing settlements, killing civilians, had ceased. Trent had heard rumors of it happening elsewhere, but this was the first time he had known it to be ordered.

The Jaguars were a Crusader Clan, among those who had pushed for the invasion of the Inner Sphere and the restoration of the former Star League. Trent had always considered himself a Crusader rather than a Warden. Where the Crusaders pressed for invasion, the Wardens believed the role of the Clans was to protect the Inner Sphere. Both had "evidence" to support their positions from *The Remembrance* and the writings of Nicholas Kerensky, founder of the Clans centuries before.

For the first time in his life, Trent questioned the Crusader position.

Jez did not seem at all shocked by the order. "It shall be done as you command, Star Colonel."

"If I may speak, Star Colonel," Trent said, still mentally reeling from the order that had been given.

Paul Moon looked at him coldly. "Proceed."

"Sir, this action seems extreme. The guerrilla actions on this planet have been minor annoyances at best. They have barely even scratched us. Perhaps we should concentrate on hitting the Kat Killers directly rather than the civilians."

Moon shook his head. "If we do not break the backs of

these guerrillas now, we risk this rebellion spreading across Hyner like a virus."

Trent also shook his head. "We have used such measures only once to my knowledge. Yes, they worked on Edo. But they can easily backfire. Do this and you may fan the flames of rebellion by creating martyrs to the Kat Killer's cause."

"My order stands," Paul Moon replied. "You will prepare your forces to execute this order to the letter. Nothing and no one is to escape from Beaver Falls alive."

From Moon's tone, Trent could tell that he would hear no more argument. He had made his decision, and probably had done so even before Trent arrived at the meeting. He glanced at Jez and saw the smirk on her face. He sensed that she savored this, just as she had savored the torture of the man Joseph. It only confirmed his belief that her mind had become twisted and sick.

The massive 'Mech bay of Planetary Command was bustling with activity as Trent entered it. He walked past half a dozen other BattleMechs before reaching the spot where his own *Timber Wolf* was parked. Judith and Master Technician Phillip stood in front of the 'Mech.

As he walked up, Judith nodded in greeting, but Phillip was obviously displeased by his presence. "Star Captain, can I help you?"

"I have come to speak with my bondsman."

"We are configuring your 'Mech per orders from your CO," Phillip said, almost as if in challenge. "I am afraid Judith is going to be very busy."

Trent was not in the mood to deal with the man. He had heard enough from Judith to know of his constant verbal and even physical abuse of her.

"I am a trueborn warrior, *Tech*," he said, stressing the last word. "Whatever is on your mind can wait until I am done speaking with her." There was a hint of aggression in his voice. He would never forget that Phillip was very likely the one responsible for his failure to win the Grand Melee.

Phillip's face flushed at the rebuke. "As you wish, Star Captain," he said, backing away.

"Star Captain," Judith said, bowing her head.

Trent took her arm and drew her closer to the massive legs of his *Timber Wolf,* out of earshot of others in the noisy bay. "This Phillip needs to be taught his place."

"You have earned his anger today," Judith said with a thin smile.

"One day, I may take even more from him. But for now, I will settle for his anger."

"The *Timber Wolf* is ready except for the exchanging of weapons pods. Repairs on the rest of the Star 'Mechs are also near completion. I noticed that you requested a switch to mostly short-range weapons. We must be preparing for a short campaign."

Trent nodded, then glanced up at the ten-meter-tall war machine that dwarfed the two of them and thought back to the orders he had been given. "Aye," he said absently, thoughts elsewhere. "Our mission is short."

Judith studied him curiously. "Is there something else, Star Captain? Some other way I may be of assistance, *quiaff*?"

He looked at her for a moment before speaking again. "I know from our talks that you share my interest in history. In the next few days we are going to take part in the making of it. But I am not sure it is a history that I wish to wear on my wrist." Trent twisted his codex bracelet as he spoke.

"I was once a warrior," Judith said. "There are times when orders are hard to follow."

"Aye," Trent returned, scanning the bay to be sure no one could possibly overhear. "Perhaps some orders should never be given. I am sure you have heard of the Smoke Jaguar action on Turtle Bay."

Judith nodded gravely. "Even by Clan standards, the action was extreme. It was an act that shocked the Inner Sphere, and it certainly had the effect of discouraging other rebellions on Clan-occupied worlds." Her face tightened as she spoke, and Trent saw the realization dawn on her. "We are going to do the same thing here?"

Trent did not have to answer. She seemed to read the reply on his face.

"Star Captain, by your leave," Judith said, "instead of crushing the Kat Killer Five, such an action risks increasing support for the guerrillas."

"Aff. But our leaders believe it is the only way to shatter their support."

"And you will take part in this?"

"I have been given my orders," Trent said, but he felt . . . guilty. Yes, *that was the word*. It was a strange and new emotion.

"You refused to obey Jez several days ago," Judith said, surprising Trent that a bondsman would be aware of his Circle of Equals with Jez. "Can you not demand a similar Trial of Refusal, *quineg*?"

Trent shook his head. "To do so would spell my end as a Smoke Jaguar. I would be branded a Warden, a sheep among a pack of hunters. And even were I to win, the command would merely be executed by another warrior who *would* follow orders."

"And so there is nothing to be done?" Judith asked.

"For now at least. It is the way of the Clan for each person to fulfill his or her role for the good of all. My role is that of a warrior. I was bred and raised for only one thing. And a good warrior follows orders."

Judith reached out a hand, hesitating a moment before resting it on his shoulder in a gesture of comradeship. "I have been among the Smoke Jaguars for over two years now," she said. "I know that the way of the Jaguars and of the Clans is different than what I was born into. I also know that you are more than a good warrior, no matter what standards apply. And I respect you for *not* blindly following orders. From what I have heard, the battle at Baker Canyon proves this point. It is what makes you who you are. It is what makes you more than my bondsmaster. I would be proud to call you friend, if you would permit. Whatever path you choose, I will go with you."

More than a warrior . . . Trent could not forget the words. Words that seemed to burn into his brain all night long as he lay in his bunk, unable to sleep.

Beaver Falls
Hyner
Smoke Jaguar Occupation Zone
7 December 3054

As the sun came up over Hyner, the early morning frost instantly turned to a foglike steam rising off the buildings of the village of Beaver Falls. Trent's Beta Striker Star moved into a cluster of trees just north of town. All that stood between them and the village was Ketchum Park. The meandering creek that broke over the rock falls was pastoral, a stark contrast to the reason the Jaguars were there.

Trent sat back stiffly in the command couch of his *Timber Wolf* and scanned the village as his Star formed up beside him. He hoped that word had somehow leaked to the Kat Killer Five, and that they would emerge from the village in their Battle-Mechs and fight. They might be bandit scum, but it was better to fight even inferior warriors than to simply kill civilians.

That was not to be. The sensors were picking up no signs of fusion-power sources. No BattleMechs, no tanks, nothing to offer a true warrior the heat and sting of battle. Trent chanted to himself many lines from *The Remembrance*, hoping to find guidance for what he was about to do in its solemn poetry. But that was not to be either.

The Remembrance celebrated the honor and glory of the Clans as expressed in the deeds of its warriors. And a warrior could find that glory only in combat against an honorable foe—another warrior. But the natives of Hyner were not warriors. What honor could come from destroying them? They were simply people who had been conquered by the Smoke Jaguars in their fierce drive to be the Clan to take Terra. Reciting aloud his favorite passages of *The Remembrance*, which expressed all that was finest and highest in the Clans, Trent only became further convinced that the attack on Beaver Falls was wrong.

What was happening to the Smoke Jaguars, to the way of the Clans?

He looked across the green to the village and shook his head. The sleepy little town was centuries old, from what he had been able to learn. Now it was going to be wiped from the map as if it had never existed. Worse yet, *he* was going to be responsible for the act.

There is still a chance. Trent switched his communication system to a secure tight-beam broadcast and locked the signal onto Jez's *Warhawk* at the opposite end of the village. There was a faint crackle and hiss as the commline came on, and soon Jez's voice filled his ears.

"Status, Trent."

"We are in position, Star Captain," he replied. "We are also on a secured channel."

"Is there some significance in that?"

Trent drew a long deep breath. " 'And Nicholas stood with the first gathering of Khans to draw up the tenets of what made a warrior. Wars have often killed the innocent, ruined entire societies. Not within the Clans. Wars were for warriors to wage and that innocents not suffer at the hands of trueborns.' "

There was a pause. "*The Remembrance*, passage ten, verse five," she said.

Trent was not surprised. All Clan warriors learned *The Remembrance* by heart as part of both their military and moral training. What did impress him was that Jez seemed unconcerned that the sacred words contradicted the action they were about to undertake. "I beseech you to abort this mission. Killing innocents is not worthy of a warrior."

"You may be right, Trent, but heed my words. We will execute Star Colonel Moon's orders." Her voice was firm, yet Trent barely recognized the tone of his longtime foe. *My quoting of* The Remembrance *got to her.*

"Why, Jez?"

"We are Smoke Jaguars," she returned. "And warriors

must respect the chain of command. We obey when we are ordered. Star Colonel Moon all but told me that the orders had come all the way from the top, from Khan Lincoln Osis on down. We do not challenge orders. We are warriors, and we have a blood obligation to serve the Smoke Jaguar. I do not like this any more than you, but we are different. I understand my place in the Clan. You question yours. You see yourself as something more than you are."

Her calm and reasonable tone caught Trent off guard, for he'd expected her usual barrage of venom. She was right—he did question the authority of the Clan. But he could not help it. Something inside him told him this thing was not right. "I do not believe a warrior exists merely to follow orders. Nor do I believe that the great Kerenskys would ever condone the killing of innocents. To do this deed makes of us mindless robots. You know it is wrong just as well as I do."

"Neg. It is my task to serve. The word of my commander is the word of the Clan, of the Smoke Jaguar itself. Our leaders think only of the good of the Clan. You fight the ways of our people. I work within the precepts of our redes and traditions. That is why I have a bloodname. And one day, I will command a Galaxy of troops. But you will remain nameless, one who is not remembered, one whose genetic legacy will never become part of the sacred gene pool to create new and better warriors."

Trent weathered her words, despite how they bruised his spirit. "The blood of innocents is on your head, Jez."

"So be it, Trent. If you refuse to obey, I will order the other Stars under me to open fire on you. You have your orders. You must comply."

Before Trent could rebut, she had switched to a wide-beam communications channel that transmitted her commands to every BattleMech in the Trinary. "Warriors of the Smoke Jaguars, the residents of this town have given aid and sustenance to bandits who have attacked our Clan, killed our warriors. It is bad enough that they are bandit scum, but they are cowards to boot. They refuse to come out and fight us face to face.

"By command of Star Colonel Paul Moon, this village is to be razed. There are to be no survivors. Every building is to be destroyed. Leave nothing alive to remind anyone that this place ever existed. Holoimages of this attack will be broadcast all over this planet so that everyone on Hyner will know the price of standing against the Smoke Jaguars. Attack now."

Trent looked at his secondary display. His people would be waiting for a confirming order from him before they opened up. At the far end of Beaver Falls, Jez's own Star began to fire. The rumblings of missile and autocannon rounds firing shattered the morning quiet. A bright flash of light illuminated the city from behind, framing the buildings that were his own targets. Russou's Star began to fire as well, hitting the city from south of Trent's position.

Trent wanted to attack his fellow Smoke Jaguars instead of the innocents of Beaver Falls, but knew his troops could not even if they shared the conflict that tore at his spirit. In the end, Trent knew that no group of warriors could stand against the Clan from within. No, only a lone warrior could. And this was not the time.

"Beta Striker Star," he transmitted through his neuro-helmet mike. "Comply with the order."

The OmniMechs of his command opened fire and began to advance toward Beaver Falls. Styx and Lior were at the head, blazing away with short-range missiles. The pair of buildings they hit collapsed instantly, sending flames billowing into the air. Trent moved forward, crossing the stream into the park as Ansel's *Mad Dog* came up alongside him. The *Dog*'s two missile racks popped open and let go with a deadly salvo that slammed into a distant warehouse.

Trent realized that he alone was not firing, and the temptation was to continue to hold his fire, but he knew that would invite an even greater loss of honor than he had risked in trying to turn Jez from the assault. Yet, some stubborn part of Trent refused to let him participate fully in this senseless destruction. Deliberately he dropped his targeting reticule onto an already destroyed structure belching flames into the early morning sky after being firestormed by Laurel's *Hellbringer*.

Trent fired his weapons—all of them.

His missiles and autocannon rounds only stoked the fire in the destroyed building. He felt a slight ripple of heat in his cockpit and heard the sound of additional ammunition cycling for another volley. He did not wait but fired again, this time imagining Jez and Star Colonel Moon in the sights of his reticule. Again an immense explosion of death and destruction blasted the gutted structure, splattering a nearby building and setting it on fire. He knew in that moment that once the storm of death had begun, there was no controlling it. Even his own efforts not to do more damage had already spread. *Such is the nature of war . . .*

Suddenly he saw a blur break from the midst of the inferno the Jaguars had set off within Beaver Falls. It was a sight that made Trent sick. A group of people, probably a family, emerged from the flames and explosions and ran toward the park where Trent and his Star were positioned.

Trent knew little of families. Trueborns were ignorant of such things, though he knew they were part of the social reality of freebirths. He might perhaps understand the concept, but the meaning was beyond his frame of reference. And yet something in his heart went out to this man, woman, and three young ones. They must have thought they had gotten free of the fires and explosions, but then they stopped in their tracks. What menaced them now were five of the giant war machines responsible for the destruction of their homes and their friends.

They prepared to break and run but never got the chance. Lior poised his *Cauldron-Born* in a low hunch, preparing to fire. Trent opened his mouth to give the order to abort, but it was too late. Lior opened up with every weapon he had. Antipersonnel cannon rounds tore up the bright green sod of the park, and missiles bore in on the family. There was a brilliant flash of light, followed by a thick stream of white smoke rising up into the stark blue sky. All that remained were a crater, smoldering soil, and the memory of five people snuffed out in an instant. The image would be burned into Trent's mind for eternity.

Lior was a member of his Star, one of his warriors. By Clan dictum, it was as if Trent himself had pulled the target interlock trigger and fired the salvo. Lior would feel no remorse. Instead he locked onto another structure, a tall one, most likely a grain silo, and began to blaze away once again.

Trent held his fire for a moment, slowing his *Timber Wolf* to a slow walk as he watched the village of Beaver Falls die in front of him. Building by building, life by life, everything that made up the tiny town was disappearing off the surface of the planet. In a few decades, there would be no memory of this spot. The Smoke Jaguar command would make sure of that.

Those lives are on my head. Their blood is mine. Unarmed innocents. Such waste should wake Nicholas Kerensky from his grave. This was not the kind of war I was bred to fight. This is not the kind of war I was born to make.

═══ **12** ═══

The portable command dome was essentially a tent with reinforced sides. With carbon-filament support rods and a hard-pressed fiber outer casing, it was designed to be raised and taken down quickly. Such was the nature of the Smoke Jaguar fighting style.

Star Captain Jez Howell stood under the built-in light in the center of the dome. In front of her, near the center of the dome, was the portable field communicator. Trent and Russou entered and stood facing her, the brief-case sized device between them.

"Watch," Jez said without so much as a preface, then activated the unit with a hand-held remote device. The gray screen of the communicator changed to crisp images of what had once been a building. All that remained was the rough outline of the structure and a massive pile of rubble belching smoke into the sky. In the midst of the debris were laborers and members of the scientist caste moving about with hand-held scanners, shovels, and gear.

"What you see is all that remains of Charlie Binary's Alpha Assault Star. They were asleep in their barracks when a truckload of explosives went off outside their compound. A message delivered to planetary command by the local media indicates that the Kat Killer Five was behind the assault."

Russou stared at the image. "There have been a rash of graffiti markings—a K-squared with a Roman numeral five—all through my patrol area. Support for these guerrillas seems to be growing rather than waning, Star Captain."

Jez nodded, her expression grim. "Star Colonel Moon ordered the razing of the city of Kimota yesterday. This action will help destroy support for these Kat Killer Fives."

Trent only shook his head. *More senseless deaths. The time has come to end this game—a game we are obviously beginning to lose.*

Jez noticed the gesture. "You have something to say, Star Captain Trent, *quiaff*?"

"Aff, Star Captain. That action will only add fuel to the resistance ignited by what we did at Beaver Falls."

"You have another suggestion perhaps, *quiaff*? Maybe you could offer one that does not show disrespect to your superior officers."

"I was raised to take the fight to warriors, Star Captain Jez," Trent said. *And so were you, but you seem to have forgotten.* "The leaders of these guerrillas are military men and women, even if we regard them as mere bandits. They are carrying out this campaign of resistance with precision, and thus far our campaign of retaliation has only strengthened their cause. But even this resistance operation must deal with military realities."

Trent reached down and slid a small circular optical disk into the field communicator. The image of the blasted building disappeared and was replaced with a map of the region that showed all the terrain features in their real-life colors and detail. That included the city of Warrenton, location of the Jaguar planetary command, and its environs for three hundred kilometers in all directions. The roadways were long gray lines, cities and villages appearing as dull red dots along them.

"We have been trying to solve the problem with brute force, but I believe the key is locating their BattleMechs. These bandits are MechWarriors. Find their 'Mechs and you find them. Even better, deprive them of their BattleMechs and cripple them once and for all. Without their war machines, they are merely a handful of men and women against the greatest of all the Clans."

"Trent, you are talking like a cadet. We have already considered such a plan. We have investigated all probable locations where the bandits might have concealed their BattleMechs, but without success."

Trent allowed himself a thin grin. "I have read those reports, Star Captain. But I have also been reading up on Hyner. Our own records reveal the possible existence of an old Star League base on this world, though it has never been found."

He reached over and took the remote control from Jez's hand and aimed it at the field communicator. The map image changed slightly. In addition to the red lights showing the locations of town and villages, a single yellow light came on between their current field camp position and Warrenton. It flashed like a warning.

"You are speaking in riddles, Trent," Jez said. "Is this where you think the Kat Killers are hiding, *quiaff*?"

"Affirmative. I believe it is a strong possibility," Trent said.

Jez's eyes widened at the sight. She fairly grabbed the control away from him and then adjusted the image scale, making the map much larger. "This is nothing but a foul swamp. How could they go there undetected? We would have seen their 'Mechs on our fly-overs."

Trent pointed to the map on the pop-up screen of the communicator. "There was a methane processing plant in that location during the time of the Star League. It provided a third of the power used by Hyner before it was destroyed during the Succession Wars that followed the collapse of the League."

"So, we are talking about ancient ruins, *quiaff*?"

"In a manner of speaking. From what I have learned in the databases, these facilities had massive piping systems, many large enough to conceal numerous BattleMechs. Given its isolation and proximity to the sightings of the Kat Killer 'Mechs, it would be a logical hiding place. If any of that complex is even remotely intact, it is the only area in the region large enough to hide them."

Jez studied the map. "And our forces have not searched this area, *quiaff*?"

"Affirmative. From what I could find in the database of missions, it was not on the search list because it could be surveyed from the air."

"Then we attack them to pay them back for what they have done to our warriors." Jez's voice rang with lust for battle.

"Neg, Jez. If we are to take them we must be like the stalking Jaguar," Trent said. "Look at that terrain. It is tight fighting, and even though it is only bandits we hunt, good warriors will die trying to destroy them. Those swamps are a quagmire, and these Kat Killers have probably booby-trapped and rigged the waters for yet other ambushes."

"We lay a trap for them, *quiaff*?"

"Aff. We tempt them with something they will not be able to resist. A target so rich and so within reach that the temptation to strike will be too great. And since we know where they will be coming from, we will pounce and crush them once and for all."

Jez looked at Trent, but her expression revealed nothing. "And what, pray, would tempt them so strongly?"

"To protect our assets, we will begin to set up smaller field-ammunition and weapons storage dumps. A convoy headed for one of these can be diverted to the roadway that runs near the swamp. These guerrillas are bound to be low on expendables, and they will not be able to resist the temptation to seize supplies passing within easy reach. To make sure, we will spread word of the contents of the convoy through the lower castes. By letting word out in the nearby towns like Chinn and New Bethesda where we have already seen graffiti in support of the guerrillas, the news is bound to reach them."

"All of that time with your bondsman has taught you to think like these Inner Sphere scum," Jez said, her tone sarcastic. "But you may have something here. I will pass it on to command. Perhaps you will yet redeem yourself in the eyes of our commander."

The image of Star Colonel Paul Moon crossed its arms in defiant thought as Jez consulted with him via the field communicator. "As you can see, Star Colonel," she said, "I believe I have located these bandits, and the plan I propose offers the perfect bait to lure them out into the open." She did not mention that the idea had come from Trent, and she did not intend to. In Jez's mind, his actions were hers. He reported to her, after all . . .

"Indeed. There are some risks. You can use only a minimal

number of 'Mechs in such an operation. Use of a large force would risk exposing your presence."

"Understood, Star Colonel. I plan to lead Alpha Star myself."

"Neg, Star Captain. This mission lacks honor. Warriors do not stoop to trickery, to the cowardly use of ambush tactics. You may accompany it if you wish, but it should be led by Star Captain Trent."

"Trent?"

Paul Moon's image grinned slyly. "Aff. Perhaps these bandits will rid me of him once and for all. And, if they do not send him home to the Kerenskys, at least we will not soil the honor of good warriors with this task."

"As you command, Star Colonel," Jez said, bowing her head slightly in respect.

"You are to be commended for this, Jez. Thanks to you, the Jaguars may yet be rid of these so-called Kat Killers."

Judith was about to enter her field tent when she saw Trent approaching. It had been a long day, and though she longed for a night's sleep, she knew she must always be at the service of her bondsmaster.

"You are out late, Star Captain," she said.

Trent smiled almost oddly. "My searches for the Star League weapons cache have thus far been fruitless, but my discovery of the methane production facility has paid off." Judith and he had spoken several times about his efforts to locate the ancient Star League base called a Castle Brian. "I now have the information needed to put an end to these Kat Killers."

"Will this be another retaliation like those of Beaver Falls or Kimota?" she asked, but she could not mask the bitterness in her voice.

"Now that you are a bondsman and a member of Clan Smoke Jaguar, you know that a warrior must follow orders, Judith. Any orders, all orders, whatever orders are given. I was there at Beaver Falls. I made whatever protest was possible. In the end, I still had to do my duty."

"What about honor?" Judith asked.

"Be careful of your tone, bondsman," Trent said. "You cannot know what is in my heart on these matters. I was there, Judith. I watched innocents die, I witnessed the senselessness of their deaths. But this time will be different. This time we shall fight the Kat Killers themselves—warrior to warrior. And when we are done, they will be destroyed and these retaliations will cease."

"I do not trust Star Captain Jez," Judith said.

"Trust is irrelevant," Trent returned. "What matters now is my own honor. The fight I have planned for these bandits grants them more then they deserve—a chance to fight and die like warriors."

"I hear your words, but I also know what I have heard from the other technicians. This Jez is reckless and seems to have an abiding hatred to you. I heard talk of your Trial of Grievance against her at Baker Canyon."

"Necessary."

"Yet it tells me that she will stop at nothing to get to you."

"You are correct. But there are times, my bondsman, that you must trust my foresight and instincts as a warrior. And this is one of those times . . ."

=== 13 ===

The north-south roadway known as the Braddock Pike was perfect for the strategy Trent had in mind. It twisted, with many tight turns cut into the hills it crossed. The road was narrow, having been built for hovercar travel in and out of the Hyner countryside centuries earlier. Surrounded by trees and with a number of steep dropoffs, the terrain forced Trent to move his 'Mech force slowly, parallel to the roadway without being seen. They were some twelve kilometers from the methane facility. When the Kat Killers did appear, he would be ready.

The fact that Jez had replaced Styx on the mission was not part of the original plan, but he had been so surprised at her endorsement of the mission that he accepted the change without comment. Trent did not care about her motivations. All he knew was that if this mission was successful, there would no longer be any need to destroy the villages and towns of Hyner.

The convoy consisted of a caravan of J-27 ammunition carriers, vehicles that had been the mainstay of Inner Sphere supply for centuries. The ones that now traveled down the pike, weaving in and out of the curves among the trees, were empty. Their sole purpose was to serve as bait for the bandits.

Trent had learned that the Jaguars had taken these very vehicles as isorla when the Arkab Legion had crumbled before the Smoke Jaguar assault on Hyner several years before. Now this same hardware would serve to entrap its former owners, whose remnants had become a resistance gang calling itself the Kat Killer Five.

Trent and his people had been waiting patiently for at least an hour, but Trent was not impatient. He was sure their prey would come for the bait. And then he saw them. Four 'Mechs. At the head was the same *Warhammer* that had tried to kill both him and Russou. In its wake was a *Crusader,* a *Grand Dragon,* and a *Grasshopper.* Trent throttled his *Timber Wolf* to life, and moved from hiding onto the road.

The *Warhammer* pilot suddenly realized what was happening, and swung to face the *Timber Wolf* as Trent brought it into the open, cutting across the convoy's path. The three other BattleMechs trailing the *Warhammer* slowed their advance, apparently realizing that they had stumbled into a well-laid trap.

As Trent dropped his targeting reticule over the computer-enhanced outline of the *Warhammer,* a brilliant flash of light came at him. The bright beams of the enemy 'Mech's twin PPCs boiled away his torso armor in a thunder-like clap of arcing electrical energy, leaving billowing black smoke where the armor had torn away. The impact was vicious, and Trent's balance swayed slightly, throwing off his targeting sight. Despite the deadliness of the attack, Trent coolly realigned his targeting reticule on the *Warhammer,* waiting patiently the milliseconds it took for the battle computer to lock onto his target.

He fired in two salvos. The first was his lasers, medium and large. The scarlet beams lanced out, one of the mediums missing, but the other, along with the large lasers, finding its mark. The lasers flayed off armor plating even as the *Warhammer* walked forward. The Kat Killer 'Mech reeled slightly under the impact just as Trent's second salvo hit, finishing the job.

The second salvo was a wave of long-range missiles from the *Timber Wolf*'s boxy missile pods. Forty in all, the missiles hit mostly in the upper torso of the *Warhammer.* Each warhead went off within an instant of the others, with spectacular results. The *Warhammer*'s forward movement ground to a halt as more of its armor was ripped away.

The BattleMech's internal structure, exposed by the earlier laser blasts, was left raw for several of the missile warheads. They were the last ones to go off, just milliseconds after the rest of the barrage. Erupting, they struck the innards of the 'Mech. The internal structure and myomer muscles were shredded by the hot shrapnel and quaking of the explosion. Trent watched as the bandit pilot lost control of his BattleMech. Its upper torso tipped back, as if trying to stop, but the legs continued to move forward. Suddenly off-center, the *Warhammer* fell backward, its stubby arm PPCs poking into the air as it lay staring upward.

"Lior and Ansel, begin your sweep," Trent said as he saw the *Warhammer* trying to use its weapon arms to help it stand. Lior and Ansel broke and ran into the rear of the guerrilla force, cutting them off from retreat. The bulky Kat Killer *Crusader* unleashed a horrific wave of short-range missiles at Ansel's *Mad Dog,* hitting the gray Jaguar 'Mech hard in its right leg.

The *Warhammer,* unable to move or stand, strained as Trent closed with it. Switching to a tight-beam laser transmission directly to his foe, he sent it over an open channel he knew his enemy could hear. "You and your force are trapped and defeated. Submit and I grant that our justice will be swift."

The message that came back was not surprising. "By Allah, you will never have my soul, you demon-cat. Help me stand and I shall fight you, one on one, warrior against warrior, as it was meant to be."

Trent surveyed the fallen 'Mech in front of him. "Impossible. You are bandits. To treat you as a warrior would be an insult to my Clan. Step out and I assure you that you will meet your fates."

The *Warhammer* rolled just enough to fire its short-range missiles. Only one found its mark in the *Timber Wolf*'s right shoulder, the others flying high and above him. Trent swung his targeting sight in on the *Warhammer*'s already battered torso. He could see the simmering fusion reactor shielding and the gyro housing under a pool of slick, sizzling green-yellow coolant. It would be a simple matter to cripple his foe and then rejoin the battle raging among the other 'Mechs.

Trent heard the tone of the weapons lock fill his compact neurohelmet when suddenly he saw the shadow of another BattleMech come alongside the mangled *Warhammer*. It was a *Warhawk* with the distinctive spotted Jaguar pattern that could only be Jez's OmniMech.

Her actions shocked him even more than her sudden appearance. She lifted the *Warhawk*'s massive leg upward, then brought it down onto the cockpit of the bandit *Warhammer*. The force of her 85-ton 'Mech smashing into the other 'Mech created an impact that shook even Tent's *Timber Wolf*. Not only did she crush the bandit's cockpit, but her 'Mech's giant foot went all the way through it with a deep grinding noise and a flash of sparks.

Trent was stunned for an instant. He glared at the *Warhawk* as Jez extracted its foot from the crushed armor plating. "You have violated the rede of honor among warriors, Jez. This one was mine to finish."

Her voice was emotionless. "Neg. These are bandits and to be dealt as we would the lowest of castes. You cannot lose honor against one of these."

Trent felt a rush of anger spread through his body. The synthskin on his face seemed to tingle with a prickly heat as he watched. Jez was right, but that did not make it any better. She *acknowledges the letter of the rede of honor, not the intent.*

Trent turned his *Timber Wolf* and began to rush toward the remaining battle. The *Crusader* was in its death dance, half-falling, half-twisting under a scything by the lasers of Ansel's *Mad Dog*. Smoke billowed from its chest and torso as its ammunition stores exploded, spreading like a fiery cancer inside the bandit 'Mech. Its shoulder and hip joints suddenly flashed with flames as the 'Mech contorted, falling into a heap.

Laurel's *Hellbringer* unleashed a series of death-blow kicks to the already felled *Grand Dragon*. Trent's secondary display gave him a reading on the downed 'Mech, and his trained eyes knew that the fight was over even before he had seen them. Laurel's maddened kicks reminded him of someone kicking a fallen foe to make sure he was indeed dead.

Only Lior still battled, engaging the last of the guerrillas as it tried to make a mad break out of the trap. Trent closed in on the fight as the Kat Killer *Grasshopper* lit into the air on a short hop, setting fire to several tree branches as it rose. Lior did not move, remaining still as he took his time to fire. A stream of depleted-uranium slugs and a Gauss rifle slug raced upward at the jumping *Grasshopper,* hitting it in the legs.

The bandit 'Mech wavered under the impacts, then the jets on the leg failed as the remaining armor blew off into the air. It dropped like a rock, autocannon rounds tearing the 'Mech apart as it fell. Trent lost sight of it among the trees, but saw a giant oak topple under the weight of the falling 'Mech. His sensors completed the picture as Lior fired into the heart of the enemy 'Mech, destroying its fusion reactor and sending a cloud of white smoke up into the air above the treeline.

"It is over," Trent signaled to his command, to Jez, and to himself. No other innocents would die now. The shameless and wasteful policy of razing villages could now end.

"Aff," Jez added on the same comm channel. "Report back to the garrison command post for debriefing and new orders."

Jaz led Trent and the other warriors of his Star crossed the parade grounds of the Hyner planetary command post. They were headed toward the looming and impressive figure of Star Colonel Paul Moon, who stood reviewing several Stars marching in parade formation.

Moon wore his gray dress uniform, and as always, the garment seemed barely able to contain his mighty musculature. The genetic engineering that had bred Paul Moon to such formidable size had made him not only strong but swift. He turned to watch the little group of approaching warriors, meeting the eyes of each one in turn. All except Trent.

"I received your message, Star Captain Jez. I would offer congratulations, but there is little honor to be won in fighting bandits. Your plan was flawless, but that is to be expected from one of your bloodline."

Her plan! Trent reeled inwardly as he realized that Jez had claimed it as her own. "I thank you, Star Colonel," she said, bowing her head slightly.

"I thank you in return. The towns surrounding that old abandoned methane plant have obviously been providing aid and information to these guerrillas. I give to you the honor of selecting which of them we will level to teach a lesson to those who aid our enemies. The choice is yours."

Trent was stunned by these words. They had destroyed the Kat Killer Five. What was the point of further retaliations? The destruction seemed more senseless than ever. "Sir," he began, knowing he must choose his words carefully. "Permission to speak freely, Star Colonel."

Paul Moon slowly turned his gaze on Trent, staring at him for a moment as though observing some disgusting alien creature. "Proceed, Star Captain."

"Sir, this step, the razing of another village, it is not necessary. We have already destroyed the guerrilla operation. What merit can there be in this new action?"

"It is not your place to tell me what has merit and what does not," Moon said, crossing his arms in what Trent now recognized as a typical gesture of authority. "We shall level one of these villages and transmit a holovid of the deed to the other cities of this world so that all on Hyner will know the price of standing in the Jaguar's path."

Trent drew a deep breath. He could no longer stand by silently. He must make a stand, even if the price was his own life. The time for waiting had passed. "I challenge you to a Trial of Grievance, Star Colonel."

"Indeed," Moon returned.

"Aff. This command violates our code of honor, as set down by Nicholas Kerensky, the founder of the Clans."

Moon chuckled slightly. "Must I remind you, Star Colonel, that this is a military command? Your opinions do not interest me, and meeting you in combat offers no more challenge than crushing a bug under my heel. But you are a blight on our Clan. For you to call yourself a Jaguar warrior brings only shame to the rest. There is no honor in combat with you, but I promise you that I shall find honor in erasing you like a stain."

"Very well," Trent said, the blood rushing in his ears as his body prepared. "I assume you wish to fight unaugmented, *quiaff*?"

Moon smiled. "Aff. And these warriors will form our Circle of Equals." He nodded to Jez and the others, who immediately moved to surround the two men. Moon unbuttoned his uniform collar and shirt, and flexed his muscles in preparation for the fight.

"You do know that I will kill you, Trent," Paul Moon said, his voice barely a whisper as he lowered his body to a fighting stance.

"But I will not kill you, Star Colonel, even if I get the chance," Trent returned, lowering his own center of gravity.

"And that is your weakness," Moon replied.

"Neg. Death is a merciful release for a warrior. Letting you live with defeat would injure you more than a death blow. Especially if I, one who you consider an unblooded failure, were to defeat you."

"No more words," Paul Moon said, then sprang out at Trent, spreading his massive arms wide to prevent Trent from escaping to either side.

Trent lunged backward as Paul Moon landed just short of him, coming down on his knees and sweeping one of his arms like a flail at Trent's legs. He caught Trent mid-stride, knocking him down hard onto the grass of the parade grounds.

But Trent knew he had to stay in motion. Any hesitation and the huge warrior would be on top of him. He was rolling before he hit the ground, moving away. He came up on his feet at the same time that Paul Moon, from a kneeling position, swung his massive fist at him. The blow hit with pile driver force against the left side of his face, breaking a tooth loose and sending Trent's entire body flying back with its force. Ringing filled Trent's ears as he turned toward the edge of the Circle of Equals. He saw the faces of Lior and Laurel, the two warriors under his command, watching without emotion.

He was too dazed to outmaneuver Paul Moon. The Elemental grabbed him from behind and encircled him with his bear-like arms. It was like trying to wrestle an Arcadian steel viper as Moon tried to squeeze the life out of him. Trent's ribs ached, and he heard a snapping sound as one of his ribs snapped. Air was being forced from his lungs. If he was going to do something, it had to be now.

Using every last shred of his strength, he managed to double over, bending enough at the waist that he could reach between his own legs to grab Moon's ankle with his right hand—the one reinforced with myomer muscles. Before Moon could react, Trent straightened up again, still holding the ankle.

Moon pitched backward, bring Trent down on top of him. Trent's weight temporarily knocked the wind out of the bigger man, and Trent broke free. His left arm ached from the crushing squeeze Moon had given him, but he would continue to fight until nothing was left of him.

As Moon rose to his feet again, Trent did not wait for the punch he knew was coming, but made a fist of his right hand and smashed it into Moon's face with every bit of power he could put into his artificially enhanced arm and fist. The blow broke one of Trent's own knuckles as well as shattering Paul Moon's nose. Blood spurted from both nostrils, but Paul Moon did not seem to care. He licked it with his beefy tongue and leveled his own punch at Trent.

No amount of agility could have allowed Trent to dodge the blow. His whole head snapped to the side on impact, and his body lifted slightly off the ground as he staggered backward. He felt something behind him, something that stopped his fall briefly before his back finally slammed against the cool of the grassy ground. Trent knew then that he had lost, and was ready to die. *I hope he takes me quickly. At least I will have served Nicholas Kerensky as I saw fit.*

He felt his body being hoisted into the air by the collar of his shirt, then the hot breath of Paul Moon in his face. "You broke the Circle of Equals under my last blow. I am still within my rights to kill you. But as you said earlier, perhaps I can make you suffer as you would have done to me."

Moon's voice was raspy as he gasped for breath. "I can hurt you more by letting you live with the shame of *your* failure."

Trent opened his augmented eye and saw Moon glaring at him like an angry bull before tossing him viciously back onto the ground.

"This Trial is done. Star Captain Jez, name the town to be razed," Paul Moon said, using the sleeve of his uniform to wipe the blood from his face.

Jez looked down at Trent and smiled. "Chinn shall perish under the claws of the Jaguar, Star Colonel." She sounded pleased.

"Good," Moon said. "Commence operations this very day."

Trent stared up at the cold sky of Hyner. He had failed to best Paul Moon, and now the deaths of the people of Chinn would also be on his head.

=14=

Smoke Jaguar Planetary Command Center
Warrenton, Hyner
Smoke Jaguar Occupation Zone
10 February 3055

"**S**tar Captain," Judith said, as Trent looked up from a hard copy report he was reviewing in his temporary office in the Planetary Command Center. True to form, Star Colonel Paul Moon had assigned him one tucked away in the bowels of the base. Small and cramped, with no windows and barely any ventilation, it was hardly a desirable work area, even by Clan standards. "I have come to ask a favor."

He looked up at his bondsman and nodded. The swelling on his face where the muscles were operative had diminished but not entirely gone. His hand was still bandaged where his knuckles had been broken fighting Paul Moon. But these were but minor injuries considering what had happened to the village of Chinn—wiped off the map because of his failure.

"What is it?" he asked.

"I request that you accompany me on a short journey."

"A short journey to where?"

"It is a surprise, Star Captain."

Her words and actions were surprise enough for Trent. In all the time that Judith had been his bondsman, she had never asked for anything. She knew her place, and did not normally overstep the bounds. The fact that she did now seemed significant.

"Very well, Judith. I only hope it is a pleasant one." Trent could certainly use something pleasant in his life these days.

She nodded. "I trust you will enjoy it, sir."

Trent and Judith did not speak much during the two-hour hovercar journey along the Braddock Pike. Judith was at the wheel, while Trent looked out the side window, taking in the last of the summer afternoon. They said nothing even when they passed the former turnoff for what had been the village of Chinn. Trent felt Judith look over at him as they sped past, but he did not turn his head. There was no longer any sign directing drivers on the Pike to the road, but Trent knew where it led. To ruins, and among them, death.

Judith turned off the pike and onto a dirt road so little used that it was overgrown with weeds. The hovercar skirts rattled slightly as the tall grasses slapped against them as Judith drove straight ahead. She was not using any map that Trent saw, which told him she had been to this place, this surprise, before.

The ground rose to form sharp hills and low ridges, all covered with grasses and brush, green against the bright blue sky of the Hyner afternoon. Judith pulled off the road and drove for nearly a kilometer cross-country before bringing the hovercar to a stop in front of a long snaking mound of dirt, obscured by centuries of growth. She stopped and shut off the car engine, then opened her door. Trent followed silently as she walked toward the long mound, finally stopping directly in front of it. He stood at her side and watched her curiously.

"Today," Judith said, "is my birthday."

Trent cocked his left eyebrow, the only one he had. "Birth day?"

"You are trueborn, Star Colonel, but I am not. I am freeborn and was raised on Terra. By tradition, we freeborns celebrate the day of our birth."

Trent did not fully understand the cause for such a celebration, but acknowledged her statement as best he could. "You are Clan now, Judith. Though we do not mark such occasions, I can understand that you were formed by other ways and traditions. If this is a day that is special for you, then I wish you a good birth day."

She smiled. "Thank you. We are not so different, though, Star Colonel. Though you were bred and born of the Clans, sometimes I wonder if you truly fit in."

At another time in his life Trent might have taken offense at such a comment by a bondsman, much less a freebirth. But Judith had come to represent one of the few supports around him. He counted on her skill, and he had come to trust her.

"You see much," he said, rubbing his jaw, which was still sore and bruised black and blue. "But that does not stand in the way of my duties and obligations, Judith. That is the way of the Clans."

"I heard from the other techs . . . what you did," she said hesitantly, as though not sure whether she might be overstepping herself even further. "They told me that you fought in protest over the destruction of Chinn. You believed it was wrong."

"Taking the lives of innocents does not strengthen the Smoke Jaguars. To the contrary, I believe it weakens us. Nicholas Kerensky never intended for us to be ruthless killers or heartless conquerors, but the upholders of a new Star League. But I lost, and that is the end of the matter."

"You say it is over, but in your heart you know it is not," Judith said. "I understand that. In the Inner Sphere, such atrocities would not have been permitted or tolerated."

"Be wary, Judith. You hover close to treason," Trent said, but he gave her a sad smile that told her he was not angry.

"I was born and raised on Terra," she said, a faraway look in her eyes. "Fourth-generation ComStar. When I was growing up, every year on this day, my family gave a party to commemorate another year of life. And it was our tradition to give gifts on the birth day."

Trent felt a slight twinge of guilt. "I have nothing to offer you, Judith. Nothing but my respect."

"I have been studying you, Star Captain," she said. "You and I may have more in common than it seems. I have seen you play chess with Star Commander Russou. It is one of my own favorite games. We both have a love of history too. That is why I brought you to this place."

She reached over and pulled back the vines covering a portion of the steep hillside. There was something underneath, something metallic. Trent was startled to see that it was a hatch-like door set into the hillside. It looked old, perhaps centuries old. He stepped forward and bent to have a better look. The door was marked with an insignia, worn down but still visible enough to make out. It was a star with one point extending outward to the right. The Cameron Star, symbol of the glorious Star League.

"On this birthday, to honor your efforts in favor of Chinn, I offer *you* a gift, Star Captain," Judith said, tugging at the door and opening it away from the hillside. The hinges groaned in protest, but Judith was strong. Trent could see that some sort of a room lay in the dark shadows, a chamber vast and almost tomblike. He stepped through the door slowly, with reverence, Judith close behind him.

"This place . . ." he began.

"Is a Castle Brian. The one you have been scouring the databases to try and find. The locals knew about it mostly by rumor. They told me of it because they do not view me as truly a member of the Clan."

Such fortifications had been scattered across the Star League at its peak. Hidden bases where the Star League Defense Forces of Aleksandr Kerensky's time had defended the worlds of the long-lost golden age of humanity. For the Clans, who had come to the Inner Sphere to reestablish the Star League, anything connected to that era was virtually sacred.

"This is venerable ground," Trent breathed as he stepped into the dimly lit room. It was thick with a layer of dust, but in one corner he saw some obviously ancient storage crates still piled up where they had been left centuries before, the wood crumbling and decayed. The walls, faded and cracked over time, still showed faint traces of the lettering marking directions to other chambers that lay within.

"It is our secret, sir," she added.

"Secret?"

"Aff, Star Captain. I offer this as a place where we can come to talk, to think. And for now, I ask that we do not tell the others about it."

"You must know how much this means to me," Trent said, gesturing around him. "The restoration of the Star League is the one and only reason we left our homeworlds and came here to invade the Inner Sphere."

"I do not wish to see this place desecrated by those who tarnish our Clan," Judith said.

Her voice was soft, but these were bold words. Trent nearly reprimanded her, but he understood her sentiments.

Thoughts of Jez Howell and Paul Moon flashed through his mind. How often he had thought that their behavior, their thinking, their manipulations, their trickery were a stain on the glory of the Smoke Jaguars.

"Aye, Judith. For now, this is a place for us alone."

"Thank you, Star Colonel," she said. "That pleases me."

Trent nodded. "This is a most honored gift. In another time and place, we would have been free to become friends. But for now, the ways of the Clan separate us." He lowered his eyes in sudden embarrassment, wishing for the first time in his existence that the taboos between castes were not so rigid.

"That is true, and yet you have made me a Smoke Jaguar. I have learned to accept my place among a people who prize honor so highly. But if honor is prized by the warrior caste— the highest and best of the Clans—how can we explain what has been happening here on Hyner?"

"A warrior serves, Judith. I know not what else to tell you," Trent hedged, fearing he would say too much. She was a bondsman and a freebirth. As a member of the warrior caste, he was bound to maintain both his dignity and his position.

"In the Inner Sphere you would have been admired for the courage of your protests. Yet here your comrades scorn you for your convictions. I also hear people say that you are reaching an age that is old for a warrior, yet where I come from an experienced warrior is honored and revered. These things I do not understand."

"It is the way of the Smoke Jaguars," Trent said. How could he admit that he understood them even less?

"We are speaking frankly, Star Captain, as we have done once or twice before. Now that you have seen other ways, the ways of the Inner Sphere, do you ever wonder what your life would have been had you not been born a Clansman?"

Trent sighed a deep breath, not minding the mustiness of the room. "I often wonder what it would have been to serve under the great General Kerensky, to have been one of those who followed him into the unknown, who turned their backs on the pettiness and greediness of the Inner Sphere."

Judith had followed him into the dark chamber, lighting the space with an electric lantern she had pulled from her pack. "Do you ever wonder about Terra? I have heard so much about how the Clans yearn to stand as victors on the soil of humanity's homeworld, and yet you have never asked me about it. You know that I was born and raised there."

"Aye, Judith. But now is a good time—tell me about Terra."

"It is like every place I have ever been, but unlike them as well. It is my home, and yet it is also the home of every other being in the Inner Sphere."

Trent nodded. "And that is what the Clans are for me, Judith. They are the home of everything I am and ever hope to be. Yet, I suddenly feel like an outsider, like one who can never go home. Perhaps you felt some of this when the Word of Blake faction split off from the rest of your ComStar."

Judith was quiet for a long time. When she began to speak it was in an almost dreamy, faraway voice. "I began my career training to be a member of the intelligence arm of ComStar, but when I showed other skills, other potentials, my superiors decided to train me as a warrior of Com Guard. I was steeped in the mysticism of the ComStar Order, and yet my training also included the pragmatism of the warrior."

"The home you left does not exist."

Judith tapped one finger at the side of her head. "As long as I am alive, it exists."

Trent nodded in agreement, tapping his own head just above the nob that had once been his right ear. "I too carry home with me."

"Star Colonel Trent, you must know this about me and know it now. I was an intelligence officer first—a member of ROM. Even from this planet, it is possible for me to activate and use my connections to ComStar should I deem it necessary. I have not done so. But that is because I am more loyal to you than to the Smoke Jaguars. I hoped that I could find a place in the Clan, but I only find myself wanting more."

She watched his face for a few moments before going on. "We could leave here, if you wish. There are no lack of units in the Inner Sphere with ties to the Star League. Not just the Com Guards, but the Eridani Light Horse and the Northwind Highlanders. All claim some link to an honorable past. Should the moment present itself, you have only to say the word and I can arrange for us to depart the Jaguars."

Hearing her speak, Trent was gripped by an inner terror he had never known before. "You have crossed the line, Judith. What you speak is treason."

"Aff, but a warrior, a *true* warrior, must always weigh all strategic and tactical options. I, like you, remember my training well. All that I am doing is informing you that other options exist."

Trent felt the seduction of her words, but he pushed away thoughts of exile, thoughts of turning against his Clan. There was still hope, still a chance to prove that the heart of the Jaguar did not beat black.

"We shall speak of this no more," he said, letting his gaze travel around the room. "In such places where honorable men once stood and breathed, treason is best left unspoken."

"Treason is determined by the victor. One man's traitor is another man's patriot."

Trent nodded. Overcome by finding this place and listening so such talk, he hardly knew what he said. "Aye, Judith, aye."

═══ 15 ═══

Smoke Jaguar Planetary Command Post
Warrenton, Hyner
Smoke Jaguar Occupation Zone
2 April 3055

Star Colonel Paul Moon stood in the very heart of the Hyner command bunker and activated the holographic imaging system so that his subordinates could see what he already knew. The circular room, its tiered floor lined with computer terminals and tactical displays, was more like an amphitheater than a command post. As the holographic display came to life, the gathered officers looked up while the technicians kept their eyes on the data flowing across their screens.

Present at the meeting was the entire command structure of the Smoke Jaguar Delta Galaxy's Third Jaguar Cavaliers—every Binary and Trinary commander and their Star commanders. This was the Cluster known as the Stormriders, and all present, including Trent, wore their pristine gray uniforms.

Looking around, it suddenly struck him how young were the others. He knew that he was approaching ripe age for a warrior, but it had not really hit him until this moment. And yet he had something they did not. He thought of the Castle Brian, his and Judith's secret meeting place. *These young warriors dream of the return of the Star League, but I have seen and smelled and touched and stood in a piece of it.*

He also had his scars, horrific proof of his life as a warrior. Some of those scars ran deeper, however, even though not visible to the eye. Scars like those left behind by his honor duel with Paul Moon several months ago. The injuries had healed, but only on the surface.

The image that came to life was a tactical display showing the planet Hyner and its three continents spinning in the air above them. Moving toward the planet were four small red dots of light, barely noticeable as they closed the distance.

"What you are seeing," Paul Moon began in his deepest command tone, "are elements of a Draconis Combine raiding force that have just appeared at a pirate jump point and begun heading toward Hyner. These raiders are traveling in *Union* Class DropShips, which tells us that the force consists of at least one Inner Sphere battalion."

"This is hardly worthy of our attention, Star Colonel," said Oleg Nevversan, the rusty-haired Star Captain of Trinary Assault. "This is a paltry force they send against us. They pose no threat either to Hyner or to The Stormriders. And besides, we no longer engage in batchalls with Inner Sphere units." A low rumble of agreement followed, and many nods of the head. Trent knew it was true. The forces of the Inner Sphere had proved so deceitful in their dealings that the Jaguars considered them beneath the dignity of the formal battle challenge, or batchall. Trent watched the moving points of red light, unable to tear his eyes away.

"From what we can tell, this is not a regular House unit, but a band of filthy mercenaries," Paul Moon continued.

"Even less impressive," Tamera Osis of the First Battle Trinary said, her gray-purple neural interface seeming to shimmer over her face in the light reflected from the holoimage. "We speak as if this were even worthy of a bid."

Jez Howell spoke up next. "Where is their projected LZ, Star Colonel?" She stood near Trent, but had left just enough distance to show she was not associated with him in any way.

Paul Moon adjusted some hand-held controls and a green image appeared around the city of Warrenton, where they now stood. "Projections indicate they intend to land on our continent."

"What is their intended target? Surely they cannot think they have enough force to take on our planetary garrison base, *quineg*?" queried an Elemental officer in charge of one of the Stars of Trinary Assault.

Moon shook his head. "Neg. I do not believe they would

risk such a goodly number of troops in a strike that could only be suicidal. I do not know what their target is. You should factor that into your bidding."

Trent stared at the continent where Warrenton was located, and saw a glowing green area that demarcated the possible landing area for the raiders. Glancing around the room, he noticed a number of his fellow Jaguars shaking their heads in puzzlement.

But Trent thought he understood. From a purely military standpoint, a raid on Hyner might not make sense, but the Inner Sphere way of life was so different from the way of the Clans. Trent was sure this force was coming to reinforce and re-supply the resistance effort on Hyner. They had no way of knowing that it was too late, that the Kat Killer Five had been crushed. All hope of rebellion had vanished forever on Hyner.

"If I may, Star Colonel, I believe I know what their target is," he said.

Paul Moon raised his eyebrows in mock surprise and gave a small laugh of contempt. "I am sure I speak for all present here in saying that none of us have any interest in your opinion in this matter, Star Captain Trent."

The nods and grunts of approval pained Trent, as did the looks of scorn on the faces around him. *This is my Clan, my blood and life. Now they treat me as an outsider, less worthy of notice than a common bandit.* He felt ashamed, not for himself, but for his fellow officers. His jaw tightened as he leaned over to speak to Jez Howell. She was, after all, his commanding officer.

"You may hate me," he whispered. "But I can help you win this bid. I know where they will land."

"You are sure, *quiaff*?"

"Aff."

"Very well," she replied. "I will bid accordingly. But know this, Trent. If you are wrong, you will answer to me."

Three days had passed, and as Trent adjusted his position in the seat of his cockpit for what seemed to be the thousandth time, he watched the sky through the trees of the dense swamp. It was from here that the Kat Killer Five had operated—the long-forgotten methane refinery. It was here that the mercenary forces would land. He was sure of it not only because of his studies of Inner Sphere history, but by a kind of gut feeling, a tactical instinct that he had come to trust in his life as a warrior.

His Star and elements of two other Binaries were positioned in the swamp, half-buried in the mire, running in a low-power mode that would make their reactors difficult to pick up until the enemy was on top of them. At the edge of the swamp, the field technicians, Judith among them, would remain concealed until needed. It was reassuring to him that his bondsman was out there near the combat she had been denied so long.

Trent was surprised when Jez bothered to include him in the bid, but then realized it would also work in her favor if he turned out to be wrong. It was not something he admired in her style of leadership, but he was coming to understand it all too well. It was not the way of the Clan as he understood it, but perhaps the ways were changing and he was being left behind.

The twilight sky suddenly had four more stars in it, fast-moving comets or meteors that were zooming down toward the swamp from the west. DropShips. They came at night, knowing that the hot burn from their fusion engines would be visible in local towns and villages. Word would spread that the Combine had come back to Hyner, if only for a short time. Trent understood and was pleased to see the ships arc toward his own position. His hand drifted down to the fusion reactor throttle on his *Timber Wolf. Not yet.* The plan was to let the ships discharge their cargo first, then the Jaguars would attack.

The bright lights of the ships came directly overhead, and Trent saw numerous smaller lights flicker around the edges of the ship. BattleMechs. Using jump packs, the mercenary 'Mechs were dropping from their DropShip and landing in the swamp less than a kilometer from Trent's current position. As one of the DropShips passed directly overhead, arcing on a course to take it away from the swamp, Trent licked his uneven lip inside his neurohelmet. *So much the better. Escape will not be quick or easy for our prey at this point.*

Jez's voice came over the speakers. "You did well in your assessment of their landing target. If the battle goes as we expect, I may yet mention it to the Star Colonel. For now, it is time for you to prove yourself worthy of the Jaguar. Attack."

Trent sent the signal to his Star to power up and commence attack. With cold precision he moved the throttle on his *Timber Wolf* up, feeling a throb of energy surge through the OmniMech from the fusion reactor under his cockpit. The lights from his heat sinks flickered on a second after the engine peaked, casting odd colors in the semi-dark cockpit. Trent felt as if the 'Mech was an extension of his own body.

Reaching for the joystick weapons controls, he began to move out. On either side of him, the rest of his Star stirred to life as well.

Abandoned Methane Plant
Swamplands West of Warrenton, Hyner
Smoke Jaguar Occupation Zone
5 April 3055

A rattle of impacts from shrapnel lanced into Trent's *Timber Wolf* as he bore down on what was left of the mercenary *Orion* knee-deep in the black waters of the swamp. The 'Mech had lost almost all its armor, and flames lapped up its torso, sending smoke into the twilight sky. Trent's lasers dug into the area from which flames emerged, mauling the internal structure of the *Orion* even more.

The Orion pilot tried to move backward, hoping to evade the *Timber Wolf* standing on the bank near it, but the move cost it what balance it had left. It fell forward into the black waters, sending a cloud of hissing steam into the evening air. As the swamp closed over the 'Mech, there was a deep rumble under the water, followed by a massive bubble of air escaping.

Trent pivoted the torso of the *Timber Wolf* and checked the short-range sensors of his secondary display. The sensors told him the grim truth. The battalion of mercenary forces had been surrounded immediately, but had put up a grim fight to break free. Before him was a pond, surrounded by dense forest growth, and beyond that was what was left of his command. Lior had been downed by the *Orion* Trent had just killed, and Laurel had ejected since the last time he had checked his display. He got no indication of what had become of Styx, but Trent assumed that the younger warrior had either met his fate or was in the process of doing so. The signals from the other two Binaries involved in the fight were intermittent at best, but the battle was not going as the Jaguars had expected.

Ansel's *Mad Dog* was at the edge of Trent's sensors limit, and from the signals he was receiving, Ansel's Omni was nearly dead. Trent wanted to signal Ansel to withdraw, but he knew the other warrior would not. It was not in his nature. The odds were stubbornly even, and even though the enemy were mercenaries, they had showed themselves well in battle.

Just then Trent saw a dark maroon *Guillotine* emerge from the other side of the bog. He dropped his targeting reticule on it as it opened up with its medium lasers. One of the mediums missed, stabbing into the bog and making it boil. The other three dragged across the chest armor of Trent's *Timber Wolf*. He held steady and let go with both his long-range missile racks as the *Guillotine* returned fire with its own short-range missiles.

The two waves of missiles passed mid-flight, and both sets found their marks. The *Timber Wolf* buckled under the barrage, its legs shedding armor plating as the warhead went off. Trent did not watch his own missiles impact, but advanced forward to make himself a harder target. Pivoting at the torso he saw the *Guillotine* come into sight on its jump jets.

His own damage display showed several breaches in his armor, the damage shimmering a deadly red. Almost all the rest of his frontal armor was outlined in yellow, showing varying degrees of moderate damage. He watched the *Guillotine* rise into the air and arc toward his 'Mech on brilliant jet flames. If this mercenary thought he was going to get control of the battle, he was far wrong.

Trent swung his *Timber Wolf* into a thick cluster of heavy-hanging trees, making it almost impossible for the *Guillotine* to land at point-blank range. He saw the outline of the maroon 'Mech drop just inside the treeline, on the edge of the bog where Trent had been standing. Its large laser and short-range missiles again flared at Trent, but this time the trees gave enough cover to prevent the missiles from striking. The steady bright red beam of laser light, on the other hand, sliced into his right weapons pod like a sword.

Armor sprayed off and green coolant dripped down his side, and for the first time since the start of the fight, a ripple of heat rose in his cockpit, stinging Trent's lungs as he breathed.

He swung to bring his lasers to bear as another 'Mech moved between him and the mercenary. He recognized the image instantly as a *Warhawk,* this one missing a weapons pod and almost all of its armor. Like a human with its skin removed, all that was left of the 'Mech were muscle-like myomer fibers and what had been armor and sensors. *Jez. Here, alive, now.*

"Star Captain, that target is mine," he said firmly as he tried to move around her.

"Surat bait," she replied over a wave of static that told him how badly she had been damaged. The *Guillotine* pilot did not care about Clan honor or tradition. He saw the *Warhawk* and opened fire with a deadly barrage of medium lasers.

Jez's *Warhawk* vibrated as if it were suffering a seizure or stroke. Flames and brilliant flashes filled the twilight as Trent moved around to get a shot. Coming up next to her, he opened up with everything he had. The crimson beams and pulses of laser light hit the *Guillotine* like a wall of red death. The right torso of the mercenary 'Mech erupted with a brilliant yellow and orange flash as its short-range missile ammo exploded. Despite the cellular ammunition storage equipment, which was intended to mitigate the effect of internal explosion, the blast still wreaked havoc on the internal organs of the mercenary machine.

The *Guillotine* careened and staggered forward a clumsy step as Trent also took a step forward, putting him closer to the *Guillotine* than Jez's machine. His foe rose just enough to let go with a salvo of medium laserfire that tore into his cockpit. Trent had not anticipated the move, and he reeled under the assault as several of his cockpit control systems shorted out, filling the air with the smell of ozone and a faint hint of smoke. Smoke in the cockpit stirred memories of the battle on Tukayyid, where Jez had also been nearby. He pushed away the memories of that nearly fatal battle, pushed them deep into his mind. This was not the moment for memories, but for prowess.

Jez attempted to lift one remaining weapon, a PPC, but the *Guillotine* pilot risked the heat in his or her machine by firing his large laser at her. A flickering of flames lapped up the side and chest of the *Warhawk,* then around the cockpit, baking the paint a sickening burned black. The sudden impact forced Jez's shots low, her PPC stabbing into the back mire of the swamp, sending dancing arcs of blue energy over the water and billows of steam into the evening sky.

Trent only noted the attack, concentrating on his own. Switching his large lasers to the same target interlock, he triggered them with one forefinger, aiming squarely at the cockpit of the enemy 'Mech. The armor remaining there exploded off as the *Guillotine* staggered back several steps. There was a flash of minor explosion as the cockpit viewport blew outward. The mercenary 'Mech shut down instantly, then toppled lifelessly forward into the deep waters of the swamp.

Trent did not hesitate. He quickly opened a channel to Jez. "We must move to the south. That way we can cut off any survivors from their DropShips."

"Neg," Jez said. "Their survivors, if there are any, are off my sensors. We will never be able to catch up in time to cut them off."

Trent looked at his own short-range sensor sweeps and saw that they were alone. He switched to long-range sweeps, mostly to confirm what Jez had reported and saw no sign of anyone nearby, enemy or ally. "The others are out of communications or sensors range."   •

There was a pause, followed by Jez chuckling cruelly. "Neg. They are dead, or near death." She paused, obviously thinking the situation through. "This is your doing, Trent. Your arrogance made us bid too low."

Trent felt his muscles tense at her words. "I cannot believe what I am hearing, Jez. You blame *me* because you failed to bid enough force to defeat this foe, *quiaff*? Warriors do not make excuses."

Again the laugh. "You are right, but Jaguar warriors also know that survival is not just battle, but the aftermath. That has always been your weakness. You have never understood the importance of politics. In the end, that has always been your undoing."

"Political maneuvering is unworthy of warriors."

"Again the fool, Trent. You do not see? You must accept the blame for the failure here. Just as you took the blame for the battle on Tukayyid. That is politics, Trent."

"Do not speak to me of Tukayyid, Jez," Trent said. "I

saved your life there. A mistake I will not make again." He glared at her OmniMech only a few meters away, his anger rising with each word she spoke.

"Actually you have already failed," she returned. "You could have let me die just now, but did not. Make no mistake, Trent. I have arranged a proper explanation for the failures here. You."

Trent's heart pounded in his ears as he remembered how Jez had falsified the truth about the debacle on Tukayyid. Now she was threatening to do the same thing again. "Negative. I am beyond your lies, Jez."

"Are you so blind that you do not see the truth of your fate, *quineg*? You are of the same age as me, yet you serve in a lesser command. We each have thirty-three years, almost beyond the peak for trueborns.

"The difference is that I have a bloodname and a proper command," she continued. "That will give me the chance to continue to serve as a warrior, while you are headed for the trash heap."

Trent bit his gnarled lower lip. "I would have had a bloodname, but was cheated out of it by spineless scum—and you know it."

"Ah, yes, *your* bloodname. I have never told you how your *good friend* Benjamin Howell nominated me in your place, did I?"

Her words caught him off guard. "You got my nomination!"

"Aye, I did. Benjamin Howell had fallen from favor in the eyes of Khan Osis. To reward my actions on Tukayyid, I, a diehard Crusader of the Howell bloodline, was granted your slot. That must eat at you, Trent, *quiaff*?"

He did not answer.

Jez laughed. "You should have demanded a Trial of Grievance, Trent. But you are so pathetic. You cower like a freeborn and let events toss you about like the wind. How unfortunate that you also failed in the Grand Melee."

"You were behind that too, weren't you, Jez? I could never prove it. Till now."

"It is of no matter to me what you think, you and that bitch of a bondsman. I assume it was she who discovered evidence of my little surprise, *quiaff*?"

"She is not the issue at hand, Jez. You are."

"You are wrong, Trent. I have the bloodname you thought would be yours. I have the command that should be yours.

My reputation is one of superiority, while you are the mockery of the Clan. You made sure of that the moment you decided to challenge Star Colonel Moon over those pitiful freebirths of Chinn. From that moment on, every Jaguar officer could see that you do not possess the heart of the Smoke Jaguar."

"Sending true warriors to slaughter innocents, even freebirths, is wrong."

Once more Jez laughed softly. "Do you really think that this was an isolated act by the Star Colonel or that Khan Osis was unaware of it? Our leaders knew what we did—they expected it of us. Even you cannot be that naïve."

Trent listened to her with a sinking heart. *My entire Clan is against me. Every truth has been twisted to fit the schemes of Jez and Paul Moon.* It was like a disease, a creeping illness eating away at the strength of the Clan. It went beyond honor, beyond Clan justice. What was at stake was not just the life of a single warrior, but a way of life, the fulfillment of what Nicholas Kerensky had envisioned for his people.

He could not help but think of Judith, of her saying there was another way, that he had a choice. At the Castle Brian, she had talked to him about other possibilities, other means to achieve honor. He knew he must turn this moment into victory or he would perish.

The decision was easy, so easy that Trent wondered if he had really decided weeks earlier and only needed this impetus to set it in motion. Pivoting his *Timber Wolf* to face what was left of Jez's *Warhawk,* he stared at her cockpit only a dozen meters away. "A Circle of Equals, *quiaff*?"

"You and I are *not* equals," Jez scoffed, "and never will be. I am a bloodnamed warrior. I do not have to accept your puny calls for justice."

"You are correct as always, Jez," Trent said as his targeting reticle swung in on the *Warhawk* cockpit across from him. Without hesitation he triggered every one of his lasers in a deadly salvo. The *Warhawk*'s viewport seemed to buckle, followed a millisecond later by an implosion. The lasers riddled the interior of Jez's cockpit, and Trent knew there would be very little trace of Jez's body left to be recovered later. The *Warhawk* billowed smoke from the hole that had been the cockpit, then tipped forward as if bowing to Trent. *Aff, Jez, we are not equals. I am alive and you are not.*

He stared at the *Warhawk* for a long minute. Then he

flipped his comm system to the channel used by the techs. "This is Star Captain Trent to Technical Command. Put me through to Tech Judith immediately."

There was a long pause and then Judith came on line. "Star Captain, this is Judith."

Trent drew a deep breath. The next step he took would set him on a path from which there would be no turning back. "I need you up here. Bring a portable electronics kit and replacement boards and chips."

"I will get a team there immediately."

"Neg. You will come alone." Trent let her know by his tone that the matter was a grave one. "There is much work to be done."

BOOK THREE

The Sword

. . . A magnificent beast, the Smoke Jaguar. It is ferocity unbound, tenacity without limit. Once it locks its powerful jaws around the throat of its prey, it never lets go.
The greatest of warriors might be shamed by comparing himself to such fierce courage. . . .

—Nicholas Kerensky, *Birth of a New Society*

The role of the warrior is to be more than the highest of castes. It is to protect the weak, defend the innocent, to be more than just a mere soldier as in ages past. No, a warrior is more than the genetics that have formed him or her. They are to be the embodiment of my vision, a new direction for our species.

—Franklin Osis, Founder of the Smoke Jaguar Clan

History will be kind to me for I intend to write it.

—Winston Churchill

$\equiv$ 17 $\equiv$

Smoke Jaguar Planetary Command Post
Warrenton, Hyner
Smoke Jaguar Occupation Zone
7 April 3055

Judith slid the battle ROM into the small module and plugged it into the communications system built into the desk of Star Colonel Paul Moon. The towering figure of Moon loomed over her as she hit the control to activate the module, and the image began to flicker to life on the screen that rose up as the system engaged. Trent stood behind her, at attention, watching as well.

What was displayed was the image of the *Guillotine* that Trent and Jez had been fighting. There was a flash as Jez's *Warhawk* fired its remaining weapons at it, and the enemy BattleMech returned fire. Then came Trent's shots, which hit true, destroying the *Guillotine* and sending it plunging into the brackish waters of the swamp.

The image pivoted and showed the burned-out cockpit of the *Warhawk,* apparently destroyed by the last salvo that made it out of the *Guillotine* before Trent had downed it. Smoke billowed from the 'Mech, and Paul Moon used the remote control to pivot the image, as if he could inspect the damage done. Silently he shut off the screen, which retracted back into the table. He looked coldly over at Judith.

"Star Captain Jez Howell's battle ROM was irretrievable, *quiaff?*"

"Affirmative, Star Colonel," Judith replied.

He stared into her eyes as if weighing her words, as if not trusting them. "And she was dead when you arrived, *quiaff*?"

"Aff."

Paul Moon paused a moment before speaking again. "Very well, Technician, you are dismissed." Judith reached down and extracted the battle ROM and module, casting only a glance in the direction of her bondsmaster. She then left the room, closing the door behind her.

"Star Captain Jez Howell is dead," Moon said like someone reciting a line from *The Remembrance*. "She died a hero in battle against a foe striking at the Smoke Jaguar. That is how she is to be remembered."

Trent nodded but said nothing. His mind was dancing with excitement, but he kept it from showing on his face. Moon stared at him. "Do you not agree, Star Captain?"

"Aye, Star Colonel Moon."

"These mercenaries have fled the planet, their operation aborted because of her actions. She alone was instrumental in their destruction, and her record will so note that."

Trent winced inwardly at those words, but again he concealed his reaction. *The lies he speaks perpetuate other lies.* "Star Colonel, her command is open now, and I have already successfully tested to the rank of Star Captain. May I assume that you will place me in command of Beta Trinary, *quiaff*?"

It was obvious by the startled look on Paul Moon's face that he had not expected Trent to make such a request. "You are a Star Captain, but your command is battered and damaged. Russou's Star has only two survivors, and your own Star only three."

As he spoke, it was obvious that Moon was verbally stalling for time.

"Until reinforcements and replacement OmniMechs arrive, I am going to take Beta Trinary off-line for refit," Moon went on. "When it becomes operational, we will discuss your place in it. Understood, *quiaff*?"

"Aff," Trent replied. He understood all too well what Star Colonel Paul Moon was saying.

Trent entered the old barracks where Judith had quartered when she had first come to the Smoke Jaguars. He could not help but remember the last time he had been here a year and a half earlier. The air smelled of mildew or mold as he closed the door behind him.

Judith emerged from behind a wall of boxes and came over. They had settled on the barracks as their meeting site prior to Trent's debriefing, knowing it was the one place on the command post that offered them at least the hope of privacy. It was not likely this place had ever been monitored.

"I assume all went as you planned, Star Captain," she said.

"Affirmative," Trent replied, looking around the room as if to verify that they were alone, then back at her. "Your editing of my battle ROM was perfect. As far as anyone knows, Jez died at the hands of the mercenaries raiding Hyner."

For Trent, there had been little choice but to kill Jez there in the swamps, but no one must ever learn that he had slain another warrior outside of a formal Trial. Working to his advantage was the fact that the possibility would never even enter the mind of a Clansman. No one suspected that he had any part in the death of a fellow warrior in combat.

"Have you thought more about what we discussed a few weeks ago?" she asked. "Is that why you asked to meet me here?"

Trent stared at her for a moment before answering. "My people have strayed from the true path of the Clans. I desire to lead in battle, but this too will be denied me. Before I killed her, Jez told me that the corruption I have witnessed reaches even to the seat of the Khan of the Clan himself. I can no longer remain among the Smoke Jaguars. I have not changed, but the Clan has. I do not understand what they have become."

"And so?" she asked.

Trent sighed heavily, but held himself tall and proud. "I wish to leave the Smoke Jaguars. If you can use your contacts to arrange it, I wish to do so as soon as possible. In exchange for what I know of my Clan, I ask only for my own command—to lead other warriors in glorious battle."

Judith listened without interrupting, then answered carefully and slowly. "It will not be so easy, Star Captain. It is true that you will bring with you a great deal of intelligence on the Smoke Jaguars. But my contacts outside the Occupation Zone seek something more. With just that one small bit of information, I can guarantee your safe exit from the Clan as well as the command you seek."

"This information," Trent said cautiously. "What is it?"

"The Exodus Road," she said firmly. "Even as we speak, the Explorer Corps is seeking the location of the Clan homeworlds, but so far to no avail. I am sure that if you could supply the data, you could also name your price for an Inner Sphere command."

Trent felt the blood rush to his face. "What you ask is nearly impossible. The location of the homeworlds is one of our greatest secrets."

"It is your ticket out of here," she countered. "The only way you can ever hope to live as a warrior again."

Trent shook his head in dismay. "The route to the homeworlds does not exist in one single location. JumpShips moving along the Exodus Road only carry a portion of the map. Routes are constantly changing, and ships dump one segment of the navigation map as part of the process of obtaining the next segment. Even our HPG traffic is segmented and bundled to prevent anyone being able to use the communications network to trace a route to the homeworlds."

"Aye," Judith said. "But there must be a way, *quiaff*?"

Trent stood shaking his head for a moment as his mind raced. "The homeworlds are something like a year's travel from the Inner Sphere. The only way I can think of to get the data would be to somehow travel to there—walk the Exodus Road. And then, somehow, we would have to find a way back."

Judith nodded. "Aye, and I think I have an idea. There are some devices I could rig on such a trip, ways to measure our jump distances. Coupled with spectrum readings of various stars along the route, we should be able to map out the road."

Trent's mutilated face had a look of semi-hopelessness. "It is a year there and a year back at best, Judith. Know this, Clan warriors of my age and status do not return from the homeworlds unless they are Khans or are bloodnamed. It does not happen. Though I hope to compete for the Howell bloodname left open by Jez's death, I doubt that anyone will sponsor me. The Star Colonel has accomplished a most effective character assassination against me. Without a bloodname, warriors like me who are getting too old for combat are often sent back home, but they do not return."

Judith seemed to light up at his words, despite what he had just said. "You are a brilliant warrior. This is merely another tactical battle. Surely there are ways to get you assigned to return to the homeworlds, especially since Star Colonel Moon would like very much to see you gone."

Trent crossed his arms and looked down in thought. His brow wrinkled unevenly between his natural and synthetic skin as he thought long and hard on the problem. As Judith said, he could view it tactically, as a battle to be won. Looking at it from different angles, he suddenly realized there was a solution, but he would pay for it dearly with his pride.

"You are right, Judith. I can think of a way to get us to the homeworlds. Getting back will be difficult, but there must be a way around that too."

"Excellent, but how?"

"The plan will require us to turn the trickery and deception of others to our own advantage. In essence, we must make Star Colonel Moon insist on sending us there . . .".

≡18≡

Smoke Jaguar Planetary Command Post
Warrenton, Hyner
Smoke Jaguar Occupation Zone
9 April 3055

Judith used the specially designed anti-static gloves to move the segment of myomer fiber into the shin of Trent's *Timber Wolf*. The myomer acted as a superpowerful muscle in the leg, and the segments she was attaching replaced the burned filaments left after her bondmaster's last battle. She struggled to get the bundle in place, then slowly pulled her head out of the OmniMech's giant leg and turned to see Master Tech Phillip standing some steps away, staring at her.

Phillip had hated her from the day she first arrived among the Jaguars, and he still did. She knew that. With the passing of time, he had come to restrain his physical abuse, but he still liked to humiliate her verbally and constantly demeaned the quality of her work. She hated him in return, but took pleasure in feigning to be terrorized by him. She had always known some day she could use that to her advantage, that it would make him unlikely to suspect that she was anything but docile and tame under his whip. And now the day had come.

"Master Technician," she said meekly, pulling off the thin elbow-length gloves and tucking them into her work belt. "May I be of service?"

He looked at her with his hard, cruel eyes. "I am here to

inform you that the Star Colonel has asked that I ration your unit's replacement parts." Judith took note of his choice of words, "asked" rather than "ordered," implying that he was at the same level as Star Colonel Moon. "Rebuilding this Trinary is the Cluster's lowest priority at this time."

In her mind, Judith had rehearsed her lines over and over, per the plan Trent had come up with. "Star Captain Trent will not be pleased at this news. He asked that I prep his 'Mech so that it will be ready when the Trial of Bloodright for Star Captain Jez Howell's bloodname is formally announced."

The chubby Master Tech raised an eyebrow. "Your bonds-master believes he will win her bloodname then, *quiaff*?"

"Aff," Judith replied almost proudly. "And since he already has the rank, he is sure that he will also win command of the Trinary."

"Indeed," Phillip said. "Even you must have heard stories of how much the Star Colonel despises Trent, *quiaff*? Many officers say he is weak, unworthy of the Clan."

"Neg, sir. I have seen him in battle. Perhaps they have not." She paused as if thinking proudly of Trent's exploits, then let her face cloud over slightly. "He is so brave that he has only one fear."

Curiosity piqued, Phillip moved closer. "And what might that be?"

Judith looked around. "He has told me this in confidence," she said, almost whispering. "Can I trust you not to speak of it?"

"I have made you the tech you are today. We are of the same caste. Trust me, Judith, my word is my bond."

Judith paused as if carefully thinking it over, then spoke. "He told me that the giftake of a bloodnamed warrior must return to the homeworld of Huntress, where it will become part of the gene pool. He fears that the Star Colonel will send him as the honor guard when Jez's gene sample is sent home. At his age, my master knows that he would never return from the homeworlds but instead be transferred to some solahma unit there. But the chances of that happening are remote, are they not, Master Phillip?"

Phillip seemed barely able to suppress his smile of cunning. "Aye," he whispered back. "The Star Colonel has surely not thought of this or he would already have enacted such an order."

Judith gave a long sigh, feigning relief. "That is good to

know. Should my Star Captain be sent to Huntress, I would almost assuredly be sent with him. And though I am curious to see the Smoke Jaguar homeworlds, I do not know what would become of me if he were reassigned."

"Of course," Phillip said, his voice returning to normal. She could tell by the look on his face that the seed she had planted was already taking root. "Do not worry, Judith. Your secret is safe with me," he said.

Trent filled his tray in the officer's mess and then sat down with it at the end of one of the long tables in the small, spotlessly clean room. He took a seat off by himself, posture stiff, almost cadet-like in its precision. He ate slowly, not looking at any of the other officers present. No one spoke to him or called him over to join them, and for once Trent did not feel anger at being treated as an outcast in the midst of his own Clan. He simply continued to chew his rations, knowing that today he would turn the contempt of his fellows to his own purposes.

Star Captain Oleg Nevversan surprised Trent when he came over. He did not carry a tray or drink, but took the seat next to Trent. Oleg had been injured in the fighting at the swamp when the mercenaries had swarmed his 'Mech. He had sustained a concussion, or at least so Trent had heard. Today, he obviously had something on his mind, and from the look on his face it was not something pleasant. Trent continued to eat, ignoring him.

"Star Captain Trent," Nevversan said slowly. "Jez always said you were weak, and now she is proved correct. She is dead and you live, unscathed."

Trent turned and faced the other man, their faces only centimeters apart. "Do you question my ability as a warrior?"

Nevversan smiled boldly, not to be intimidated. "All I know is that Jez Howell, an honored warrior and officer, told us you knew where the enemy would land. She encouraged us to lower our bids for the combat. She is now dead, as is one of my own warriors. Yet you live."

"What are you trying to say, Oleg Nevversan?" Trent said evenly, taking another slow and methodical bite of his rations.

"Some say that you would do anything for a command. Tell me, Trent, what was it like watching a true warrior like Jez die?"

Trent looked into Oleg's eyes, and gave him a defiant

grin. "Her death was as she deserved. And in the end, her command is mine."

"There will be many who oppose you, a mangled older warrior, assuming command," Nevversan said.

"Perhaps. But there is nothing to stop me now. I will be eligible to compete for the Howell bloodname as well as for her command." Trent smiled, making it as smug and satisfied as his ruined face would allow. "And now all that is left is for Jez's giftake to be sent back to Huntress as soon as possible."

Nevversan was obviously thrown off guard, not hiding his curiosity. "Why is that so important?"

Trent chuckled for the first time since Jez had perished by his hand. "That is not your affair, Star Captain," he said, pushing his chair back and getting up. He did not bother to clear away his tray, and could feel Nevversan still staring at him as he crossed the mess hall and left the room.

Star Colonel Paul Moon looked across his desk at Phillip, his personal technician and Master Tech of the Cluster. Through the window behind him, the evening stars were beginning to show through the clouds as night settled over Warrenton. The day promised to end calmly and peacefully.

"The information you have brought me seems consistent with information one of my officers has also provided," Paul Moon said.

The portly Phillip bowed his head in acknowledgment. "I exist to serve the Smoke Jaguars and the warrior caste, Star Colonel."

"And you do so well," Moon replied. "I will handle matters from this point forward, Phillip. You will speak of these things to no one."

"Aye, Star Colonel," Phillip said as he backed his way to the office door.

As the door closed behind the tech, Paul Moon smiled broadly as he sat back in his chair and pondered his good luck. He finally had a way to deal with that stravag Trent once and for all. Neither he nor his trashborn bondsman would any longer taint his command. They would be sent back to the home of the Smoke Jaguars, not as heroes, but destined for the dung heap.

"Sleep well tonight, Trent," Moon said softly. "For tomorrow your worst fear will come to haunt you."

Star Colonel Paul Moon swiveled his chair around toward the window, and sat back in contentment to contemplate the stars of Hyner.

═══ 19 ═══

Smoke Jaguar Planetary Command Post
Warrenton, Hyner
Smoke Jaguar Occupation Zone
11 April 3055

Stone-faced, Trent stared intently at Star Colonel Paul Moon. "Would you repeat that order, Star Colonel?"

With just the slightest sneer, Moon repeated his words. "I am designating you as honor guard for the giftake of Jez Howell." He moved the small silver metal cylinder that contained her gene sample across the table. It was sealed and locked with several built-in mechanisms and bore the markings of the scientist caste on the side. Impressed into the thick lid of the device was a circuit chip, the memory core of Jez's codex bracelet. Once Jez's giftake reached Huntress, it would become part of the sacred gene pool of other honored warriors from which the scientist caste was constantly breeding new and better generations of Smoke Jaguar warriors.

"You will accompany her giftake back to our homeworlds for honorable internment," Paul Moon went on. "A ship waits in the system as we speak."

Trent tightened the muscles on his face, which had the effect of twisting it slightly because of his scarring. "Star Colonel, what of the open Howell bloodname?"

"The Trial of Bloodright is slated for three weeks from now. You will already be out of the system by then—not that anyone in your House would be willing to sponsor you."

"And the chance to win Jez's command, that will be lost as well?" Trent spoke in the low, almost menacing tone sometimes used by Jaguar warriors.

"You know that the trip back to the homeworlds is a long one. I cannot keep her position open. For the time being, however, Beta Trinary is off-line until I receive the appropriate replacement parts and personnel. I may hold the appropriate Trial of Position to fill the slot should I opt to reactivate the unit."

"After I am gone, *quiaff?*"

"Affirmative," Moon said curtly.

"I must protest this action," Trent replied.

"Noted."

"Neg, that is not enough. I challenge you to a Trial of Grievance, Star Colonel," Trent spoke the words as if they were a formal slap.

Paul Moon looked amused as he stood and faced Trent. "I refuse your request for a Trial, Star Captain."

"You fear that I will defeat you?" Trent prodded.

"Negative, though I applaud you for a good try at provoking my anger. No, I refuse it because that is my right. Furthermore, your refusal to serve as Jez's honor guard is an insult to your fellow warriors. None, to my knowledge, has ever refused posting to such duty. As genetically engineered warriors, we have obligations beyond the bounds of combat and position. We must all be concerned with maintaining the bloodlines for future generations."

"Neg, Star Colonel," Trent said. "This is not about honor or duty. This is about your hatred of me. This posting is a way to remove me from your presence. You know that my age is thirty-three years. By the time I reach the homeworlds I will be thirty-four, an age when a warrior is considered past his prime. You know they will never send me back.

"In the meantime you strip me of my last chance to compete for a bloodname or to lead fellow trueborns in battle. Neg, Star Colonel Moon, I demand this Trial of Grievance because you are betraying the ways of our people. You are playing politics like a merchant rather than behaving like a warrior."

"That will be all," Paul Moon barked back. "You give me too much credit, Trent. You have me orchestrating your removal from the Inner Sphere as if it were something I had planned, something I had plotted and carefully manipulated.

I *am* a warrior. As such, I merely fulfill my duty. I do not have time for such plotting and scheming. You were sibkin of Jez, reared in the same sibko and fought by her side in many battles, including Tukayyid. You were with her when she died. My decision does not reflect my dislike for you. It reflects a wish to honor you as the best individual for this task."

"You deny that you are sending me back because you know the chances of my return are nearly impossible?" The unspoken accusation lingered in the air, *liar*.

Moon shook his head. "Think what you will, Trent. I have said all I am going to." He took up a sheet of hard copy from his desk and scanned it for a moment, then he slid it across the desk toward Trent.

"A number of warriors will be accompanying you on this trip. Most have been declared solahma, though one is also dezgra. They are assigned to report to our garrisons on Huntress. You will be the ranking officer, so these troops will report to you for the duration of the mission." He gestured for Trent to take the sheet with his new orders. "You will also find a full manifest of the cargo of your DropShip as well."

"Disgraced and old warriors and a ship already loaded for my departure," Trent said, picking up the sheet and glancing at it scornfully.

"Coincidence, I assure you," Star Colonel Moon replied. "Ever since Tukayyid, many of my fellow officers have been seeking to purge the Jaguars of the baggage that cost us victory there. I am confident that you will find much in common with the members of your new command."

Trent narrowed his good eye in a cool glare. "If I share so much in common with them," Trent said slowly, "then I am sure they must be among the best warriors ever to uphold the glory of Clan Smoke Jaguar."

Paul Moon chuckled slightly. "Perhaps you will still get your chance to fight and die in battle, Star Captain. The ships of the Explorer Corps have become most aggressive in their efforts to discover the Exodus Road. Who knows? Maybe you will encounter one of them."

"Either way you win," Trent said. "The chances of an encounter on the Exodus Road are slim. If I die, you are content because my lack of a bloodname means that my genes will never become part of the sacred gene pool. If I live, you will make sure I never return to the Inner Sphere."

"Again, Trent, you give me too much credit. The plotting you imagine is all in your mind."

Trent crossed his arms in defiance as he stared at his senior officer. "You have doomed me."

"Neg, Trent," Star Colonel Moon replied. "You have doomed yourself."

Trent stood in the doorway of the barracks as Judith finished her packing. His personal kit bag was flung over his left shoulder, and in it were all his worldly possessions. An entire lifetime as a warrior crammed into one small bag.

Judith looked up as she stuffed the last article into her own bag. "I notice that we are taking several BattleMechs back."

"Isorla, captured goods. They represent new technology that the Inner Sphere is attempting to employ against us, and our scientist caste on Huntress no doubt wants to examine them."

Judith returned to fastening up her bag as she spoke. "So far, so good for our plan. You outfoxed Paul Moon this time. Getting him to name you as honor guard for Jez's gene sample gives us just the opportunity we needed to try to map the route to the homeworlds."

Trent shook his head slightly. "I never imagined that my life as a warrior would lead me down the path of deception. If it helps us get what we need, I suppose I may find a way to live with it one day. In the meantime, have you come up with anything?"

Judith held up a small black pad-like device. It was the size of a wallet and had only one visible control surface. "This is a basic neutrino scanner. We use these to manually monitor the readings of 'Mech reactors to make sure they are not releasing too many neutrinos."

"But how will that help us map the Exodus Road?"

"When a JumpShip arrives in a new star system, its core emits EMP, an electromagnetic pulse."

"That much I know," Trent said, still puzzled. "If another ship happens to be at the same jump point, it can read the arriving ship's EMP and determine its configuration."

Judith nodded. "Aff, but what most people do not know is that the drive also emits a neutrino pulse. The neutrinos actually emerge near the outer hull of the vessel and travel less than a hundred meters before dissipating. At that point they are indistinguishable from the low-level neutrinos constantly emitted by the ship's fusion drive."

"That means you could not use it as a means of measuring another ship's course. The pulse dissipates almost instantly, and besides you have to be practically on top of the ship to measure the neutrinos emitted by the jump. Obviously, no JumpShip ever gets that close to another one."

"Correct," Judith said. "From a military standpoint the neutrino pulse has no real value. You can detect the presence of the ship, but not how far it has traveled. But for our purposes it does offer something. With this device mounted either to the JumpShip's hull or in an airlock near the outer hull, the scanner will measure and record the level of neutrinos released by the pulse. There is a direct correlation between the neutrino level and the distance of the hyperspace jump. Taking these readings, we can determine exactly how far the JumpShip has traveled between stars."

"Which could also help us figure out almost exactly where we have jumped to." Jumps had to be made from jump points. Usually these were at either the zenith or nadir points of the star's gravity well. There were also pirate points, locations where gravity was a null factor in a star system, but these were riskier to use. Despite the fact that there were thousands of stars on the path between the Inner Sphere and the Clan homeworlds, knowing the exact distance of a jump narrowed down the number of possible star systems dramatically.

"Affirmative, sir. And when coupled with simple spectral analysis that I can run once we arrive in a system, we can not only pinpoint the exact stars, but the route the Clan uses to travel between them."

Trent looked at the device in his hands and then handed it back to her. "Getting it into an airlock on the JumpShip will be difficult. Passengers are usually confined to DropShips during such voyages." Where JumpShips traveled between stars, the DropShips attached to them were the vessels that carried personnel and cargo. DropShips could travel to and from a planet in a star system, but the only way they would travel between stars was by hitching a ride on the hull of a JumpShip.

"As a warrior, you might be able to get around more, despite regulations. You will probably have to be the one who finds a way to get the scanner in place."

"I am not so sure," Trent said. "As a technician, you might be able to come up with a better pretext for getting aboard the JumpShip."

"Aff, but my specialty is BattleMech tech. Only a Master Technician would have more general technical skills. My presence during a jump would be suspicious. I still think you would have more opportunities to move about freely."

Trent looked at her. "Can it be so easy?"

"It is a weakness of the Clan. The Jaguars are concerned only with protecting themselves from external threats. No one expects a warrior to threaten security from within. The only security measure vaguely related to that is the test of every passenger's genetic identity prior to lift-off to make sure no spies have infiltrated the crew."

Trent nodded, a sadness suddenly overwhelming him. "As you say, a weakness of the Clan . . ."

"No Smoke Jaguar would ever consider the possibility that one of its own might reveal information."

"Our code of honor prevents it." Trent shook off his sadness. He had set his course, and now was not the time to change his mind.

Judith smiled slightly. "The very same code our own superior officers have been violating all this time."

Trent nodded. "You need not worry, Judith. My path is laid before me as surely as the Exodus Road leads back to the homeworlds. It is too late for me to turn back now."

20

Trent floated into the airlock of the docking ring, using the handholds on the bulkhead to balance himself against the weightlessness of zero G. The DropShip *Dhava* had just locked onto one of the docking rings along the JumpShip's kilometer-long spine, and this was the one airlock passage between the two vessels. He looked out at what he could see of the docking rings. Its relatively simple technology was all that held the two ships together, all that kept him and the others in the DropShip from being blown out into the vastness of space and death. He and Judith had decided that either the airlock or the hull itself were the optimal places for measuring a JumpShip's neutrino surge. Trent glanced about for an inconspicuous place to mount the device—when the time came.

A small reinforced viewing port allowed Trent to see down the length of the ship. Two other DropShips, *Union* Class vessels like the *Dhava,* were also locked along the long spine of the *Odyssey* Class JumpShip. One docking ring was empty, but Trent had no doubt another ship would occupy it sooner or later. Returning to the homeworlds was no small undertaking, and the Clan would never abide the waste of sending a JumpShip all the way back to Huntress not fully loaded.

He felt a hand on his shoulder and turned to see Judith hovering next to him above the deck. "We are going to be jumping soon, Star Captain."

"Aye, I just heard the ten-minute warning," he said. "I trust you found your quarters, *quiaff*?"

"Aff." She raised her eyebrows and gave a slightly mocking smile. "And they are nearly as luxurious as my quarters back in Warrenton," she said.

Suddenly another figure entered the airlock alongside them. It was an Elemental, a giant of a man with sandy blonde hair tied into a collar-length pony tail that hung down the back of his tree-trunk like neck. In the small space of the airlock, the man's figure seemed even more enormous than normal, almost as if he were intentionally pushing himself into Trent's personal space.

"I assume you are Star Captain Trent, *quiaff*?" the Elemental said.

"Aff," Trent replied. Judith stood at his side looking up at the impressive warrior. "I am Trent of the Howell bloodline."

"I am Star Commander Allen of the Moon bloodline," the other man said coolly. "I was informed by our JumpShip captain that you were finally aboard. As security officer I reviewed your files while you were making the trip from the surface of Hyner. You served in the Stormriders, *quiaff*?"

Moon, bloodkin to my former CO, the man who sent me out here to rot away as a solahma. "I served under Star Colonel Paul Moon of the Stormriders. You two are bloodkin, *quiaff*?" Trent decided he had better be careful what he said to this man.

"Affirmative," Allen replied. "More precisely, we were in the same sibko." He seemed somewhat guarded, probably measuring Trent's reactions as well.

"You are his comrade and friend then, *quiaff*?" Trent fished boldly.

Allen laughed, a deep belly roar of sheer amusement. "Negative, Star Captain Trent. I loathe Star Colonel Paul Moon." With a sudden, swift movement he pulled up his left shirt sleeve and revealed a long scar running from wrist to elbow. It was deep and had obviously torn muscle.

"A warrior does not cry over spilled gruel, but I can tell you one thing about Paul Moon. I took him on in a Trial of

Position for the rank of Star Captain, and he feigned injury, then attacked me unawares. It nearly cost me this arm, and in the end, is why I serve on a JumpShip as a Marine rather than a true warrior in the field."

Trent gave a short, humorless laugh. "Then you will be displeased to know that he is well."

"Freebirth," cursed Allen as he pulled his sleeve back down. "And if you are aboard this ship, I can only assume that you have crossed him somehow."

"Aye," Trent said. "It is one thing you and I have in common."

"Indeed." Allen extended his big hand to Trent.

Trent shook the Elemental's giant hand, then gestured to Judith with his head. "This is my bondsman Judith."

Allen shook her hand as well. "What Clan is she from, Star Captain? Nova Cat or perhaps Diamond Shark?" It was an obvious joke, for both Clans were long-time rivals of the Smoke Jaguars. As security officer, Allen must have looked over Judith's file as well as his. Trent suddenly realized that none of this conversation was as casual as it seemed. The man was doing his job.

"Neither one. Her blood is Inner Sphere. She was once a MechWarrior of the Com Guards, but I bested her in honorable combat. In admiration of her prowess, I took her as isorla on Tukayyid." Trent spoke proudly, both for himself and for Judith.

Allen cocked one eyebrow as he looked at her, then back to Trent. "You fought on Tukayyid and made a Com Guard your bondsman. No small feat, *quiaff*?"

"Aye," Trent said, with a sense of pride he had rarely experienced since arriving on Hyner long months ago.

Star Commander Allen looked over at Judith. "You are going to receive a gift beyond description, bondsman. You are traveling into Clan space. How many of your former kinsmen can make that claim? One or two, at most? You will be following in the footsteps of the great, who first made the voyage from the Inner Sphere centuries ago. You will visit the homeworld of our Clan. This is a great honor."

"Aye, Star Commander," Judith said, bowing her head slightly.

"Keeping an Inner Sphere as a bondsman is a rarity I have not encountered before, Star Captain Trent."

Trent nodded and gave his off-kilter smile. "And one that

has earned me the scorn of more than a few of my fellow warriors," he said. "It made me a pariah, but perhaps that was a good in disguise. If nothing else, it kept me from playing politics, a game that seems to find such favor among weaker men." He could not help but think of Jez and Paul Moon and the way he had turned their own games of ambition and self-interest to set in motion his own plan of escape.

Again Allen laughed. "Now I know why Paul Moon disliked you. You sound like a warrior who is true to the way of our Clan." He gestured to the passageway back into the JumpShip. "As the senior security officer of the *Admiral Andrews,* I invite you to join me at jump station. We have much in common, Star Captain Trent. I am hoping to hear some good tales of you and Paul Moon. I also long to hear of Tukayyid—not the stories of those who wish to bury it in the past, but of one who fought there and lived to tell the tale."

Trent glanced over at Judith. She nodded imperceptibly, and no one else would have understood her slight smile of satisfaction.

Later, after the ship jumped and he and Judith had retired to their respective quarters, Trent looked over the hard copy records of the other Smoke Jaguar officers either on board one of the two docked DropShips, or due to arrive in with the final one. A dozen in all, each with orders to report to Huntress and assignment to Zeta Galaxy, referred to as The Iron Guards.

It was to be their last posting, he knew that. He was also sure that a set of orders assigning him to The Iron Guards would also arrive on Huntress. *Solahma.* The word was like a curse to a Clan warrior. If a warrior did not die in glorious battle or achieve a bloodname by a certain age, he or she was judged to be virtually useless. Such warriors were being sent back to Huntress, the homeworld of the Smoke Jaguars, where they would be relegated to the scrap heap of a solahma unit. Most would be assigned various noncombatant tasks, though there was still a chance—if one were fortunate—that his or her unit might serve in some suicide mission that would offer one final opportunity to die with honor. That, after all, was the only death worthy of a warrior—on a field of battle.

The unit Trent was shepherding to Huntress would be assigned to guard the homeworld, but that was a sham. What possible threat could exist with all of the fiercest Clans still focused on the invasion of the Inner Sphere? And surely no one on Huntress feared an attack by the forces of the Inner Sphere. Trent was surely the only Smoke Jaguar who knew that an attack by the Inner Sphere had suddenly become a real possibility. He had no illusions about the uses of the Exodus Road data he and Judith intended to gather and hand over to her contacts.

Perhaps he would be doing the solahma warriors in Clan space a good turn. All they had to look forward to was slowly and ingloriously rotting to death. Should he succeed in providing the Inner Sphere with a means to attack the homeworlds, some solahma warriors on Huntress might still get their chance to fight and die with honor one day. It might be years from now, but the chance was real.

And if he failed, Trent would be facing a similar fate worse than death—assignment to a solahma unit. Paul Moon would have won. Solahma units generally were assigned second-line 'Mechs, if any. Sometimes they were sent into battle against BattleMechs with nothing more than sidearms and knives.

That was not how warriors should die.

It was not how Trent planned on dying.

Age had nothing to do with a warrior's skill or prowess. He knew that at least one of the warriors with whom he was traveling was truly dezgra. Disgraced and dishonored for attempting to conceal a violation of the bidding ritual in a Trial of Combat. The others were, like Trent, simply older warriors, some of whom had also served on Tukayyid.

He could imagine their bitterness and resentment, and how they would be clinging to the hope that fate might yet send them some means by which to prove themselves one last time. Whatever they were, whatever they thought or felt, this group of warriors was, for the moment, his command. If all went well, Trent would have another chance even if they did not. But he could not simply dismiss them. As warriors, they deserved his respect, and he would forge them into some sort of a unit.

We will be traveling together for nearly a year, and by the time we arrive on Huntress, we shall show the other Jaguar warriors that solahma is merely a word. We shall stand with backs proud and heads high when we set foot once more on the homeworld.

A gentle rapping at the stateroom door interrupted these thoughts. Trent rose and opened it to find Judith floating there in the corridor. He motioned for her to enter, then carefully secured the door as she drifted into the room and grabbed onto a chair to come to a stop. "I thought you would be sleeping by now," he said.

"I wanted to thank you for earlier today," she said.

"Thank me?"

"Aye, for your praise of me before Star Commander Allen. You made me remember the pride I once felt as a warrior. And it made me certain we are doing the right thing."

"I only spoke the truth," he replied.

"This Star Commander seems like a good man," she replied. "His company will help make the long trip pass quickly."

"Aye, and his friendship can help get me access to the *Admiral Andrews*." Star Commander Allen had given them a tour of the JumpShip, which had already been a help in their plans. Help they would never be able to thank him for.

"Everything seems to be falling into place," she said.

Trent shrugged slightly. "It is a long way to Huntress, Judith. Many things can happen before we get there. Many things can go wrong."

≡ 21 ≡

***JumpShip* Admiral Andrews**
Zenith Jump Point
Richmond
Smoke Jaguar Occupation Zone
2 June 3055

Trent walked through the corridor of the JumpShip using his deck shoes. Mounted with light magnetic plates, the shoes allowed contact with the deck and at least some degree of normal walking and movement in the weightlessness of zero-gravity. The shoes were not common on most short trips, but on a journey that would last for the better part of a year, ship's personnel used them to help maintain their personal stamina. Muscles tended to weaken during long space flights, and the exercise of walking was important to keep up health.

He stopped near the maintenance airlock and glanced both ways down the corridor. He punched in the access code given to all officers aboard the ship, and the inner door hissed and whirred as it opened. Trent stepped into the airlock, then reached for the neutrino sensor hidden behind a handhold and tucked it into his belt. This was a trial run, one of several he and Judith had carried out in their trip across the occupation zone. As he exited the airlock, Trent punched the stud that would close and seal it shut.

Later tonight Judith would analyze the device to make sure that it was working properly. They would probably never get another chance to travel to Clan space, and if the device was not in proper calibration, the whole operation would be for naught.

As he moved down the corridor parallel to the jump drive core that ran nearly the length of the ship, Trent thought about how far they had come already. The brilliant orange star of Richmond shimmered below, a beacon marking the outer limits of the Inner Sphere. Beyond Richmond was the Deep Periphery and the first stars on the Exodus Road.

He stopped at the end of the access corridor and checked himself over. He had donned his dress gray uniform, complete with regalia, for the meeting with his new officers. The fourth and final DropShip had docked onto the *Admiral Andrews* at the last recharge station at Idlewind, bringing with it the last of the warriors in his charge. He had sent them orders to meet in one of the small briefing rooms so he could take their measure and let them know what he expected of them.

Trent opened the door and stepped in. Half the warriors rose to attention, careful to hold their positions in place with one foot so that they did not drift up off the deck with their sudden standing movement. The others remained seated, some of them looking bitter and defiant. Trent walked over to a table set up at the head of the room, then turned to his command. "At ease," he said, taking the end seat for himself. "I am Star Captain Trent, your commanding officer during this trip."

One of the men who did not rise leaned forward on the table with his elbows. "In other words you are our warden, here to take us back to Huntress so we may serve out the rest of our lives as prisoners."

"Negative," Trent replied. "I know that you have been declared either solahma or even dezgra, but that means nothing to me. In my eyes you are still Smoke Jaguar warriors, and as such you will behave accordingly." He rose from his seat, and the warrior who had spoken took his elbows off the table and pulled himself up straighter.

"Bold words from an officer so aged that he will most likely not return from this mission," said a female Star Commander who Trent easily identified from her file as Krista. "Is there a point to this meeting, Star Captain Trent?"

Trent understood both her bravado and her comments regarding his own status. "I am sorry for disturbing your schedule, Krista. I thought I had come to address warriors

worthy of being called Smoke Jaguars. Apparently you are
not that, but are some foolish freebirth who has no sense of
command or duty. Perhaps I should contact security and let
them know that the bandit caste has infiltrated this ship and
can be rounded up here in this room, *quiaff*?"

Her face and the faces of several others turned bright red
with anger. "I *am* a warrior," Krista said. "I am merely
denied the chance to prove it." Others in the room echoed
her sentiments. Trent did not smile, but felt like it. He had
struck a nerve.

"Good, Krista, and the rest of you. It is encouraging to
know that the blood of the Jaguar still runs through your
veins. I understand your sentiments, but this is not a time for
such matters. Now is the time to show those who sent us here
that they were wrong in doing so. That we are not worthless
chaff of the Clan, but true warriors, now and forever."

"Your words have no meat behind them," a slightly over-
weight officer said from the far end of the table. Trent recognized him as Marcus, the warrior declared dezgra. His
violation of Clan custom had cost him his command and
posting to a brig for several months. "Why not just leave us
be, Star Captain? You have nothing to gain by taking your role
with us so seriously."

"Negative, Marcus," Trent said sharply. "I have everything to gain in my own self-respect as an officer and a
member of the Clan. You need not participate, however, if
you think serving under me as a warrior is pointless or a
waste of your time. Do note, though, that as your superior
officer I will treat your insubordination as outright mutiny
now that we are about to depart any formal authority of the
Smoke Jaguars."

"Mutiny?"

Trent saw that the word stung deeply. What Clansman did
not know about the mutiny in the Deep Periphery of the *Prinz
Eugen,* one of the ships accompanying General Kerensky's
great Exodus? Once captured, General Kerensky had ordered
all officers aboard the vessel executed. Mutiny was the gravest
of betrayals among the Clans.

"Aff," Trent said, again knowing this barb had hit home.
"Those of you who do not follow orders will be treated as
mutineers. Punishment will be swift and suitable to the crime. I
will order the Marines to throw you into an airlock and jettison

you into space." Trent meant everything he said, and he wanted to leave no doubt about it.

There was a long pause while the dozen officers seated at the table seemed to reflect briefly on what they had heard. Trent surveyed their faces and was satisfied they had understood.

"Any other questions?" he asked. No one spoke.

"Does anyone wish now to declare that my program is not in his or her best interest?"

Universally, the warriors responded, "Neg."

Trent took the opportunity to smile. "Excellent then. There are four simulator pods aboard the *Dhava*. We also have several isorla Inner Sphere BattleMechs in our bays. I will instruct my technician to begin any repairs necessary in case we need the 'Mechs operational. In the meantime, I have established regular instruction and simulator sessions for each of you. We will meet every day for calisthenics and to go over tactics drills and scenarios I will post for you daily."

"Star Captain." It was a bearded warrior who Trent knew was named Stanley. "An indulgence, *quiaff*?"

"Aff," Trent said, granting him permission to raise a question.

"The rest of us have spoken together informally before this meeting. We understand why we are here. How is that you come to be our commanding officer?"

Trent pondered the question for a full five seconds. A part of him was tempted to say what he really thought. *I am here because of internal politics, because of distortions of Nicholas Kerensky's vision, because of failed policies, and because I believe that warriors are more than murderers of unarmed civilians.* He resisted the temptation, however.

"I am here as honor guard for one who has fallen. I have the task of accompanying her genetic legacy to Huntress and making sure it is properly interned there. She and I were sibkin, and I was deemed the most appropriate to make sure she achieves the fate she deserves." Speaking the words, Trent knew he was the only one to appreciate the irony of them.

"Over the coming months we will come to know each other well. And, by the time we arrive on Huntress you will be the best warriors to ever emerge from their sibkos."

Judith stood with her back to the door of his cabin and looked at the neutrino scanner, inputting the information into her digital pad perscomp. "Everything seems to be going as planned, Star Captain. I have used simple hand-held imaging binoculars to give me the spectrum readings to correlate your data."

Trent stood next to her, holding out his wrist and the attached watch. "You will download the information into my wristscomp for storage."

Judith began to move, then hesitated slightly. "Sir, it would be better to keep the information stored in two places. Is your wrist computer for backup or primary storage?"

"Neither, it is the only place that the information will be stored," Trent said.

"I do not understand."

"I trust you implicitly, Judith. You have proven yourself to be a worthy warrior in battle and one I might call friend. I believe that you are honorable or you would not be alive now," he said, remembering the sabotage of his *Timber Wolf* after the Grand Melee. "These people you are dealing with, however—your 'contacts' on Hyner. They are strangers to me. I know nothing of them, and so will retain possession of the data until I am sure of their honor."

"Star Captain," she said, carefully weighing her words. "They are ComStar, as was I."

"Do you know them personally and can you verify their integrity from experience?"

"Negative."

"After today I realized something, Judith. This thing that we are doing is no small matter. The information we are gathering can only be used for one purpose, to take the fight to the very heart and soul of the Smoke Jaguar Clan. I am prepared to deliver that information, but I will not take that risk foolishly.

"What I will be giving your 'contacts' is the means to crush a deadly enemy, a rabid animal who is no longer able or willing to control itself. In doing so I am placing both our lives at risk. If captured we will be tortured to death, at best."

"The risks are shared by us equally, Star Captain," she said firmly.

"Neg, Judith. I am your bondmaster still. Your life and actions are my responsibility and mine alone. If we are to fail, then I am the one that must pay the price."

She nodded and began to transmit the information from her datapad computer into his wristscomp. Trent could tell from her face that Judith understood that no matter what happened, he was still a true Clan warrior. Not a Smoke Jaguar warrior, tainted by failed policies and leadership. Neg. He was the warrior in the true tradition of Nicholas Kerensky, founder of the Clans. No matter what he did, it must be with honor. He wore the mantle of warrior proudly, yet the weight of it seemed to grow heavier with each passing day.

22

DropShip Dhava
Nadir Jump Point, Unnamed Star System
The Exodus Road
15 November 3055

Trent stood behind Lucas' simulator pod, where the tactical and damage indicator and sensor displays were being relayed. He had a good view as Lucas moved in for the kill.

There were only a handful of functional BattleMechs on the DropShips attached to the *Admiral Andrews*. Most had suffered some damage, having been taken in battle or captured after a fight. Judith had been able to get five up and working.

Faced with a command of twelve warriors and only five BattleMechs, Trent had let Clan tradition determine who would pilot a 'Mech should the necessity arise. A Trial of Position was being fought for each 'Mech. He himself had tested, earning the right to pilot an isorla *Marauder II,* a machine that reminded him of his *Timber Wolf*. The other warriors were vying for the 'Mechs that remained. Thus far Lucas was showing great potential, while Trent was silently pleased that Marcus had failed in the first round, falling to a tall female named Tamara.

From the multi-screen displays, Trent was able to monitor Lucas' status as he waded in against the warrior named Stanley. Both warriors were piloting in the same model of 'Mech for which they were competing, which would show how well each would handle the machine in battle. Lucas was a determined fighter, pushing his simulated *Hatamoto-Chi* to its limits of speed and endurance. Despite having lost more than half his armor, Lucas unleashed a driving assault that forced Stanley to seek cover for his simulated 'Mech in a small forest in the holographic battlefield where they fought.

Unrelenting, Lucas did not try to flush out his foe by firing into the woods, a tack many warriors might have tried. Instead he charged in after Stanley's own *Hatamoto-Chi,* holding his fire and venting as much heat as possible. The charge caught Stanley unprepared as he tried to turn and fire. Lucas did not engage his weapons, but instead ran at full throttle into his foe. The impact shredded the remaining armor off both 'Mechs, and belches of computer-simulated smoke filled the space between them as Stanley's 'Mech wavered under the attack. Still not done, Lucas threw a barrage of punches so violent that his simulator pod rocked to its maximum pitch with each blow.

It was over in a matter of seconds. Stanley's simulator pod lights and external screens went off as his engine went into a failure. Lucas' pod door opened, and he almost leaped out of it. His body was drenched in sweat, and the pungent aroma stung at Trent's nostrils. He had set the internal temperature of the pods to what would actually be encountered. The *isorla* 'Mechs were Inner Sphere models that suffered much higher heat levels than their cooler-running Smoke Jaguar counterparts.

"The victory is yours, Lucas."

"Now all we need is an enemy," Lucas said.

Trent hoped Lucas and the others would find what they were seeking. He himself had already found his enemy, the greatest foe he had ever faced—his own Clan. "Perhaps, Lucas, time will bring you your wish."

As he made his way through the JumpShip, Trent stopped near the small maintenance airlock where he had planted the neutrino scanner. The ship had jumped thirty minutes ago and was now in the process of deploying its solar sail. The vast solar-collection sail would gather the free-floating charged particles from the unnamed star system, and store them in the JumpShip's drive core. Once fully charged, in four to five days, the ship would be able to jump again.

In the meantime, Trent had to recover the device, store its readings, then plant it again before the next jump. Being commander of the warrior contingent aboard the DropShips had proven useful to Trent. It had made it a simple matter to persuade Star Commander Allen to let him know the jump schedule in advance so that the jumps would not interrupt his training regime. It was a perfectly legitimate request, though, of course, no one would ever guess his true purpose.

Stepping into the airlock, he glanced out through the small viewing port before pulling the neutrino scanner down from its hiding place. Visible less than a kilometer away was another ship. Not simply a JumpShip, but a WarShip. Shimmering in the external lights on the hull was the insignia of a pouncing gray Smoke Jaguar.

Destroyer, Trent told himself. *Whirlwind Class, from the looks of it.* His warrior instincts kicked in immediately, the statistics for the ship playing through his mind. While Jump-Ships generally stayed out of a fight, WarShips were built to plow right into the heart of battle.

WarShips were not a common sight away from the Inner Sphere these days. The few not active in the occupation zone were positioned every few jumps on rotational duty along the Exodus Road. They were there for protection and to transmit a small piece of the ever-changing navigational map of the path back to Clan space to other vessels in route.

WarShips were powerful and impressive, but they offered very little of interest to a warrior. Aboard such a vessel a warrior was merely a passenger. Only riding high in the cockpit of a 'Mech did he or she truly live in service to the Clan. Or, so thought Trent.

As he slipped the neutrino scanner into his pocket and turned to go, he discovered that he was not alone. Standing behind him in the narrow doorway to the airlock was a young man with an unruly mop of sandy-colored hair and wearing the uniform of a ship's tech. Trent's heart skipped a beat, but he did what came most naturally to him. He went on the offensive.

"Is there a problem, Tech?" Trent eyed the man's ID tag and saw the name Miles. Trent had no idea whether this Miles had seen him with the scanner or had just come to the door.

"Negative, sir. I just noticed that the airlock was open." There was a hint of nervousness in the man's voice, but Trent knew it could be merely the fear the lower castes felt toward an angry member of the warrior caste.

Trent gestured to the viewport. "I was observing the destroyer. It is an impressive vessel, is it not?"

Miles rose on his tiptoes to look over Trent's shoulder through the viewport. "Aff, it *is* impressive, Star Captain."

Trent gestured toward the passageway. "I must attend to my duties," he said. "You will be sure to seal the airlock behind you, *quiaff?*"

"Aff," Miles said, still looking out the port at the fearsome sight of the Clan WarShip.

Judith moved in close to Trent at the feet of his *Marauder II,* which she was working to repair in the 'Mech bay. She spoke in a whisper as Trent held onto the *Marauder*'s massive leg strut to keep himself from drifting off into the open bay. "You are not sure whether he saw the scanner?"

"Neg," Trent whispered back, eyeing the storage bay cautiously. "He did not seem very intelligent, but he may have been trying to conceal his suspicions."

"Miles is a risk, not just to this mission, but to our lives," she said.

"That is an understatement," Trent nodded. "I must deal with him."

"Negative," Judith retorted. "I will deal with Miles."

Trent shook his head. "Neg, Judith. I am the warrior. This is my mission."

"You will never get access to Miles. He is a tech. I have become friendly with several of the ship's techs. I can get to parts of the JumpShip and the DropShips that you would never be able to, even as a warrior. I will make sure he does not speak of whatever he may have seen."

"You talk beyond your station as a bondsman, Judith," Trent said.

"I have been beyond my station since the day you agreed to my proposition back on Hyner. All I ask, Star Captain, is that you permit me to perform one of the duties for which I was trained in my former life. It is true that I am no longer a warrior. But this is not an honorable act. And thus far you have shouldered all of the risks of this operation. This is something that I can contribute. Allow me to be what I once was." Judith spoke from the heart, and it was not a tech Trent saw standing before him but another warrior.

"Aye, Judith. Do as you must."

* * *

The drive core of the JumpShip *Admiral Andrews* was its most delicate mechanism. The Kearny-Fuchida titanium/germanium alloy core ran the 740-meter-long length of the vessel. Charged via the solar sail and suspended in perfect balance in a helium housing, the core was a massive superconductive capacitor. The helium suspension shaft itself was surrounded by a larger maintenance tube that ran the length of the ship.

The maintenance of the inner core was accomplished via this tube, and it was sealed during hyperspace jumps between stars, and with good reason. During a jump, the field initiator at the aft end of the ship tapped the massive power stored in the core to warp the space around the JumpShip and its attached Drop-Ships, essentially moving it through hyperspace from one star to another instantly. During the field generation that took place, the core filled the maintenance tube with an incredible static charge. The maintenance tube was protected on the outside. However, anything inside the tube, which stood next to the helium-suspended and -encased core, would be reduced to pure carbon in a matter of milliseconds, so intense was the heat and electrical charge.

Tech Miles was making a last check of the forward alignment system, sealing the control plate back into place before leaving the maintenance tube. It was a routine inspection, one he carried out in the few minutes before every jump. There was no risk. The drive-core maintenance hatch was open only twenty meters away, and he had the electronic key needed to lock it. As long as the hatch was open, the safety overrides prevented anyone from engaging the jump drive.

He didn't even think about the hatch as he finished his work. Miles was a busy tech, after all, and there was a jump scheduled in a few minutes. He was intent on finishing the task at hand, while the back of his mind contemplated with pleasure the thought of the card game planned for later that evening in Cargo Bay Three. There was a sound behind him, but he did not even bother to turn and look. It was only his tool kit shifting. No one ever came into the jump core. Because of the risks, this was the last place even the techs wanted to work.

There was a blur out the corner of his eye as Judith brought the wrench down on the back of his head. Then everything in his world went black.

His lip tasted the metallic surface of the floor of the jump chamber, his ears still ringing from whatever had hit him. He was dazed and his limbs felt cold and numb and as if he couldn't control them. A flash of red lights in the chamber made his heart suddenly begin to race. Red lights in the drive core—a jump was about to take place. Miles pulled himself up like a drunk, staggering toward the hatch. Reaching down, he grappled for the access key. It was gone! In a blur he reached for the intercom and pressed the emergency button, but nothing happened.

He did not suffer. A bright flash of light filled the corridor and enveloped his body in a final embrace.

Judith half-walked, half-floated into Trent's quarters, closing the doorway behind her. Her stomach was still rolling from the last jump. She stood before him, her face blanched of color. Trent stared at her for a long moment before speaking.

"It is done, *quiaff?*"

"Affirmative. It will appear to be an accident. There still is a risk that he spoke to his seniors and told them about you."

Trent nodded. "I considered that. That is why I thought it best if I were the one to perform this act."

Judith shook her head. "You are proceeding from a misinterpretation, Star Captain. You think that I have not killed before."

"I know that you were a warrior, Judith."

She shook her head violently. "Negative. I was a member of ROM before I joined the Com Guards. I have had to murder before. I do not enjoy it, but I have done it."

Trent ran his fingers through what hair he had and nodded. "And what I did to Jez was close enough to murder that I would not know what else to call it. But our acts are justified. We are doing what is necessary to put an end to a corruption—that of our own Clan."

Trent spoke boldly, but he still remembered how he felt after the death of Jez on Hyner. The mix of anger, frustration, guilt, and bitterness. Now he and Judith were bonded in still another way. "Do you play chess, Judith?" he asked.

She was puzzled by this sudden shift of conversation. "Aye. Though, I have not played in many years."

Trent opened the small drawer above his bed and pulled out the box containing his chess set. "I used to play, before

Tukayyid. Star Commander Russou played me, but he did not have the finesse I enjoy."

"Is this not a breach of etiquette, Star Colonel? You would be gaming with a lower caste member."

"When we are alone Judith, you and I are equals from this moment forward." Trent set up the board and deployed the white pieces on his side. In the slight gravity of the Drop-Ship, they just barely stayed in place. It was going to be a long night . . .

23

Trent set the small packet of food on the table in his room, and it drifted slightly above the surface in the gravity-less environment. He was eating alone, as he did most of the time on the DropShip. It was not that he did not care for the other warriors. Quite the opposite, he found their company a pleasure on the few occasions he had joined them in the mess room. They were, like him, all trueborn, with many common interests, viewpoints, likes and dislikes, and so on.

Despite that, he knew in his heart that they were also very different from him. And that was what made him keep to himself. The feeling that he stood apart, as much here among warriors who respected him as back on Hyner among warriors who scorned him. Where he had decided on a path of action to preserve himself, they were willing to submit to orders, to walk obediently into their solahma assignments without so much as asking why. Their complacency frustrated Trent, a situation made even more difficult by the fact that he could express his thoughts and feelings to no one. No one, that is, except Judith.

There was a firm knock on his door that stirred him from these dark thoughts. "Enter," he said and was surprised to see

Star Commander Allen hovering in the doorway. Behind him he glimpsed a light gray of a jumpsuit, which told him that Judith accompanied the big Elemental. Every time he saw Star Commander Allen, Trent's heart beat slightly faster. *Does he know or even suspect what happened to Tech Miles? Does he suspect that Judith or I had something to do with it?*

"I hope we are not intruding," Allen said, moving through the doorway with an elegance that seemed to defy his giant stature. Judith followed, closing the door behind them. "But this is a special eve. We have reached Pivot Prime, and there are traditions we must share."

Trent raised his one real eyebrow. "Pivot? I do not understand."

The big man lowered himself somehow into the other chair across from Trent and placed a cloth sack on the table. Judith drifted into the room but stayed back, acknowledging her position with the two warriors.

"This place, the planet below, is known as Pivot," Allen said. "We are at the edge of the Caliban Nebula. This was the first point from which the great General Kerensky and the Exodus Fleet could view the Pentagon Worlds, which everyone knows were the first homeworlds of our ancestors. It is an important point, a place of great significance."

"I do not understand," Trent said with a puzzled expression.

Allen chuckled. "I am not surprised. We Marines and the spacers who travel these lanes treat this point like the crossing of Terra's equator or the rounding of Cape Horn in ancient times. For us, this is a crossing point on the Exodus Road, and we mark it accordingly."

He pulled his gray uniform shirt sleeve back and revealed a small set of marks. They were stars, Cameron Stars of the former Star League, tattooed in a small row on his bicep. They were small, but brilliant yellow, almost golden. "Each one marks my passage past Pivot. We commemorate the past with these symbols of why we have launched the invasion of the Inner Sphere—the restoration of the Star League." Allen pulled a small black device four centimeters by two centimeters out of the sack.

"This is a laser tattoo marker. I have programmed it for the symbol of passage, the Cameron Star. I wish to share this rite with the two of you."

"With both of us?" Judith asked.

Allen nodded once, firmly and quickly. "Aff, Tech Judith.

You and your master have brought me many good stories of combat. We are of different castes, but our ship techs have a similar ritual, so perhaps I do not err too gravely in sharing this one with you. I have read the official reports of Tukayyid, but your tales have made me feel that I was really there."

Trent could well imagine that even stories would some-what feed the hunger for combat of one who had been raised and trained as a warrior. Ship duty offered little chance to fight in true battle except in Trials of Possession, a rarity for the precious JumpShip assets. He pulled up his right sleeve, exposing the artificial skin of his arm, which retained a small patch of real skin near the shoulder. "I am honored," Trent said. Judith also pulled back her sleeve and bared her arm.

Allen reached over and pressed the device against Trent's arm. There was a clicking sound and a slight whir. As the big man pulled the marker away, Trent saw a golden Cameron Star about the size of a fingernail permanently lasered into his skin. Allen then reached over and performed the same action on Judith.

"Is there more to this ritual?" Trent asked.

"Aff," Allen said, reaching into the bag and pulling out a bottle with odd markings. "This is an alcoholic drink. Whiskey. Tradition calls for us to share a drink from the same cup, the mark of kinship."

Trent did not drink alcohol. It dulled the senses, which no warrior could afford. But this was a rite, even if not an offi-cial Clan ritual. To refuse would be insulting. He reached over to his nightstand and pulled out a small collapsible cup, which he handed to Star Captain Allen.

Allen looked at the cup for a moment, as though his mind were suddenly distracted by other thoughts. "There was a death aboard the JumpShip, one I am investigating," he said.

"A death?" Trent said.

Allen opened his mouth to speak, but was interrupted by a siren coming from the hallway and over the small speaker in the ceiling over Trent's bed. A red light flashed in the room, and the festive mood suddenly changed. Allen rose to his great height and lifted his wrist communicator to his lips, opening a direct channel to the bridge of the JumpShip. He spoke in short muffled tones of command, and listened intensely to the responses coming over the tiny speaker in the communicator.

He looked over at Trent, his expression grave. "We must go, Star Captain. An emergency situation has arisen."

"What kind of emergency?"

"A JumpShip has been detected at this jump point. It is an Explorer Corps vessel."

Trent had been in the Combat Information Center, the CIC, of the *Admiral Andrews* several times since the journey had begun. It was the perfect command center in a crisis, with all JumpShip and DropShip operations able to be coordinated from this single command post. Trent was also impressed with the rapidity with which the captains of the *Andrews* as well as those of the docked DropShips had been summoned.

Star Captain Jonas of the *Admiral Andrews* was a lanky man. He was also well past his prime from the looks of it, but had somehow dodged a solahma assignment. He stepped up to the holographic projector in the center of the CIC and let his eyes travel over all the faces gathered around. "Sitrep is as follows. Apparently a ComStar Explorer Corps *Scout* Class JumpShip arrived several hours before we did. Our sensors only just detected her when we sounded the alert. The other ship was in midst of deploying its jump sail at the time and has not tried to flee. Most likely it does not yet have the charge for a jump."

"DropShip?" Star Captain Walter Stiles, master of the DropShip *Dhava,* asked.

"One detected in-flight on a fast burn for Pivot Prime," he said, mentioning the name of the single planet in the system. "Ship class is *Union*. Pivot is a habitable world with a single Clan outpost on it to defend the HPG relay there. According to Ops the vessel has a four-hour head start."

Trent spoke up next. "Garrison strength on Pivot?"

Jonas stroked his goatee. "At present one Star. Two Points of BattleMechs, three of Elementals."

"And a *Union* Class vessel could be carrying upwards of two and a half Stars worth of 'Mechs," Trent said.

"Operational orders for all units traveling the Exodus Road are specific regarding Inner Sphere encounters," Jonas said. "We are to use any and all force necessary to capture or destroy these forces. Under no circumstances are they to be allowed to escape."

Trent understood. Should the Inner Sphere obtain information of a Clan settlement on Pivot, that data would put them a step closer to learning the location of the homeworlds. He could have used Judith there to advise him of what she knew of the Explorer Corps from her days in ComStar. That, of course, was impossible. No tech would participate in a council of warriors. "We must deal with two threats then," he said. "One is the JumpShip, the other is this force currently burning for the planet."

"Aff," Jonas said firmly. "If they seize that HPG it will not give them all of the coordinates of the Exodus Road, but they will get enough to map out several other star systems on the way." .

"We cannot permit that to happen," Star Commander Allen stated.

"Aye," Captain Jonas returned. "We should detach the *Mohawk* and the *Stealthy Cat* along with fighter escort. They can intercept and disable the JumpShip within the hour. The Marine forces should be ample to seize control of the Jump-Ship or to make sure she does not jump."

Star Captain Walter Stiles spoke up next. "I assume that leaves me to go after the ground force with the *Dhava*." He glanced at Trent. "Perhaps this is a chance for our solahma forces to prove themselves worthy of the Smoke Jaguar one last time."

"They will not fail," Trent said. "But the enemy forces are not inconsiderable. I have six operational BattleMechs and the warriors to man them. Let me also take one Star of Marines for close-combat support."

Stiles nodded and glanced at Star Commander Allen, his grin broadening from ear to ear, then back to Trent. "Well bargained and done. Commence launch operations in fifteen minutes. We will download all tactical data on Pivot Prime and relay a priority message to the outpost there. May the will of the Kerenskys guide you."

Judith double-checked the cockpit seal on the hatch to the *Marauder II* from the access gantry as Trent climbed in. "Are you sure this is the course you wish to follow?"

Trent scowled slightly in response.

"The Explorer Corps is seeking the same thing we are, the path of the Exodus Road. You will be killing those we hope to one day assist."

"Aff," Trent replied. "I will do my duty to the best of my

ability, Judith. To do anything else would risk us appearing to be something else besides a Clan warrior and his tech."

She bowed her head. "I understand," she said. "You must be careful, though. Ammunition is minimal, half-loads for every 'Mech. These machines were isorla, meant for analysis and investigation by our scientists, not for use under battle conditions. They work, but some may have problems we did not discover through routine testing and diagnostics."

"As with all people and all things, Judith," Trent said, pulling on his neurohelmet, "we do what we must."

24

Smoke Jaguar HPG Station
Pivot Prime, Caliban Nebula
The Exodus Road
30 January 3056

"**S**moke Jaguars, this is Captain Bryant Foster of Meredith's Marauders. We have beaten the force defending this HPG and claim it in the name of ComStar. Withdraw your forces immediately and no one else need die."

Trent sat back in the cockpit of his *Marauder II* and surveyed the scene. Pivot was a desolate and barren world of rocks and brown dirt. The only plant life consisted of mosses and lichens, and his force kicked up a cloud of dust that rose nearly a hundred meters up as they advanced. They had been on the planet a full day, after being dropped off by the *Dhava*. Six lone BattleMechs against at least ten mercenaries in the employ of ComStar.

The mercenaries had done well. They had hit the Clan HPG facility from two different sides at once. The defenders, solahma warriors all, had made a futile but heroic effort with their pitiful second-line 'Mechs and generations-old battle armor. Now Meredith's Marauders held the small outpost. The problem they faced was that they had suddenly become the defenders, and Trent's force was on the advance.

He had reviewed the situation tactically and knew that it would be difficult to take the base because he was outnumbered. Computer simulation indicated less than a forty-five percent chance of success, but Trent was counting on a few things even the Clan battle computers could not factor in. Timing would be the key to victory. With that thought, he pressed the keypad on the cockpit console and overlaid the image of a digital clock on the secondary display. It slowly ticked off the remaining minutes before battle would commence.

Trent signaled his small force to stop at the top of the last ridge before they reached the HPG compound. Lucas in his *Hatamoto-Chi* was on his right, while on his left was Deleon in his isorla *Komodo,* sending up a flurry of dust as he came to a halt. On his far right flank were the rest of the solahma under his command. The ever-arrogant Krista in her dark maroon *Gallowglas,* Geronimo in his *Daikyu,* and Winchester's incredibly light and fragile *Venom,* missing paint where its armor plating had been replaced. Trent surveyed them, then checked the chronometer display in the cockpit.

"You all know the plan and the risks associated with it. I know that some of you are viewing this as a chance to die with honor in battle. Remember that victory is the most important thing here. Whether you live or die today, your codexes will reflect the honor with which you fought to protect our Clan from its enemies." He glanced again at the time display. "Jaguars, attack!"

They raced up the ridge and cleared it in unison. The compound lay before them. Surrounded by a hexagonal dull gray stone wall, the five structures composing the facility appeared impenetrable until Trent spied the holes where the Marauders had blasted their way through. Inside the base, moving to firing positions behind the waist-high walls, the remaining BattleMechs of the mercenary unit prepared to weather the assault.

Trent fired his PPCs at the largest of the 'Mechs as the rest of the Jaguars rushed toward the compound, each one with weapons blazing. The brilliant blue bolts of man-made lightning hit a Marauder *Atlas* in its upper chest just below the skull-like head, sending armor plating ricocheting off in every direction as the bolts seared their way in.

Two minutes, Trent noted as he moved down the ridge. In front of him Deleon's squat *Komodo* stopped and opened up on a lanky *Quickdraw* with his ten medium lasers. The scarlet beams reached up and over the defensive wall, and sliced the right arm off the *Quickdraw,* but not before the mercenary let go a salvo of missiles that seemed to swallow the *Komodo* and showered Trent with dirt clods and debris.

The *Gallowglas* and *Daikyu* poured their destructive energies into the defensive wall, blasting most of it away in a single salvo, pushing debris back onto a smaller mercenary *Sentinel*. Trent raised his targeting reticule as the *Atlas,* now recovered from his attack, returned the favor. The Gauss rifle slug hit his Mech's right leg with such force that it nearly knocked him off balance, but he fought the *Marauder II*'s controls and kept it upright—just in time for the wave of missiles and lasers to hit.

His secondary display showed yellow all over his upper torso and shoulders where his armor had been mangled in the attack. Trent brought his PPCs and LB-X autocannon on the same target interlock, firing the moment he heard the lock tone in the neurohelmet speakers. The damage was mostly on the left side of the fearsome *Atlas,* smoke billowing from the holes where his PPCs had cut deep. Trent swallowed hard as the heat level in his cockpit spiked for a moment. This was an Inner Sphere 'Mech, not Clan equipment, and it was much more susceptible to the dangers of overheating.

The *Atlas* fired again, hitting again with its Gauss rifle, the slug twisting and ripping armor as it tore a gouge into the upper leg of Trent's 'Mech. From his cockpit he saw a *Thunderbolt* lay a deadly salvo into Winchester's *Venom*. The light 'Mech staggered for a moment, then crumpled, its leg struts giving out under the weight of the undamaged portions of the 'Mech. There was a brief flash of explosion as it fell, and Trent knew that the pilot inside had died. Lucas stood over the fallen *Venom* in his *Hatamoto-Chi* and avenged Winchester with every weapon he had. The *Thunderbolt* pilot lost his balance under the barrage and fell, the 'Mech disappearing behind the rampart wall.

A wave of missiles jarred Trent's *Marauder II* as he tried to locate the *Atlas* through the smoke and dust that now filled the air. The missiles slammed into his torso, ripping armor plating and throwing one of his heat sinks off line.

One minute, he thought as he glanced at the chronometer on the secondary display. The *Atlas* moved closer to the defensive wall and suddenly broke through the wave of smoke. Trent fired at the same time the mercenary MechWarrior did, their shots passing each other in less than a heartbeat. This time the *Atlas* missed, the Gauss round slamming into the ridge next to Trent and instantly gouging out a crater. The enemy 'Mech's lasers and missiles found their mark, however, pitting and demolishing even more of Trent's precious armor, causing his own PPC shots to swerve and break off off target.

He swung the *Marauder II* around and saw the damage he had inflicted. The *Atlas'* skull-like cockpit was badly burned, with a long black scar running diagonally across its surface. Deleon's *Komodo* and Lucas in his *Hatamoto-Chi* advanced toward the hole in the wall, firing blindly at the defenders on the other side as they pumped every bit of their firepower out at the Smoke Jaguars. The *Komodo* wavered under a steady stream of autocannon and laser fire, its armor literally shredding and flying off backward as it seemed to evaporate into thin air. There was an explosion, then the 'Mech was no more.

Trent concentrated on his own foe. His *Marauder II* carried only one more salvo for its autocannon, and Trent knew it was better to use the ammo than risk having it explode. Activating the weapon, he sent a long stream of autocannon rounds up the surface of the wall in front of his enemy, then into the torso of the *Atlas* itself. He held his aim steady and true as the autocannon rounds burrowed into the internal workings of the *Atlas,* blasting myomer and reactor shielding on the way.

The *Atlas* wavered, sending another Gauss rifle slug streaking out and into his right leg, making the *Marauder II* quake violently under the impact. He glanced at the secondary display and smiled inside the neurohelmet at what he saw on the digital time readout. *Now . . .*

Suddenly from the other side of the compound came a deafening roar that penetrated even the soundproof Battle-Mechs. The DropShip *Dhava,* flying low and fast, swept across the HPG compound only a dozen meters above the transmitter dish. Its turrets cut downward at the defenders from the rear. The 'Mech bays opened and Star Commander Allen's Elemental Marines leaped out, their leg jets flaming fully to slow their descent. They dropped down quickly onto the mercenary BattleMechs, firing their short-range missiles as they went, then grappling with the 'Mechs as they landed. The *Dhava* swung away, but in the confusion, Trent and the rest of his force were able to race forward through the gaping hole and directly into the compound. The sudden chaos had worked perfectly in their favor—just as he had planned it.

The battle was over from that moment, and there was no one on Pivot Prime who did not know it. The fighting lasted another five minutes or so as the suddenly panicked mercenaries tried to rally, then flee. The *Atlas* Trent had so viciously engaged attempted to rush him, but Trent charged also, slamming into the mercenary with such force and skill that the *Atlas,* or what was left of it, fell down, its gyro too badly mauled for the 'Mech to stand.

Geronimo's *Daikyu* had run out of ammunition but kept on fighting, engaging in a slugging match against the *Thunderbolt,* which had gotten back on its feet. The mercenary's last attack, a deadly punch, had gone through the cockpit of the *Daikyu,* sending up a black greasy cloud of smoke as Geronimo died, crushed instantly under the impact. The moment Geronimo was dead, Trent declared the *Thunderbolt* as his own and opened up with both his PPCs. There was a flash of a large laser, a brilliant emerald beam that seared into his *Marauder II,* then there was nothing, deadly silence. The *Thunderbolt* dropped, its chest section ripped wide open and pumping bright green coolant over the hot and torn armor. The *Daikyu,* still stuck onto the mercenary 'Mech's fist, went down with it.

Trent looked around at the debris that had been the battle site an hour earlier and rubbed his neck to relieve the tension. Smoke still spiraled from the fallen BattleMechs, and the compound technicians and MedTechs moved about, caring for the wounded or tending to the damage done. Judith was there, studying the staggering damage his *Marauder II* had taken.

Star Commander Allen stood at his side as the MedTechs went off bearing Deleon's charred remains on a stretcher. Trent looked down and saw the odd look of serenity on the burned flesh that had been a face only a few minutes earlier. The Elemental at his side rested his hand on his shoulder.

"Your plan was well laid, Star Captain," Allen said.

"And executed," Trent replied nodding to his comrade warrior. *Those who died did so with honor—Deleon, Geronimo, Winchester, and the others who might never recover from their wounds.*

"Thank you for allowing me to fight again in true battle. Such pleasures are rare for me."

Trent was about to tell Allen that no thanks were needed

between fellow warriors when the MedTechs passed with another stretcher, this one bearing a man in a white jumpsuit with the ComStar logo on one sleeve. The injured man was soaked in blood and was almost as white as his uniform, but somehow still conscious. Judith came up alongside Trent and looked down at the man on the stretcher, who locked eyes with her.

"I know you, Judith—Judith Faber . . ." he said, attempting to reach for her.

"Precentor Purdon," she said softly. Trent saw the pain on her face, a flash of memories of her life before the Clans. "I am just Judith now. I am a bondsman of the Smoke Jaguars." It was obvious that the use of her former surname had disturbed her.

The man on the stretcher coughed painfully. "It's true, then, what I've heard. Some said you were MIA, but others said you'd changed colors. That you'd turned against us. You're a *traitor!*" he said, coughing so hard that his whole body shook.

"Neg," she replied. "I am part of Clan Smoke Jaguar now."

The injured man's voice was weaker, almost fading at moments. "No, you're worse than a traitor. It's not just ComStar you've turned against, but the . . . the whole Inner Sphere."

Trent nodded for the stretcher to be carried away, but the man's eyes continued to glare at Judith even as the MedTechs hurried off with him.

"You are not a traitor, Judith," Star Commander Allen said firmly, seeing the look of pain on her face.

"Neg," she said, looking at Trent. "I am not a traitor."

Trent nodded, understanding her hidden meaning. Neither was he a traitor. Not yet.

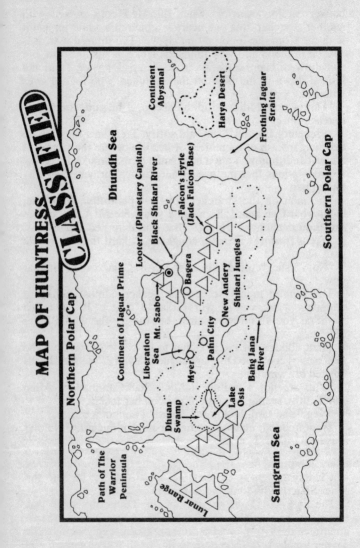

25

DropShip Dhava
Huntress
Kerensky Cluster, Clan Space
19 February 3056

Trent looked out of the DropShip *Dhava*'s viewing port into the globular cluster that hid the Clan homeworlds and saw the flicker of reflection that was the recharging station they had left several days earlier. Docked to it, he knew, was the *Admiral Andrews*. From what Star Commander Allen had told him, the ship was due for a month-long overhaul before beginning the return trip to the Inner Sphere.

It was a return trip that Trent was also determined to make. Moving his gaze downward, he saw the green and blue planet growing larger below them as the *Dhava* sped closer for a landing only a few hours away. *Huntress*. The home of Clan Smoke Jaguar. After almost a year of travel, during which he and Judith had secretly gathered data on every jump and star along the way, they had finally arrived in Clan space. Now, all they had to do was get back to the Inner Sphere with their precious data.

The sway of light gravity as the DropShip spun was enough to let him take a seat in the small observation lounge. Judith sat there too, quietly drinking in the same view of the Jaguar homeworld. The door to the small room opened, and the giant figure of Star Commander Allen filled the doorway as he bent his head enough to clear the portal.

"Welcome to Huntress," he said proudly. "It is a magnificent sight, is it not?"

Trent nodded. "This is my first time here. I noticed that the ship's computer included no maps of the planet."

Allen nodded. "Security protocols prohibit any of our ships from carrying maps of any Clan world."

"A wise precaution," Judith said sagely. "Should anyone from the Inner Sphere get his hands on knowledge of Clan space, they might use it to strike at our homeworlds." She spoke in her most loyal Smoke Jaguar tone.

"Aff," Allen returned. "And the risks are real. For some time during our trip here I suspected a spy, or at least a murderer."

Trent's heart raced. "Neg! A spy in our midst?"

"Aff," Allen continued. "A tech named Miles was killed in the jump drive core. It could have been an accident or it could have been murder. I investigated, but the only one of his contacts we were able to verify throughout the day was with you, Star Captain."

"Me?" Trent said. "Impossible. I do not even know a tech named Miles. But I do remember you mentioning the incident just before the action on Pivot Prime."

"Aye. The very one. It is possible that Miles did not die a natural death, but you certainly had no hand in it either. I would stake my life on that," Allen said. "I have come to know and respect you during our long voyage together, Star Captain. You are an honorable man."

"So, was it murder?" Judith said quickly.

Allen shrugged. "I judged it to be accident. If it was murder, he was most likely killed by one of his own caste. No matter how closely we monitor security, members of the lower castes sometimes lack control. His loss is a waste of resources, but in the end he was merely a freebirth tech."

The *Dhava* rolled just then, bringing the planet into view. Allen's eyes turned back to the image of Huntress through the viewing port. "Look, you can see the green waters of Lake Osis from here." He pointed to the largest continent.

"Tell me more about Huntress, Star Commander," Trent said, relieved that he was not under suspicion in the death of the Tech Miles. He was also pleased that Judith had held her tongue at the freebirth comment, remembering her station in the Clan.

Allen nodded. "The largest continent is where our people live. It is called Jaguar Prime. The other, smaller continent is

Abysmal and is aptly named. It is mostly barren desert, and the only thing there is a small training base.

"We will be putting down in the capital city of Lootera. Someone told me that is the Hindu word for predator. A fine name, *quiaff*? Lootera is on the eastern coast, sitting at the point where the Black Shikari River runs into the Dhundh Sea. It is a fine city, a tribute to the suffering and sacrifices by which our people survived and flourished. Overlooking the city is Mount Szabo. From anywhere in the city you can look up and see the mountain. It is truly stunning and a reminder that the Smoke Jaguar rules Huntress."

Trent nodded. He had heard of Mount Szabo. Carved into the face of the steep peak overlooking Lootera was a lunging jaguar, symbol of Clan Smoke Jaguar. Etched and lasered into a nearly two-hundred-meter high rock face, the image was lit at night and visible just below the cloud line. He had heard many stories of how impressive was the sight.

"The genetic repository is in Lootera, is it not?" Trent had not had to think of Jez or her giftake for months. He had deliberately put the whole business out of his mind, but that was no longer possible.

"Aye," Allen replied. "I have never been inside, but I have admired the building often. It is at the base of Mount Szabo, a pyramid marked with an eternal flame. If you are in the Warrior Quarter, it is hard to miss."

Trent rose and looked at Judith. "We have much to do. I must ready our warriors for arrival. I am to turn them over to the garrison commander." Thoughts of Jez stirred memories of fire and burning flesh. He walked out of the room. It was time to prepare himself for landing on the homeworld of the Smoke Jaguars.

Trent had called his command together in the ship's 'Mech bay. Gathered around him were the remaining solahma warriors, each wearing his or her pristine gray dress uniform. The BattleMechs standing silently in their storage bays spoke of the battle they had fought on Pivot, the 'Mechs burned and badly damaged in the fight against the mercenaries on Pivot Prime. They were secured and barely moved as the DropShip brought them down to the surface of Huntress.

At the head of the line stood Krista, a scar running down her cheek from the fighting on Pivot. She had survived, as had Lucas, though his survival had been uncertain for two long days while the MedTechs tended to him. A full pace behind them stood Marcus and the others who had not tested out to pilot 'Mechs. Trent was proud of his small command, and saw that his training and their stand on Pivot had restored some of their pride and confidence.

"Ten, hut!" he barked. His warriors snapped to attention.

Trent took his position at the head of the formation and began to lead their march with the same drilling precision he had learned in his sibko. He led the way to the unloading door and out onto the soil of Huntress.

The air outside was heavy, full of moisture and unfamiliar smells. On the tarmac, the techs were busy unloading the *Dhava* of her cargo. They did not seem to notice Trent and the handful of warriors coming down the ramp. The city of Lootera rose in the distance, but what Trent could see was disappointing.

The only thing that seemed to stand out was the peak of Mount Szabo to the north. On its face was the enormous carved image of the Smoke Jaguar looming over the city. *It is gray and bleak. I expected so much more after all the talk I have heard of this place.*

There was a small band of Jaguar warriors in the distance, standing and talking among themselves, barely noticing either the DropShip or Trent and his little group. Trent marched toward them, back ramrod-straight and head held high. He stopped less than five meters from three officers and went to full attention. He waited while the bright sun beat down on them and drew a sweat from the real skin on the left side of his face. Finally, the officers turned to him, and the sight of one of them lit a deep angry fire in Trent.

He showed none of that, however, as he stepped forward smartly. "Star Captain Trent, Delta Galaxy, Third Jaguar Cavaliers," he barked with precise tones. "I hereby turn over command of the warriors of the DropShip *Dhava*."

Galaxy Commander Benjamin Howell stepped forward, smiling broadly at the sight of Trent.

"I, Galaxy Commander Benjamin Howell of the Zeta Galaxy, accept these warriors into my command. Word of your engagement on Pivot was transmitted to us several days ago while you were on approach. Any warriors who have distinguished themselves in the service of our Clan are welcome in Zeta Galaxy in the defense of Huntress." Howell motioned to one of the other officers, who took Trent's place at the head of the group and began to lead the group away.

"It does me good to see you again, Trent of the Howell bloodline," Benjamin Howell said.

Trent said nothing. He held his jagged lips stern and narrowed his eyes as he restrained his anger. This was the man who had cheated him of his right to vie for a bloodname—all in the name of ambition and petty politics. This was the man who, in essence, had awarded the bloodname to Jez instead—the bloodname Trent had believed was meant for him. Because of things Benjamin Howell had done, or failed to do, Trent had come to question all that the Smoke Jaguars represented.

"You are bitter and angry," Howell said. "This I understand. Let us meet in my office and talk. We were once friends, Trent. There is no reason we cannot be so once again."

"Is that an order, Galaxy Commander?" Trent asked coldly.

Benjamin Howell smiled thinly. "If that is what it takes, aye, it is."

Howell turned and walked away, and Trent realized that he did not like Huntress. No, he did not like Huntress at all.

$\equiv$ **26** $\equiv$

Hall of the Hunter, Zeta Galaxy Command
Huntress
Kerensky Cluster, Clan Space
19 February 3056

Trent's ride to the base of Mount Szabo was accompanied by a mist-like rain that only seemed to add to his feeling of gloom. The hovercar moved silently down the wide avenues, driven by an infantry trooper who was, no doubt, an older solahma warrior. The man did not try to speak with Trent, and Trent was grateful.

He was impressed with the relative splendor of the Warrior Quarter of Lootera. The main boulevard was wide and lined with inscribed gray stone pillars on either side. At the end of the avenue was a circular fountain with a statue of General Alexsandr Kerensky, the great man who had led the Exodus several centuries earlier.

Beyond the fountain was a pyramidal structure standing almost at the foot of Mount Szabo. It was surrounded by a wide stone parade field. Around its perimeter were statues of BattleMechs facing outward. At the base of each an inscription was carved. Kent could not read them from here, but guessed that the inscriptions commemorated certain warriors and a great deed he or she had accomplished as a defender of the Clan and its sacred gene pool. The stone 'Mechs stood for all time, eternally guarding the future of the Clan.

Trent's hovercar sped past the statues and rounded the

perimeter to reach the base of the mountain. He knew the function of the structure before he saw the eternal laser flashing upward into the sky from the base of the pyramid. The *genetic repository*. He reached down to the satchel at his side and patted its side. Inside the satchel was Jez's giftake.

The car stopped, and Trent got out, then looked up again at the image of the Smoke Jaguar towering over him. He had come to the Hall of the Hunter. The planetary command post of the Smoke Jaguars, buried deep in the heart of Mount Szabo. He stopped at the small security post, where his codex was scanned and verified. The guard also checked his retina with a hand scanner. Then the warrior who had driven Trent here motioned for him to follow.

It took nearly twenty minutes and a long elevator ride to reach the office of Galaxy Commander Benjamin Howell. Trent was escorted to the door and then left standing there alone. For a moment he stared at the door and considered simply walking away. But then he changed his mind. At one time he and Howell had been friends, the best of friends. Perhaps a fragment of that friendship still remained, a fragment worth salvaging. Perhaps even something Trent could use to arrange a trip back to the Inner Sphere . . . He knocked three times and heard a muffled "Enter." Which he did.

Unlike the office of Star Colonel Moon on Hyner, the office of Galaxy Commander Benjamin Howell was much larger. Though lacking a window, its atmosphere was not so forbidding, perhaps a because the illumination from the desk lamps was softer than the ceiling lights common throughout the rest of the complex. Sitting behind the black stone desk was Benjamin Howell. He motioned for Trent to sit. Slowly, without a word, Trent complied.

"It has been a long time, Trent."

"Perhaps not long enough," Trent replied.

"Drink?" Howell asked, pulling a bottle from a lower drawer. "It was isorla from our conquests in the Inner Sphere. I have kept it all this time in hopes of enjoying it one day with a friend."

Trent glared, a flicker of red light from the circuitry coming to life around his artificially enhanced eye. "I still do not drink, Galaxy Commander. And I am no longer sure we are still friends."

Benjamin Howell took out a glass and poured himself a drink. "I read the battle reports of your encounter with the

Explorer Corps on Pivot Prime. Interesting engagement. As always, I admired your tactical acumen. Hitting the compound and forcing them to commit on one flank, then dropping the Elementals on top of them . . . very impressive touch."

"One works with what one has at his disposal," Trent said, leaning back against his chair.

"An impressive victory nonetheless. You always prove that my faith in you was well placed, Trent. And you were working at an extreme disadvantage in my 'Mechs."

" 'Your' BattleMechs? According to the manifests they are intended for the scientists here, for research purposes."

"Paper and digital records," Benjamin said, then took a sip of his drink. "You must know the truth, Trent. This command, defending Huntress, is where they send warriors like me. I am old, over the hill. We have two Galaxies on planet, The Iron Guard and The Watchmen. I tested into this position shortly after my arrival here. As the elder officer, I am technically in charge of both. But they are more men than machines. All new equipment is shipped out with reinforcements—headed for the occupation zone and intended for the day when the invasion of the Inner Sphere begins anew. We get nothing here."

Trent began to understand. "So you have made an arrangement with the scientist caste. They request the BattleMechs for research purposes, then you get them for your own use."

Howell nodded. "Very good Trent, you always had a good grasp of tactics. It is pleasing to see that strategy is also part of your skills."

"Why?"

Benjamin smiled and took another sip of his drink. "The solahma and sibko forces under my command do not have the weapons needed for defense. What I do, I do for the protection of the Jaguar homeworld and our Clan. By borrowing these 'Mechs, I am able to enhance the old SLDF equipment assigned to us. The scientists have also given me a number of prototypes that would normally have been scrapped. My work over the last year and a half has turned these two Galaxies of rifle carriers into a sizable 'Mech-equipped force."

Again, Trent suddenly understood. Huntress was not a heavily armed fortress. Instead it was defended by solahma units and cadets training in their sibkos. By Benjamin Howell's logic, he was acting in the best interests of the Clan.

"You have been refitting your forces covertly. Why not simply go to the Khans and ask them for what you need?"

Benjamin Howell chuckled. "You were always innocent in the ways of politics. Khan Lincoln Osis sent me here in exile. He asked me to nominate Jez in your place for the bloodname—a diehard Crusader in the house of Howell. Then, like the consummate politician, immediately ordered me here to assume command. A command on paper only. No other Clan has waged a Trial on Huntress for over a decade. The only other Clan here is a small base of Jade Falcons in the mountains, and they keep to themselves."

Jade Falcons, on Huntress? Neg! "Why are the Falcons here?" Trent asked.

"It was a gift from ilKhan Leo Showers prior to the start of the Crusade. They have a small base in the mountains called Falcon's Eyrie. I simply call it desolate. While it may rain almost every day here, up there they do not know what the sun in the sky looks like."

"Why not simply challenge them to a Trial and drive them off?"

"Huntress is a large planet, and they keep to themselves. We only see them from time to time. To pursue them would be a waste."

This time it was Trent who chuckled. "Listen to you, Galaxy Commander. There was a time when the mention of the Jade Falcons or any other Clan would have boiled your blood into a battle rage. Now you seem almost complacent."

"Neg," Benjamin parried. "I merely have a broader view than when we were invading the Inner Sphere together. I understand that on the battlefield of politics I am no match for those who lead us. I also know that my main duty is to defend Huntress."

"Defend it from what?"

Howell's eyes narrowed. "At some point the Inner Sphere commanders will learn our location. It may take them at least another ten years, but it is inevitable. When they do, I will be here, waiting for them. And in my command will be fresh warriors and seasoned veterans, trained warriors willing to do my bidding for one last chance to die gloriously in battle. All I have to do is stay alive, and eventually the war will come to me. That is why my actions are so necessary."

Trent looked down at the satchel at his feet. "If you have read the records, you know why I am here."

"You have come to intern Jez Howell. And knowing how well you got along with her, I am sure you want to get the task over as quickly as possible. I must admit, I was a little surprised that you, of all people, were named as her honor guardian."

"Aff," Trent said in a relaxed tone. "My Cluster Commander hates me. He considers me a failure, just as everyone who fought on Tukayyid is a failure in his eyes. He sent me here so that I could ultimately be reassigned—to you. Then he will not have to deal with me. Sending me to Huntress as honor guard was a way to get rid of me, while also handing me a final insult. I have been tasked with guarding the genetic legacy of my greatest foe. And, then, he never has to deal with me again."

"I did read the reports. Your Star Colonel Paul Moon is well known to me. I once thought I could master the seas of Jaguar politics but I ended up here. One day, he too will take my place perhaps, *quiaff?*"

"Aff," Trent said softly, but secretly he was hoping that Paul Moon would meet his fate at Trent's own hands, in battle. "I must go," he said, picking up the satchel and holding it tightly in his grip. "There is an obligation that I must attend to, as you have pointed out."

"Indeed, Trent," Benjamin Howell also rose to his feet. "Your tone has changed since you first came in. Have you decided—are we still friends, you and I?"

"Aye."

"Excellent," Howell said. "Then we shall dine together like in the old days. And perhaps a game of chess as well."

Trent nodded, but his mind was on the duty he had still to perform.

The interior of the genetic repository was a massive chamber carved from stone. Its marbled floors, black, gray, and white, were tiled with the shapes of running Jaguars. The walls, dark and forbidding, all bore dozens of seals. Each showed a name and a digital code, each was the holding place of a giftake. Copies of all genetic samples were also maintained on Strana Mechty, but these were the originals, the very stuff that shaped the warrior caste of Clan Smoke Jaguar.

In the dim lights a white-robed scientist, flanked on either side by Elemental warriors dressed in dark gray, stood in the center of the room. The incense burners on the walls wafted pungent smoke into the air, heightening the solemnity of the moment.

Trent stepped forward and stopped ten meters from the scientist. The man was older than anyone Trent had ever seen, and he wore thick eyeglasses and spoke in a rough voice. "I am the Keeper of the Jaguar kin, the blood of our warriors. Who disturbs this most sacred of places?"

The voice echoed deeply from every angle in the chamber, seeming to shake Trent to his bones. He was sure the vault had been intentionally designed this way, to instill awe and fear in those who came here.

Trent drew a long breath. "I, Trent, of Bloodhouse Howell, stand as honor guard for one who has served with honor." He had rehearsed the lines during the trip in and spoke it in his deepest ceremonial voice.

"Has a blooded warrior passed to nothingness?"

"Neg. A warrior has died, but she lives on." Trent held up the silver container holding Jez's giftake. "I bring you Star Captain Jez Howell of the Delta Galaxy. She died with honor." It was a lie, but it rolled off his tongue as easily as truth.

One of the Elementals took the container and handed it to the scientist, who held a small scanner to the codex embedded in the lid of the cylinder. A flashing green light on the scanner told Trent that all was in order. "I stand here before all assembled to say that a new generation of warriors will carry Jez Howell in their blood. Her substance will live on after we are all gone."

"Seyla," Trent and the Elemental said in low, solemn tones.

"Honor guard, you have fulfilled your duty. Know that this warrior has come home. You have braved the darkness of the stars to intern her, as our ways demand. You serve the Jaguar with honor," the old scientist said, bowing his head.

Trent bowed his in return. He no longer served the Jaguars, but only what Nicholas Kerensky had intended them and the other Clans to be. All that remained now was the journey back to the Inner Sphere, where Trent would seek the chance to fulfill his own honor.

Technician's Quarter
Lootera, Huntress
Kerensky Cluster, Clan Space
19 February 3056

Trent pulled the collar of his raincoat up around his neck as he entered the doorway of building where Judith was staying. The Technician's Quarter of Lootera was far less grand than the Warrior's Quarter. Lacking were the parade fields, the massive granite and marble structures. Here the streets were narrow, the buildings older, yet very well kept. The Tech Quarter had a darker, closer feel to it. More human and inviting than the impersonality of the Warrior Quarter, and oddly quiet.

He had received Judith's message telling him where she had finally managed to billet for the evening. He was more than willing to meet in the Technician's Quarter rather than under the gaze of his fellow warriors. She was waiting for him in the small entrance hall, and then led him up the stairs to her room.

Trent was surprised to see that the Spartan conditions of his quarters were not much better than what his bondsman enjoyed. She closed and secured the door and sat on the edge of the bed as Trent hung his wet coat on a wall hook, then took the lone chair.

"I take it your efforts thus far have been successful, Judith?"

"Aye, Star Captain," she said, producing several optical diskettes from out of her jacket pocket. "There is little military data available on Huntress, but I was able to get maps of the city and some topographical details of the planet." Judith had been scouring the databases for information on the Jaguar homeworld via the terminal in her quarter. Though the data available was limited, it had apparently been enough to keep her up all night making copies of files and appropriate notes.

"Huntress has only a handful of settlements, and these are relatively close. Pahn City and New Andery are agricultural centers and the site of chemical facilities that apparently exploit the jungles for everything of value. Myer and Bagera are mining and processing centers." Like everything in Clan society, things were built with a purpose. "Given enough time, we should be able to get an accurate picture of this world from a military standpoint."

"What are your impressions of the place now that we are finally here, Judith?"

Judith paused, caught off guard by the question. She thought for a moment, then said, "To speak plainly, I am disappointed," she said. "I expected much more. This is the homeworld of the Jaguars, yet from what I have been able to ascertain, it is defended by only two Galaxies. Mount Szabo is a powerful fortress, that I grant you, but a static defense position is a throwback to the ways of the past. And defending the homeworld are warriors the rest of the Clan considers washed-up and past their prime. It seems illogical."

Trent shook his head. "Not really. The focus has been on the invasion of the Inner Sphere. Besides, there is no threat to the homeworlds. The Inner Sphere does not know the path of the Exodus Road." *Yet . . .*

Trent gave Judith a questioning look, which she read immediately.

"No bugs," she said, and Trent was relieved. He was confident of Judith's ability to detect any surveillance devices. Besides, a tech's quarters on the homeworld were not likely to be monitored.

"And the people you have encountered?"

"Content. Yet everything seems subdued compared even to Hyner. It is as if everyone were pre-programmed and is simply going through the motions. I have never been in such a place where I should feel comfortable and do not."

"It is only one day, Judith."

"Aff," she said. "But I do not wish to stay here long for fear of boredom."

"Hopefully we will not be here long."

"Did you meet with your former Commanding Officer?" she asked.

"Aye," Trent said. "Benjamin Howell is now a Galaxy Commander and in charge of the defense of Huntress."

"Impressive." Judith studied his face as though trying to read his thoughts. "Any ideas yet on how we can get re-assigned to the Inner Sphere?"

"Perhaps," Trent said. "Howell is involved with smuggling goods from the Inner Sphere to Huntress."

Judith shook her head slightly. "That does not sound very honorable."

"Neg, it is not what you think. He sees it as the only way to get equipment for his solahma troops. The Khans do not equip the two Galaxies here with sufficient gear. They get whatever old equipment happens to be around and whatever he has been able to improvise. This smuggling he is running is not aimed at profit, but at making sure that the defense of Huntress is sound."

"It is ironic. On the way here, we were forced to destroy an Explorer Corps mission whose goal is the same as ours. Now, you speak as if this smuggling operation might offer us a chance to return to the Inner Sphere . . . Yet it is an operation aimed at strengthening the defense of this place."

Trent nodded. It was truly a paradox. "I am meeting him this evening and hope to put a thought in his brain. I have an idea, and I think I know how to get Galaxy Commander Howell to see things from my point of view."

"Good luck. The information we have gathered on the Exodus Road is of no value unless we can get it away from here and back to the Inner Sphere."

"Aye, Judith. That is so."

Trent entered Galaxy Commander Benjamin Howell's quarters and saw that the small work/dining table was set for a formal meal. Howell wore a casual uniform and smiled as he motioned for Trent to have a seat. Howell was different than Trent remembered from years past. Gone was his sharp edge. *Perhaps his failures have taken the fight out of him.*

"I am pleased that you have come to dine with me this night," Howell began. "Tonight the members of the Golden

Fang Sibko are executing their Trials of Position for a new Galaxy that is being formed."

He activated the holoviewer against one wall. "The Trials are broadcast to all officers, and I thought you might wish to watch." The holoviewer flickered to life, showing an arena with five OmniMechs poised at the outer edges. The Trial had not yet begun.

Satisfied that the image was clear enough, Howell turned back to Trent. "I have a traditional Huntress meal for you—not what our mess hall cooks usually prepare. Bolton steaks, leeks from the Dhuan swamps, Steel Viper eggs from the depths of the Shikari jungles. I think you will find it pleasing."

Trent looked at his plate, happy that it was not the typical military fare he had been on since leaving Hyner. "From one warrior to another, such food is appreciated, Galaxy Commander."

"There is no need for formality here, Trent. I am Benjamin."

Trent took a bite of the steak, its taste hot and peppery in his mouth. "Spending time with you is appreciated," he said, "but I hope to begin the trip back soon."

Benjamin's fork hesitated on the trip to his mouth, and he lowered it back to his plate. "Interesting that you mentioned this. I received a communications packet from Star Colonel Paul Moon almost three weeks ago, Trent. He has petitioned me to accept your transfer into the Iron Guards Galaxy. He cited your age and lack of bloodname as justification."

Trent was not surprised by the news and maintained his composure. "And your thoughts on this?"

"You will be of an age for assignment to a solahma unit by the time you would return to the Inner Sphere," Howell said slowly as though not wanting to offend. "And I must admit, having you, an old friend and protégé, here has some appeal. There are several special projects underway, operations hidden in the jungles south of here. Our breeding program has been expanded greatly, and I have several of the new sibkos assigned to testing these covert projects. When they are complete, the Inner Sphere will be facing a new technological terror and will again fear the roar of the Jaguar."

"New technology, *quiaff*?"

"Affirmative. Our scientist caste is remarkable. While our comrades in the Inner Sphere have allowed those filthy freebirths to catch up with our technological edge, here on Huntress we are forging the new weapons to retake Terra."

Trent wanted to press further, but he was afraid of tipping his hand or putting Howell on guard. For now, his curiosity would have to wait. "I have been thinking," he said between bites. "I can be of use to you in the Inner Sphere."

Benjamin tipped his head and raised one eyebrow. "How is that?"

"You need arms and armaments for your forces here. As a warrior, I could gain access to a wide variety of equipment. My having a bondsman as a tech could also prove useful to your efforts. Combined with whatever operations you already have in place, you might find me a great asset, *quiaff*?"

On the holoviewer, the Trial began as the OmniMechs swept in on each other, weapons blazing. One of the 'Mechs fell quickly in a holographic explosion, the warrior ejecting just as his 'Mech went up in flames. Trent and Howell cast occasional glances at the holovid as they spoke, then turned back to each other.

"What you say has merit, Trent. Why would you make such an offer, though? My actions must seem on the far side of honor."

"Aff, but I understand your logic. You know me well enough to understand that I seek only to fight and die in honorable combat. I will not find that here on Huntress. If I did return to the Inner Sphere and then eventually get re-assigned back to you, the knowledge that I had helped equip Zeta Galaxy would mean a great deal to me. From my perspective, I can only win from such an arrangement."

Howell had turned back to the holoviewer, watching for a moment as a *Summoner* toppled over in response to a barrage by a devastating *Warhawk*. "I have neither acknowledged nor accepted the request from your Star Colonel Moon."

"I am grateful," Trent said. "And I would consider it a personal favor if you would let me return instead to the Inner Sphere." He paused and thought hard about his next words before speaking. "After you withdrew my nomination for the Howell bloodname, I wanted to kill you. But now I see that you have been as much a victim of politics as I have and that my lust for revenge was misplaced."

The two fell silent again as they watched another one of the

Trial contestants, a *Mad Dog*, being shredded and destroyed by the sheer firepower of the battered *Warhawk*. The *Warhawk* walked backward, putting enough distance between itself and the remaining contestant, a *Timber Wolf*, to unleash his 'Mech's deadly PPCs. The *Timber Wolf* sagged under the brilliant blue lightning, then tipped over, slowly, almost drunkenly.

"Spectacular, is it not?" Howell said, shaking his head in admiration.

"He may have earned the rank of Star Captain with that kill," Trent said, reading the name of the combatant appearing on the holoviewer. *Kerndon . . . this was one to watch.* "So, Trent, you would like to be sent back to the Inner Sphere?" Howell took a sip from his glass. "Perhaps this would be a chance for me to right a wrong I have done you. I cost you your bloodname, but will not deprive you of a chance to die as a real warrior.

"For your actions on Pivot, an engagement that successfully protected the location of the homeworlds from our enemies, I hereby refuse the request of Star Colonel Moon. You will return to the Inner Sphere on assignment. And when you do, you will 'assist' the special operation I have revealed to you."

"I will not disappoint you, Benjamin," Trent said in a calm tone that belied his true feelings.

"You never have, Trent." Benjamin Howell set his glass down. "The *Dhava* and the *Admiral Andrews* will complete their maintenance in a few days. You will take command of a Trinary of replacement troops and equipment on its way to the Inner Sphere."

"Tonight," Trent said, lifting his glass in a toast, "let the Smoke Jaguar roar at the moon and our enemies tremble in their skins . . ."

= 28 =

Jaguar Spaceport
Lootera, Huntress
Kerensky Cluster, Clan Space
12 March 3056

The fifteen warriors followed the sibko instructor out onto the spaceport tarmac to where Galaxy Commander Benjamin Howell and Trent stood. It was mid-afternoon, the only time of day when the sun managed to break through Huntress' seemingly endless murky skies. The Kit Master, a warrior older than Trent, bore the rank of Star Captain. Her hair was black but streaked with gray.

She was a warrior who now spent her days training a sibko of cadets, and Trent wondered if she felt bitter at being deprived of the only thing for which she had been born and bred—a life in the field. A life of combat. He would never understand that this was all a Clan warrior had to look forward to if he or she did not earn a bloodname or die in battle. What else could a warrior do but make war?

She held a small noteputer in her armpit as she stood at the head of the formation of newly qualified warriors. "I am Star Captain Glenda, Kit Master for these so-called warriors."

Trent was familiar with the nuances of the Smoke Jaguar ritual of assuming command from another officer. "I am Star Captain Trent, and these warriors are now mine to lead."

"Command is not assumed but taken by the prowess of blood in battle," she replied.

Trent bowed his head to acknowledge her words. The ritual called for the shedding of blood, and was sometimes simply a gesture, sometimes a full-blown test of combat skill. Trent had already decided which it was to be. He stepped forward and threw a furious jab with his right fist. Enhanced by myomer muscles, his attack was faster than any normal warrior's, though Glenda did try to dodge to the side. His fist dug into her cheek, twisting her face and head under the impact. She lost her balance, spinning and falling to the steaming surface of the tarmac. She was quickly back on her feet, a thin stream of blood trickling out the corner of her mouth.

"Blood has been drawn," she said, picking up the note-puter and handing it to him. "Duty fulfilled." Rubbing her jaw once, Glenda then pivoted and marched away, leaving Trent with the Trinary of troops.

He faced them squarely and barked his order clearly. "Trinary, fall in!" In swift precision they marched off toward the DropShip *Dhava,* which stood awaiting them in the distance. Trent watched them walk off, then turned to Benjamin Howell, who stepped up next to him.

"You know the names of my contacts in the Inner Sphere, *quiaff*?" Howell said.

Trent nodded.

"Excellent. This Trinary is intended as replacements for Delta Galaxy. Your Star Colonel Moon will be receiving word in the coming months that his request for you to be assigned to Huntress is denied, but I may see to it that the message is lost in transmission. Either way, you must depart immediately.

"One day, Trent, you may be returned here as solahma. Should that day come, I will be proud to have you under my command."

Trent did not think he would ever see Benjamin Howell again, but said nothing. If he returned to Huntress, it would be at the head of a force against it—never to fight here in defense of the Smoke Jaguars.

He gave Howell a salute, executed his most precise pivot, and set off toward the waiting DropShip.

In the near-zero gravity of the *Dhava*'s exercise room, Trent jogged on the specially designed treadmill, sweat glistening over his natural skin as he pushed for yet another kilometer.

His shirt was mostly soaked in sweat, as were his shorts, but he knew the importance of staying fit, especially on such a long journey. He looked up and saw Judith enter the room, using handholds to navigate her way to the harness straps for the weight resistance gear.

"May I join you?" she asked.

Trent nodded as he puffed each breath out steadily. Reaching up, he tapped the button to cut his speed, lessening the tension on the harness that held him over the device.

Judith finished strapping herself into the trainer and keyed in the amount of resistance she desired, then began bench-pressing against the resistance pads. "I did not see you in the observation lounge during liftoff," she said, catching her breath after one set. "Over the past week you have become so quiet and withdrawn. Is something wrong?"

Trent switched off the treadmill and came to a stop, leaning on his forearms and drawing in several gulps of air. "Now that we are actually heading back to the Inner Sphere, I have much on my mind."

"What we have accomplished in the last few weeks is remarkable, do you not agree, *quiaff*?"

"Aff," Trent said. Judith was right. The data they had gathered on the Huntress system and its defenses was priceless. They had stumbled onto a number of interesting details from their contacts in the warrior and technician castes—everything from information about the undersea base to hints of the covert sibko and training project deep in the jungles. "We have more than enough information for your contacts in ComStar. They should be pleased with our work."

She waited to see if he would say more, then asked, "Do you wish to talk?"

Trent toweled away the sweat that clung to the left side of his face and unfastened the harness. "My resolve has not wavered, Judith. It is just that I am thinking not of our actions, but the results of those actions."

"I do not understand," she grunted, pushing up on the resistance bar with all of her might.

"What we are doing is the right thing. Once I reached that decision I never questioned it. But what will the Inner Sphere do with the coordinates and locations that we are providing them? I am a warrior. I can only assume they will use it to mount some sort of assault against the Smoke Jaguars."

Judith stopped for a second and sat up, looking at Trent as he stepped off the treadmill. "Aye, I expect they will."

"If the Inner Sphere brings war to Huntress, many innocent people will die, people who have no concept of the Inner Sphere's way of waging war." Clan tradition called for warriors to only fight other warriors. There were no raids on industrial facilities. If a commander wanted to seize a town, he would simply issue a batchall for it, a combat trial would be fought, and the victor would control the town.

It was different in the Inner Sphere, where the Jaguars and the other Clans had faced an enemy who struck at resources as well as opposing warriors. The simple elegance of the Clan way was lost in the Inner Sphere. They did not seem to abhor waste if it meant victory, while to the Clans the destruction of resources was nearly unthinkable.

Judith nodded in understanding. "From what I have seen here, the lower castes and the Jaguars as a whole would be appalled at the way the Inner Sphere fights. The people of the homeworlds are far from what has happened in the Inner Sphere. What information they do get is carefully filtered and distilled for them. What they consider to be 'barbaric' is the norm in the militaries of the Inner Sphere—including even the Star League Defense Force from which the Clans evolved."

Trent heard her words and closed his eyes, rubbing the metallic circle of silvery circuitry around his right eye as if it would ease his mind. "The question I have been pondering is whether I am taking the Smoke Jaguars into a potentially genocidal fight?"

"Trent," Judith said, using his name rather than his rank for the first time since she had known him. "You are doing what must be done. You are humane. When the people of Chinn were going to be annihilated, you risked your own life to save them. From what I have been taught and read, the great Kerenskys never envisioned their people as destroyers. But that is what our Khans would turn us into. Think of those who were murdered in Edo, Chinn, Beaver Falls—all in the name of retribution, revenge, punishment. They were innocents, innocents who were executed in the name of Jaguar justice."

"That is the point, Judith. I have had much time to think of what will be the outcome of our plan, and I fear that I will be

doing to my kindred what my superiors have done to innocents of the Inner Sphere."

"Neg," Judith replied. "The warrior caste wages war
because they are bred to it. That is who they are, all the know.
The commanders play politics with their officers' lives, yet in
the same breath condemn such actions if challenged.

"The truth of the matter, Trent, is that our plan is on the
side of right. If the Inner Sphere ever does strike at the
Smoke Jaguars—if they take the fight straight to every
member of the Clan in every caste, maybe then this invasion
and the killing can come to a stop."

Trent wrapped a towel around his neck and turned to
leave. Judith's logic was sound. He had mulled it over thousands of times and had arrived at the same conclusion.

"We will take readings along the way back," he said,
"checking both the neutrino and spectral analysis from our
voyage in. Oftentimes ships follow different jump routes
along the Exodus Road, and we need to take that into
account.

"If we are going to complete this act of honor, we must do
it right."

=== 29 ===

DropShip **Dhava**
Zenith Jump Point, Unnamed Planet
The Exodus Road
27 May 3056

Trent felt a slight wave of dizziness as the JumpShip *Admiral Andrews* emerged at the jump point of this unnamed world. He was finding the long trip back to the Inner Sphere even slower and more tedious than before, especially since their ship had been forced to wait at two recharge stations while priority went to several other starships bound for the Inner Sphere. Star Commander Allen had not said much, other than that those ships were headed for a planet called Wayside V and were assigned to the newly formed Tau Galaxy. It made no matter to Trent. He had his own concerns. They could not wait, but he had no choice.

The Trinary given to him to command while the unit traveled to its new posting in the Inner Sphere was proving to be a real challenge. It was not their skills that were lacking. On the contrary, from what Trent had seen of their ratings in the simulator pods and in workouts, they were skilled. It was their attitude that was disturbing. Among themselves, they behaved as warriors should toward one another, but they were contemptuous of him, almost to the point of insubordination. Compared to the solahma warriors he had brought back to Huntress, these green trueborns were arrogant.

Trent was in his cabin dressing, readying himself for a

meeting with these green troops. He looked in the mirror and touched the synthskin on the right side of his face. He rarely thought about the scars and changes to his face, but seeing his reflection now, he suddenly remembered what his face had been before the bloodbath on Tukayyid, the face he had worn before the fires changed him forever. It had been the face of a younger warrior . . . *like the warriors in my command.*

Examining his ruined face, he thought he understood what was wrong and what his charges saw when they looked at him. Their minds had been corrupted by those who trained them. They had been told the lies about what happened on Tukayyid.

This was nothing new. He had seen this before. There was only one way to clear up the matter, one way these young warriors would not fail to understand.

Judith was on her way to the 'Mech bay for routine maintenance of the replacement OmniMechs the ship was bringing to the Inner Sphere when she ran into Trent apparently headed in the same direction. After all their time together, she had learned to read the expressions on his mutilated face. "Is something wrong, Star Captain?"

"Aye," he replied. "It is a matter that has been brewing for some time."

Judith nodded. She too had been concerned about the green troops. "Your new command?"

"You see much, Judith."

She smiled. "Your chess game has been off thus far on the trip, and you have added nearly two hours to your exercise routine. Something is bothering you, and it is not the data on Huntress. I have seen how the greenies act around you, and I have overheard their comments in the 'Mech bay when you leave and they remain."

"They hate me," Trent said.

"They do not know you."

"Exactly. But I intend to remedy that within the next few minutes." They had reached the entrance to the 'Mech bay, and he tapped the control to open the door.

As he entered, Trent saw his young charges standing around a portable holoviewer in the simulator area. They were reviewing a tactical map and discussing the various ways to deal with a scenario, a common training practice before a simulator run. Some warriors glanced casually in his direction as Trent approached, but none so much as acknowledged his presence.

No, Trent thought. *Not this time.* He reached down and hit the control on the side of the table that shut off the holoprojector. The three-dimensional map winked off into nothingness.

"Is there a problem, Star Captain?" one of the warriors, Kenneth, said.

"Aff," Trent said. "The problem is with you." He pointed at Kenneth, then to another pair of them. "And you and you. In fact, the problem is with all of you."

"Yes, there is a problem," a shorter muscular female named Alexandra said. "You have interrupted our simulation for no reason."

"I am your ranking officer. I need no reason."

"You have caused waste in erasing that simulation, and waste is not to be tolerated," she said.

Trent gave her a pencil-thin smile. "Alexandra," he said, "your tone is insulting to me as your senior and as a warrior. I challenge you to a Trial of Grievance."

"Over mere words?" she said.

"Neg, over behavior unbecoming to a Jaguar officer. You will fight for your sibkittens," he said, using the derogatory phrase Kit Masters often favored in sibko training. "If you dare."

The other warriors moved into a rough circle around Trent and Alexandra. Trent knew she was one of the best among them, destined one day to lead. He had seen that in her.

She balled up her fists and lowered her stance. Trent did not. He remained almost casual, as seemingly indifferent to her as she had been to him just moments before. He looked around at the other warriors. They were watching intently as if they savored the beating she was about to hand him. Trent knew there were risks, but he had survived so many more fights than she had. Her edge was speed, but even that could be defeated by the skill that came only with experience.

Moving into position, he glimpsed Judith, perched atop a stout *Cauldron-Born* in one of the nearby stalls. She gave him a thumbs-up sign. Trent also saw Star Commander Allen appear near the bay entrance, arms crossed as he watched. Somehow word had gotten to him that something was going on in the 'Mech bay.

"You hate me, kit," Trent said as he lowered his own stance. "Why is that?"

Alexandra's expression seemed to harden as the muscles of her face and neck tightened. "You were there. You had your chance to lead us to victory and failed. Because of the likes of you, we are not traveling to a new Star League, but to an 'occupation zone.' " She spit out the last words as if they tasted bad in her mouth.

"You think I am weak, Alexandra?"

"Affirmative. Weak and a pitiful excuse for a warrior. Our Kit Masters have told us how your generation of warriors failed our Clan. How failures like you led to our defeats on Luthien and Tukayyid."

Trent saw others nodding in agreement. *So much the better* . . . "Let us end your torment now, kit," he said in a low tone, thrusting his artificially enhanced arm and fist at Alexandra with lightning speed. She moved almost fast enough to dodge the blow, but not quite. He hit the side of her face in a glancing shot, ripping at her ear. She swung back, hitting him hard in the side, and his ribs screamed at the blow.

Trent pulled back as she tried to throw another punch, blocking her this time with his left arm. It was enough to slow her, enough for him to bring his powerful right arm back into play, hitting her with sledgehammer force in the stomach. The impact of the blow threw Alexandra backward and knocked her to the ground, but she skidded to a stop in zero-g and sought to regain her breath.

He moved in close to her as she lifted herself to a squatting position and leapt at him, her face a mask of fury. She struck him with the full force of her body, wrapping her arms around him in a crushing hug. Trent's arms were pinned at his sides as she hefted him off the floor slightly. Even his myomer-enhanced muscles were unable to break her powerful grip. She squeezed tightly, as if she wanted to see the life ooze out of his body. He had the use of his legs, and kicked her in the shin with all his might, but Alexandra held on.

Face to face she held him, gritting her teeth. Sweat ran down her brow. "Warriors like you dishonor us all," she said, squeezing him more.

Trent too was slick with sweat. "You have so much to learn, kit," he said. His tone was as calm as he could muster, mocking her efforts to crush him.

She lifted him up and carried him closer to the edge of the Circle of Equals. She was going for the easy way. She would toss him out of the Circle and declare victory. But it was not going to be easy for her, even wearing her magnetic shoes in the light gravity of the 'Mech bay. Trent tipped his head back slightly, then brought it forward, smashing it into her skull with incredible force.

The head butt was made worse by the optical control circuits around his eye. The circle of ferro-titanium circuitry was surgically cemented to his skull, and dug into the skin of Alexandra's forehead like metal prongs. She let him go, staggering backward, stunned.

Trent saw his chance. Swinging his right fist furiously, he caught her as she swayed near the edge of the Circle. The blow lifted her upward slightly, then dropped her unconscious onto the deck. Trent's lungs ached as he bent to grab her by the uniform collar. Using his enhanced muscles, he lifted her up off the floor and held her in the air with the one hand. Blood ran down from the wound on her brow, then floated as droplets in the air. He held her up like a dead animal for the others to see.

"Look at her," Trent said coolly. "And let this be a lesson to your arrogance." He swung her limp body around in the nearly non-existent gravity so that everyone in the Circle of Equals could see her, crushed and defeated.

"I was like you once," he said, drawing a difficult breath of air, his side aching from Alexandra's earlier blow. "I thought I and my kind were superior. But then I fought in many battles and learned what it means to be a warrior. I risked all, and lost much." He looked at his own oddly muscled arm that held Alexandra and winced in memory of what he had lost in the service of the Jaguar.

"Yes, I fought on Tukayyid," he said, still holding her body like a limp doll. "In battle against a worthy foe, I slew many of the enemy. As proud a Smoke Jaguar warrior then as I am now."

He tossed Alexandra directly at two of the young warriors, who stepped quickly aside as her body fell outside of the Circle. "She was your best, yet I, one who you scorn, have bested her. I, Trent, Star Captain of the Jaguar, was once again victorious."

He looked into the eyes of Kenneth, then Rupert. "Today your training begins anew. Today I will teach you what I know so that one day, you too may survive . . . survive that you too may live to tell of what you have seen and learned."

Trent could see that they feared him now, but he saw something else in their eyes too. He had broken them by defeating Alexandra. Gone were the cockiness and arrogance. What he saw in their eyes now was respect. Trent knew that for the rest of the journey, he could lead and they would follow.

Judith moved her rook forward to an aggressive stance on the portable chessboard, then lifted her fingers hesitantly. She watched Trent across the small table. He was studying the board with deep concentration. A minute or so passed, and he suddenly looked up at her.

"Is there something wrong, Judith? Why do you stare at me so?"

"Nothing is wrong, Star Captain," Judith said. "I was just thinking about what happened earlier today. I never expected you to take much interest in these new warriors we are escorting back to the Inner Sphere. Yet you confronted them to win their respect. You did not have to do this."

"You have read *The Remembrance*," he said. "In one of the most famous passages Nicholas Kerensky said, 'The highest calling a warrior can have is to honor—even beyond allegiance to his Clan.'"

"You are answering a higher calling then, *quiaff*?"

Trent smiled as he moved his remaining knight, taking out her bishop. "Aff. I believe many Smoke Jaguars have lost sight of true honor as taught by Nicholas Kerensky. But I must not. No matter what I have done or will one day do, I am still a Clan warrior. I have a duty to fulfill and will carry it out to the best of my ability. It is something my superiors cannot crush out of me."

He reached across the table and pointed to her king. "Checkmate, *quiaff*?"

═══ 30 ═══

A knocking at his door made Star Colonel Paul Moon look up from the display built into his desk. "Enter," he said, and Star Captain Oleg Nevversan came through the door.

"Star Captain," Moon said cordially.

"Sir," Nevversan began nervously, not even bothering to close the door all the way.

"What is it, Star Captain?"

"Sir, you were expecting the replacement troops to arrive this morning, *quiaff*?"

"Aff," Moon said. "Two of the Stars will be used to reactivate Jez Howell's former Trinary. Has the ship been delayed?"

"Neg," Nevversan said. "They arrived at the spaceport an hour ago, complete with the 'Mechs and supplies we were expecting."

"Then everything is in order," Moon said.

"Neg, sir. There is something you should know—" Nevversan was cut off by a knock at the door, a movement that made the door swing open. Seeing the face of the man who stood there, Paul Moon rose from his chair, stunned.

Trent, garbed in his finest dress uniform, stood in the doorway and saluted as Oleg Nevversan made way, stepping to the side. Paul Moon looked as if he were seeing a specter from beyond the grave. His mouth hung slightly open for a long embarrassing moment as Trent took a formal stance in front of his commanding officer.

"Star Captain Trent reporting for duty, Star Colonel."

"Neg!" Moon stammered. "What are *you* doing here?"

"This is what I was trying to tell you," Star Captain Nevversan said in a low tone. Moon shot him a furious look and gestured for Nevversan to leave the room. Nevversan bowed his head quickly and departed, this time closing the door tightly.

Trent allowed himself a thin smile of satisfaction over the distress aroused by his return. "I am reporting for duty, Star Colonel Moon. Having fulfilled my obligation as Star Captain Jez's honor guard, I was assigned command of the warriors arriving here as replacements."

Moon's face turned a bright red, and every muscle in his body seemed to tense as he glared at Trent. "I filed a formal request to have you posted to the homeworlds as a solahma warrior. You have no business here."

Trent tipped his head slightly. "Galaxy Commander Benjamin Howell informed me that you had made such a request. Frankly, I am surprised that he has not contacted you to advise you of the status of your request. On the trip back to Huntress our ship encountered an Explorer Corps force attempting to seize one of our HPG relays along the Exodus Road. I and the other warriors you had decided were fit only for the scrap heap recaptured the relay station and, as a result, prevented the enemy from obtaining knowledge of the Exodus Road."

"And for this he refused my request?"

"Affirmative. He said that despite my age and lack of a bloodname, I still had much to offer my Clan."

Moon pounded one of his massive fists against the desk top, shaking it with the force of his blow. "Your return here is a violation of our Clan traditions. You are old, and by all rights should be serving with fellow solahma warriors. You do not belong here, Trent."

"Permission to speak freely, Star Colonel?"

Moon stared at him in pure rage. "Aff," he said through gritted teeth.

"I *am* here and there is nothing you can do about it . . . sir. Your request to transfer me has been denied. Until I prove myself unworthy of command, I am still on active duty with The Stormriders. In fact, I know from reports I downloaded during approach that you have formally announced plans to reactivate Star Captain Jez Howell's unit with the new forces I have brought with me today."

"Aff," Moon said.

"Then as a ranking Star Captain, I want to compete to lead this Binary."

"Neg! Impossible!" Moon shouted. "I will not have the likes of you serving in my command."

Trent remained calm and collected in his speech, as if he had rehearsed it numerous times. It was that which seemed to stir the blood of the Star Colonel, making him even more furious.

"Star Colonel Moon, you do not have a choice. Having tested as a Star Captain, I qualify for command of a Binary or Trinary. Even if you attempt to thwart me and do not reform the unit, I will qualify for at least a Star to command."

Moon grinned viciously. "You are correct. You are entitled, but I can call for a Trial of Position for any command you covet."

"Affirmative, and I will win, Star Colonel."

"Arrogance is unbecoming a warrior," Moon growled.

"You would know, *quiaff*?" Trent snapped back.

Moon's eyes narrowed, and he leaned across the table, his reddened face glistening with a thin film of perspiration. "Listen here, Star Captain Trent. Words are not victories. I have shown you once before what happens when you attempt to oppose me. Go down that road, and I assure you, the next time we face off in a Circle of Equals, I will kill you. I will drink your blood and urinate on your giftake before I see you serve under me again."

Trent said nothing. He threw his superior officer a quick salute, performed a perfect about-face, and left the office.

"Trent!" an excited voice called from behind him. As the autumn sun beat down on him, Trent spun and saw Russou, his sibmate and comrade in arms, racing across the parade grounds toward him. Trent walked forward to meet him, and the two gave each other a firm handshake of friendship.

Trent smiled at the sight of his old friend's name patch, which now read "Russou Howell." *Much has changed since I departed.*

"I heard you had returned," Russou said with an answering big smile. "Somehow I always knew you would."

"Much to the disappointment of our commanding officer," Trent replied. "It is good to see you, Russou."

"As it is you," Russou said. "Huntress . . . you really traveled all the way to the homeworlds and back? Tell me, Trent, what is Huntress like?"

Trent searched his mind for the words to describe the Smoke Jaguar homeworld. "Impressive, yet at the same time bleak. It rained most of the time we were there. Lootera's Warrior Quarter has many signs of tribute to the Jaguar, and I have stood on the observation deck of Mount Szabo and seen the jungles beyond the city. It is beautiful, yet it seemed small to me even compared to Hyner."

Trent clapped Russou on the back. "And you, old friend, it seems you have not been idle since my departure." He gestured to the name patch.

"Two weeks after you left I won Jez's bloodname. It was not so easy to get a nomination, but in the end I bested the other contestants. If I had not won it, Star Colonel Moon would surely have sent me back to Huntress to join you."

Trent stared longingly at the name tag. *Jez's bloodname— my bloodname.* She had cheated him out of the chance to win a bloodright, and because of that, Russou now claimed what might have been his. "Congratulations, old friend," was all he said.

"And you, returning in time to compete for a command. That is either very good or very bad timing."

Trent laughed softly. "Bad for both of us. The Star Colonel is reforming Beta Trinary, *quiaff*?"

"Aff."

Trent drew a deep breath as he thought of what he would say next. "There will be a Trial of Position for the command I seek. We may face each other, old friend."

Russou nodded. "Aye, I have taken a new command recently, but I too desire Jez's former command. We will fight, and I am sure one of us will win this prize."

Trent smiled. "Then it will be settled in the way of the Clan, in battle."

"Just remember, Trent, you are fighting me, not our Star Colonel."

"Were that the case, I assure you the battle would be to the death."

"He hates you too, Trent. He has left no doubt about that since the day you left. He sees you as one of those to blame for our failure on Tukayyid. He sees me as weak simply for being your friend."

"It is something he will have to get over—in time."

"Affirmative," Russou added. "But in the meantime you must tread carefully, my friend. Our Star Colonel is surely brewing up some scheme to get rid of you once and for all."

"You!" came a voice from behind Judith as she set down her kit pack. She spun and saw Master Tech Phillip walking across the 'Mech repair bay in a fury, his bulky frame seeming to ball up in anger at her sight.

Judith had expected this reaction. It had been almost two years, but she was sure Phillip would not welcome her return. He had thought to be rid of her for good. Added to that, she had reported to the 'Mech bay rather than to his office first, a subtle insult intended to spark his rage.

It was not the most prudent move, but Judith knew she had to end the cycle of his abuse, and the pretext of her return from the homeworlds would do that. Besides, besting him once was all it would take.

She stood facing him, hands resting defiantly on her hips. "Master Tech Phillip, I was just coming to report to you for active duty."

He stopped in front of her and drew his hand back to deliver a blow to her face. He had done it before, dozens of times. The memory of the abuse she'd endured at his hands fueled her own wave of rage. *Not this time, Phillip.* His fist flew toward her face, but before it could make contact, Judith had swung her arm up and blocked it with her forearm. Then, she slammed into his stomach with a rapid jab of her other fist.

Phillip was caught totally unprepared for her return strike. She had never done anything like that before. He rose slowly to a semi-upright position and rubbed his gut to ease the pain he still felt. Judith stood ready to throw another punch if necessary.

She did not give him a chance to talk. "You may be the Master Tech, but I am of your caste and do not intend to tolerate anymore of your abuse. This"—she tugged at her bondcord, holding it in front of him—"no longer grants you permission to strike me at your whim. I have proven myself to the Clan time and time again. I have been to our homeworld, walked in the jungles at night, seen the Smoke Jaguar on the prowl. You will treat me as an equal or you will die."

"You will pay for your insolence," he spat, finally standing upright.

"Negative, Phillip. You attempted to manipulate the Star Colonel in sending me and my bondmaster away. But we are back. And if you ever raise a fist against me again, it had better kill me. Otherwise I will take your life with my bare hands. Do we have an understanding, *quiaff*?"

Deep red flooded the chubby face of the Master Tech as he stared back at her. He said nothing until she barked out again. *"Quiaff!"*

"Aff, Judith. For now, you have the upper hand."

As it should be forever, Phillip. . . .

═══ 31 ═══

Smoke Jaguar Planetary Command Post
Warrenton, Hyner
Smoke Jaguar Occupation Zone
30 August 3057

The hovercar sped out of Warrenton with Judith at the controls. Neither she nor Trent said anything as they drove away from Warrenton. Both seemed to be breathing in the midmorning sunshine, so welcome after more than a year of traveling by JumpShip from Huntress, not to mention the foul weather of that place. Judith felt the sun's heat penetrating her lightweight jacket and warming her gray shirt underneath. She remembered the first time they had taken this trip almost two years ago, the first time she had brought Trent here, to this special place, the one place on Hyner they could call their own.

Trent had been pensive since his victory in the Trial of Position, quiet, almost withdrawn into his own thoughts. The contest had, in the end, resulted in Trent's victory. It had been close, but now Trent commanded Beta Trinay, Jez's former command. Russou, despite losing to Trent, had behaved like a true warrior and bore no ill will.

But Judith knew everything would be fine once they were in the Castle Brian. In that place she was more than a tech and he was more than a warrior. There, in those ruins, they had stood among things that had not been disturbed for centuries and breathed the same air as men and women of a greater time in the history of humankind. There, she and Trent seemed to gather power and strength anew.

This was their first trip back since returning to Hyner. Both had been kept very busy with duties. Trent was reorganizing his new Trinary of warriors, including Russou and his Star. He had the members of his new command constantly drilling in their new 'Mechs—which in turn kept Judith and the other techs busy.

As she made the turn onto Braddock Pike heading north, Judith sensed Trent becoming uneasy. She knew why. They would once again drive past the ruins of Chinn, and she knew he had never ceased to blame himself for its destruction. Judith had even more urgent matters to talk about this afternoon, and hoped it would help chase away the ghosts of Chinn.

"I have encountered some problems in reaching my contacts," she said.

Trent stirred slightly, as though unwilling to break the silence in the hovercar. "Problems?"

She did not take her eyes from the road. "My contact was present on-planet when we first returned, but when I tried to contact her again, she was gone."

"Do you think she has been discovered?"

Judith shook her head. "Neg. I know several techs in the medical center of the command post. If someone was being interrogated, I would have been able to find out. I think my contact has gone to ground for some reason."

"We have no way to pass on the information we have recovered then," Trent said.

Judith shook her head, but did not take her eyes from the road. "Not at this time."

He pounded his fist into the dashboard, startling her with this uncharacteristic show of rage.

"This is beyond belief, Judith. We have traveled to the Kerensky Cluster and back. We have managed to plot the position of every jump point between Huntress and the Inner Sphere. We possess information that every House Lord would kill for, and we cannot get that information away."

"I have an idea," she said. "With my ComStar contact in hiding or otherwise detained, it might be possible to make use of the HPG here on Hyner to get a coded message out."

"Do you think your Com Guard compatriots would come to Hyner to attempt to recover us?"

"I assume you want me to answer honestly."

"Aye."

"No," she said. "I do not think they will come here to extract us. The risks of crossing the Occupation Zone border are much too great. To do so might be interpreted as a violation of the Truce of Tukayyid. Besides, our entire Cluster is here. The Stormriders are a potent threat—a front-line unit. Somebody would have to show up with nearly a regiment of their own troops."

"There has to be a way for us to get off Hyner and take the information with us," Trent said. "I have heard reports of the Wolves carrying out raids against Jaguar targets, but I see no way for us to leverage that to our advantage. Even if the Stormriders are pressed into that fight, we would not be sent anywhere that would put us within reach of ComStar."

She understood the urgency of his need to pass on the Exodus Road data. Trent had told her all about Galaxy Commander Benjamin Howell and his operation. They had spent many hours discussing the small-time smuggling operation during chess games aboard the *Dhava* on the long trip back from Huntress. Some of Benjamin's lower-caste cronies had been trying to contact Trent, but he had managed to evade them thus far. He had never really intended to get involved in that operation.

The problem, as she had pointed out to Trent, with such operations is that sooner or later they unravel. And when they do, all parties connected with them are exposed. In this case, that would include Trent. And the Exodus Road data stored in his wristcomp would fall when he did.

This was not a time to panic, but the moment for making careful plans. After all they had been through, a foolish and hasty mistake now might cost them everything.

"I suggest that we both remain on guard, but otherwise exercise patience," she said. "Sooner or later something will present itself, some way for us to leave Hyner. When it does, we will take advantage of it and depart. It is also possible that my contact will surface at any time. If she does, we can at least get some direction from ComStar on how to proceed."

"Affirmative," Trent replied. "There is nothing we *can* do but wait. The problem is that patience is not a virtue drilled into us in the sibkos. The Smoke Jaguar is always first to pounce into battle. I do understand the tactical necessity of waiting for the right moment to strike, but it does not come naturally to me."

Judith nodded. "I had the same problem," she said.

"What changed you?"

She looked over at him. The man next to her was horribly scarred, and despite the synthetic skin that covered half his face, a stranger would probably see him as a monster—burned and disfigured. She saw something else, something beyond the scars, something deep inside him. He was a man of honor and integrity, and she respected that.

It is time to say it out loud, to speak it to him. "My lesson in patience was you."

"Me?"

"Aff. I told you that I was once a member of ROM, which is an intelligence branch of ComStar," she said, watching the road carefully. "What I did not tell you was that I never left ROM. I had been trained for special missions, covert operations, black operations. When the Clans invaded I was posted to the Com Guards, not as a soldier so much as an infiltration—should the opportunity ever present itself.

"My superiors were sure the Com Guards would one day engage the Clans in battle. If they did, I was to use any and all means at my disposal to penetrate the Clans and learn all I could. If possible, I was to search for clues to the Exodus Road. My mission orders left plenty of room to improvise. My Com Guard superiors had no idea that I was still in the employ of ROM. Only the Precentor Martial himself was aware.

"On Tukayyid I fought you in order to survive. It was sheer luck that you took me as a bondsman. It has been years, but now we are on the brink of achieving what I set out to do."

Trent was silent for a moment. "I am merely a mission to you?"

She bit her lip. "Neg, Trent, you are more than that." So much more. Judith felt a longing for him that sometimes left her whole body tingling with frustrated desire. Even as she drove, she felt the air between them charged with invisible sparks of electricity. "I have come to care for you, Trent."

Trent lowered his head. "I understand what you feel, Judith," he said almost softly.

"You do?"

"Aff. But here, now, we are still Smoke Jaguars. Coupling

between the castes is illicit. Perhaps Judith, once we leave here . . . we can be . . . more."

She was about to try again to express her longing and desire, but something in the road ahead suddenly took all her attention. Two laser rifle-armed infantry stood behind a barricade in the road, weapons in hand. Their armored vests, thigh pads, and tinted-glass helmets made them appear totally menacing. She took her foot off the accelerator and let the hovercar slow.

Trent shot her a quick glance, then smiled. "Remain calm, Judith. I will deal with them."

She stopped the vehicle, and the guards moved to either side of it, looking in at Trent and Judith, who had lowered their windows. The faces of the helmeted troopers filled the open windows, air hissing out of the filter systems in their headgear. "This area is restricted access only."

Trent held up his wrist codex, which the trooper on his side scanned with a hand-held device. "I came here to walk, relax. I am Star Captain Trent, Third Jaguar Cavaliers."

"And her." The trooper motioned to Judith with his rifle butt.

"My bondsman. I pressed her into service as a driver. It is a task befitting one of her position, *quiaff*?" *A lie, but a necessary one.*

The trooper nodded and spoke in a muffled voice. "Affirmative, Star Captain. You must be new to Hyner."

"Neg. We have been away for some time, however."

"This is sacred ground, Star Captain. Our scientist caste discovered a Star League Castle Brian in the hills there." The man pointed up toward the mound.

Trent feigned surprise "I had no idea, trooper. Such a site—where the Star League once stood. I should like to see such a place."

The trooper shook his black-helmeted head. "Negative. I am sorry, Star Captain, but Star Colonel Moon has declared that only the bloodnamed of the Clan can visit this site."

"But I am a trueborn warrior," Trent said.

"Aff, but not blooded, sir. Bloodnamed from other units come here under invitation of the Star Colonel, but we have orders that no other may pass."

Trent took the words like a physical blow. He lowered his head and wiped his face with his hand. "Very well, trooper," he replied. "Judith, take us back to base."

She nodded, sure he must be feeling the same suppressed rage as she. The Castle Brian was their place. She had discovered it first. She had brought him there. It was there that Trent had become more than a bondsmaster to her. Now the Smoke Jaguars had taken that from them. What had once been their place of freedom was now restricted to the elite bloodnamed of the Clan. She was sure that this was Paul Moon's way of using the site to play the game of political favors with other units.

Judith reversed the hovercar and closed the windows. Neither she nor Trent said a word on the trip back to Warrenton. They did not have to. Their secrets had bound them together more tightly than any bondcord.

≡ 32 ≡

Trent entered the briefing room along with all the other offi-cers of the Third Jaguar Cavaliers Cluster, but he might as well have been alone. There were hostile glances in his direction from the likes of Oleg Nevversan and Ramon Showers, but he did his best to ignore them. Only Star Cap-tain Nanci of Binary Elemental seemed willing to have any-thing to do with him. She stood at his side, dwarfing him with her massive muscular bulk, oblivious to the looks the other officers were giving him. *She, like me, is unblooded. In her eyes, we share that in common.*

Trent looked up at her, his own arms crossed in a relaxed, yet obstinate mode. "Do you know why we were summoned, Nanci?"

"Affirmative," she said in her voice so deep it sounded almost masculine. "At least I think so. Rumors have been flying that Galaxy Commander Hang Mehta is here with the commander of the Nineteenth Striker Cluster."

"A raid then, *quiaff*?"

"One can only assume that Star Colonels Paul Moon and Thilla Showers are bidding against each other for some sort of mission. And since the bidding is taking place here, it is only logical that the strike would be against the Draconis

Combine." Trent thought her logic sound, given that Hyner was poised on the border with the Draconis Combine.

Trent held back a grin. A raid into the Combine would give him a chance to remain in the Inner Sphere and pass on the information he and Judith had gathered. "I hope you are correct. I would welcome an opportunity to get my unit into battle."

"Only if you have been bid. Though you have nothing to worry about there, Trent."

"Why do you say that?"

She shrugged slightly and lowered her tone so that their fellow officers would not hear. "All in this room know the contempt Star Colonel Moon feels toward you."

"Aff," Trent replied softly. "I would expect him to keep me out of the bid for this fight."

"Neg," she said. "I have heard him speak openly of you. Paul Moon will make sure that you are bid, no matter what. His intentions toward you are, I believe, crystal clear."

Trent understood. Unable to dispose of Trent by shipping him off to a sorry fate on Huntress, Moon would make sure he was killed in battle. Trent had no illusions. Even if he were successful and died a glorious death, Paul Moon would find a way to sully his name. No matter what, there would be no honor for him.

Before he and Nanci could say more, the door at the far end of the room opened and two figures entered. Trent recognized one as Star Colonel Paul Moon. The other was a shorter warrior who wore the rank of Galaxy Commander. It had to be Hang Mehta, Moon's commanding officer. Though much smaller than Moon, her stride was a full step ahead of the big Elemental, and the cast-iron expression on her face easily identified her as the superior officer. Every officer in the briefing room snapped to attention as the pair came to the head of the room.

"Third Jaguar Cavaliers, Stormriders of the Smoke Jaguar," bellowed Galaxy Commander Mehta in a ceremonial tone, "you will once again draw blood in the name of our Clan and show that we are not as wounded as our enemies think. The Wolves attempted to raid us to restore their own honor, and Khan Lincoln Osis has decreed that Delta Galaxy will show both our kindred and the barbarians at the gate that we are far from weak."

"Seyla," came the solemn approval of all the Jaguars in the room.

"Our target is the Combine border world of Maldonado, one jump from here. There are several military bases there. This strike will stun the forces there and demonstrate to both the Combine and our fellow Clans that the Smoke Jaguar can still hunt and destroy." She looked up and over at the Colonel who stood at her side.

"Star Colonel Moon has successfully won the bid to attack Maldonado. Under his command, you will strike with a fury that will echo across the stars."

"Seyla," they all responded again.

Moon stepped up beside his commanding officer. "Storm-riders, my bid was as bold as the fires in your hearts." He glanced over at Star Captain Oleg Nevversan. "Trinary Assault, you will rend our foes." He pointed to Ramon Showers. "And Supernova Striker, you will send our enemies howling in fear." Then he turned to Trent, his voice dropping an octave. "And Beta Striker Trinary, you shall rush into the valley of death to slay those who would oppose us. Two DropShips are being prepared and you depart in three days' time."

"Into the valley of death they rode . . ." Trent remembered the words from an ancient poem he had once read many years ago. His sought the eyes of Star Colonel Paul Moon, who fixed him with an icy stare.

Trent sat in the cockpit of his *Cauldron-Born,* adjusting the seat again for what seemed like the thousandth time since his return. He missed his *Timber Wolf,* which had been re-assigned since he had left and returned to Hyner. Instead he had been assigned one of the replacement 'Mechs that had come with him from Huntress. Though he had successfully tested at a higher weight class, he had opted for the *Cauldron-Born.* Trent was still having trouble getting used to the fact that the 'Mech's stance was lower than the *Timber Wolf*'s.

Judith climbed into the cockpit hatch opening and slid into the tight space behind the command couch. The cockpits of BattleMechs, unless modified, were designed to hold one MechWarrior. Two could ride in one if need be, but the confines were seriously cramped. She pulled the hatch shut behind her.

"I received your message—that we needed to speak."

"Aff," Trent said, setting his neurohelmet on the communications console to his right. "Our unit is being dispatched on a mission to Maldonado in the Draconis Combine."

Judith smiled. "Excellent. I knew this would come."

"Aye, but you will somehow have to get word out to ComStar. We leave in three days, and a JumpShip is fully charged and waiting for us. We should be arriving in the Maldonado system on May seventh. We touch down on planet seventeen days later."

"That is not much time," Judith said.

"I do not control the time table, so the arrival time is out of my hands. But who knows when such an opportunity might present itself again? We must strike while the iron is hot."

"Agreed," Judith said. "I only hope someone monitoring the message traffic in ComStar will recognize the codes I'm using. They are old . . . very old."

Trent reached over and put his hand on her shoulder. "We have come a long way for this, Judith. Perhaps the end is finally in sight. If so, we are close to righting a great many wrongs."

Star Captain Oleg Nevversan leaned across the holographic projection table in the heart of the command center and studied the terrain where they would be landing. It was a long and twisting canyon, nearly a kilometer deep, but with rolling grassy hills in the lowlands on either side of the river that cut through the middle. The hills ran a short distance along either bank before cutting sharply up the sheer rock sides of the canyon. The rock faces were so steep that it was impossible for anyone to enter the canyon except at established roadways. The base was well positioned for defense. *Defense—something the Jaguars scorn.*

"With my Trinary and Supernova Striker dropping on the west side of the Shenandoah River, and Trent's Trinary on the other side, we will be in poor position to provide him support when we do engage the enemy."

"Affirmative," Star Colonel Paul Moon said, pointing to the northern rockface that jutted out in an area where the reports placed a military complex. "Trent's Trinary will engage them first, drawing them out. However, the depth of the river will prevent you from crossing when he needs you. You will have to ford the river three kilometers north of the base. By the time you get there, it will be too late for Trent and his command."

Oleg looked at the wide river, which glowed green on the projection. "Trent is no fool, Star Colonel. If nothing else, he has proven himself to be a very good tactician. When he sees his map of the region, he will spot the problem almost instantly."

Moon nodded and pressed several of the built-in control studs on the edge of the table. The holographic image of the river shrank in width to only a scant dozen meters, more than enough to permit a BattleMech crossing. "Unfortunately, a mistake has occurred. Trent's copy of the tactical plans for this operation were constructed from a model of the river in summer. We are arriving at the start of Maldonado's spring season. During the summer months, the river is a narrow ribbon that can be easily traversed. When you and he arrive there, the spring thaw will have turned that creek into a raging, turbulent river that no known BattleMech could cross."

"The odds of him surviving are thin at best," Nevversan said.

"Aff," Moon said, feigning an expression of concern. "And if he somehow manages to last until your arrival, you should use your discretion to make sure he does not leave Maldonado alive. Do you understand, Star Captain?"

"Affirmative," Nevversan said, beads of sweat forming on his brow as he realized just how far Star Colonel Moon would go. "From what you say, Star Colonel, I assume you will not participate in this mission, *quiaff*?"

"Correct. In the official orders, you will be placed in charge of the overall operation."

Oleg Nevversan understood the implications. *Plausible deniability.* Whatever he did on Maldonado, whether he followed Moon's command or ignored it, the blame would rest on his head—never on the Star Colonel's. It was an unsettling feeling.

"Understood, Star Colonel."

"Very well," Moon said, shutting off the holographic display. "This meeting never happened."

═══ 33 ═══

When Star Colonel Moon was awakened at 0400 hours by the comm officer, his first reaction was anger. When he learned that it was to attend an HPG message from the Galaxy Commander—his senior officer—he moved with vigor and purpose. He dressed quickly and hurried down to the large HPG receiving room, where he now stood with the comm officer on the other side of the soundproof glass giving him the signal that the message was coming in.

The holographic projection system was built into the floor near the center of the room. As it flickered to life, it gave form to the image of the stout Galaxy Commander Hang Mehta. Paul Moon knew that this was important. Direct holographic projecting between worlds was expensive, and from what he gathered, something of a technical nightmare to coordinate and maintain. It was usually reserved for only the most important of transmissions. Moon snapped to attention quickly as he stood face to face with his commanding officer.

"I assume that you are alone and that this room is secured, *quiaff*," Mehta said, returning the salute. Paul Moon activated a small switch that closed off a wall section so that even the technicians could not see what was going on.

"It is now, Galaxy Commander."

She rubbed her brow in thought, then looked back at Moon. "A potential emergency has arisen involving one of your officers. Star Captain Trent of your Beta Trinary. He is to be apprehended immediately and placed in sequestered security facilities—no contact with anyone."

Moon felt the blood flow out of his face in an instant. "Star Captain Trent and his Trinary are currently en route to their JumpShip for the strike on Maldonado, Galaxy Commander."

"Contact the DropShip and abort the mission," Mehta said.

Paul Moon hesitated for a millisecond with his reply. "I am unable to comply, Galaxy Commander. Our mission protocols state specifically that DropShips and JumpShips on such a raid are to disregard any and all transmissions once en route." Hang Mehta had apparently forgotten the protocol, even though it was she who had who originally set it up. The Combine's network of spies and so on were known to broadcast messages transmitting conflicting orders or other dishonorable trickery to outbound DropShips. The mission protocol was in place to ensure that no one tampered with the orders for a Jaguar raid. Now it was suddenly turned to their disadvantage.

"Freebirth!" she cursed.

"If I may inquire, Galaxy Commander," Moon began cautiously, "why is the apprehension of Star Captain Trent called for?"

Mehta looked at him sourly. "Zeta Galaxy Commander Benjamin Howell was found to be conducting a smuggling operation from Huntress. During narco-interrogation he revealed that Star Captain Trent is one of his operatives."

Moon's mind raced. *Trent—betraying our caste?* He was tempted to tell the Galaxy Commander that he had set Trent up, that the man's chances of returning from Maldonado alive were not even minimal. But he had already seen her rage once before and did not want to incur it again. Worse yet, Trent had a knack for surviving. "Smuggling is an act worthy only of merchants and bandits. It is far below the code of a warrior."

"Do not be such a fool," Galaxy Commander Mehta said angrily. "This is not about a mere violation of caste, you surat. Do you not see the threat, *quineg*? Trent has been to Huntress and back again. He has traveled the Exodus Road. Our operatives in The Watch indicate that such a man, one who would turn against his own caste, might turn against the Clan itself. Trent is a potential traitor. And if he is one, he may have our greatest secret with him—the location of the Clan homeworlds."

"Traitor?" The concept of a Clan warrior, even Trent, betraying his people was unfathomable. Perhaps these intelligence-gathering fools in The Watch were having nightmares, seeing ghosts where there was nothing. A warrior would never turn against one of his own. . . .

"Do not be blinded to the danger, Star Colonel Moon. I took the liberty of having my Watch operatives on Hyner check his and his freebirth wench's access to your garrison computer system."

"You checked my network without informing me?"

"Aff, you fool, because there is more at stake than just your petty ego and territoriality. Trent and this Judith spent a total of four hours downloading the complete strategic and tactical overlays and deployments of our Clan in the Occupation Zone. This information was obtained piecemeal, and because the two of them accessed it using the maintenance procurement system as well as Trent's access as a Trinary commander, no security alarms were sounded. She tracked our logistics flow and pinned down certain units, while he checked our TO&E on other planets. The data the two of them have compiled and carry with them consists of every bit of knowledge about our troop deployments within the Inner Sphere."

Moon was stunned at the news. "He has no reason to do this unless he plans to turn against us."

Hang Mehta's tone grew darker and more forbidding. "I know that you tried to shuffle off Star Captain Trent as a solahma warrior. You may very well have forged the instrument of our own destruction."

"I do not understand," Moon said. "You approved those orders. Khan Osis himself has stated that the warriors who fought on Tukayyid were inferior and were what had cost us our victory."

"Enough of this prattle," Mehta barked. "Rest assured, Star Colonel, that you and you alone will suffer the blame if Trent is a traitor. In the meantime, you have a great deal of preparation."

"I do not understand."

"You have DropShips and JumpShips at your disposal, *quiaff*? You are a Cluster Commander, are you not? Mount as large a force as possible immediately. You will proceed on to Maldonado. You are to take whatever actions necessary to make sure that Star Captain Trent is apprehended. If you cannot apprehend him, then you will destroy him. Either way, if he is indeed a traitor, he will not pass any information on the Smoke Jaguar to our enemies."

Moon felt his whole body tense as she gave the orders. It was not going to be easy. The Maldonado raiding force would have almost reached the jump point and the waiting JumpShip by now. They would jump out of the Hyner system immediately upon arriving there. He could muster a Star or two and one of the *Broadsword* DropShips. If he took one of the lithium-battery JumpShips and made an in-system jump to a pirate point, he would be able to link up with the other JumpShip in perhaps four or five days. Then it was a single jump to the Maldonado system.

"I will not fail you, Galaxy Commander," he said with a quick salute, which she did not return. A part of him was suddenly happy. If his original plan for Trent failed, he would be on Maldonado to kill him personally. Either way, Paul Moon would make sure that Trent did not live.

"No, Paul Moon, you will not," she replied in an icy tone as the holographic image shut off and normal lighting came back on. Moon knew that the price of failure would be the end of everything he had worked so hard to build.

The dim lighting of the cramped DropShip mess doubling for a briefing room had the kind of musky smell one normally associated with pilot ready rooms or locker rooms. Trent looked at the display showing the Shenandoah River Valley, where the Twelfth Dieron Regulars were based on Maldonado. With his skill at tactical analysis, Trent saw several problems with the plan, the least of which was the deliberate splitting of their forces.

The Regulars were sheltered in a fortress-like complex built into the east wall of the river valley—the side where Trent and his Trinary would land. In that fortress, they would be hard to root out. From Trent's understanding of the plan, his unit was going to be the bait, a force small enough to lure out the Regulars. Then the Jaguar force on the other side of the river would suddenly cross over, using the twisting canyon as a sensor screen, and hit the Regulars as well.

"We can accomplish the same goal by all landing on the

same side of the river," Trent said to Star Captain Oleg Nevversan. "If you hold your force back far enough, I can still be effective in luring them out."

Oleg Nevversan shook his head. "Negative, Star Captain. This plan has no room for modification. It comes from Star Colonel Moon himself."

The statement did not reassure Trent in the least. "Warriors always have the right to alter deployments as long as they accomplish the actual mission objectives."

"Not in this case," Nevversan said firmly. "We deploy per orders, Star Captain." His tone was almost smug. Trent glanced at Star Commander Russou and Alexandra, who had tested to take his former command of Beta Striker Star. Russou cocked his right eyebrow, indicating that the plan seemed questionable. Alexandra simply looked back at the map.

Nevversan shut off the display unit. "We will be docking and jumping in three days. Have your units ready for action upon your arrival."

With those words the briefing came to a quick end. Trent said little other than giving orders to Alexandra and Russou to review the battle plans. Then he drifted out into the corridor and down to his small stateroom. Once inside he closed the door and saw Judith hovering near the fold-down cot.

"Problems?" she asked, watching his face.

"Perhaps. We have had little time to talk since our departure. I am curious about how you and I will be extracted once we arrive on Maldonado."

Judith gave a slight shrug. "Unknown. I have rigged your OmniMech's IFF transponder. On normal bands, the signal will simply identify your *Cauldron-Born* as either friend or a foe—the way the IFF is supposed to do. However, if scans are run at the high end of the frequency bands, they identify you as a blue target on any T&T system that is monitoring those bands."

"We have no way of knowing if your ComStar accomplices ever received your message?"

She nodded. "That is correct."

"What of you, Judith? You cannot be with me in my 'Mech when we land on Maldonado. How will you get away?" The concern in his voice was genuine, and more than a bondsmaster might normally express. But to Trent, Judith was more than a normal bondsman.

She smiled slightly. "I did not come this far to be left

behind. Do not concern yourself, Trent. I will get away from the other techs. If ComStar is there and you are extracted, I will be at your side—of that you can be sure."

"But if the ComStar forces do not show. What then?"

"Then I will stand beside you to the end. We started this together, and if necessary, we will die together."

The red-haired Precentor IV Karl Karter stroked his beard as he looked one more time at the hardcopy printout of the transmission. The planet Pesht's largest moon shone outside the window, its yellow-white light shimmering down on this key Combine world. Here, in the safety of the ComStar base in the foothills of the Kincha Mountains, the moon seemed far away.

His staff filed into the room, their gray Com Guard uniforms showing the unit patch for the 308th Division, Winged Divinity. Most of his forces were on Tukayyid, but what he had on this flank of the Clan Occupation Zone was a quick-response unit, ready to deploy at any moment to blunt any major Clan intrusion.

The officers entered the room, and he waited until the door was closed before speaking. These were good men and women. They had almost all seen action against the Ghost Bears on Tukayyid, been tempered in the fires of the greatest battle in the history of mankind. The First Army of the Com Guards were almost all veterans of the Ghost Bear assaults—hence their nickname "The Bear Maulers." Since the glorious and costly victory on Tukayyid they had not seen much action. The message he had just received would change all that.

"All right, people, listen up and listen good," he began as the last officer took a seat. "We've been tossed this one from the boys upstairs, and we have no choice but to pull it off." He held a printout in front of him.

"By direct order of the Precentor Martial and of Precentor Katrina Troth of the First Army High Command, we are ordered to take any and all available forces to the planet Maldonado on or before May twenty-fourth."

"What is the mission, sir?" piped up Demi-Precentor Frakes.

"A defection and extraction. Apparently one of our ROM operatives has convinced a Smoke Jaguar warrior to defect. Our job is to get them out of there, no matter what."

"The Smoke Jaguars are not on Maldonado," pointed out Demi-Precentor Loxley.

Precentor Karter smiled. "They *will* be on the twenty-fourth of May. Our ROM operative indicated that they intend to execute a raid at that time. And per direct orders from the Precentor Martial, we are to use 'any and all force and means necessary to ensure that the defector be extracted alive.' "

Karter scanned the printout one more time, searching for one line in particular. "In fact, my good officers, 'the 308th Division forces are to be considered expendable in the successful execution of this mission.' "

The air in the room went silent. "What of the local command?" Frakes asked. "I believe the Twelfth Dieron Regulars are on Maldonado now."

"According to a copy of a command order I received, Theodore Kurita himself has sent a message to the Regulars. They are to provide full and total cooperation in this mission."

"This warrior must be very important," another officer said.

"That's not for us to know. We only have about a battalion of troops ready, but we must leave immediately. Our Jump-Ship is still at a pirate point only a few days out. We have to load up, get there, and get to Maldonado on the double."

Demi-Precentor Frakes spoke up again. "We've fought the Clans before and beat them. I can't wait to do it again." Murmurs in the room seconded his boast.

"I agree, Demi-Precentor, but we are not going to defeat the Jaguars. We are going to pull out our agent and one warrior." Karter cocked his head slightly and narrowed his eyes. "But if we get a chance to send a few more Clanners into the great beyond, then by Blake's blood, they'll dread the day they ever met Winged Divinity."

34

Emerald Landing Zone
Shenandoah River Valley
Maldonado
Draconis Combine
24 May 3058

The Smoke Jaguar DropShip opened its 'Mech deployment doors as it hovered over the LZ on the far southeastern bank of the Shenandoah River. The giant metallic echo of the doors locking into place was lost against the roar of the fusion engines. The night was lit by the brilliant fires of the thrusters burning away the sod of Maldonado as the BattleMechs jumped the short distance down to the ground, then began moving away with almost uncanny military precision.

Trent glanced back at the DropShip as it throttled its engines and lifted off the ground and away, leaving the three Stars of his Trinary moving into position in the sudden and enveloping darkness of the Maldonado night. Somewhere in the hills across the river, the same scene was being played out by the mission's other two commands. The DropShips would continue south for another twenty kilometers, heading for the point where the troops would rendezvous with it when the raid was over. His long-range sensors silently pulsed their signals around the landing zone, confirming that everyone in his command was present, operational, and intact.

What was not in order was the terrain feedback coming back from the sensors on his secondary display. It was not what he expected to see. Not at all. The Shenandoah River, which should have been further away, was not. The hills off to the east rose gradually at first, then sharply into a low range of jagged rocks—impossible terrain. But it was the river that concerned him most. It was wrong, dead wrong. The surface scans he was getting off it indicated one of two things. Either his sensors were malfunctioning or the Shenandoah was much bigger than he thought.

He activated the command channel. "Star Captain Russou," he said into his neurohelmet microphone. "Please confirm the readings I am getting on the river."

"Working . . ." Russou said. A moment later, Trent heard him curse. "Stravag! This is impossible!"

"Aye," Trent shook his head and closed his eyes. "That is what I thought." He switched to the channel used by the Binary and Trinary commanders. "Star Captain Nevversan, this is Star Captain Trent."

"Go, Trent."

"The river has apparently flooded. I show it to be almost a kilometer wide."

"Confirmed. We cannot make it across from here. You will proceed on to the mission objective."

The primary premise of the assault was that all three Jaguar units would combine their efforts and converge on the base of the Twelfth Dieron Regulars. Going in alone would put Trent's command at risk of being outnumbered four or five to one, and wiped out piecemeal. "Say again, Star Captain."

"You have your orders, Beta Trinary," Nevversan replied.

"Oleg, how can I carry out my orders if you and Supernova Striker are unable to get over to provide us the supporting fire necessary to successfully execute this assault? Sending my Trinary in alone is akin to suicide."

"Neg, Trent. We will find another place to ford the river and join up with you. The Star Colonel's orders are clear, and I aim to fulfill them to the best of my ability. We will begin deployment within the hour, and you will also begin your approach at that time. By the time you engage these Combine surats, we should have found a place to cross."

Trent looked at the tactical map on his secondary display. *Nevvarson is ordering me to my death and he knows it. Either he is incompetent or he does this at the bidding of Star Colonel Paul Moon.* Trent understood then that Moon must have known all along that the river would be much

wider than indicated by the briefing material he had given
Trent. That Moon would stoop to trickery and lies to kill
honorable warriors only confirmed for Trent the necessity of
taking the path he and Judith had chosen. It was the only way
to preserve what honor was left him as a warrior of the
Smoke Jaguar.

"Aye, Star Captain," he said. There was nothing to do now
but obey.

Judith tossed the small kit bag into the front seat of the
mobile repair vehicle and prepared to hoist herself up. The
small tracked vehicle had no armor to speak of but was
equipped with a fast and powerful engine, towing cables, a
power winch, and a cutting assembly. It was used to move
rapidly onto the battlefield to perform emergency surgery on
fallen 'Mechs.

This one was ready for deployment, even if it had yet not
been ordered into action. She adjusted her goggles to make
sure their fit was good. Though the polarized viewscreen of a
BattleMech cockpit would filter the bright light of the Maldonado sun, a quick glance at it could be blinding to an individual. It would take several more days of exposure before
her eyes were adjusted enough to tolerate the sunlight on this
planet.

She put her foot on the small lip of the running board and
was about to step up when she heard a voice that chilled her
soul. "Judith, what are you doing? No one has ordered the re-
covery vehicles into action yet."

She turned and faced Master Tech Phillip for what she
knew would be the last time. He had been assigned to the
operation, since it involved almost all of the Third Jaguars
Cluster. Indeed, Paul Moon himself would be here if not for
his bold bidding, in which he had removed himself from the
bid. Judith reached into the vehicle as though seeking a grip
to balance herself on the running board. Her hand closed
around the laser pistol on the seat. "I was merely readying
this vehicle for deployment, Master Phillip."

"I gave no such order," Phillip said, coming closer to
where she hung half out of the door of the mobile repair
vehicle.

"Aye," she said, glancing around quickly to be sure they
were indeed alone. Then she swung the laser pistol and leveled it at Phillip, aiming it at the bridge of his nose—squarely

between the eyes. "I do not think you will be handing out orders for some time." He was stunned by her action, his mouth dropping open at the sight of the weapon. Phillip took a step back, then stopped, apparently frozen with fear.

"It—it is illegal for a member of the lower castes to possess a weapon," he stammered in disbelief.

Judith smiled thinly. "Neg, you jackass. I am a warrior and something more. You tried to beat that out of me, but you could not. And soon, I will have my honor again." Then she fired the pistol. A brilliant burst of ruby-red light flashed and burned through Phillip's nose, skull, and brain. A wisp of smoke floated in the air as his body dropped back, motionless.

Quietly she dragged his corpse into the rear of the repair vehicle. Taking him with her would mean that no one would find his body and start asking untimely questions. For now, only two techs would be missing, hardly something worth mentioning to Star Captain Nevversan. *Time to go home. . . .*

As the first rays of dawn reached into the depths of the valley, melting the frost off the trees and grass, the lead elements of the Twelfth Dieron Regulars had begun their assault on Beta Striker Star. From almost half a kilometer back, Trent saw the flames and the blasted armor flying off as a barrage of enemy missiles hit Alexandra's *Cauldron-Born.* She fought to keep her new 'Mech upright amid the beating she was taking from the missiles.

Bombardier, Trent concluded, identifying the enemy 'Mech from a long-range scan of the bend in the river and hills just ahead of his unit. *Plus seven more—two full lances.* The missile-boat 'Mech and several of the others had opened up at their maximum range, rising just above the ridge, firing, then quickly moving down to where his forces could not return the compliment.

The progress along the river had been slow and methodical by Smoke Jaguar standards, but Trent understood the need for such caution despite several prompts from Oleg Nevversan to the contrary. "Star Commander Russou, bring Charlie Star along the river bank and provide suppression fire. Star Commander Alexandra, bring Beta Striker up onto the ridge and fire down." From what Trent saw on the tactical display, all things being equal, the Dieron Regular BattleMechs would be caught in a cross-fire . . . all things remaining equal.

Beta Striker swept up the ridge that provided cover to the

Combine BattleMechs. As they reached the top Trent saw a fiery barrage of lasers, explosions, flames, and the blue beams of charged particles. Most of the volley hit the Omni-Mechs of Beta Striker like an instant tornado. Armor rained back toward his Alpha Attack Star, rattling off MechWarrior Teej's *Mad Dog* and Dex's *Shadow Cat*. The missile salvo followed a second later, hitting Beta Striker again with a wall of fury and explosions. Alexandra's *Cauldron-Born* vibrated madly at the edge of the ridge, and the *Hankyu* piloted by MechWarrior Kutt seemed to pivot on its right leg, then stumble backward, toward Trent's Star.

At the edge of the ridge, where it dipped downward toward the river to the west, Trent watched as Charlie Star paused and returned fire. Star Commander Russou's *Mad Dog* unleashed its long-range missiles, which hit behind the ridge line where Trent could not see the havoc they were wreaking. His secondary display suddenly started showing more Combine BattleMechs on his sensors, data fed him from the tactical displays of Charlie and Beta Stars. It was not a mere two lances, but suddenly three lances—a full company of twelve BattleMechs—squaring off against his Trinary. Readings at the edge of the long-range sensors told him that even more might be hiding just beyond his sensor range, skirting the edge of the fight.

He sent a short digital signal to Star Captain Nevversan, the pre-arranged code to let him know that Trent's command was engaging the enemy. Then he throttled up the fusion reactor in the bowels of the *Cauldron-Born* and moved it forward. "Charlie Star, report," he said.

"Confirm twelve, neg, make that eleven 'Mechs," Russou said as an explosion seemed to light up the area on the other side of the ridge, making Alexandra's force stand out in silhouette for an instant.

"Copy." Trent then opened a channel to his own Star. "Alpha Attack, move in and form up alongside Beta Striker. All units engage." He walked his 'Mech forward without fear, but he could not help wondering whether he would survive the fight. *It would be ironic to die now, here, so close to escape. Neg. Today, I will not die. Today, I will become the Smoke Jaguar I always wanted to be.*

Trent reached the top of the ridge just as Alexandra's force began to start down the other side. From this vantage point he saw visually for the first time what his Trinary was facing.

At his feet lay the burning remains of a camouflage-green Combine *Panther* that had apparently rushed up the hill straight into the face of Beta Striker Star. The remaining Combine 'Mechs were carefully poised at the bottom of the ridge. The two greatest threats were the mantis-like *Daikyu* and its sister *Naginata,* both of which were firing at Beta Striker and his own force as it cleared the ridge top. To Trent's left, Rupert in his *Summoner* took the brunt of the *Daikyu*'s deadly PPC and autocannon fire as it slashed away at the surface armor of the *Summoner*'s right side. Arcs of blue-charged electrical energy, residue from the PPC attack, crackled around the *Summoner* as it swayed under the impact of the fire.

Rupert struggled to maintain his balance, but a blast of medium laser pulses from a SDR-9K *Venom* stitched the torso of the *Summoner* one more time, reaching deeply into the gouges already created by the first wave of damage. This time the shots were not slowed by the ferro-fibrous armor, but seared directly into the heart of the Jaguar OmniMech, hitting engine shielding and the balancing gyro that kept the machine stable. The *Summoner* swayed drunkenly toward the river as Trent locked his own Gauss rifle and LB5-X autocannon on the *Venom.*

The Gauss rifle slug, propelled on a magnetic pulse, flashed at supersonic speeds into the *Venom* as the light 'Mech tried to drift back. It was just about to ignite its jump jets when the round hit the green and brown-painted 'Mech in the leg. The impact was furious, shattering the knee joint and bending it backward as the autocannon laced a series of pot holes up the 'Mech's front torso. The Combine Mech-Warrior never stood a chance as his 'Mech rattled violently and fell over, its stump of a leg leaking coolant and venting a white cloud of steam. It fell at the same time that Rupert dropped at Trent's side.

On his right, Dex's *Shadow Cat* paused about twenty meters further down the hill and leveled its pair of large lasers at a retreating *Wolf Trap.* The Combine MechWarrior, walking deftly backward, unleashed a deadly barrage of autocannon and missile fire that merged with a blast of LRMs from the *Naginata* nearby. A total of fifty-five missiles spiraled in on Dex's 45-ton *Shadow Cat,* only four of them missing and plowing up the turf instead. The others did horrific damage to the cockpit and chest of the low-slung 'Mech. The eruption of the warhead sent armor-ripping shrapnel against the cockpit glass of Trent's *Cauldron-Born*.

The impact on the lighter *Shadow Cat* was more devastating. Billows of gray and black smoke poured from the deep holes in the torso as Dex attempted to keep his 'Mech upright. Trent swung his medium long-range laser and short-range missile pack into play on an HM-1 *Hitman* that had broken off from the melee with Charlie Star still brewing to the west, down at the low end of the ridge not far from the river. The missiles tracked the moving *Hitman*, pockmarking the armor under the armpit while the laser scored only light damage on the right arm.

Trent watched as the *Shadow Cat* was bathed in a blast of PPC fire from the *Daikyu*, taking the hits just under the already gaping damage. Dex's fight to keep his *Shadow Cat* upright and able to fight was coming to an obvious end as the 'Mech toppled onto its side. Dex ejected up and back, away from the falling 'Mech, rising upward into the air on a streaking cloud of solid rocket plumes until his chute deployed.

Trent stared back down into the foothills of the small valley, then realized he was not being fired upon, not even targeted. It was as if he was not even there, totally invisible to his would-be enemies and allies. *They are not firing at me. Judith's message must have gotten through.* His heart lifted for a moment at that thought. Instead of firing, he started looking for an opportunity to break through the Combine line. *Perhaps I could make a sprint for their base . . .*

Then a roar filled the air from behind him on the ridge. A glance at his scanners showed a massive airborne object—a DropShip—moving in swiftly from the rear. He pivoted the *Cauldron-Born*'s torso and saw the ship looming over him, its drop bay doors open. A *Broadsword* . . . a Smoke Jaguar *Broadsword*, from what he could see of the insignia in the early light of sunrise. *Where had it come from?*

Then a voice came down from the ship over a wide-band communications channel that everyone in his Trinary could hear.

"Star Captain Trent, this is Star Colonel Paul Moon. You are hereby charged with treason against your caste and your Clan. Surrender or be destroyed!"

=== 35 ===

Shenandoah River Valley
Maldonado
Draconis Combine
25 May 3058

Judith saw the flashing bursts of light just ahead of her, and they told her she was closing with a battle. The tracked mobile repair vehicle was slow and loud, but she had made good time since leaving the DropShips. She slowed slightly and tried to use the limited communications set, hoping to pick up some of the combat chatter from the ridge in the distance, but thus far with no luck. *Who are they fighting? The Dieron Regulars?*

She steered the vehicle to the east, toward the foothills, hoping to get to the top of one of the hills to get a better look at the battle site. That point was two kilometers away, however, and the steam of fog rising as the Maldonado sun burned away the morning frost and dew made visual sighting difficult at this distance. She kept heading north by northeast, constantly adjusting the comm set to pick up any sort of communications.

Suddenly from in front of her she saw a squad of troopers emerge from hiding in a small trench. Most carried shoulder-launched short-range missiles and, from their aim, she was sure they would be more than willing to blast her vehicle. The troopers did not fire, however, but held themselves steady, the reflective faceplates under their helmets hiding their expressions. Their light green uniforms and the green and black field patches they wore made her smile. On the chest of one of the troopers she made out a familiar circular symbol with two star points dipping downward.

"Freeze!" one of the men commanded through an amplified speaker in his face plate. She slammed the vehicle to a stop and slowly shut it off, then held her hands in front of her so the troopers could see she was making no overt moves.

The men fanned around the vehicle, some holding the missile launchers while others switched to laser rifles. All of their weapons were trained on her. The officer in charge moved slowly and cautiously to the half-opened window of the vehicle, ready to fire his rifle at the slightest provocation. She knew these were forces friendly to her, but they still did not know that.

"Sir, we have a body in the back," one of the men at the rear of the vehicle barked. The officer glaring at her from the side seemed to tense for a minute.

"Hands where I can see them," he commanded. She nodded as he opened the door with one hand, keeping the laser rifle trained on her face with the other.

"Name?"

Judith used the code phrase and password she had sent in her covert message. "Archangel."

"Password?"

"Redemption," she stated firmly.

The officer lowered his rifle and motioned to the others in the squad. They dropped their weapons aim from the transport and spread out, providing the officer and Judith with cover. The officer pulled out a small communicator from his belt and activated it. "Bear Claw, this is Rapier. Archangel is in the bag. You are clear for phase two."

"Roger, Rapier," came a voice over the speaker. Judith looked into the distance and saw the hillside suddenly come alive with movement. Hidden until now under camouflage and sensor concealment tarps, more than two dozen BattleMechs seemed to rise out of the hillside and come alive. She smiled. Trent's force had gone right past them in the foothills, never knowing that his rescue was so close at hand.

Suddenly there was roar near the river, and she saw a gray Smoke Jaguar DropShip sweep down toward the ridgeline in the distance. In the pit of her stomach, she knew that this was not going to be easy. . . .

* * *

The sleek, almost polished gray battle armor of the Elementals under Paul Moon's command dropped from the *Broadsword* Class DropShip and deployed on the south end of the ridge, where Trent and his command had been only a few minutes before. Elementals were usually imposing figures, but their threat seemed dramatically diminished when viewed from the cockpit of Trent's 'Mech. He was not seduced by that, however. He knew how deadly Elementals were when they swarmed a 'Mech. And he knew that Paul Moon would stop at nothing to destroy him.

"All Stars, continue your attack," Trent commanded. "Keep the Combine forces on the run."

"Negative!" countermanded Moon. "Beta Trinary, this is Cluster Commander Paul Moon. Star Captain Trent has been implicated in a violation of our code of honor." On the other side of the ridge the battle still raged as Beta Striker and Charlie Sweep Stars waded into the remains of the Twelfth Dieron Regulars company. Explosions and errant flashes of laser beams and PPC shots stabbed up into the air. "I order you to break off your assault against these Combine freebirths and to apprehend Star Captain Trent immediately."

Trent studied the tactical sensor feed that showed the area on his secondary display. He held the high ground on top of the ridge. Russou's force was driving back the DCMS forces, while Beta Striker Star, or what was left of it, was still advancing. *That leaves only my own Star and the Colonel's as a threat.* His communications system was set for a wide transmission.

"This is Star Captain Trent. Disregard Star Colonel Moon's command. His charges are unfounded and unworthy of the warrior he claims to be. Maintain the assault on the Combine force."

A check of his long-range sensors showed that the Colonel's Elemental Star, numbering twenty-five armored infantry, were forming a wide semi-circle around Trent's position on top of the ridge. Facing south, with the battle raging behind him, Trent knew he was being drawn into a confrontation in which he would be dramatically outnumbered. His own Alpha Star seemed stymied, unsure of how to respond.

Moon's deep voice bellowed over the channel again, "Star Captain Trent, surrender or die."

Trent decided to take advantage of the confusion created

by Moon's arrival. "Beta Trinary, you know me. I trained you, taught you the ways of the Smoke Jaguar warrior. Paul Moon's accusations are illicit and unfounded."

"Sir," signaled Teej from his *Mad Dog*. "I must follow the orders of a superior."

Trent knew that his time was up. "Very well, Star Colonel Moon. This ends now," he said, charging the *Cauldron-Born*'s autocannon, short-range missiles, and medium laser. Against Elementals, his powerful Gauss rifle was virtually impotent—unable to hit the small, man-size targets.

"Attack!" Moon shouted. More than two dozen Elementals suddenly lit up on their jump jets, rising into the air and soaring toward Trent. Instead of charging down the ridge toward the assault force, he rapidly backed up his *Cauldron-Born,* moving down the hill to the fighting still raging below. He triggered his weapons and sprayed the Elementals just before he dropped out of line of sight with them. His laser beam cut the air horizontally like a knife, striking one of the jumping Elementals in mid-leap and severing his arm. Trent's autocannon rounds missed their mark, but the shrapnel and debris they threw up skewed the flight paths of two more Elementals. His pair of short-range missiles streaked out and went off near the lead Elemental. One missed altogether, but the other blew half the leg off the rising power-armored trooper.

He heard a scream of agony over the wide channel and knew the voice was Paul Moon's. Trent did not see him drop, but from his angle of flight, he knew he had taken off Moon's leg at the knee joint at least.

Trent grinned.

"Kill him!" howled Moon as the Elementals seized the top of the ridge and opened fire with their shoulder-mounted missile packs. The armor-piercing warheads raced down the hillside at Trent from the front and flanks as he slowed his pace and turned to break to the north. He thought he might make it to the Twelfth Dieron's command post if he could punch through the base. At least fifteen of the missiles found their mark on him, blasting armor plating off the *Cauldron-Born*'s arms, legs, and torso. Teej's *Mad Dog* rose to the ridge and blazed down at him with its pulse lasers, filling the air with brilliant crimson dots of light and rupturing even more of his torso armor.

Trent opened up again with his autocannon as another clip

signaled as loaded in the firing chamber. This time the LB-X rounds tore up the top of the ridge before the Elementals could take flight. One of his attackers disappeared in a cloud of black and gray smoke and others dove for cover. Almost a half-kilometer away, Charlie and Beta Stars had pushed back the Combine 'Mechs and were turning to the south to face him. He saw one of the Elementals pull himself onto the ridge top and knew that it was Star Colonel Moon, his armored suit having sealed the severed limb and no doubt pumping sedatives to mask the pain from his stump of a leg. Normal men would have passed out in agony, but Elemental warriors and their suits were designed to allow them to fight on to death.

"You will not get away, Trent. Not this time."

Suddenly from all sides of the crippled Elemental, a row of BattleMechs assumed the ridge line, opening fire on Moon's Elemental Star from the rear at point-blank range. They ignored Moon and his damage. Two grappled with Teej and fell backward, out of Trent's line of sight. *Reinforcements?* Then he saw the 'Mechs in detail on his tactical readout. *Thug, Raijin, Nexus, Black Knight, King Crab . . . and the color . . . gray-white.* He had seen some of the 'Mechs and the logos they bore once before, for two days on a planet called Tukayyid.

A new voice came on line in his ear speaker. "Smoke Jaguars, this is Precentor Karl Karter of the Com Guards 308th Division, crusher of the Ghost Bears on Tukayyid and terror of the Clans. We have beaten you before, and stand ready to do so now. Withdraw, power down, or die. The choice is yours!"

The Elementals did not waver in their assault on Trent. They rushed forward, but were no match for the Com Guard forces firing at them. Trent took four more hits from missiles as the Elementals attempted to close with him. Finally convinced that they could not reach him, they turned and mounted a counterattack on the Com Guard force. They rose into the air on their jets, lasers and machine guns blazing away as the Guards blasted back at them with lasers and missiles.

The remains of Beta Striker Star charged into their flank on the ridgetop, and soon the entire hillside was a melee of carnage and death. The ground shook under Trent's *Cauldron-Born* as his short-range missiles hit one of the Elementals still coming for him. His fire cut the gray-clad warrior in half as the machine gun rounds splattered against Trent's viewport, just short of penetrating.

Trent turned and saw the three remaining 'Mechs of Charlie Sweep Star moving slowly toward him. He recognized the lead one instantly as Russou's *Mad Dog*. It was pitted with black missile hits and the still-steaming scars where lasers had slashed off its armor protection. His junior officer's gait looked almost weary as the 'Mech moved toward him. Trent knew there was no way to avoid this confrontation. He accessed his battle computer terminal via the small keypad on the console and tapped in the self-destruct sequence controls.

BattleMechs rode atop fusion reactors. Though the reactors could be breached in the midst of combat, they were equipped with a series of fail-safe devices intended to protect the reactors from exploding except under the most extreme conditions. A warrior could, however, on his own accord, self-destruct a 'Mech.

Jaguar 'Mechs were default-coded with a ten-second delay. Once activated, the magnetic shielding that held the fusion reaction suspended would drop. The reaction of the core dropping out of alignment would release a compact nuclear explosion in an incredibly tight area, taking out the 'Mech and everything near it. Trent's carefully coded commands changed that timing, significantly . . .

Behind him came a series of explosions, but Trent ignored them. Instead he walked toward Star Commander Russou Howell, one of the few Smoke Jaguars he called friend. He heard Russou's voice, almost longingly, on a private channel. "I do not understand this."

"You do not have to, Russou," Trent said calmly, checking the tightness of his safety harness.

"Is what Moon said true?"

Paul Moon's voice came over the wide-band channel to both of the warriors. "Crush him, Russou. He is a traitor to you and your Clan. Kill him!"

Trent studied the *Mad Dog* as it slowly approached him. Russou's Starmates formed at his sides, waiting for him to make his move. "You will have to destroy me, Russou. You know that."

"I do not want to."

"You have no choice. This is how this must end," Trent said, wrapping his hand on the locking toggle for his ejection system as he heard a blast of autocannon fire to his rear. It was the Com Guards advancing down the ridge toward him, fighting Star Commander Alexandra's Star in close-quarters combat.

There was a pause during which Trent wondered how Russou would react. Then he saw the *Mad Dog*'s weapons pods come up as Russou ordered his Star to attack Trent with everything they had just as the Com Guards rushed to Trent's side. The initial barrage was weathered by his remaining armor as he staggered back under the shuddering impacts of the weapons. Fighting the wave of heat that spiked in his cockpit, Trent struggled with the controls and balance as the *Cauldron-Born* swayed under volley.

He raised his Gauss rifle in front of him and tilted his 'Mech backward slightly, pointing it at an angle back toward the ridge. Enemy fire ripped the weapons pod off at the elbow joint, tossing it into what was left of his legs as lasers and missiles ate away at the 'Mech's myomer muscles and ferro-titanium internal structure. His secondary display switched to show him the damage as the 'Mech died around him.

He fired the autocannon in his other arm in a steady stream into the sod in front of him, sending up a massive explosion of dirt and grass between him and Russou's Jaguars. The ComStar *King Crab* moved to his flank eighty meters away and blasted at Russou, but missed. The red warning indicators on his *Cauldron-Born* flared in front of him as Trent braced himself.

This is where I die in the eyes of my former Clan. This is where I become a dead traitor. He keyed the self-destruct sequence and reached to hit the ejection control. A burst of laser fire tore at the heart of his 'Mech as the reactor went critical. There was a blast of cool Maldonado morning air. Then there was an explosion. A brilliant flash almost as bright as the sun rising in the sky. Trent closed his eyes and his vision seemed to tunnel as he passed out into a darkness that was warm, wet, and comforting.

$=$ **36** $=$

Trent stood at parade rest between the two Com Guard bodyguards, as if an unspoken order still held him at bay. His warrior's gray jumpsuit had been cleaned, but still had a worn look about it. It was the same clothing he had worn for most of the journey from Maldonado to Tharkad. Judith stood at his side, silent and yet he could read her nervousness. She had been sequestered away from him for days at a time, obviously being interrogated and debriefed.

Though he had been unconscious during the end of the battle along the Shenandoah River, he knew how it had turned out. The explosion of his *Cauldron-Born* had been sudden and rapid, the low-level EMP from the blast overloading the sensors of many of the surrounding 'Mechs. Russou and a handful of Omnis had managed to get clear, but what they saw was Trent's honorable death.

Precentor Martial Anastasius Focht, infamous among the Clans as commander of the Com Guards, entered the room by the far door. Trent studied him curiously. The other man's appearance was striking, with his stark white hair and a black eye patch over one eye. The lined, leathery look of his face betrayed not only his age but years of exposure to wind and weather. Focht walked over to his desk and gestured for Trent to have a seat.

Trent went to the chair and sat down slowly, its leather creaking as he did. Anastasius Focht, the man who had orchestrated the greatest defeat the Clans had ever known, sat facing him.

The room itself was spartan in appearance, with only one bulletproof window, simple wooden furnishings, and a deep blue carpet. So unassuming was it that Trent forgot for a moment where he was, seated in a room on the capitol world of the Lyran Alliance. From what he understood, the leaders of the Inner Sphere had gathered on this world for a kind of grand council. That was why Focht was here.

"I am Anastasius Focht," the man said in a deep tone. He gestured to an aide standing beside him. "This is Precentor Klaus Hettig, another veteran of Tukayyid."

Trent nodded to each of them. "I am Star Captain Trent, formerly of Clan Smoke Jaguar."

Focht cast a quick glance at Judith, then back at Trent. "My aides tell me you have information to offer ComStar. Information that would be of interest to us . . ."

Trent slowly pulled out the optical disk onto which he had dumped the data from his wristcomp. As he did, the bodyguards leaned forward, hands massaging their weapons, perhaps fearing that he had somehow smuggled in a weapon. Focht took the disk and slid it into the small holovid unit built into the desk and pressed a control stud. There was a flicker of light as the holoviewer came to life, projecting the image of a world hovering in the space between the two men. The planet spun slowly, its principal cities dots of red light on the surface.

"There is no need for bodyguards," Trent said. "On my honor, I do not pose a threat to you or those around you."

Focht said nothing but simply gestured to his guards. They stepped outside, though everyone in the room knew they would be just on the other side of the door. Trent waited until they were gone, then began to speak. "Precentor Martial Focht, I present to you Huntress, homeworld of the Smoke Jaguar Clan. In this datafile you will find everything I was able to obtain regarding the defense of that world."

"Huntress," Focht said, staring at the glowing holoimage. "Impressive. But it is merely a point of light somewhere in the sky. Which point of light, we do not know."

"That is the reason for our meeting, and why it is of such import. I also bring with me the path to this world, the Exodus Road, the route taken by Aleksandr Kerensky and the Exodus Fleet when they left the Inner Sphere forever."

Focht's one good eye continued to hold Trent with its fixed stare, as if he found the words hard to believe.

"I also bring with me the current placement of the Smoke Jaguar units posted in the Inner Sphere," Trent went on. "In short, I present you the whole of Clan Smoke Jaguar, everything needed to bring them to their knees."

Focht nodded slowly, and when he spoke, his tone was musing, almost as if he was talking to himself. "Huntress. It all began there, didn't it? It began when our own Explorer Corps ship stumbled onto the world years ago. While exploring the stars we spawned the very invasion that might have destroyed us."

Trent was not exactly sure what Focht meant by that, but it did not concern him right now. "This information is encrypted, Precentor Martial, and I have the only cipher. Any attempt to extract the data stored on that disk would result in the information being irrevocably purged."

"This information, I assume, has a price attached to it. I know you do not want our money. No Clansman values coin. What *do* you want then, Star Captain Trent?"

Trent sat back in his chair and paused to give weight to what he was about to say. "In exchange for everything I know of the Smoke Jaguars, I ask for a command to call my own."

"Command?"

Trent's tone went from formal to impassioned. "I am a warrior, but my own people consider me past my prime, of no value. But I know differently." He cast a quick glance at Judith still standing nearby. "I am one who has been genetically bred for war, trained to lead others into battle. Being a warrior is all I am, all I will ever be. I want to know that I might one day lead others into battle again."

Focht said nothing for a moment, then turned to Precentor Hettig at his side. Hettig whispered something to Focht that Trent could not hear. Focht pondered whatever his aide had said, then turned back to Trent.

"You must forgive me, Star Captain. But you come here, having been rescued by our own Com Guards, promising me the unimaginable. You offer me the beating heart of the most brutal of our Clan foes. You bring me this information at a time when I can use it most. But, frankly, Star Captain I must mistrust this offer. Why should I believe you?"

The words caught Trent off guard, and his face tingled with heat. "I am more than thirty years old. As my bondsman, your former warrior, will attest, my people would have discarded me. As I sit here facing you, they think of me as dead. I was a tool, forged by the leaders of the Jaguar Clan to obey and serve mindlessly. What independence they could not crush out of me, they tried to destroy through ridicule and ostracization. And yet, Precentor, I did not succumb. I survived instead."

Precentor Hettig cut him off with a snort. "Yet you come here willing to turn against your people. A Clansman willing to turn traitor? That is hard to believe."

"Neg," Trent snapped back. "It was my own Clan that betrayed *me* years ago when they began to betray the vision of Nicholas Kerensky. Each day they mock his spirit, defy what he saw as our true destiny. The leaders play politics among themselves and favor those who learn the rules. They do not make honorable combat, but take innocent lives with impunity. This is my only chance to set matters right." *My only chance to cleanse the blood of innocents from my hands.*

Focht also sat back with a sigh. "Politics is always the foe of true warriors," he said. "That is something we both understand, Star Captain." Trent waited, sure that the Precentor Martial was going to say more.

"My fear is that you are bait," Focht said, "sent here to lead us into some kind of trap. An action doomed from the start."

Trent shook his head. "I will submit to interrogation if you doubt my integrity."

Precentor Hettig leaned forward to speak. "Perhaps we can simply extract the cipher you spoke of and need not negotiate with you at all."

Trent gave him a thin smile. "You may try. But if I give you the incorrect code, you will lose everything on that diskette." His voice was confident and firm.

"That is not necessary," Anastasius Focht said to his aide. "He comes from the Clans, and I have spent time with these people. His word is his bond. Attempting to spoil what he offers nets us nothing, but we will verify, with his consent, the validity of the data—should I accept his offer."

For the first time since he entered the room, Trent relaxed. This was a true warrior, the man who had led his forces to victory over the Clans. Trent suddenly knew Focht was someone he could trust.

"Tell me, Star Captain," Focht said, "can you be sure that the Smoke Jaguars do not know you are alive and carry this information?"

"Aff," Trent said.

"How can you be so sure?" Hettig demanded sharply.

"Because if they knew I was alive, they would stop at nothing to kill me and destroy this information. There is a fatal weakness in our warrior caste. It is impervious to attack from without. But, from within, a lone warrior can break the spine of an entire Clan. If they even suspected I was alive, their Galaxies would swarm across the truce line seeking me out." Another long silence followed his words.

"I understand," Focht said finally. "That is why we placed ROM operatives within the ranks of the Clans. Almost all were rooted out. But it only takes one, a single agent"—he glanced at Judith, who bowed her head in respect—"to bring one warrior to us with the right information, and we knew that the Clans could be bested. It has taken years, but you and Judith have brought us what hundreds in the Explorer Corps could not."

"I am pleased you think the data useful," Trent replied. "But what say you to my request for a command?"

Focht smiled enough for his teeth to show. "I, Anastasius Focht, Precentor Martial of ComStar, hereby extend the offer of a command of a Binary's worth of troops. You would serve in the Com Guards, under my personal command. You shall provide insight and counsel to me and my allies regarding your former Clan. You will see battle, but only when I decide it is to be so."

Trent was pleased at these words. "Well spoken, Precentor Martial. But a Binary is hardly worth the very heart of the Smoke Jaguar. I should think a Cluster would be more worthy of this information I bring you."

"Perhaps so, Star Captain. But you have yet to prove yourself to me as a commander. When that time comes, I will see to it that you are considered for such a command. I can extend to you a Trinary of warriors to lead when you do eventually enter combat. Certainly enough for a warrior such as you to prove your worth to the Com Guards, would you not agree?"

Trent stared at the holographic image of Huntress spinning over the table in front of him. He was thrilled at the prospect of leading warriors into battle once more. But another thought struck him. *To turn traitor to a people should never be so easy, yet it is so.*

"Well bargained and done, Precentor Martial," he said. He reached over to the controls on the desktop and keyed in the eight-digit code for the cipher. Above them the image of Huntress shrank to a small dot of light and raced upward toward the ceiling. Dozens of other dots of light, star systems, came holographically into view, filling the space between Huntress and the table top. The three-dimensional map shrank as another one took shape. Within moments the vastness of the Inner Sphere was imaged over the table top. A fine red line flickered among the stars, shimmering all the way from the Inner Sphere, through the Deep Periphery, to Huntress, now poised just at the height of the ceiling.

"I give to you the Exodus Road," Trent said as the other two men studied the shimmering red stars, unable to hide their excitement or their awe. "May we follow it in the spirit of the great Kerenskys. And may it one day lead us to victory over those who defy the ways of honor."

Epilogue

JumpShip **Admiral Andrews**
Zenith Jump Point
Unnamed Planet, The Exodus Road
Deep Periphery
15 November 3058

Russou Howell looked at the new rank insignia on his gray field jacket in its holding rack on the wall. *Star Colonel.* He had been practically ordered to undertake the Trial of Position, even though he did not know where the command was. Star Colonel Paul Moon had pushed him into it, and he had complied. That was what a warrior did—he followed orders. But he thought he should feel differently about it, prouder, more excited. Instead, winning the new rank felt hollow, as if the Trial had been rigged in some way. As if the command had been bought with Trent's blood.

Once he had won over the other two aspirants in Trials of Combat, he was informed of his new posting—the world of Huntress. *They are shuffling me away because of my age, sending me back to Clan space so I will never see action.* Russou tried to force the thoughts from his mind, but he was sure he would never see combat again. Not combat as he had known it thus far.

Hovering over the small table in the null gravity of the room was a dark wooden box. All that was left of Trent. He opened it and saw the chess set his friend had been so fond of. As the warrior who killed Trent, Russou had been given his only possession as isorla. He had considered refusing it, but did not out of respect for his longtime comrade. He fidgeted with a black knight and a white bishop, both pieces worn by time.

A slight rapping came at the door. "Enter," he said slowly, lost in memories of the friend he had killed. An Elemental entered, his head nearly scraping the ceiling. "You did not come down for dinner, Star Colonel Russou. I was concerned. Is all well?"

Russou looked up at the muscular officer. "Aye, I am fine, merely spending time honoring the memory of an old friend. I apologize for standing you up, Allen," he said.

The big man smiled and closed the door. "No apologies necessary, Star Colonel. If you wish me to leave, I will."

"Neg," Russou said, motioning to the chair next to him. "Please sit. Since the incident on Maldonado, I have spoken with no one of what happened there. Since Trent's death . . ."

"Trent, you say? Star Captain Trent of the Delta Galaxy?"

Russou nodded. "You knew him?"

Allen smiled broadly. "Aye. We traveled to Huntress and back aboard this ship. He is dead?"

"Aff," Russou replied. "They said that he might be a traitor, that he might have actually turned against our caste." *And now he is dead, at my hands.*

"That is not possible," Allen said, shaking his head. "I fought next to him on Pivot Prime. He risked his life to save the Clan. Such a man would never turn against our people."

Russou rubbed his forehead where the hairline had receded years before, hoping to relieve the pressure he felt there, to no avail. "I too believe as you do. But others, those caught in the web of politics, do not. They implicated him in smuggling and believed that he might have posed a significant threat to our Clan's security."

"These 'others' . . . they ordered his death?"

"Aye," Russou said. "Star Colonel Moon ordered me to do it. And like a good warrior, I obeyed."

"Did Trent die with honor?"

Russou only nodded.

Allen lowered his head. "Then let us talk this eve about the Trent we knew, the warrior we remember. . . ."

Trent glanced down at his new off-white uniform with blue cape and liked the fit and feel. Only twenty-four hours had passed since his initial meeting with the Precentor Martial and in that time he had attended what seemed like an endless series of meetings and debriefings. The various experts had gone over his data on the Exodus Road and the map of Huntress with a fine-toothed comb, in the process questioning him minutely about every detail.

This was the first time he had been alone, if he could call it that. Outside the door was a pair of guards, posted there not to prevent his departure, but to protect him. They had shuffled him to a secure area, elegant by his Clan standards. If the room lacked anything, it was a window, but Precentor Hettig had explained that Trent needed the protection of guards because he was now a "threat" to the Clans. *I do not feel like a threat. Nor do I feel like a traitor.*

What he did feel was a sense of release, as if he had finally dropped a burden he had carried for too long. There was a pang of regret as well. Paul Moon had not died on Maldonado. Or so said Precentor Karl Karter, who reported hearing Moon barking curses and final challenges to the Com Guards even as his force was withdrawing. The raid had been a failure for the Jaguars, but Trent was sure Moon would find a way to twist the truth to his advantage. And if the Jaguars had been forced to withdraw from Maldonado, Moon would probably still find comfort in the fact that he believed Star Captain Trent had died there.

That, perhaps, was Trent's only regret. Russou was still alive somewhere believing that he was responsible for killing his closest comrade. Knowing Russou, Trent was sure the guilt was burning like hot coals in his mind. He wanted Russou to know that he was very much alive, and that he preserved all that was the spirit of Clan Smoke Jaguar—honor, duty, obligation. But that was not to be. And in the end, Russou would end up a victim of politics as well. One day, men like Star Colonel Paul Moon would discard Russou as old and worthless, shuffling him off to the solahma trash heap as he had tried to do with Trent.

But what Paul Moon had done or did not do no longer mattered. Trent had beaten him at his own game. And that was enough.

A knock came at his door, and he went to open it. Standing there was Judith. She stepped in as the guards gave her a nod and then closed the door. At first she said nothing, looking at Trent in his new Com Guard uniform with pride, and something more . . .

"It is pleasing to see you, Judith—Faber," he said, attempting to make use of her surname.

"It has been so long since I heard that name that I hardly recognize it. But between us, it isn't required." Trent noted her use of a contraction but made no comment.

"Aye," he said, putting his hands on her shoulders and holding her in front of him. "I did not see you in my meetings. Where have you been?"

"Debriefings, just like you. The Precentor Martial has told me that I will be given a new posting in ROM, but thus far I don't have any specifics. It is a 'reward for service above and beyond the call of duty.' But I did what I did because it was the right thing to do. Not just for ComStar, but for everyone."

Trent nodded. "In the end, what matters is not rank, position, or place. What matters is what is in here." He tapped his chest twice, then his temple.

"Affirmative. But our new places in the universe mean that we will be apart. In the last few years, I have come to depend on you, to *need* you. And now that we are both being reassigned, we'll be separated for some time."

Trent smiled, but he did not know how to respond to that. "You have not seen your family in some time," he said instead. "You spoke of them before. Perhaps you could go to Terra and see them, *quiaff?*"

"Neg," she replied. "News did not travel well into the occupation zone. We did not learn what has happened to ComStar. Apparently the Word of Blake splinter group seized Terra earlier this year. Travel there is prohibited to anyone who serves ComStar."

Trent bit his lower lip, not just for Judith but for himself as well. He had hoped to visit Terra, to stand on the soil of the mother world of humankind. Now that was not to be. Instinctively he pulled Judith closer to him, hugging her stiffly, but firmly. He felt her warmth against his chest, her breathing matching his own. "I am sorry."

She pulled back. "You have nothing to be sorry about. I had a mission, and together we completed it. What happens next is left to those with more power than either of us would ever want to have. But in the end, we did what was right."

"Affirmative," Trent said, pulling away from her slightly,

allowing his hand to graze her dark hair as he did. "Here I am now, a Demi-Precentor in rank. But in my heart, I am the last of the Smoke Jaguars. The others are lost, corrupted by men like Paul Moon. As long as I live, I will continue to serve the wisdom of Nicholas Kerensky."

Judith shook her head in disagreement. "You are wrong, Trent. You are not the last of the Smoke Jaguars. I think of you as the first of a new breed." Her words pleased him. Bending forward he pressed his lips against her warm mouth. They kissed slowly, then furiously, their bodies pressing tightly to one another as if they were clinging for life itself. Then she pulled back and looked into his face, running one hand along the synthetic skin on the right side, caressing him.

"I have waited a long time for this," she said.

Trent looked down at the lone gray cord on her wrist. He reached to touch it. "This is no longer required. You are not my bondsman, Judith Faber. We are now equals."

She tugged at the cord and let it snap back against her wrist. "We will be apart for a long time, Trent. I will wear this as a reminder of my precious time with you." Then she put her arms around his neck and pulled him close. They held each other for a long time, not knowing when or how they might ever be together again . . .

About the Author

Manassas
The Old Dominion
Terran Hegemony
United States of America, Terra
14 October 1996

BLAINE PARDOE was born in Newport News, Virginia, Terra, pre-Star League 1962, but grew up in Michigan. He attended Central Michigan University, where he earned his undergraduate degrees. BattleTech® is one of his true loves, next to his family. He has written a number of books for the game line, as well as his two BattleTech® novels, *Highlander Gambit* and *Impetus of War*, published by Roc Books.

He also has written a number of computer game books for the Brady Brooks imprint MacMillan.

In his "day job" Blaine is an Assistant Director for one of the "big six" accounting firms outside of Washington, D.C., where he is in charge of national technology training for the technology support staff.

He and his wife Cyndi have two children, Victoria Rose and Alexander William, who lovingly tolerate his nightly trips into the 31st century, where most of his writing takes place. He resides in Manassas, Virginia just outside of the Bull Run battlefields where he often stands in the footsteps of Stonewall Jackson and contemplates battles of the past and those of the far-flung future.

For those who wish to contact him, he can be reached at PARDOE@EMCS.COM.

Triad National Cemetery
Tharkad City, Tharkad
District of Donegal, Lyran Alliance
30 September 3058

The moist breeze wending its way through the labyrinth of monuments in the Triad National Cemetery dragged on Victor Ian Steiner-Davion. The premature arrival of spring had reduced September's normal blanket of snow to islands of white floating in muddy oceans. The bright green of new leaves and grasses peeked out, seeking sun. The early spring had created a general feeling of well-being that had been greatly in evidence on the media broadcasts the Prince had caught while his DropShip burned toward the planet.

One good frost and it all dies. Standing before his mother's memorial, Victor remained immune to the spring fever infecting Tharkad. Her death had come as a result of power grabs by just two Inner Sphere nobles. Victor had come to Tharkad to participate in the Whitting Conference, where dozens of Inner Sphere nobles would make power grabs. The conclusion that things would be a disaster was all but inescapable.

Victor frowned. *Things will only go bad if you allow them to go bad.* He shifted his shoulders and winced at the aches he felt. Most of them, he knew, came from the grueling trip from

Coventry to Tharkad. JumpShips were capable of tearing a hole in the fabric of reality, allowing them to move from point to point, up to thirty light years at a jump. Tiring though they were, those jumps didn't bother him so much as had the high-G DropShip burn in to Tharkad. *Being as small as I am, laboring under more than one gravity is a chore.*

He managed a smile. "Not that such a consideration stopped Kai or Hohiro from beating up on me." He fingered the fading bruise around his right eye. He'd gotten it when he failed to pick off a right-cross delivered by Hohiro Kurita. *I saw it coming, but couldn't do anything about it.* While chagrined about getting a black-eye, he was also proud of it.

Too much of his life had become politics and appearance. He accepted the necessity of such things, but politics still grated on him. It struck him as completely ludicrous to have to take a position far more extreme than he ever intended to carry out, just so he could later compromise with opponents, finally getting what he wanted in the first place. The time and effort wasted in those games could be better spent actually doing things.

Setting up the Whitting Conference was a prime example of the waste politics caused. Fourteen weeks earlier, on Coventry, he had proposed building a united force to take the war to the Clans. Within two days his sister, Katherine, Archon of the Lyran Alliance, had offered to host the Whitting Conference on Tharkad. In doing so she had assumed the burden of organizing the meeting, inviting the leaders of the Inner Sphere and, quite deftly, positioning herself to be seen as the unifying force for the future of the Inner Sphere.

Victor acknowledged that she'd played her part well and that her orchestrations dictated his actions. Though Coventry was less than ninety light years distant from Tharkad—a trip he could have made inside three weeks—there was no reason for him to show up before the first of October, since that was the date Katherine had chosen for the conference to start. Victor had remained on Coventry along with his staunchest allies, putting their troops through training exercises.

Though the delay had annoyed him, the time spent on Coventry training had not. The insulation and isolation from life that Victor often felt vanished as he spent as much time as possible in the company of his troops. For the first time since his ascension to the throne of the Federated Commonwealth, he actually felt he had a grasp on the concerns of ordinary citizens.

He'd also taken the time for personal training. Victor had always been fit—blessed with the Steiner metabolism that prevented him from piling on pounds—but physical inactivity had begun to sap his strength. He began a program of exercises, then supplemented it through kendo training with Hohiro and learning aikido with Kai Allard-Liao. In return he found an old grizzled sergeant who was willing to teach the royals the intricacies of boxing.

And Hohiro learned a lot faster than I wanted him to. Victor shook his head, wondering for a moment what his mother would have said if she could have seen him with his black-eye. She'd have been concerned for him, but she would have smiled and told him it was good that he was getting more exercise. *She always knew what to say to make someone feel good.*

He looked down at the dancing, crackling fire of the eternal flame at the granite base of the monument. Unlike the countless statutes memorializing his mother scattered throughout the Federated Commonwealth, this one lacked a physical representation of Melissa Steiner-Davion. And yet it had something of her. Its blocky stone strength like the foundational strength she had provided to the union of the Federated Suns and the Lyran Commonwealth when she wed Hanse Davion thirty years before.

Victor bowed his head. He knew he should drop to his knees to offer a prayer for his mother, but the thaw surrounded her gravesite with a chilly moat that had already soaked the hem of his long, steel-blue greatcoat. Since most of the citizens of the Lyran Alliance—the name his sister Katherine had given to the Lyran half of the Federated Commonwealth after she seceded—thought he had murdered his mother, kneeling in a puddle before her grave would probably look to them like the wild behavior of a killer overcome with remorse.

He crossed himself and offered a brief prayer for the repose of Melissa Steiner-Davion's soul. He took a deep breath, then nodded toward the granite tomb. "What you and father built thirty years ago has dissolved in just two years after your death. Were you alive, uniting the Inner Sphere to face the Clans and destroy them would have easily been possible. Now

I just hope the chance to destroy the Clans won't be frittered away."

A flicker of movement near the entrance to the cemetery caught his attention. Looking up through a gravestones, he saw a trio of black hoverlimos vaporizing puddles on the cemetery roadway as they sped toward him. The lead and rear limos had flashing lights playing against their windscreens while the middle vehicle—the largest of them all—moved between its escorts with a certain serenity.

From back behind him he heard the click of his own hoverlimo's door opening. Victor turned and in an effort to forestall rash action, held up a hand to restrain the icy-eyed man emerging from the limo. "No need to be anxious, Agent Curaitis."

"Given who is in that vehicle, and what she has done to obtain power, is there a reason I shouldn't be anxious?"

Victor thought a moment, then nodded. "You have a point there."

The black-haired bodyguard closed the hoverlimo door and stood beside the vehicle. Victor knew better than to expect further comment from Curaitis. _The man makes a rock seem talkative._ In addition to that, the approaching limos had Curaitis' full attention.

The lead limo veered off, allowing the larger one to come to a stop barely ten meters from the nose of Victor's limo. The gull-wing door in the back third hissed and swung up. Victor saw movement in the darkened interior, then his sister emerged, unaided, and stalked toward him.

You never change. Taller than him, Katherine emphasized that by wearing knee-length white boots with high heels. Her white sable coat hung down to the tops of her boots and was matched by the furred hat perched on her head. Her long, golden-blond hair played over the shoulders of the coat as her steady, long-legged stride brought her closer.

She gestured lazily toward him with a gloved hand. "Good afternoon, Victor."

"And you, _Katherine._" He made certain to pronounce every syllable of her name with care and precision. Though she had taken to calling herself "Katrina," Victor refused to acknowledge the change. Katrina Steiner had been his grandmother, an Archon and undoubtedly the most shrewd and powerful woman ever to rule one of the Successor States of the Inner Sphere. For his sister to have usurped Katrina's name and image seemed a crime to him. "I'm surprised to see you here."

"Are you?" Her ice-blue eyes held his stare defiantly. "I missed you at the spaceport."

"Ah, so that was *you*." Victor gave her a slight smile and let his gray eyes show the venom he kept out of his voice. "I should have realized it was a welcoming committee, but I really wanted to come here before I did anything else."

She stopped at the other side of the monument. "Easing a guilty conscience?"

"Guilt? Over what?"

Katherine smiled coldly. "You missed her funeral. You didn't care to make it."

Though Victor had thought himself ready for this encounter with his sister, her remark still got past his defenses. Having no reason to think of her as an enemy at the time of his mother's death, he had told her to use her discretion in scheduling Melissa's funeral. Since their mother had been blown apart by a bomb, having her lie in state until all her children could gather was not really an option. Katherine staged the funeral almost immediately, and Victor alone among her children had not been able to get there in time.

"I wanted to be there, Katherine, but there are times the responsibilities of leadership prevent us from doing what we want to do."

Katherine allowed herself a throaty little laugh. "Ah, yes, what were you doing then? Preparing to chase after some Clan bandits?"

"They were a threat to the Inner Sphere and the truce."

"No, Victor, they were your chance to play soldier one more time." Katherine opened her arms wide. "Look around you, Victor. This cemetery is full of people who have been seduced by the lure of BattleMechs. Six hundred years ago they were created to rule the battlefield. Three centuries ago Aleksandr Kerensky took the Star League Defense Force away from the Inner Sphere because he feared the Battle-Mechs that had hitherto been used to protect life would become instruments of its destruction, and he was right. For three centuries wars raged in the Successor States, with leaders mounting up in 'Mechs to win glory for themselves and some tiny piece of an entropic universe for their realms. Then Kerensky's people returned to show us just how destructive a 'Mech can be."

Katherine toed Melissa Steiner's grave. "Even our mother was caught up in that MechWarrior mystique. She gave birth to Yvonne, took over as Archon from her mother, then announced she would become a BattleMech pilot. She became obsessed with these ten-meter-tall engines of destruction. She went so far as to pursue a course of study at the Nagelring, all because it was traditional for an Archon to be a pilot, a warrior—though history shows that being a warrior is in no way related to being a leader."

She peered down her nose at him. "*That* is a lesson you still need to learn, Victor."

Victor's blue-flecked, gray eyes narrowed. "I doubt I will learn that lesson from you, Katherine."

"I could teach you much, Victor."

"I'm sure of that, Katherine." Victor fought to keep his voice even and his anger in check. He had evidence, very strong evidence, that his sister had conspired with Ryan Steiner to have Melissa murdered. *I don't have the proof I need to expose you, Katherine, but Curaitis says it should be forthcoming. Then I will teach you a lesson—one concerning justice.*

He raised his chin. "I'm not certain I want to learn the lessons you could teach me."

His reply seemed to take her a bit by surprise. "You spend too much time playing warrior, Victor. It's not good for your realm."

"If I'd not played warrior on Coventry, you'd be a Clan bondswoman right now."

Katherine's cheeks flushed crimson at the idea, and for the barest of moments Victor thought she might actually thank him for stopping the Clans at Coventry. "Oh, what you did at Coventry was interesting, Victor. Your decision to allow the Jade Falcons to flee without punishment has played well here. In fact, it is said that your fear of the public reaction to your cowardice is the reason you didn't dare appear here until the day before the conference."

"Not that you think that."

"Not at all, Victor. I think you had your reasons for delaying."

Victor nodded. "I did. In fact, my delay came from something you did teach me."

"Oh?" Vanity pulsed a spark into her blue eyes. "What was that?"

"I learned how to make an entrance." Victor folded his arms across his chest. "I waited for everyone else to arrive first, then I came, along with my troops. And then I went at once to my mother's grave, to pay my respects. And look who came to me! I'm sure your rushing to my side will also play very well in the media, Katherine."

She took a step toward him and he thought for a moment that she would slap him. Instead she reached out with her left hand, letting her fingertips linger at the edge of his jaw. With her thumb she traced the outline of the bruise around his right eye. "Oh, Victor, you think you have won this one, don't you? I hope you don't bruise easily because I think you will find this conference very battering. I set the agendas, I guide the discussions, I run the whole thing. If you do not play by the rules I lay down, you'll be left in the dust. It is as simple as that."

He shook his head slowly to make her pull back her hand. "No, Katherine, it's not going to be that simple. Somewhere deep down inside you have to know that the reason we're coming together here is not to entertain you, but to find a way to destroy the threat the Clans pose to us. If you interfere with that, if you stand in the way of what must be done, *your* realm will bear the brunt of the Clan retaliation. And *then*, sister dearest, the people of the Lyran Alliance will wish they had a warrior as their leader again, because only a warrior will be able to save them."

He took a step backward, then tossed her a brief salute. "By the way, I'm appropriating Bifrost Hall at the Nagelring as my headquarters while I'm here. It will provide me with the facilities I need."

Katherine's eyes half-lidded. "And it is convenient to the ComStar compound."

"And the Luvon Foundation, which is where Morgan Kell and Phelan will be staying."

Katherine's eyes grew wide. "I did not invite them."

"I know. I corrected your oversight." Victor walked to his hoverlimo, but turned back toward her before getting in. "You're right that being a warrior doesn't necessarily confer the skills needed to be a good leader and ruler. It also doesn't bar one from picking them up."

Katherine snorted derisively. "What you should be asking yourself, Victor, is whether you can pick them up fast enough."

"Perhaps, Katherine. Or maybe it's you who should be wondering if you can prevent me from doing so." He gave her a cold smile. "If you can't, you'd best make sure I'm pointed at an enemy because you don't want me coming after you."

Timber Wolf (Mad Cat)

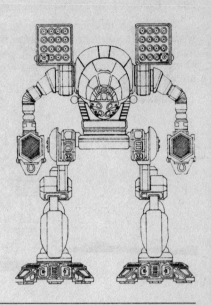

Warhawk (Masakari)

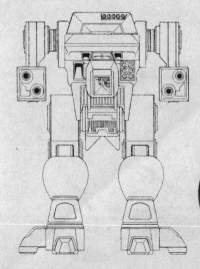

Atlas

Crab

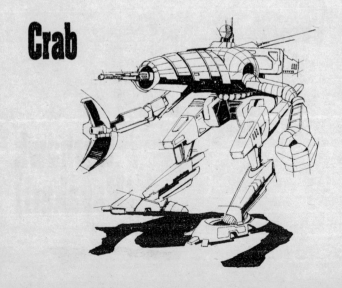

Daikyu

Venom

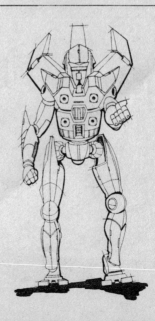

Shadow Cat

Komodo

Elemental

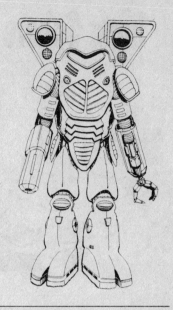

J-27 Ordnance Transport

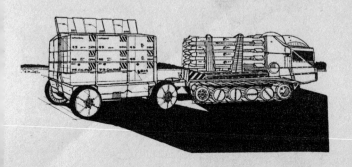

Inner Sphere Union Class Dropship

LOOSE

Clan Union-C Class Dropship

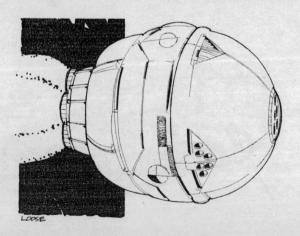

LOOSE

Clan Odyssey
Class Jumpship

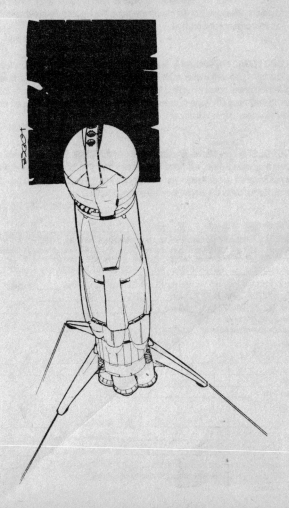